D0456625

*It just might be the deadliest literary
discovery of all time.*

continued...

WHAT TIME
DEVOURS

A. J. Hartley

BERKLEY BOOKS, NEW YORK

THE BERKLEY PUBLISHING GROUP
Published by the Penguin Group
Penguin Group (USA) Inc.
375 Hudson Street, New York, New York 10014, USA
Penguin Group (Canada), 90 Eglinton Avenue East, Suite 700, Toronto, Ontario M4P 2Y3, Canada
(a division of Pearson Penguin Canada Inc.)
Penguin Books Ltd., 80 Strand, London WC2R 0RL, England
Penguin Group Ireland, 25 St. Stephen's Green, Dublin 2, Ireland (a division of Penguin Books Ltd.)
Penguin Group (Australia), 250 Camberwell Road, Camberwell, Victoria 3124, Australia
(a division of Pearson Australia Group Pty. Ltd.)
Penguin Books India Pvt. Ltd., 11 Community Centre, Panchsheel Park, New Delhi—110 017, India
Penguin Group (NZ), 67 Apollo Drive, Rosedale, North Shore 0632, New Zealand
(a division of Pearson New Zealand Ltd.)
Penguin Books (South Africa) (Pty.) Ltd., 24 Sturdee Avenue, Rosebank, Johannesburg 2196,
South Africa

Penguin Books Ltd., Registered Offices: 80 Strand, London WC2R 0RL, England

This is a work of fiction. Names, characters, places, and incidents either are the product of the author's imagination or are used fictitiously, and any resemblance to actual persons, living or dead, business establishments, events, or locales is entirely coincidental. The publisher does not have any control over and does not assume any responsibility for author or third-party websites or their content.

WHAT TIME DEVOURS

A Berkley Book / published by arrangement with the author

PRINTING HISTORY
Berkley edition / January 2009

Copyright © 2009 by A. J. Hartley.
Cover design by Rita Frangie.
Interior text design by Stacy Irwin.

ISBN: 978-0-425-22623-0

BERKLEY®
Berkley Books are published by The Berkley Publishing Group,
a division of Penguin Group (USA) Inc.,
375 Hudson Street, New York, New York 10014.
BERKLEY® is a registered trademark of Penguin Group (USA) Inc.
The "B" design is a trademark of Penguin Group (USA) Inc.

PRINTED IN THE UNITED STATES OF AMERICA

10 9 8 7 6 5 4 3 2 1

What is love? 'tis not hereafter;
Present mirth hath present laughter;
What's to come is still unsure:
In delay there lies no plenty;
Then come kiss me, sweet and twenty,
Youth's a stuff will not endure.

—SHAKESPEARE, *TWELFTH NIGHT*

PART I

Since brass, nor stone, nor earth, nor boundless sea,
But sad mortality o'er-sways their power,
How with this rage shall beauty hold a plea,
Whose action is no stronger than a flower?
O, how shall summer's honey breath hold out
Against the wreckful siege of battering days,
When rocks impregnable are not so stout,
Nor gates of steel so strong, but Time decays?
O fearful meditation! where, alack,
Shall Time's best jewel from Time's chest lie hid?
Or what strong hand can hold his swift foot back?
Or who his spoil of beauty can forbid?
   O, none, unless this miracle have might,
   That in black ink my love may still shine bright.

—Shakespeare, "Sonnet 65"

CHAPTER 1

Thomas Knight froze, one hand on the coffeepot, the other extended to the faucet over the sink. It was still dark outside and the kitchen light should show only a fringe of green from the yew in the yard, but there was something else. Something at the window. He wasn't sure if he'd gotten a flash of it in the reflection from the percolator, or caught a glimpse with the corner of his eye, but he knew something was there, something strange. Something *wrong*.

He stood there motionless for three or four seconds, as if waiting for it to move, but he knew it wouldn't and that he would have to turn and look directly at it. Right now it was just an impression of colors that shouldn't be there—a pale oval touched with yellow and red—sharp against the blackness of the yard beyond, but when he looked at it, it would take shape and meaning. He didn't want to look.

He turned to it slowly, and even though he wasn't surprised, the fact of the thing almost made him cry out. A woman's face was pressed up to the glass.

Her eyes were wide, like she was staring at him, but Thomas didn't wave her away, or threaten to call the police. There was something too fixed and vacant about the eyes. They were unaware of him.

She was standing at the window, he supposed, but there was an awkwardness to her posture and a slight smear of something on the glass: sweat? Makeup? She didn't move at all, and Thomas took a small, reluctant step toward the window, half hoping the figure would turn out to be some store mannequin, dressed and propped there by one of his more enterprising students as an end-of-term gag.

But she was real enough. He took two wary steps toward the window.

The glass reflected black everywhere but where the face was pressed to the window, lit by the kitchen light so it seemed to float like a party balloon. He supposed she was in her late fifties. Her pale skin looked delicate and had the beginnings of translucence. She was expertly made up, her lips a trifle redder than suited her, and her teeth were unnaturally white. But it was the eyes that he couldn't shake. They were wide, fixed in something that might have been surprise.

Or terror.

One was a dull, muddy green, the other an uncanny violet.

Thomas put down the coffeepot and picked up the wall-mounted phone, his eyes still on the motionless face pressed up against the window, but he didn't dial. He would go outside first. He needed to know for sure.

The kitchen had two windows, one facing south—into the backyard—and one facing east, which was where the woman stood. Thomas stepped out into the predawn chill, cinching his bathrobe tighter as he walked barefoot onto the cold path. She wasn't visible from the front of the house and it was only when he went around the dark yew that grew on the corner and turned down the narrow path between the house and next door's dense privet hedge that he saw her. She wasn't standing exactly, which meant that she was rather taller than he had imagined, but was slumped over one of the gold-flecked aucubas that were planted along the shady foundation. Down here the only light was the startling and flat brilliance of the kitchen window, which had given an unearthly vividness to the woman's face from inside. Out here the light only brushed a little green and gold over the edges of the aucuba. The woman herself was no more than the silhouette of her head, her body lost in shadow.

Thomas approached her slowly, watching for movement, anything that would shift the nature of the morning's strangeness into something more mundane. She could still be just some disturbed old woman who had fixated on his house for reasons known only to herself, and who might yet bustle off muttering incomprehensibly.

"Excuse me," he said, and when she didn't respond, didn't move at all, he put his hand on her shoulder.

Then he knew. He felt the cool slickness of fluid on her shaded shoulder and he recoiled.

Too late. His touch made her shift. She rolled as she fell away from him, and the kitchen light showed the terrible concave shape of the back of her head and the blood that soaked her back like a cloak.

CHAPTER 2

Thomas was already two hours late for work but the police were still there. He had recounted every detail of the morning's grisly discovery but hadn't had much to offer. No, he had never seen her before, and no, the spot where she was lying was not where he'd found her. She'd fallen when he touched her, and he was sorry for disturbing the crime scene, but he hadn't been sure she was dead . . .

He told the story twice, once to a uniformed officer who treated him like some half-wit who had willfully compromised his investigation, and once to a female plainclothes detective called Polinski who was merely efficient. He gathered they didn't know who the dead woman was.

"No purse, no credit cards, no ID," she said. "Mode of attack suggests a mugging."

"The mode of attack?" said Thomas, unnerved by his own curiosity, but also trying to suggest he had nothing to do with it. Thomas was a big man, six foot three and broad across the shoulders. People who didn't know him expected him to be rough, physical. He had noticed a couple of the policemen sizing him up, though he suspected some of them already knew who he was.

"Looks like she was hit from behind with a half brick. We found it under the hedge. The lab has it now."

Chastened, Thomas said nothing.

They kept him sitting around for another forty-five minutes and then said he could go. When he went back inside to get his things together, he found that his hand was shaking. He checked his face in the mirror. He was pale, dead looking. Suddenly he felt nauseated and ran to the bathroom, but when he got there, nothing happened. He sat for five minutes on the edge of the tub, then drank a long glass of ice water and felt better.

Thomas dressed for work, feeling the silence of the house now that everyone had left and the strangeness of putting on his tie in the middle of the morning. He wanted to call his wife, Kumi, in Japan, just to listen to the sound of her voice until the world felt closer to normal. It wouldn't matter what she said. It was enough that they were talking again.

The wheezy grandfather clock in the hall chimed eleven. He brushed his teeth again, ran his hand over his stubbly chin, and decided to shave. He wasn't sure why, but it seemed important to go to school looking composed and professional, looking different from the way he felt.

Perhaps if everyone else assumes it's an ordinary day, he thought, *it will be.*

But it wasn't an ordinary day and not because of the corpse at his window. In the morning's chaos, he had forgotten that his early classes had been canceled, and the school had been closed for the Williams memorial. Thomas remembered as soon as he pulled into the empty parking lot behind Evanston Township High School.

He cursed, turned the car around and drove over to Hemingway Methodist on Chicago where Ben Williams had volunteered in the soup kitchen. The service was already over and people were drifting out, clustered together, so Thomas sat in the car by the curb, radio off. He recognized a lot of the kids, including a number who had graduated five or six years ago, most of them black. Was it that long since Williams had been here? It didn't seem so, but then it never did, these days. Thomas was thirty-eight and had been teaching high school for a decade. Ben Williams had been twenty-three; a smart, thoughtful, popular kid and a wide receiver for the Evanston Wildkits. He had only joined the National Guard because it helped pay for college. After his tour he had planned to be a teacher, like Thomas. A week ago he had been killed in Iraq. Thomas didn't know the details.

Thomas had been his English teacher. He couldn't remember what they had studied that year. *Julius Caesar*? As soon as the title came to mind he was sure it was right, sure also that Williams had taken the lead in organizing a staging of two or three scenes from the play. The memory came back so powerfully that Thomas couldn't believe he had forgotten it, or the charismatic kid at its core. Williams had played Mark Antony. Thomas thought they had done the assassination scene and its immediate aftermath, maybe even both sets of funeral orations, but the only thing he could recall clearly was Ben Williams talking to the class as the people of Rome:

> *The evil that men do lives after them;*
> *The good is oft interred with their bones;*
> *So let it be with Caesar. The noble Brutus*
> *Hath told you Caesar was ambitious:*
> *If it were so, it was a grievous fault,*
> *And grievously hath Caesar answer'd it.*
> *Here, under leave of Brutus and the rest—*
> *For Brutus is an honourable man;*
> *So are they all, all honourable men—*
> *Come I to speak in Caesar's funeral.*

Thomas was surprised at how well he recalled the lines, but had forgotten—or half forgotten—the boy who had made them memorable.

Twenty-three. If he had merely read about this in the paper, if he had never known Williams, the memorial service might have produced a private diatribe about the war, but he felt no outrage, only loss and futility. He started to frame thoughts of Williams's frustrated potential but pushed them away as clichéd. He wanted a stronger connection to his former pupil but couldn't grasp enough of him beyond that classroom *Caesar* to make the boy real. He thought of Williams but found that his own thirty-eight years weighed too heavily on him. At twenty-three he had been teaching in Japan, had not even been to graduate school yet. He *had* already met Kumi, had already fallen in love with her, in fact. Twenty-three.

Strange, he thought, *that so much of who you are was already in place so early.*

He remembered it all, the scent of his apartment in Japan, the feel of the bicycle he had ridden every day, the thrill of visiting Kumi. It was so long ago, but felt so fresh that he smiled as if he were still there in that moment, as if he had not dropped out of graduate school, had not separated from his wife, and had not found a body at his kitchen window. He stared at his hands as they sat at ten and two on the steering wheel: big hands, they were. Strong. But the skin was tougher than it had been, not quite as smooth. He looked back to the church and wondered if losing a former student was at all like outliving your own children.

Amazing, he thought, *the way you can make everything about you . . .*

"Nature of the beast," he said aloud.

"The beast" being?

Life, he supposed.

He sat there, replaying all he could dredge up about Ben Williams, and watched the kids filing out to cars and yellow buses, while Ben Williams's former classmates hugged, shook hands, and swore to keep in touch.

CHAPTER 3

By evening, the morning's horror seemed a world away and he was not entirely surprised to find the house deserted when he got there, the only sign of the investigation being a mass of yellow tape designed to keep people away from where the corpse had been, and a squad car down the block. A couple of uniforms were going house to house. He had almost forgotten what had happened, pushed it into some dark part of his mind and tried not to look at it. Now he was back, and it was real again. As he walked up the path to his front door, something of his former nausea returned.

Inside, Thomas had another glass of water, reached for the phone, dialed a sixteen-digit number, and waited.

"Hello, Tom," said Kumi.

"You don't say *moshi moshi* anymore," he said, smiling.

"Not to you," she said. "You are the only person who calls at this ungodly hour."

"So how's Tokyo?" he said, the sound of her voice unwinding him like a hot bath.

"Oh, you know, the usual. The State Department wants to involve me in intellectual property issues with China, about which I know nothing."

"And they understand that you speak Japanese, which is not the same as Chinese?"

"Yeah, they got a research grant."

"So why you?"

"Who knows. They think I look friendly."

"Boy, do they not know you," said Thomas.

"No one knows me like you do, Tom," she said, wry as ever. "Or at least there are bits of me that only you see."

"I should hope so," said Thomas.

"That's not what I meant," she said. "You have a mind like . . ."

"A graduate student?"

"I guess so," she said. "Aren't you getting a bit old for that?"

"Probably," he said. "But sometimes it feels like I only really knew you in my twenties."

He thought he heard her sigh. For years they had been separated, furiously so. Now they were at least speaking again, perhaps more than that, though it was hard to be sure. They had never stopped being married, at least technically.

"How are your classes?" he asked.

Kumi had decided that since she was going to be in Japan, she might as well tap into her cultural heritage. She had signed up for three courses, karate, traditional Japanese cooking, and ikebana: flower arranging. That had been the first to go.

"Those women drove me nuts," she had said. "Everything had to be *just so*. And there was only one way of doing it. They're sticking two bits of bamboo and a camellia flower on a rock and they act like they're defusing a tactical nuclear missile. They'd look at mine and say, 'This is incorrect.' *Incorrect?* It's flower arranging! I had to get out before I killed someone."

That had been two weeks ago.

"Not sure how long the karate is going to last," she said tonight. "They say I'm unfocused, too aggressive."

Thomas chuckled.

"Laugh it up, English teacher," she said. "I'll come by there and kick your ass."

"When?" he said.

"When I've mastered rolling my sushi," she said. "I'm better at that. The Zen thing makes more sense when you're making rice and seaweed snacks than when someone is trying to kick you in the head. Go figure."

"Listen," he said. "Something happened and I need to talk to you."

He told her about the dead woman and she asked the right questions until he had no more answers, and there was a silence. Then he told her about Ben Williams's memorial service.

"I don't think you ever mentioned him before," she said.

It wasn't supposed to be a criticism, but Thomas bristled.

"You weren't talking to me then, remember?"

"It takes two to . . . I don't know," she said. "Whatever the opposite of 'tango' is."

"True," he admitted.

"I'm sorry I can't come back to the States right now, Tom."

"Oh, I know," said Thomas, pleased that she would even consider it. "I'm not sure which bothered me more, the murder or the memorial service. He died at the same age I was when we met."

"Yes?"

"Makes you think, doesn't it," he said. The hollowness of the phrase stung him into saying more. "I mean, makes you realize how little time you have—or might have—how much you should . . ."

"Seize the day?"

"Something like that, yes."

"Are you okay, Tom?"

"Yes," he said. "Sorry. I'm just feeling . . . melancholy, I guess. I'm thirty-eight, Kumi, you know? *Thirty-eight*. That makes me about halfway through."

"Halfway through what?"

"Life," he said. "I mean, given average life expectancy. More than halfway if something happens . . ."

"Oh, *this* is a cheery conversation," she said.

"Sorry."

"I'm sorry I'm not there, Tom, but you didn't want me back before."

"Not true," said Thomas. "I did, even if I didn't know it."

She laughed at that, and he pressed what he took to be an advantage.

"So how long are we talking? Six months? A year?"

"Tom," she said, and there was that caution again, that refusal to get caught up in him, in *them*. "I'm not sure. I can't think about it right now. This project I'm working on is starting to show some real promise. I complain about my job but it's a part of me. Between you and me, I'm actually pretty good at it, and most of the time, I love it. Let me get this assignment off my desk and then we'll talk. Promise."

"Weeks?"

"Two. Maybe three."

"Okay."

"Good," she said. She laughed, a short exhaling sound that blew the tension out of her chest, a noise so familiar he could almost see it, and he knew what it meant. It was relief, joyous and grateful, and he knew she had been steeling herself to tell him she wasn't coming yet, wasn't even ready to discuss it, long before he had called.

"Okay," he said again, wondering when he would see her next, wondering also why these calls always made him feel like a contestant on a game show, the one who comes in second and goes home with the kinds of consolation prizes you either already have or never wanted. "I just want you here again."

"Soon," she said. "Promise."

CHAPTER 4

Thomas was clearing out the book-filled lumber room that he
mockingly called his library when the phone rang. He read
novels obsessively all year round. Even after hours of grading papers he would curl up in a corner with a glass of something and a book, till he could barely keep his eyes open. It
was what he did. He read slowly, weighing each phrase in his
mind no matter how pulpy the genre, and always finished,
even if it took weeks, regardless of how bad the book was.
Every third book was, he decided, a waste of his time, and
though he could usually predict which those would be inside
a few pages—as he could usually predict what grade a student paper would get inside the first paragraph—he couldn't
put them aside. It was, he thought, as he set down a stack of
pristine paperbacks and went looking for the phone, a fault of
which he was secretly and absurdly proud.

"So how've you been, Mr. Knight?"

The voice was odd.

"Fine," said Thomas, reflexively. "Who's this?"

"It's David Escolme. You've probably forgotten me."

"Not at all, David," said Thomas, thinking that he had, in
fact, forgotten him right up to the moment the phone rang.

David Escolme had been a student of his, what? Ten years
ago? Something like that. Before Ben Williams for sure. And
unlike Williams, Escolme had been a geeky, acne-faced kid,
unathletic, socially awkward, and a bit too clever for his own
good. They had talked about music, what used to be called alternative rock and its various forebears, from grunge to those
older, quirky, tough-to-categorize bands like XTC. In fact,
Escolme had been the one to introduce Thomas to some of
those groups, and had made a gift of one of XTC's albums to

him when he left school. Thomas still played it from time to time.

As if hearing his thoughts, Escolme said, "You still listening to music?"

"Some," said Thomas. "I'm a bit out of touch these days. Still playing the same stuff I did when you were here, probably."

"And reading Sherlock Holmes? You introduced me to him, remember?"

Thomas didn't remember, and hadn't read Conan Doyle for years. Escolme didn't wait to hear his answer but quoted in a ludicrous British accent.

"*You see but you do not observe!* Great stuff. Do you remember the TV version with Jeremy Brett? Awesome."

"They were good," agreed Thomas.

It was more than a surprise to hear from Escolme after all these years. There was something strange about it. Underneath the young man's hurried explanations about how he had come to look up his old high school English teacher, behind the amiable banter about the years since last they spoke, there was something calculated. He sounded like he was working from a script, not with the bored detachment of the telemarketer, but with a studied nonchalance, like an actor trying to pass off as spontaneous what was actually memorized.

"Did you know Ben Williams?" Thomas asked.

"No," said Escolme. "Read about him last week. It was the memorial today, right?"

"Right."

"Tough break."

The inadequacy of the remark irritated Thomas, and he decided to press the conversation to a close.

"Was there something particular on your mind, David?" he asked.

"Well, it's a funny thing," the voice was saying over what seemed to be a cell phone line, smiling as if it really *were* funny, though Thomas didn't believe him. "I didn't really know who else to turn to. I know it's been years, and we've sort of lost touch, but I mean . . . Who else do I know who reads Shakespeare?"

Thomas frowned.

"Shakespeare?" he said.

"Yes," he said. "I need a little help with Shakespeare."

He was almost giggling at the obvious absurdity of the request, and Thomas wondered for a moment if the whole thing was some kind of practical joke. Maybe there were a bunch of them, fresh from the memorial, huddled around a phone trying not to explode with laughter as they prank-called their old teacher . . .

"You must know other people who read Shakespeare, David," said Thomas.

"Maybe," said Escolme, not even bothering to dodge, "but you were doing a doctorate on him, right? I remember that. That's why you were such a good teacher."

Thomas smiled at the non sequitur.

"I never finished," he said, "and that was all a long time ago. Why don't you talk to someone in the English department at . . . Where did you go to school again?"

"BU!" he said, momentarily genuine in his surprise. "You helped get me in, remember?"

"Of course," said Thomas. Boston University: his old alma mater, from which he had finally fled to teach high school back in Chicago, trying to shut out his professors' mutterings about wasted talent as he had shut out the groaning fault line on which his marriage sat.

That was a long time ago.

And the ground beneath his marriage had stopped shifting. For now. Thomas's mind went back to the conversation he had had with Kumi, and he wondered vaguely when he would see her again.

"Anyway," Escolme was saying, "I didn't get real friendly with the faculty there."

"What about Randall Dagenhart?" said Thomas. "Is he still there?"

"I guess," said Escolme, a little too quickly. "I had a class with him but it was one of those huge lectures. He didn't even grade my papers. In the end, I spent more time with the theater guys. Anyway, I *trust* you."

There it was again, that edgy nervousness. Thomas didn't like it.

"Thanks, but . . . ," he began.

"I'm serious," said Escolme. "*This* is serious."

And then he inserted a little autobiographical news to prove it was serious. Escolme's news—that he had since completed a master's degree in English, then worked for a boutique literary agency before being head-hunted into one of the largest literary management companies in the country—was surprising only because it made clear what such conversations always made clear, that the time had slipped unnoticed away. Thomas knew nothing about the world of publishing, but he had heard of Vernon Fredericks Literary, if only for their movie division whose agents were routinely thanked on Oscar night.

"I don't understand what that has to do with Shakespeare," said Thomas. "Or with me, frankly."

"Mr. Knight," he said. "I promise. This is not like anything you've dealt with before. Honestly. I want it to be you."

Thomas paused.

"To do what?" he said.

"I have to show you. I'm at the Drake. Room 304."

Thomas suddenly felt weary beyond words. He wanted to say that he had spent a miserable and horrific day dealing with the corpse he had found propped up against his kitchen window, but even the idea of saying such things made him want to forget them. He paused and then said simply,

"When?"

CHAPTER 5

As soon as he had hung up, he Googled "Escolme, Vernon Fredericks Literary." Thomas wasn't sure what he expected to find: a story in the *Tribune*, perhaps, local boy makes good. Something like that. What he found was a professional-looking website, all cool blues and grays, surrounding a similarly professional blurb about the literary awards won by its (unnamed) "talent" along with a set of submission guidelines. At the bottom of the page, it listed VFL's locations: New York, London, Beverly Hills, Tokyo, and Nashville. No Chicago branch. Thomas clicked the New York link and found a roster of agents.

David Escolme was two-thirds down the list.

There was a picture. The boy Thomas had known was still recognizable, but only just. The acne was gone, the eighties glasses had been replaced by sleek black frames with oblong lenses, and the boy was now a man, smiling confidently into the camera. He looked comfortable in his elegant suit, a man for whom the slings and arrows of adolescence had long since glanced off and been forgotten, a man immune to the future. It was the face of a businessman.

Nothing wrong with that, he reminded himself. *And let's see if we can spare him your tiresome lectures on the state of the arts in America, shall we?*

He grinned sheepishly to himself and his gaze fell on the kitchen window. The evening light was dwindling fast and the window was like a hole into the swelling night, a picture frame whose canvas had been slit out. For a second he saw the dead woman's face as clearly as if she was still there, her staring eyes (one green, one violet) turned blank upon him.

He turned abruptly away and checked his watch. He had

time for one of his slow, pounding runs around Evanston's twilit streets before going on to meet Escolme. Anything to get that face out of his mind.

His phone rang once and he snatched it up.

"Hello?"

"Mr. Knight, this is Lieutenant Polinski. We spoke this morning. You have a second?"

"Sure."

"We're still trying to get an ID on the victim, but I need to ask you again if you're sure you didn't know her."

"I'm sure. I wouldn't forget." *Those eyes.* "Why?" he asked.

"You keep your garbage by the kitchen door?"

"Yes."

"And it gets collected when?"

"Wednesday morning, from the front."

"The crime scene guys turned up a piece of paper— actually, a yellow Post-it note—in a bush a few yards from the body. It could just be garbage, but it seems unlikely that it's been lying out there for almost a week, particularly since we had that rain over the weekend."

"What did it say?"

"It just had your name and address written on it in pencil. Have you thrown anything like that out recently?"

"No. I already know where I live."

"Right," said Polinski. "That's what I figured. When we know who she is we'll be trying to match the handwriting, but for now we're working on the assumption that the note was hers."

"Which means . . . ?"

"That she was coming to see you. You sure you didn't know her?"

Thomas stared blankly at the wall and she had to prompt him before he said, again, "I'm sure."

It was only after he hung up that he began to wonder if that was true.

CHAPTER 6

It was hardly surprising that Escolme was staying at the Drake. Thomas took the Red Line to Chicago and State and walked down to where the Magnificent Mile began. The hotel itself—muted Deco elegance outside and red-carpeted opulence inside—always reminded Thomas of some fine old English theater, some place built by Henry Irving where you might find a young John Gielgud having a quick smoke by the stage door. It wasn't squeaky clean like most of the glass-and-chrome high-rises, and its prestige lay in a certain gilded shabbiness that spoke, in so far as Chicago could, of venerable age. Thomas liked it, but he felt like an impostor.

He walked quickly under the paneled ceilings and overwrought chandeliers, dodging vast floral arrangements set up like defensive gun casements, till he found the reception desk where he brandished Escolme's room number as if he were claiming sanctuary. The uniformed black man pointed the way to brass-doored elevators flanked by potted palms.

Thomas was wearing faded jeans and a flannel shirt with a leather jacket, and when he caught a woman in a Chanel suit looking at him skeptically, he gave her a defiant look that set her fiddling with her purse.

The defiance was bravado. Places like this always left him tucking his shirt in and standing up straight as if he were trying—vainly, of course—to blend in, or worse, to impress someone. He felt a flush of irritation that Escolme had insisted they meet here, as if the agent were rubbing his former mentor's nose in his success.

But that didn't feel right either. Escolme had been a good kid. Quirky, perhaps, a bit neurotic, but neither arrogant nor mean spirited.

The elevator door opened and Thomas stepped out, checked the room numbers, and moved down a hallway till he reached 304. The door was a rich heavy timber that might have been teak—more the door of a family home than a hotel room—and was fitted with a similarly heavy brass knocker.

He knocked and waited.

When nothing happened, he knocked again.

Suddenly the door flew open and Thomas saw David Escolme for the first time in a decade.

It was a momentary meeting. Having flung the door open, Escolme peered at Thomas for a moment, then turned his back on him, muttering, and went quickly back into the room, leaving the door open. Thomas stepped uneasily inside and, for a moment, watched his host as he riffled vaguely through books on his desk, then hurled them to the floor with a shout of rage. Whatever he had heard in David Escolme's voice over the phone had intensified exponentially.

The agent seemed to have forgotten him. He was pacing, his lips moving constantly, stopping periodically to rub his temples with both hands, a picture of frustration and despair. He was wearing what were probably his work clothes, including wingtips, but had discarded his jacket and tie and unfastened several buttons of his rumpled shirt. The room Thomas was standing in was a mirror of its owner: what had been elegant and sophisticated overturned as if by a whirlwind. The floor was strewn with books and papers, a coffee table had been upended, and the vase of tulips that had been sitting on it lay in pieces on the carpet. A familiar CD case lay on the floor: XTC's *English Settlement*.

"David?" said Thomas. "Is everything okay?"

Escolme turned, as if just remembering he wasn't alone, produced a hollow bark of laughter, and went back to his pacing, picking his way between overturned drawers of clothes and what looked to be champagne bottles, at least half a dozen of them, strewn across the floor like howitzer shells.

"I'm sorry," said Thomas. "This looks like a bad time. I'll let myself out and maybe, if you'd like to give me a call sometime . . ."

"No!" Escolme shouted. "Don't go."

The vagueness in his eyes was suddenly gone, and he looked earnest and desperate.

"You are obviously busy," Thomas continued. "I can come back . . ."

"No," said Escolme again, crossing quickly to him and grasping Thomas's arm in a knuckle-whitening grasp. "Please. I am . . . not quite myself. But I need you here. Please, sit down."

The inadequacy of the phrase "not quite myself" and the fact that there wasn't an upright chair in the room that wasn't covered with discarded books and papers made Thomas hesitate. Escolme turned a leather-backed wing chair, swept a stack of legal briefs onto the floor, and motioned to it.

"Please," he said again.

Slowly, his eyes on the agent, Thomas sat down.

"Perhaps you would like to join me," said Thomas, cautiously.

Escolme nodded thoughtfully and repeatedly, as if mulling the suggestion, then took a seat opposite him, crunching the broken vase underfoot as he did so.

"What's going on, David?"

For a long moment the young man was quite still, and then, to Thomas's horror, he put his hands in his face again, rocked forward, and emitted a long, breathless sob. At last he lowered his hands, but his face was still set in a grimace of grief, mouth stretched wide in the parody of a smile, eyes squeezed shut, tears smeared on his cheeks.

"I lost it," he breathed.

"What?" said Thomas, still tense and uncomfortable, his voice barely more than a whisper.

Escolme looked at him then, as if steeling himself to say the words.

"*Love's Labour's Won.*"

"What?"

"*Love's Labour's Won,*" he repeated. "The Shakespeare play."

Thomas stared at him, incredulous.

"But that never existed," said Thomas. "Or if it did, we don't have it. It's lost."

"Not lost," said Escolme. "I held it in my hands only hours ago. And now it's gone."

CHAPTER 7

"What are you talking about?" said Thomas. All the tension had suddenly evaporated and he felt curiously relaxed, as if the whole thing had been a joke or a misunderstanding. "*Love's Labour's Won*? There's no such thing."

"There is," said Escolme. "There was. I had it."

"David, it doesn't exist," said Thomas, kindly. "It never existed."

"It did," said the agent, calming now, so that the frantic despair was turning into exhaustion. "It does. I had it," he said, his eyes closing again. "Here."

The energy drained out of him again and he slumped in his chair.

"How could you have had it?" Thomas said, trying to keep the disbelief out of his voice, trying to protect the man from what was surely a delusion.

"I had it." He sighed. "I had it, and it's gone."

This was becoming a mantra. Thomas tried a different tack.

"Where did you find it?"

"Oh, I didn't find it. I was loaned it," said Escolme. "By a client."

Thomas breathed out slowly so that the air whistled. It was one thing to have lost something Escolme thought was a lost play by Shakespeare; it was another thing entirely to have lost something a client had entrusted to him, something *the client* believed to be a lost play by Shakespeare. It wasn't of course; it couldn't be. But if someone thought it was—or merely *claimed* it was—and then put it into their agent's safekeeping . . . No wonder Escolme was freaking out. This could destroy him.

"Okay," said Thomas. "So when did you last have it?"

He might have been helping Kumi find her car keys.

"I put it in the hotel safe when I arrived," he said. "I got it out an hour ago to show you."

The agent's eyes flashed at Thomas as if this were some-how *his* fault. Thomas ignored the idea.

"And you kept it in here?" he said.

"Yes," said Escolme. "It was here. Right *here*," he said, slapping the bed with his hand. "It was in this black attaché case. I took a shower. Changed my clothes. I didn't notice it had gone till . . ." He glanced at his watch like a man who had no idea whether it was day or night. ". . . twenty minutes ago. But it must have gone while I was in the bathroom."

Thomas scowled at the evidence of the search around him. This was Escolme's own desperate work, not the act of an intruder, and it had been done not as the rational search of someone who had mislaid something, but in the desperate chaos of hoping against hope. The briefcase was open on the bed, slewed into the stripped sheets. If the agent was right, someone had timed their entrance perfectly and had known what they were looking for and where to find it. Everything else in the room, champagne bottles included, had been un-settled by his own subsequent panic.

"Is anything else missing?" Thomas asked.

Escolme stared at him.

"You mean, did I have any other priceless artifacts lying around?" asked Escolme with sudden scorn. "A forgotten Van Gogh still life, maybe, or a long-lost Michelangelo marble . . . ?"

"That's a *no*, then," Thomas cut in.

"That's a *no*," said Escolme, deflating again.

"Then we should call the police," said Thomas.

"No," said Escolme. "Absolutely not. You might as well call the *Tribune*. I'd be finished."

"The owner, then."

"Again, no," said Escolme with the careful emphasis of someone warning a persistently irritable child. "And for the same reason."

"Who knew you had it?" he said.

"No one," said Escolme. "Just my client."

"Who is—?"

"I can't tell you that," he said.

Thomas snorted.

"Maybe I should go," he said.

"No," said Escolme. "Don't. I just can't tell you that."

Thomas checked his watch.

"Other people at the agency must have known?" he said.

"No. VFL gives us a lot of leeway. No one stands over us because we're so *good* at what we do." He grinned wolfishly, his eyes empty. "I answer to no one."

"I'm sorry, David," said Thomas. "I don't think I can help you. I don't understand why you called me."

He picked up one of the fallen champagne bottles for something to do and set it on the bedside table. It was full, the foil still tight over the wired cork. Thomas studied the label to break Escolme's hold on his eyes. It was French, labeled Saint Evremond Reims. He'd never heard of it. He risked a look at Escolme.

The agent's fiery defiance had crumbled so that the schoolboy he had been shimmered into view like the picture on a faulty TV. He looked lost and wounded and alone.

"Sounds like a Sherlock Holmes story, doesn't it?" he said, quietly. "Locked rooms and missing papers. " 'The Naval Treaty.' Remember that one?"

"Vaguely," said Thomas. Something about the reference bothered him, and that showed in his face.

"You *have* to help," Escolme said, suddenly pleading.

"I don't know how," said Thomas.

And that was the truth, though the full truth was that he wasn't sure he wanted to help. He didn't like the feel of the situation and was relieved to be able to extricate himself— honestly—on the grounds of his undeniable ignorance.

"I really don't know what to do," he said. "I'd talk to your client or the police, but I understand why you don't want to."

"I see."

"I'm sorry," Thomas said. "I'm going to go now. If there's anything I can do to help, call me."

Escolme looked numb. He nodded, his eyes glazed, but said nothing.

"You okay?" said Thomas. "I mean, if you need me to stay . . ."

"Daniella Blackstone," he said.

Thomas thought for a moment. The name resonated but unspecifically.

"That's your client?" he said.

"As in Blackstone and Church," said Escolme, "yes."

Thomas whistled in spite of himself.

"Don't be too impressed," said Escolme. "I can't get anything of hers published. She's not that great a writer."

"Then she's incredibly lucky," said Thomas. "I can't remember a week when Blackstone and Church weren't on the *New York Times* bestseller list."

Blackstone and Church wrote mysteries set in England starring a detective inspector who also happened to be a peer of the realm, and who handled cases with a supernatural bent. Thomas had read two and had found them both preposterous and hugely entertaining.

"But that's Blackstone *and Church*, isn't it?" Escolme shot back. "Not just Blackstone. The woman couldn't write a decent story if her life depended on it. She's been a stone around Elsbeth Church's neck for over a decade. They wrote their last co-authored book two years ago, and a year after that announced that they would be writing solo stuff for the foreseeable future. Blackstone hasn't been able to get published since, and given the crap publishers spew out, that should tell you something."

"So why do you represent her?" said Thomas.

"Because all my other authors are waiting for the Nobel committee to call, you mean?" said the agent, caustic again. "Because she separated from her representation when she split with Church, and because her publisher had done such a great job of hiding how little of Blackstone and Church was actually Blackstone, that we snapped her up. Of course, it took about ten minutes—or more accurately, ten pages—to see that she was dead weight, and about another ten minutes for her former publisher to leak that out to further Elsbeth Church's solo work. So for eight months I've been pushing her crap, trying to get a press to pay a ghostwriter to get in on the act, and had no bites. Then she shows up in New York with a play, of all things, handwritten."

Thomas stared at him. None of this felt right.

"Handwritten?"

"Oh, not in Shakespeare's hand," said the agent. "Her own. First, she says she wrote it as a response to Shakespeare and could she get it copyrighted? I knew she was lying after reading the first ten lines. The woman could no more have written that than flown to the moon. I called her on it and she took it away in a sulk. A week later she calls me up. No she didn't write it, she says. She copied it. The original is Shakespeare's and no one knows it exists. Can I figure out how to secure some form of rights for her that will ensure she never has to write another lousy word? I tell her that if it's Shakespeare it will be public domain and she'll have no rights to the content beyond the value of the manuscript itself. 'Then we'll have to restrict who sees it,' she says. 'I can't copyright the work, but I can copyright the edition, and make sure everything comes from that.' I tell her the first step is to very quietly verify that it is what she says it is. She tells me to go ahead, carefully, and brings me these handwritten pages. She dares not even photocopy it in case someone sees it. She sure as hell won't give me the original, so I have only her transcript. Any investigation of the text thus hinges on the words themselves, not the composition of the ink, the age of the paper, and so on."

"I don't think I understand," said Thomas. "I mean, if it's just her copy, then the thing you've lost has no value, right? And she still has the original. So what's the problem?"

"Because no one can know about it!" he said. "If there's another copy floating around out there, there's no way she can keep the content secret. Next thing you know the whole thing is on the Web, it's public domain, and no one makes a cent."

"There can't be that much money riding on this," Thomas began. "Surely . . ."

"Are you joking?" Escolme snapped, his voice rising, the muscles of his face tense and still. "A quarto of *Hamlet* was auctioned for twenty million U.S. a year ago, and that's a play we already know inside out, and one that exists in multiple copies of multiple early printings. Can you put a price on the only extant version of a lost Shakespeare play? I can't. But it's not about the value of the artifact itself. Even if the copyright were considered public domain, the owner of that one copy could pluck numbers out of the air while the film, theater, and book producers lined up to get a look at it."

"I know . . . ," Thomas began.

"No," said Escolme with an earnestness tinged with menace. "You don't. This would be the art discovery of the century. It would make headlines in every newspaper in the world. In the *world*," he repeated. "Because Shakespeare is global, the bedrock of culture and education all over the planet. It doesn't matter if the play is obscure or even bad. It doesn't matter if it's the original Shakespearean manuscript or a copy made by some kid in crayon. It's a new Shakespeare play, and if people agree that that's what it is, that's all it has to be. Within a year, you'd be looking at a blockbuster movie starring everyone you've ever heard of, and book sales that would make Dan Brown and J. K. Rowling weep. Billions of dollars, Mr. Knight. *Billions.* That little stack of paper wasn't a book, it was a potential industry."

Whatever skepticism Thomas might have felt about the status of the missing pages themselves, he guessed Escolme was right. If the play was legitimate, it would be a diamond mine for far more than literary academia. But he didn't know what he was supposed to do to help or why Escolme had called him in the first place.

"It's not about who owns the original," Escolme concluded. "That will be worth money, but it's nothing to what will be made by whoever gets this thing in print first. That's the issue. *That's* the problem. Daniella Blackstone could still have some perfect Renaissance quarto version sitting in a safe-deposit box somewhere that she'll be able to sell for a nice little nest egg, but the real money is in the first modern edition and everything that flows from it. The only way she can control that is by making sure no one sees it except in her copyrighted printing. Do you see now, Mr. Knight? We had control of the thing and we lost it. *I* lost it, and with it, the kind of money you can't begin to imagine."

Thomas said nothing for a moment. All this talk about money was distracting him, but even if Escolme was right, it didn't change the question that had been in Thomas's mind since their first conversation on the phone.

"Why did you call me?" he demanded. "I don't understand why I'm here."

"I wanted you to read it," said Escolme. "Tell me what you thought. Whether it was real."

"I'm a high school English teacher!" Thomas exclaimed. "You need experts. Academics. Those guys who run word choices and spelling variants through computers so they can figure out who wrote what. That's an entire field of study that I know nothing about. Even if you had the thing in front of you I couldn't begin to help. I never even finished my doctorate, David!" Thomas said, getting to his feet. This had gone on long enough. "I'm sorry. This has been a very strange day. I'm glad to see you again, David, but I'm not the person you need."

CHAPTER 8

Thomas Knight returned home to 1247 Sycamore Street, the Skokie end of Evanston—Escolme's business card tucked into his breast pocket—baffled, frustrated, and with a sense of failure he knew was wholly unreasonable. It wasn't Thomas who had lost the manuscript, after all, nor could any reasonable person expect him to aid significantly in recovering it.

If it had ever existed.

And that was another part of the deflation. Like all teachers, Thomas had been proud of his former student's success, however much Escolme wore it like a peacock wears its tail. But if Escolme was just a scam artist, or—worse—deluded, then all that success amounted to nothing at all.

The alternative—that he was telling the truth—was no better. If Escolme really had found a lost play by Shakespeare, any glory he might have achieved would be wiped out by his losing it again—and then some. It was a nasty irony that the moment he had re-entered Thomas's life, the peacock agent was in the process of having his feathers rudely plucked. Thomas couldn't decide which would have been worse, to have never heard from Escolme again, or to be invited into the agent's confidence in time to have a ringside view as his former student's life went down the toilet.

Assuming all this is real.

That reference to "The Naval Treaty" bothered him. Escolme was right that the Sherlock Holmes story was similar: a valuable manuscript disappearing from a locked room so that suspicion fell on the man charged with its safety. Holmes stood by the suspect, proved his innocence, and discovered the manuscript.

All very tidy.

Which was why it bothered him that Escolme had referred to it. It too neatly made him the aggrieved party. But what if that was a blind? The evening had felt so strange, and not just because of this tale of the missing play. It felt like Thomas had walked into a play when it was halfway through, that the ravaged hotel room was no more than a set. What had Escolme said about being involved in theater in college? Was it possible that all his anguish and panic was no more than a performance, and if so, why?

Still, he thought, *imagine finding a lost play by William Shakespeare!*

It was an exhilarating idea, however preposterous. Sure, it would be worth money, whatever the legal issues of copyright, but just the thought of bringing such a thing to light, sharing it with the world . . .

Thomas Knight, graduate school dropout, makes the single greatest discovery in the history of Shakespeare scholarship . . .

Wouldn't that be something? He considered this as he poured himself one of the two drinks he permitted himself a night. He rarely indulged in the second, but tonight he would.

I think we'll make exceptions for days that begin with corpses at your kitchen window, he thought.

Beginning tomorrow, he would be mired in final papers from his English classes, so he would be on the wagon till the weekend whether he liked the idea or not.

It was the first week of June and the kids could smell the summer vacation, redolent with the aroma of barbecues on the shores of the great lake, suntan lotion, and the cordite edge of fireworks. They just had to fight their way through his palisade of essays and exams, and they'd be free. Thomas could almost remember the scent of it himself, and the infinite expanse of glorious school-less days that it heralded, all those end-of-year hurdles like a crossing of the river Styx to the Elysian fields beyond.

These days the summer brought little change in his daily rhythms, beyond giving him more time to read. He had hoped to see Kumi, but he doubted he could afford the flight, and she was likely to be tied up at work even if he made it out there. He sipped his whisky and savored the aroma of peat, smoke, and the tang of seaweed, then took his glass out to the back porch where he could sit and listen to the night.

Thomas had a small yard, a square of unruly lawn edged with ancient rosebushes that had been there when he moved in, and hedged from the neighbors with privet and holly. It was private and still. From the rickety deck he could sit, glass in hand, and listen for the screech owl that roosted in his prize elm at the bottom of the yard. Back here in the green, cool shade, the city could be a thousand miles away. He suspected he longed for these moments like his students longed for summer.

God, he thought. *What a day.*

It seemed impossible that everything—the dead woman, the memorial service, Escolme and his bizarre assertions— had all happened in the last twenty-four hours. Less, actually. It was surreal and exhausting.

One day, one normal, ordinary day, Kumi will come, and we will sit together in the silence and watch for the owl. Then on Saturday morning we'll take the L into the city and go to Lula's for breakfast. She will have the strada, like she always used to, and we'll talk about the books we are reading, then we'll go for a walk along the shore . . .

He didn't pay attention to the sound until he realized that he had heard it at least three times. It was faint, a short, ring-ing clink like a tiny bell. He listened for a second and it came again.

A neighbor's wind chime?

Not unless it had just been put up, and besides, the night was still.

He tried to focus his hearing to place the sound. It came again and he realized two things at once: it came from the passage between the hedge and the house, and it was the sound of footsteps. He didn't know why they rang like that, but that was what they were.

He put his glass down very slowly. The sound had stopped. He stood up slowly, listening.

Nothing.

Thomas's body was tense, his breath held, his head cocked, listening.

Still nothing.

Then it came again, muted this time but just as close. If it was footsteps, whoever was back there was being careful. Perhaps they knew he was here.

The nearest phone was in the kitchen. He looked around the porch. There was nothing out here but his old rocker and a faded wooden table he had started to strip down and never finished. The closest thing to a weapon he had was his whisky glass.

Oh yes, he thought, *that'll work. Because a killer returning to the scene of the crime will burst from the shrubs brandishing a brandy snifter . . .*

Shut up. Listen.

The sound came again, a shrill metallic *ping*, this time close enough that he could hear the other sounds that came with it; the shifting of fabric, the infinitesimal creak of shoe leather, the faintest hint of breath.

It was getting closer.

If he could get into the kitchen he could reach for the phone. Or a knife. Slowly, his eyes locked on the dark tangle of green where the passage down the side of the house began only fifteen feet away, he took a step sideways toward the kitchen door. Then another.

He checked the kitchen door. It was open, but the screen was closed to keep the bugs out of the house. He took a step toward it, then returned his stare to the passage. The porch light gave him nothing beyond the deck itself. Whoever had crept down the side of the house could probably step out into the yard and still be largely invisible. Thomas stared at a shape beside the hedge, a dark bulge about the height of a man, unsure if it had been there before. He found himself inventorying the plants that grew along the hedge, trying to remember if anything was big enough to create that shadow.

Another sound. This time not the ring of metal but the crunch of grit beneath a shoe.

Thomas took another step toward the kitchen. The phone was no longer good enough. Whatever help it brought would be too slow by far. He needed a weapon. His left hand found the mesh of the screen door and fumbled for the latch. It was stiff, had needed oiling for weeks. He pressed it, his eyes still on the mounding shape beside the hedge. For a moment it wouldn't budge, and then it gave with a snap and the door juddered and creaked as it swung open.

Thomas winced at the noise. In the yard there was a sudden and absolute silence, then came that *ting* again, louder and crisper this time, followed rapidly by another, then another.

Whoever it was, he was running away.

Thomas released the door handle and sprang down from the porch. In two long strides he was turning into the passage at a full run.

If the yard had been dark, the passage, screened by the house and shrouded by the overgrown shrubbery, was almost completely black. The sound of his own echoing footsteps drowned out any sound the intruder might be making, and Thomas was too full of nervous energy and anger to process what happened next. He heard one more tiny metallic ring, then realized too late that the figure in the dark had stopped running, had turned to meet him.

As Thomas barreled into him he was caught with a hard roundhouse punch to his jaw, a punch he never saw coming, a punch he ran into with such force that his head snapped back and the night went white as lightning. It took a real punch to stop a man as big as Thomas in his tracks, but this one did just that. He stumbled into the wall and as he fought to stabilize himself, he was kicked hard in the stomach. Through the shock and the pain he heard the tiny ring of metal as the shoe connected, and then he was slumping to the ground, trying to breathe, silently shouting with panic as the air refused to come. He collapsed to the ground, his lungs empty, unaware of anything but the desperation of his body.

CHAPTER 9

It was probably only a matter of seconds that he spent huddled breathless on the concrete path, just time enough for his attacker to get away without having to run. Thomas heard the jangling steps as he walked and felt only a dumb fury at his incapacity. Later he would feel relief that the killer—if that was indeed who it was—had not come back and done to him what he had done to the woman. Thomas, after all, would not have been able to stop him.

He phoned the police and, when a uniformed officer arrived, told him what had happened. There was precious little to report, and the only significant detail he could offer—that his assailant wore bells on his shoes—made little impression on the policeman.

"People think they hear all kinds of weird noises when they're under stress," he said. "Especially if they've been drinking."

"Just make a note of it, will you?" said Thomas.

"Bells. On. His. Shoes," wrote the policeman. "Okay?"

"Okay," said Thomas, knowing the detail was useless, unless they were going to broadcast an APB for one of Santa's elves.

He also knew the police had their work cut out for them and that his minimal report wasn't helping, but he still felt frustrated and, if he was honest with himself, a little scared. It seemed likely that his attacker was connected to the dead woman with the strange eyes, and if so, then who was to say the man wouldn't come back?

Thomas tried to sleep but kept waking up, sure he had heard something. At five, exhausted and frustrated, he abandoned the attempt, showered, read, and made it over to the

Dominick's on Green Bay Road by a little after six. It was quiet, which he liked. He liked grocery shopping, or at least he did when he knew the store's layout as he did this one. He had two modes in shopping and usually did both in sequence on each visit. The first was swift, businesslike and faintly Zen, the stocking of the cart with the staples he did not have to search for or consider—milk, juice, eggs, bread, and so forth. That done, he relaxed into the fun part, the inspection of meat and vegetables and the imaginary arrangement of menus and recipes in his head as he planned his dinners for the next few days. His fridge and freezer were not as large as he would have liked, so the process took discipline as well as imagination.

Thomas liked food, though he was not what some would call a "foodie," and not solely because he loathed the word. He had, he liked to think, an eclectic palate, and could appreciate a fast-food burger for what it was, even if he'd rather be dining on oven-roasted pork shoulder with spigarello, pattypan squash, and chickpea barigoule at Avec on Chicago's Randolph Street. He was not a gourmet, just an enthusiast.

He picked over a few ears of corn. Supply was apparently depleted, though whether by drought or flooding (there had been a lot of both lately) he couldn't say. He chose a pork loin that was on special, which he would roast with rosemary and thyme from the garden, and chose a suitable beer. He had a poor palate for wine and couldn't afford to educate it. Beer, he knew. He picked up some chicken, navy beans, and coarse sausage for a cassoulet, and chose from the fruit selection. The peaches and nectarines seemed best, so he added several of each. Then salad greens, tomatoes, pine nuts, and a bottle of extra virgin olive oil (*how can anything be EXTRA virgin?*), and he was done. And, more important than filling his shopping bags, he had rebuilt some version of normalcy.

He was home by seven and was just about done unloading the car when he caught the strobing flare of blue lights through the living room window and was on his way to the front door when the bell rang. Even though he had glimpsed the cop car, the sound made him jump.

He opened the door and found a policewoman standing with her back to him, looking casually across the street. She turned to him, pale and smileless. Lieutenant Polinski. She had a long oval face, a thin broad mouth, and a mane of unruly black hair. She was probably in her midthirties but had the eyes and complexion of an older woman.

"Good morning, Mr. Knight," she said. "Can I come in for a moment?"

"Sure."

"Sounds like you had an eventful evening. You okay?"

"Kind of," he said.

"Tell me about it."

He did, though there wasn't much to tell, and when he finished she just nodded seriously and said, "Going after him wasn't real smart, especially if you thought he might have been the killer."

"I know," said Thomas. "I was just . . . Someone was sneaking around my yard. I don't know. I was angry."

"Still, it was a reckless thing to do."

"That's me." Thomas grinned. "Mr. Reckless."

She gave him a hard look.

"This isn't a game, Mr. Knight. This is a murder inquiry and you could have gotten yourself into serious trouble. The kind of trouble you don't wake up from. You hear what I'm saying? Let's try to be a little more careful—and by that I mean smart—in the future, okay?"

"Okay," he said.

Polinski gave him another look, sure he wasn't really getting it, then shrugged.

"There are several officers going door to door to see if anyone might have seen anything. They started yesterday."

"Oh," said Thomas, unsure of what to say. "Right. I haven't remembered anything else, I'm afraid. But I'm glad to have them around. After last night, I mean."

"And you are still sure you didn't know the woman?"

"Sure."

"Right," she said. She seemed unusually watchful, and Thomas wondered why the officer in charge of the investigation was talking to him, when uniforms were deemed sufficient for the shoe-leather work at his neighbors' houses. "Does the name Daniella Blackstone mean anything to you?"

Thomas stared at her.

"The novelist? That's who the dead woman was?"

"That's right," said Polinski, her gaze steady. "You knew her?"

For a moment Thomas did not know what to say.

"Only through her books," he said.

CHAPTER 10

It wasn't an adequate answer, he knew, and though he had been able for a moment to convince himself that it was an honest answer in a very limited sense of the word, he knew that it was also an evasion. Polinski had sensed something in his hesitation, and though she had left, he knew she'd be back. It couldn't be a coincidence that Daniella Blackstone had died outside his house, not with his address in her pocket, not when her agent was a former student of his.

What had been strange and scary in the way dreams can be scary before you get out of them, suddenly became a good deal darker, more alarming. Because what had seemed like a series of weird but unconnected events—the dead woman, Escolme's mad obsession, the nocturnal stalker—now felt uncannily like parts of a whole.

Escolme had set him up. He must have. He had given the woman his name. She had wanted to get some outside authority to confirm the identity of the play, someone who wouldn't try to muscle in on her ownership of it as a way of making a name for himself as an academic, and Escolme had sent her to him. As a result she had been killed on his doorstep, and Escolme had hidden the fact that he knew she was dead, and that he had already implicated Thomas. Maybe he had hidden more than that, worse.

"Sounds like a Sherlock Holmes story, doesn't it?" Escolme had said. *"Locked rooms and missing papers. 'The Naval Treaty.'"*

" 'Naval Treaty' my ass," Thomas muttered. The whole thing had been a shell game. He just had to find out why.

He called the Drake.

"I'd like to connect to a guest room," he said. "David Escolme."

"Can you spell that please, sir?"

Irritably, Thomas did, and waited for the ring of the room phone. What he got instead was the receptionist again.

"I'm afraid we have no one of that name staying here," he said.

His irritation spiked, touched now with something like apprehension.

He hung up, and forced himself to stop staring at the clock.

None of this felt right. He put his coffee down, crossed the room quickly, and went out the front door.

Polisnki and the other cop were nowhere to be seen, and whatever crime scene work had started in the small hours had apparently been completed. The patch of sidewalk up the block was still taped off, but no one was there now. Thomas fished in his pocket for Polinski's card and went back into the house.

She didn't answer her phone, and he didn't take the automated service up on being connected to another officer. Instead, he waited for the recording to start and said, "This is Thomas Knight from 1247 Sycamore. We spoke briefly this morning. I have something to say about the Blackstone murder. It's probably not important, but please give me a call."

He left his number and hung up.

It was, he knew, more backpedaling, more inadequacy. He was playing it down because he didn't want to be involved, not because it would be somehow inconvenient to be caught up in a police investigation, but because he hated the idea that he or someone he had once taught could be responsible—however indirectly—for a woman's death.

He then called five different home-security companies and inquired about installation costs. He had never had an alarm system before, had never seen the need. Suddenly he wanted one, and soon.

CHAPTER 11

He was fractionally late getting to school, and his students were restless. He did his best to marshal his thoughts and their attention, but he couldn't focus and found himself relying on the very teacher's book that he usually referred to—rather pompously—as the "Antidote to Learning." *Okay, now that we've worked out some answers of our own, let us consult the Antidote to Learning . . .* At the end of his first class he apologized for his distraction and promised the students to be his usual self the following day. They nodded solemnly and exchanged significant looks.

They know you've been talking to the police. They may even know why.

Sometimes Thomas wished that there were a national exam that would test the kids' capacity to get to the heart of secrets and mysteries involving the faculty. They'd all ace it.

At lunchtime he checked his phone for messages. There were three, two of them from alarm companies asking for details of his home and whether it was "prewired" for a security system. Thomas wasn't sure what that meant but called them back and said it probably wasn't. That would raise the costs, they said. He told them that was okay and set up an appointment for both companies to come by over the weekend.

The third message was from Polinski requesting that he call her back. He did so and, this time, got her on the first ring.

"This is Thomas Knight," he said.

"You have some information for me," she said, businesslike.

"I'm not really sure," said Thomas. "It's pretty flimsy. More of an odd coincidence really . . ."

"Go ahead," she said.

He told her everything: Escolme's call, their meeting at the Drake, his panic at the lost Shakespeare play, and his claim that it had belonged to the novelist who had been killed at Thomas's window. There was a momentary silence when he finished, and Thomas waited, half expecting a polite thanks and tacit dismissal.

"Can you spell that name for me? Escolme?"

He did so, and there was another pause.

"A lost Shakespeare play?" she said. "Does that seem likely to you?"

"Not really, no," said Thomas. "I don't know that much about it."

"Seems like he thinks otherwise," she said. "Anything else?"

"I think that's everything."

"I'll be in touch," said Polinski, and then she was gone.

In the teachers' lounge, he unfolded his *Tribune* and stared at it. Periodically he turned the pages, looking vaguely for anything about the murder. His eye snagged on a single word in the headline for a small story in the Living section: SHAKE-SPEARE.

His unease seemed to surge, then stilled as he focused. Seconds later, he relaxed. It was nothing. Apparently the National Shakespeare Conference was taking place right here in Chicago. Eight hundred or more Shakespeare professors from all over the world gathering to lecture and debate. Thomas grinned bleakly. He had attended this conference when it came to Boston in his graduate school days, and he had found it by turns impressive, daunting, and absurd.

It was nonsense, of course, to think that the conference was in any way relevant to what had just happened. It would have been arranged months, even years before. Thomas hadn't been a part of that world for more than a decade, had not, in fact, ever really been a part of it since he had abandoned his doctoral dissertation before it was a quarter complete. Yet, as an English teacher, he had never been able to let go of Shake-speare completely, though sometimes he felt as if it were Shakespeare who would not let go of him. Now the conference was arcing back into his city, into his life, and Thomas couldn't help feeling that it was significant. Somehow.

He looked up, frowning, and decided. He would leave school as early as his classes would permit and head over to the conference. He looked back to the paper to see where the meeting was being held and caught his breath.

The conference was at the Drake.

Naturally . . .

CHAPTER 12

Thomas arrived at the hotel having heard from neither the police nor Escolme, but he had barely thought about either since lunch. The idea of attending the Shakespeare conference had filled him with an excited curiosity. There would surely be people he knew there, by name if not by face, though the latter wasn't out of the question. There would be the dinosaurs still plugging away at scholarship everyone else had abandoned thirty years ago, the hotshot theory heads with their jargon, the Bardolators (often stray actors) and those who treated them as unthinking fans. More to the point, he would be immersed again in all that old energy, the crackle of intelligent debate, the thrill of discovery, but also the nitpicking and bluster, the intellectual outrageousness and pedantry, the stupefying political correctness worn like zealotry, and the oppressive careerism, everyone poised like vultures for someone to say something unutterably stupid. It would be like dropping in on his own funeral.

And being glad to be dead, he thought with a grim smile.

If that was what being out of academia meant, perhaps so.

The Drake felt different this time, and though he had no clear idea what he hoped to discover there, Thomas entered confidently, as if he belonged. One of the ballrooms had been given over to the book exhibit, another to registration. He made for the latter.

A couple of dozen academics were lining up at three alphabetized tables, picking up conference programs and name tags. He needed one or the other to be able to come and go as he felt. He approached the nearest table and made a study of the letters—P–Z, in this case—as if unsure what his name came under, resting his hand casually on one of the clear plastic name tags. He palmed it and made a beeline for the nearest bathroom.

In one of the stalls, he filled his name in on a piece of notepaper and slid it into the plastic sleeve, then walked purposefully back to the reception area, chose the A–K table, and sidled up to the front, looking apologetic.

"I'm sorry," he said to the harried graduate student at the front. "I seem to have mislaid my program. Do you mind if . . . ?"

"Help yourself," said the girl, gesturing to the pile of parchment-colored booklets.

Thomas walked away, thumbing through the program to see what session he might catch before the day ended and feeling pleased with himself.

"Knight? Thomas Knight?"

Thomas turned quickly. Standing a few paces away was a man in his sixties with a face like a bloodhound and large wet eyes. He had a laptop case slung over his shoulder and he was dressed in professorial mode—a heather-colored tweed suit—that might have been de rigueur fifty years earlier. He was a large man, rounded off at the corners but otherwise quite square, with linebacker shoulders despite his silvered hair. He was looking shrewdly at Thomas with something like disbelief. Thomas knew him at once.

"Professor Dagenhart," he said, smothering the sense of panic that he had been so quickly found out, but glad that it was Dagenhart. "How are you?"

"I'm fine," said the older man, smiling, but still looking quizzical. "What about you? I never thought I'd see you here again," he said, taking Thomas's hand and shaking it firmly.

Here *doesn't mean Chicago or the Drake*, thought Thomas. *He means at the National Shakespeare Conference.*

The location didn't matter. The conference would be largely the same whatever city it happened to be in, and most of the delegates would see little beyond the hotel walls.

"My hometown," said Thomas, lamely. "Thought I'd check it out."

Check it out? He was reverting to graduate school mode, talking like his students.

"Not presenting then?" said Dagenhart.

"God, no," he said, with a frankness he instantly regretted. "Just wanted to see what's hot in Shakespeare studies these days."

Dagenhart smiled at the phrase, though it was a dry smile, amused, and Thomas rushed to close up the silence.

"Are you presenting, Professor?" he said.

"I'm not reading a paper, if that's what you mean," said Dagenhart. "I'm in a seminar on gender in the early comedies."

"Right," said Thomas, nodding as if nothing could be more fascinating, trying to think of something intelligent to say, trying to impress as he once might have in class.

"And you're still teaching high school?" said Dagenhart, with that same slightly disbelieving smile, as if Thomas had said he was a steeplejack or a lion tamer.

"For my sins," Thomas smiled.

"And no plans to finish the doctorate?"

"God no," he said, with too much gusto. "I mean, I love teaching at this level. I feel like . . ."

"You're making a difference?" said Dagenhart, still wry.

"Well, yes," said Thomas, trying to keep the defensiveness out of his voice. "A bit. You know."

"Well, I guess someone has to be in the front-line trenches," said Dagenhart. "Better you than most. Still, I don't know how you put up with it."

"With what?"

"The laziness. The institutionalized mediocrity. All that damned testing to prove the opposite of what we all know: that they aren't really learning and nobody cares."

"Well," said Thomas, "it's not all that bad. I mean, I'm at a good school. And if you really care about your subject and the kids . . ."

A woman tapped Dagenhart on the shoulder and he turned. She was also in her sixties, tall, and vaguely regal in her bearing. She somehow managed not to see Thomas at all.

"We're heading in," she said in a bored, British voice.

"Yes," said Dagenhart, "I'll be right there." As an afterthought he said, "This is Tom Knight. Former student of mine. Teaches high school now."

"Do you, indeed?" said the empress. "How public-spirited of you."

Thomas smiled and nodded, checking the name badge she wore on her lapel: Katrina Barker.

His mouth fell open.

"Miss Barker," he said, "I loved your book. Really . . . great."

"The new one?" she said.

"Probably not," said Thomas. "The one on city comedy."

"Oh God," she said, "that was a former life. Not really doing that anymore. But I'm glad you liked it."

"I thought it was wonderful. Your treatment of religion in Jonson and Middleton . . ."

Dagenhart checked his watch, then turned his moist, shrewd eyes back onto Thomas. "Well, good to see you again, Knight. All the best."

Barker framed an apologetic smile, and her eyes were kind. Thomas opened his hands and shook his head: he understood, the gesture said. She was busy and important, while he was neither . . .

Then she was following Dagenhart, who was moving into the crowd easing through double doors into the conference hall, leaving Thomas standing there, checking his program as if he knew what he was doing, as if he had a right to be there.

He had enough dignity not to sit near Dagenhart for the three papers that followed, though his eyes constantly strayed to where he was sitting, as if expecting him to turn and smile, suggest they get together in the bar to catch up and meet his cronies properly. But the damage was done, and the papers that followed served only to reinforce to Thomas how the world of academia had forgotten him and moved on, that far from him rejecting it for its arcane pettiness and navel-gazing, academia had rejected him.

He wished he'd been able to say something intelligent to Katrina Barker, who was, he thought, genuinely brilliant: the kind of scholar whose work transforms the way you thought about a play or the context that produced it. He wanted to rush out and buy her new book, just so he could come back and talk to her about it, but he knew he would do no such thing.

The paper session was a plenary, and the hall was almost full. The three presenters, two men and a woman, were all in their later thirties or early forties, and all looked like they could be powerful executives at some slightly offbeat West Coast corporation. Thomas understood little of what they said. He got glimmers of salient points from time to time, and it was only occasionally that the vocabulary itself derailed him—so he couldn't blame theoretical jargon—but he just didn't understand what they were talking about. Shakespeare himself barely entered the papers (a couple of references to *Lear* in one, some lines from *Twelfth Night* and *As You Like It* in another), as if the plays themselves were taken as read. What dominated instead was historical detail about obscure people and events or, more accurately, *conditions*, all of which the audience seemed to see as relevant, because they applauded enthusiastically and gave each other sage nods and whispers as the moderator opened the floor to questions.

"All this is very well," said a young man in black, leaping to his feet, "but it's all based on the idea that these plays were written by William Shakespeare, a man of no breeding, little education, no travel or courtly experience . . ."

People were groaning and rolling their eyes.

"I would remind you," said the moderator, "that this is a Shakespeare conference, and that for our purposes *Shakespeare* was a man from Stratford-upon-Avon . . ."

There was a pattering of applause and a few cheers. The questioner continued to babble, dropping references to the Earl of Oxford and the impossibility that the son of a Stratford glove maker could have produced poetry of such delicacy and worldly experience . . .

Thomas fled.

Leaving the conference entirely felt like admitting defeat or, worse, failure in larger terms, but he hated the idea of just loitering, hoping to get attached to some group of clever people who had known each other for years and treated conferences like this as a species of reunion. He went to the bar. At least with a drink in his hand he'd look like he was doing something.

The Coq d'Or was darkly paneled, with red leather chairs. He fancied a gin martini, but didn't feel like spending what he'd usually lay out for dinner, so he ordered a Honker's Ale. He had taken no more than two swallows when he looked up, sure he was being watched. Standing by the main entrance was Polinski. She was quite still, her eyes on him as if she had been there for some time, considering him. In her face Thomas saw something like skepticism, even hostility, and his half wave stalled in the air.

She hesitated a second more, then sauntered over, her gaze steady.

"Mr. Knight," she said. "What brings you here?"

"Shakespeare conference," he said, tapping the program by his beer glass. "It's kind of what I used to do. Almost. I thought I'd stop by, see if there was anyone here I knew."

"Like David Escolme?"

She was still standing.

"He checked out this morning," said Thomas. "Didn't I tell you?"

"No," she said.

"So you came here to see him? I'm sorry. I could have saved you the trip."

"It's not a problem."

She was still giving him that level, considering look. Thomas moved the opposite chair away from the table for her, and she sat slowly, a strange, studied motion as if she were cradling something fragile and expensive. She put her hands on the table. They were big, strong hands, the skin rough, the nails untended.

"So you were studying Shakespeare at Boston University," she said, "when you were in graduate school."

Thomas started to nod and then caught himself.

"You've been reading up on me."

"Let's say you've left quite the paper trail over the years," she said. It could have been a wry observation, almost a joke, but her eyes said otherwise.

"Man's got to speak his mind," Thomas said, taking a sip of his beer. He had once had a habit of holding forth on everything he thought wrong with the city and the school system to whoever would listen, particularly to journalists. They were impolitic rants, often fueled by other kinds of disappointment and failure, and one of them had finally cost him his job. For a year or so.

"You didn't make the papers last year for speaking your mind," she said.

"Not most recently, no," he conceded. The strange stories that had come out of the Philippines the previous Easter had made for screaming headlines, and though there was a lot people didn't know, the story of what he had found as he worked to unravel his brother's death had gotten a lot of attention. At school he had refused to discuss the bizarre blend of paramilitary fanatics and ancient archaeology that had led him from Italy to Japan, or the spectacular and bloody chaos of that Philippine beach where his brother had died and the whole business had finally ended, but the city would remember him for a while. Being at the center of such sensational events, it could hardly be otherwise.

Ironically, those very events had turned his life around. Without them, he would never have gotten his job back, would never have reconnected with Kumi. It didn't make up for the loss of his brother, but it helped that good things had come out of all that death.

Thomas matched Polinski's stare and shrugged.

"If you think I'm some publicity hound trying to relive last year's fifteen minutes of fame, you've got me all wrong," he said. "I went through a lot of stuff last year, as you know, and yes, it was all as overblown, as intense, as crazy as the papers made it sound. But I'll tell you, I didn't look for any of it, certainly not the tabloid response, and if I could trade it all in for the life of my brother and my friend, I would do it in a heartbeat."

She listened, and then nodded, giving ground, but some of her reserve remained.

"Tell me about Escolme," she said.

"He was a good student," said Thomas. "This was ten years ago. Bright. Hardworking. Socially a little . . . *awkward*. Not the most popular kid in school. Unathletic. Pimply. But, as I said, very academic. Got great SATs. I wrote him a reference and he got into several good schools. He went to Boston University to do an English degree. Wrote to me once or twice: one of those thanks-for-inspiring-me kinds of letters teachers get from time to time, then . . . Nothing. I hadn't heard from him in about eight years till he called yesterday and said he wanted to see me."

"Did he give you an address?"

"Not a home address, no, but I have his business information."

Thomas fished in his wallet and drew out the VFL card. Polinski glanced at it, but didn't pick it up. She still seemed wary, like she was testing him.

"And he claims to have had a lost play by William Shakespeare that he got from Daniella Blackstone."

"*Love's Labour's Won*, yes."

"And you believed him?"

"I don't know," Thomas admitted. "He said that he and Blackstone had it and were going to get it printed so that they could hold copyright on the only modern edition. Copyright only lasts for a limited amount of time—seventy years, I think, in the United States—before the work becomes public domain. After that, it's only the individual edition that can be copyrighted. Even if Shakespeare had living descendants, which he doesn't, they wouldn't make any money off his plays anymore."

"So Blackstone was trying to get an edition published without the original leaking out? Is that possible?" said Polinski.

"I have no idea. Writers manage to keep their stories secret until publication, I guess. But in this case the value of the book would hinge on it being clearly by Shakespeare. She'd need outside confirmation of that by experts, which she couldn't get without showing it to scholars, any one of whom could leak it. Once the original manuscript was out there, say photocopied and posted on someone's website, then the play would become public domain, and any edition Blackstone released would have to compete with others by other people. I think. Escolme didn't say she had any scholarly background as a Shakespearean, so you have to assume that her edition would have been basic, to say the least. If actual academics had been able to put together other editions, hers would be worthless. It had to be kept secret."

"What about that outside confirmation?" said Polinski. "You can't just *say* something's by Shakespeare, right?"

"If the publisher felt it could make that claim in good faith, I don't think they'd be prosecutable if it turned out not to be. I figure they were going to publish the play as Shakespeare's quickly, let the scholars fight over its authenticity for a while, and rake the money in off the book sales while they did so. Unless it was blindingly obvious that it *wasn't* Shakespeare, they'd make quite a profit for a while and then the whole thing would go away. But so long as there was a controversy over the text, they'd be coining it, and if enough scholars came out in favor of its authenticity, they'd make a mint, at least until better editions came out, which would probably take years."

"For a high school teacher you seem to know a lot about this."

"Most of this is from Escolme, so you can ask him yourself when you see him."

"Right," she said, and there it was again, that slightly sardonic skepticism in her long face and thin, wide mouth.

"What?" said Thomas. "Have you spoken to him already?"

"No," she said. "In fact, we've no idea where he is."

"Did you call Vernon Fredericks Literary?" said Thomas, nodding at the business card.

"Yes," she said, and she smiled at last, a humorless, knowing smile that left her eyes hard and fixed.

"And?"

"Well, it's interesting," she said.

"How so?" said Thomas. He was beginning to feel toyed with.

"They've never heard of him," she said.

"What?"

"He doesn't work there. Never did. And nobody with the name of David Escolme has been registered at this hotel. Ever. See," she added, smiling again, "that's why it's interesting."

CHAPTER 13

It was like walking into a room and finding yourself on the ceiling.

"No," he said for the third time. "Escolme. E-S-C-O-L-M-E. First name, David. He was here last night in room 304."

"I'm sorry, sir," said the concierge, "but he wasn't. There's no one of that name in the system."

"I was in there with him," Thomas insisted.

"He wasn't registered in that room."

"But when I called this morning I was told he had checked out," said Thomas.

"If that was, in fact, what you were told," said the concierge with a look at Polinski, "the desk clerk made a mistake. I suspect that all she actually said was that he wasn't registered and you assumed she meant he had checked out. We're pretty careful about keeping guest information private around here."

Thomas knew the woman was probably right, but he couldn't let it go.

"Right," he said, marching away and calling to Polinski over his shoulder. "Come with me."

The policewoman said nothing as he led her into the elevator and hit the button for the third floor. She remained silent when they got off and made their way down the hallway to room 304, where Thomas rapped incisively on the door.

They heard movement almost immediately, and Thomas turned his stare on Polinski, as if certain he was about to be proved right.

He wasn't. The door opened slowly and a woman in her seventies peered anxiously into the hallway.

"I'm looking for David Escolme," Thomas snapped.

"Who?" the woman said, through the crack. She looked

alarmed, and though Thomas couldn't do anything about it, he knew it was his manner that was bothering her.

"David Escolme," he barked. "Medium height, midtwenties . . ."

The woman was shaking her head.

"When did you check into this room?" Thomas tried.

"This morning," she said.

"That's enough," said Polinski. "We're sorry to have bothered you, ma'am."

She took Thomas by the arm and began to propel him down the hallway. He shrugged out of her grasp with a splutter of irritation, but the old woman was already closing the door.

Thomas fumed silently as the elevator descended, and when he felt Polinski's eyes on him, he turned on her.

"You think I made it up?" he spat. "What kind of lunatic would come up with a story like this? He was here, Goddamn it. Right there in that room. I could describe the pictures on the walls, the color of the drapes, anything to show I was in there last night."

"You know that those kinds of details would prove nothing," said Polinski. "You could have been in there anytime."

"Why would I make this up?" he demanded as the doors opened. "Obviously it doesn't get me off the hook as far as Blackstone is concerned. If anything, it just puts me in the frame more. *I* came to you about Escolme, remember?"

The two of them stood there, staring at each other, until they became aware of a woman, preposterously dressed in mink, with a bellhop waiting at her elbow. They walked out.

"Come here," said Thomas, leading her back to the concierge's desk. She followed a couple of steps behind as Thomas tapped the computer screen.

"Is this hooked up to the Internet?" he demanded.

"Sure," said the concierge, with another look at Polinski.

"Can I just . . .", Thomas began, moving around the desk and inserting himself into the concierge's chair. He felt the other two looking at each other, but he didn't care. He Googled VFL and pulled up their home page.

"See," he said, "look at the New York office."

"What?" said Polinski, now at his shoulder.

"The list of agents . . . ," Thomas began.

But there was no list of agents. And as he clicked hurriedly on the other branches, none of them listed their agents.

"His name was right here," he said. "He had his own page."

There it was again, that sense of walking on the ceiling: chandeliers where coffee tables should be, all the doors upside down. It made no sense.

"Can I use your phone?" said Polinski.

"Knock yourself out," said the concierge, who was watching all this like she'd stumbled into a sideshow.

Thomas typed Escolme's name into the search engine.

"There!" he said, triumphant. "David Escolme, Vernon Fredericks Literary." He clicked on the link.

The computer hesitated, then loaded the page. It was instantly clear that this was not what Thomas had consulted before. At first he thought it was a weather site, but then realized that the weather map was merely filling space. The key piece of information was underneath it:

"Site unoccupied. If you are interested in purchasing this domain name . . ."

Beside him, Polinski was giving Escolme's name to another switchboard operator. After a moment she said, "So it's not company policy to post any information on agents? And this has not changed over the last few days?" There was a pause and she nodded and then said, "No, that's fine. Thanks."

She hung up.

"This is crazy," said Thomas. "The page was right here."

"Look at the URL," said Polinski. "It's not part of the VFL site. If there was a page for Escolme here, someone just copied the style of the agency, placed some links to it from their own page and posted it through some other provider. And there's something else. We ran Escolme's New York address."

"And?"

"Seems he moved out. No forwarding."

Thomas felt outmaneuvered. Nothing made him angrier.

"And you were planning to mention that, when?"

"I wasn't." She shrugged. "Because I'm the cop and you . . ."

"Aren't," he concluded for her. "So now what?"

"I'm going to talk to the concierge some more—privately—find out who was registered to room 304."

"Meaning I should leave."

"I expect you'll be hearing from me soon," said Polinski.

"Is this one of those 'don't leave town' warnings?" said Thomas.

"It would be helpful if you made yourself available for further inquiry," she said.

Thomas smiled.

"Of course," he said. "Now, if you don't mind, I'm going to finish my beer."

But he didn't go straight to the bar. He swung by the Shakespeare Conference's notice board, snatched a lime-green flyer for a staged reading of some obscure Middleton play off an adjacent table, and scribbled on the back of it: "David Escolme (in case you're skulking around here, masquerading as a Shakespearean). Re *LLW* or anything else. Don't call me again. Ever. TK."

With two furious slashes he underlined the *Ever*, took a thumbtack from the corkboard, and punched it through the paper with such force that the backing cracked. A heavy woman who had been peering at the board flashed him a look of alarm and backed hurriedly away.

Thomas walked back to the Coq d'Or, his head low and bullish.

CHAPTER 14

"Where's my beer?" he said to the startled barkeep. "I was sitting there. I had to step outside for a minute and . . ."

"I'm sorry, sir, I just dumped it. Thought you were gone."

"Well, I'm back," he said. "And I'm thirsty, and I'm a teacher, which means I can't afford to take two sips of a six-dollar beer and then throw it away."

He was still hissing mad, and knowing that he was taking it out on the bartender didn't make him feel any better.

"Let me get you another," said the bartender. "It was one of the Goose Islands, right?"

"The Honker's Ale," Thomas nodded.

"I'm partial to the Wheatmiser, myself," said the bartender.

"Maybe I'll try that next," said Thomas.

"It's got a punch," said the bartender.

"So do I," said Thomas.

"I see that." The barman grinned.

"Sorry," said Thomas. "Strange day."

"They all are," said the bartender, putting the freshly poured beer in front of him. "Enjoy."

"Cheers," said Thomas, sipping and savoring. "Good. You know anything about champagne?"

"Some," said the bartender. "Our selection's limited, though. What did you have in mind?"

"Ever heard of Saint Evremond Reims?"

"Reims is a town in France, in the Champagne region, specifically," said the bartender, pleased to have the answer, or part of it. "You know the French don't think that anything from outside that region can be called champagne? If it's from California, it's just sparkling wine."

"What about Saint Evremond?"

"Probably the house, like Moët or Krug, you know? But I've never heard of it. Maybe they produce primarily for the French home market, like Mercier."

"Thanks," said Thomas, impressed.

"We even now?"

"The moment you poured my replacement pint," Thomas grinned.

"Never get between a Shakespearean and his beer," said a voice to his left.

Thomas turned. It was a woman, slight, professional looking in a brown pantsuit. Her hair was a straight chestnut tied back in a disarmingly girlish ponytail, but her eyes were cool and mature. She was probably in her midthirties, but the smirk, like the ponytail, took a decade off her. She looked attractive. And familiar.

"Actually, I'm a civilian," he said.

"I thought you said you were a teacher," she said.

"High school," he said.

"Oh," she said. "I'd say something encouraging about your attending the conference, but that would be patronizing, wouldn't it?"

"Probably," he said. "And I'm not actually attending the conference."

"Your lapel badge would suggest otherwise, Thomas," she said.

"Oh," he said. "Yes. I was just stopping by."

"Hear any interesting papers?" she said, then caught herself. "Wait. Don't answer that. You walked out during questions after mine, so don't be *too* honest."

He smiled, recognizing her.

"A bit over my head," he said. "I'm sure it was very smart."

"What does that have to do with anything?"

"Coin of the realm here, isn't it? Smart, I mean."

"That's the official story," she said, flashing that slightly impish grin. "We're all incredibly clever and saying deeply insightful things, and if you don't understand them, then you obviously aren't clever or insightful and don't really belong. It's a bit like the Emperor's New Clothes."

"I remember," said Thomas, adding, "I was a graduate student for a while."

"In Shakespeare?" she said. "Where?"

"Boston University."

"Who did you work with?"

"Dagenhart," said Thomas.

"My God, did you really?" she said, clearly delighted. "Randy Randall Dagenhart! He's here, you know."

"Yes, I saw him."

"Used to be a terror to virginal graduate students everywhere."

"The way I remember it, that's a pretty small constituency," said Thomas.

"True," she said. She looked at him directly as if concluding an assessment, one he passed. "I'm Julia McBride," she said. "Jules to my friends or what passes for them in academia."

"Thomas Knight," he said, shaking her hand.

"Pleased to meet you, Thomas," she said, toasting him with a cream-colored cocktail in a stainless steel martini glass. "I shouldn't make fun of Randall. He's had his share of hardships, after all."

"I don't know much about him."

"Oh, you know, the usual. Bad marriage. Or went bad. So he became a bit of a hound, I'm afraid. For a while."

"Then what?"

"Not sure. His wife got sick. Something serious and debilitating. A stroke, maybe. He had to look after her. I don't think she was disposed to be very appreciative. Anyway . . . He's in a session on early comedy tomorrow," she remarked. "You going to go?"

Thomas shrugged. He had not thought that far.

"It's reputed to be little more than a commercial for the seminar he's running at the institute in Stratford next week," she said. "There's a special mini conference over there, since it's an off year for the ISC, and all the rules are different."

"The ISC?"

"Sorry. International Shakespeare Conference. Meets every two years. Invitation only. The word is that if you miss twice without a damned good reason, you get stricken from the list. But this thing is different. Smaller. A little less intense. They are even allowing graduate students to present, if you can imagine that. All the old-school textual critics have been recruited. I'm using it as an excuse to get over to the U.K. and see some shows, but I probably won't attend a lot of the sessions. Not really my speed. At least we won't have to deal with the Oxfordians there."

"Oxfordians?"

"Those lunatics who claim the Earl of Oxford wrote the plays, and Shakespeare—for reasons passing human understanding—took the money and the credit. Bonkers, of course. Stratford is the one place those people avoid." She turned to the barman and raised her empty glass. "Same again, please."

"What is that?"

"They call it a Drake Chocolate Kiss," she said, with a playful grin. "Sorry you asked now, aren't you? You can have a taste if you like."

Thomas felt himself color a little.

"I'm good," he said. "What do you know about *Love's Labour's Won*?" said Thomas.

She seemed taken aback by the question, but that might have been the sudden shift in tack.

"Not much," she said. "We don't have it."

"But it existed?"

"Maybe," she said. "I don't recall the details. Why?"

"If one turned up now," said Thomas, "I mean, if someone found a copy of the original . . . that would be a big deal, right?"

Her face shifted, and this time her perplexity seemed deeper, but there was something else, something like wariness or caution.

"I'm not a wacko," Thomas added hastily, "I'm just curious."

"It's a curious subject about which to be curious," she said, arch again. "But yes, I guess it would be a big deal. Why?"

"Like I said," said Thomas. "Just curious."

Her drink arrived and she sipped it. Thomas could smell the chocolate. Her eyes were fixed on a spot over his shoulder. Thomas followed her gaze to a tall, earnest-looking young man who was hovering near the door as if debating whether to join them.

"You know him?" asked Thomas.

"Graduate student of mine," she said. "Let me introduce you."

"I really should be going," he said, rising.

"At least finish your beer," she said.

"Can't argue with that," Thomas replied. He sat again and took a drink of the Honker's Ale. By the time he had put the glass down, the kid had joined them.

Thomas thought of him as a kid but he was probably twenty-five. He was balding, with the kind of goatee favored only by graduate students and baseball players.

"Thomas," said Jules, "this is Chad Everett. One of my doctoral candidates."

Thomas nodded and shook his hand. Chad's eyes were cautious, watchful.

"Are you a graduate student too?" he said.

"Recovering," said Thomas. "A decade gone and still clean."

Jules laughed, but Chad didn't. He was still standing.

"You want to join us?" said Thomas. "I'll be going in a minute . . ."

"No," he said, brusque. "I've got to do some work on my paper."

"Chad is presenting tomorrow," said Jules. "His first conference."

He looked at her at that, a quick, stung look, as if she had announced that he wet the bed.

"There was just something I heard today that I wanted to check," he said, pointedly not to Thomas.

"Okay, Chad," she said with elaborate weariness. "Pull up

a chair. Would I be right in thinking that you have your paper with you?"

"Yes, actually," he said, humorless, opening an antique satchel.

"Isn't that handy," she said. "Thomas, I'm afraid we're going to talk shop."

"My cue to go home," said Thomas. He drained his glass.

"Maybe we'll meet again soon," she said.

She held him with a frank, amused gaze that made him flush like a teenager.

"Maybe," he said, getting up. "Chad," he added, in farewell.

The graduate student didn't look at him.

On his way out, Thomas remembered the petulant dismissal he had left for Escolme on the notice board. Maybe it was the beer, or the conversation, but he was feeling forgiving. Escolme surely hadn't meant for Blackstone to die at his house. He couldn't blame the guy for not advertising how he had inadvertently dropped his old teacher in the thick of things.

Thomas walked briskly across the silent lobby, found the notice board, and looked for the green flyer. It was nowhere to be seen. Escolme—or someone—had taken it down.

Now why, he thought, *does that bother you?*

CHAPTER 15

It was a little after four in the morning. Thomas wasn't sure why he had woken, but he knew how tired he was, and he immediately rolled over, trying to get comfortable again. He thought he might want to pee. His bladder didn't feel especially full, but he knew that he would struggle to get back to sleep, now that the idea had struck him. He rolled out of bed, his eyes barely open, and shuffled toward the bathroom. He was almost inside, standing on the landing at the top of the stairs, when he froze.

At first he thought he had heard something, but then he realized that it hadn't been a sound. It was something about the air. He could feel the faintest hint of a breeze coming up the stairs and on it the heady and distinctive scent of the flowering tobacco plant by the front door. He stood quite still, listening and thinking.

Someone was in the house.

For a second he couldn't think of anything at all. Any other day he might have thought that the best way to scare off some common burglar was to move around noisily. But not today. If there was someone downstairs, it was no common burglar looking to rip off his stereo and his TV . . .

This was something different. Something much worse.

Thomas stepped noisily to the bathroom, opened the door, reached in, and turned on the cold tap. He closed the door, letting it snap noisily in the stillness. Then, with the sound of running water spilling out into the house, he cautiously picked his way over the floorboards back to his room, and the phone.

The house was old and the floors creaked, but Thomas had been there long enough to know the telltale spots, and he was back in the bedroom without making a sound. He had almost reached the phone when he heard the groan of wood under pressure.

The stairs, he thought. *He's coming up . . .*

Thomas did not own a gun, but he suspected that whoever was coming up the stairs with such confidence might. He reached for the phone but knew that with all the speed in the world it would take the police rather longer to get there than it would for the intruder to hear and kill him.

Should have thought of that home security system sooner, he thought.

He had only one advantage: the running tap. He looked quickly around the room for something he could use as a weapon. The bedside lamp was too clumsy and fragile. He scanned the cast-off clothes and stacks of books. Nothing. Then he heard the top step squeak. The intruder was outside the open bedroom door now, standing outside the bathroom. The sound of the tap might drown out any movement he might make, but the stairs were blocked and there was no other way down.

Thomas spread his arms wide and grabbed the bottom corners of the duvet. Then he stepped out onto the landing.

There was a man at the bathroom door, his back toward Thomas and a gun in his hand. His head looked strangely oversized, but by the time Thomas registered that, he was already charging and flinging the outstretched duvet over the intruder's head.

The man turned into it, grunting in surprise as Thomas launched himself, drawing his arms around him so that the bedding bound tight, muffling and stifling.

The gun cracked loudly and a puff of feathers blew out of the duvet. The bullet shattered the hall window and Thomas's ears rang. He felt himself flinching away from the weapon.

Don't back off! his brain shrilled at him.

If his attack hesitated, he was dead.

He clamped with his arms as the other fought to get free, and when he thought he knew where the intruder's head was, he snapped his own hard into it. The duvet softened the blow, but it still felt hard and irregular, like the man was wearing some sort of helmet or mask. Thomas recoiled and caught an elbow in the ribs. Then the gun turned back toward him, and as Thomas fought to control the arm that brandished it, it went off twice in rapid succession. It was so close in the confined space that it sounded like a cannon, and the sound alone nearly drove Thomas back. But he wasn't hit, and that was what counted.

Not hit, but tiring.

Thomas was a big man, and not in bad shape, but the gunman was stronger. Another few seconds and he wouldn't be able to keep that gun from turning into his face. He channeled all the energy he had left, compressing it into the center of his chest like he was squeezing a tight spring in the muscles of his back and shoulders. Then, with a cry of release, he surged forward, shoving like a rocket-powered bulldozer. The gun arm came free—Thomas had no choice but to let it go—but it couldn't turn on him because the intruder's momentum was carrying him over the top step and down.

The gunman fell hard, losing the duvet in his tumble, and the pistol snagged against the banister rail and tore from his grasping fingers. It fell into the hallway below and clattered on the wood floor as Thomas began his hasty descent. The living room window made a pale rectangle of streetlamp where the intruder had fallen, and Thomas knew now why the man's head had seemed so distorted. He was wearing night vision goggles: an array of straps with what looked like field glasses lashed to the front.

The realization alarmed Thomas, slowed him. If he had had any doubts before, this made it clear: this was not some street thug looking to pay for his next fix. This guy was serious. It was all connected: Blackstone, Escolme, the intruder in the yard. Thomas had no idea what was going on, but this guy was part of it, and that was bad.

And the intruder could see. Which meant he would find his fallen gun in another second or two . . .

Thomas's right hand swept the wall and found a switch. He snapped the hall light on and the intruder winced away from it. At least now they were even. Thomas could see where the gun had fallen, and he figured he had about as much chance of reaching it as the guy who had brought it into his home. But he would have to get over the prone intruder first.

Thomas came barreling down the stairs like a charging rhino, but the intruder held his ground, and it was only when he was too close to stop that Thomas saw the flash of bright steel in his hand: a professional-looking combat knife, drawn from God knew where. He slashed with it and Thomas felt a long wound open along his forearm. The pain flared as if the knife were hot, and Thomas pulled back. He was still a couple of steps higher than his attacker, and his instinct was to kick, hard as he could.

His bare foot caught the man on the side of his head, knocking him back into the hall. Thomas felt the blood coursing down his arm and threw himself at the prostrate knifeman.

The intruder stabbed upward with his blade, and Thomas twisted away, immediately regretting the attack. The blade scythed through air, and Thomas landed awkwardly on his side. Less than a second later he was scrambling to his feet and looking frantically for the gun.

It was lying half under the couch by the living room fireplace. He took two loping strides and flung himself onto it, turning and aiming at the open doorway into the hall as he did so.

Then there was darkness again. The intruder had shut off the lights. Thomas squatted there, the gun trained on the open doorway, waiting.

For a moment, nothing happened, then a dark blur sped past the doorway. As it moved, Thomas glimpsed the muzzle of another gun—smaller, a revolver—as its black eye opened with a flare of yellow-white brilliance and another roar of sound. Thomas shot back blindly, squeezing the trigger twice. It was only then that he realized he was hit.

CHAPTER 16

The shock came first. Then the pain. Both surprised him with their intensity. The bullet had gone into his right shoulder. He didn't know if it had passed right through, but he feared his clavicle was broken. He slumped against the wall, wondering vaguely—absurdly—if his blood was staining the paint. He wasn't going to die, not unless the gunman came back to finish him off. Not tonight. Whatever damage the bullet had done, there was no spurting, no loss of air, which meant that nothing major had been ruptured. There was only the pain.

Well, that's good, he thought. *Only the raging, searing, screaming pain. Three cheers for me. Hip hip . . .*

He had to get to a phone. The only one downstairs was the portable in the kitchen. It was only a few yards away, but he didn't like the idea of crawling back into the dark hallway. He had no idea where the gunman was, and in what shape. Thomas had fired twice. The automatic was large and heavy, a nine-millimeter, he thought. If either round had hit him, the intruder could be dead or dying.

Or he could be sitting out there, waiting to see if you come crawling out so he can finish you off.

Thomas listened, but he couldn't hear anything over his own breathing. Was that getting harder? He inhaled and felt a stab of pain, not in the shoulder where he was hit, but lower, more central. He breathed again, and the pain came back. The breath itself was weak too, like he was trying to suck air in through a straw.

Maybe this is shock, he thought.

His hands and face felt cool and clammy, and he was sweating more than the fight merited. But it was his breathing that bothered him. It was fast and shallow, and it seemed to be getting harder. He could also feel himself relaxing despite the pain, his whole body getting heavy as if he were starting to float away on a warm, dark tide.

Sleep, he thought. *That's all I need. Rest.*

His eyelids fluttered. Then closed.

He fought back to consciousness. His eyes snapped open and he took a deep breath that felt like it tore something in his chest. He wasn't getting enough air. He gasped another mouthful, but it was clear now. His lungs weren't filling properly.

Something was wrong. His delight that he was merely in pain had been premature. The bullet had nicked something inside. His lungs were filling with blood. If he didn't get to the phone in the next couple of minutes, he thought, he was going to die. Maybe even if he did.

CHAPTER 17

Thomas slumped onto his side, then rolled to his knees. Carefully, biting back the agony in his shoulder, he started to crawl toward the door, still clutching the pistol. He had no idea how many bullets he had left and didn't know how to check, but he kept it anyway. If the intruder was still out there, he wanted a fighting chance. In truth, he knew that unless the guy was already dead or gone, he wouldn't have one. He could barely move and doubted he could raise and aim the gun at all. His right arm had no strength so he had switched the weapon to his left, but he knew that however lousy his right-handed shooting was, his left would be a good deal worse. He found himself wondering about those switch-hitting baseball players who could drive in home runs from either side of the plate . . .

There you go, he thought. *Think about the Cubs. Don't think about the pain. Don't think about your lungs. Imagine you're at Wrigley . . .*

He wasn't so much breathing now as panting, thin, rasping inhales and exhales. Each one brought a shudder of pain through his chest. They were getting worse. He reached the door and peered into the darkened hallway, pushing the futile pistol ahead of him as if it might help.

There was no sign of his attacker.

That was the good news. The bad news was that it was another five yards into the kitchen and at least that to the phone, which was wall mounted. He could barely crawl. There was no way he would be able to stand and lift the receiver.

Zambrano's on the mound, he thought. *Derrek Lee is healthy and Mark DeRosa is on fire . . . There's still hope.*

He thought of Kumi and the do-over he had started to

build of their lives. After all those years apart, they might finally give it all another try, and nothing in the past decade had seemed as good as this one frail truth. He started to crawl. The pain was getting worse. He wouldn't make it.

He managed a yard, then another. As he reached the door, his strength gave out and he crumpled hard where the wood met the cool tile of the kitchen floor. He was starting to shiver, and the desire to stay where he was, sleep it off like some nasty hangover, was back.

Just lie back, he thought. *Unwind. A little sleep can't do you any harm.*

He climbed back into his crawl as if he were forcing his way through a hundred push-ups. His shoulder shrieked and his arm buckled, but he forced it to stay steady. There wasn't much light coming in from the window—the window where he had seen the dead face of Daniella Blackstone imploring him to let her in—but he was sure the skin of his hands was turning blue.

Not good, he thought.

And the phone was still a thousand miles away, floating beyond any possible reach. His eyes were watering, though whether that was physical or emotional, he couldn't say. He lurched another couple of feet and then collapsed at the foot of the fridge. He rolled painfully onto his back, sucking in the air, feeling the room beginning to swim.

Only another moment or two now, he thought.

Unconsciousness was coming to greet him like a smothering embrace. He beat it back with his mind, as if swatting away crows, and squinted down the side of the fridge.

There was a broom, one of those old-fashioned long-handled affairs with a head of plaited grass, just like the one his parents had had.

He reached for it, first with his imagination, then with his left hand. He couldn't reach, and had to shift inch by inch, hunching his back up and to the right like a dying sidewinder. He stretched out his hand again, but he was still inches short.

Not much longer now.

He squirmed and stretched again, and this time his

splayed fingers caught the coarse bristles of the broom and brought it crashing down on top of him. The handle hit the tile like the popping of a champagne cork.

Not dead yet.

Bracing the tip of the handle with his lifeless right hand, he used his left to poke the brush head up to the counter. He shoved it hard, stabbing it upward like a spear. Nothing happened. He tried again. Still nothing. He yelled, and thrust it again.

This time he heard the clatter of the phone as it fell to the tiled floor. He flailed his left hand, grabbed it, and pushed the talk button. With what little concentration he could still muster he squeezed blindly at the keypad, mouthing as he did so, "Nine. One. One."

He mashed the receiver to his head and listened, his eyes clamped shut. When he heard a voice, he managed "Twelve forty-seven Sycamore," before slipping into unconsciousness.

CHAPTER 18

"I hate to say I told you so," said Polinski, considering the hospital room approvingly.

"No, you don't," said Thomas. His chest was strapped and it was hard to speak.

"You're right, I don't," she said, shrugging. "Was it Escolme?"

Thomas shook his head, felt a shot of pain in his shoulder, and said, "No."

"You sure?" said the policewoman. "You said he was wearing night vision goggles."

"I guess not," Thomas conceded. He lifted his head from the pillow cautiously. "I don't think it was him. It was dark for a lot of the time and then . . ."

He shrunk away from the memory. Polinski nodded, her thin lips pursed.

"Was it the same guy who attacked you outside the night before?"

"Couldn't say," said Thomas. "I'd say no, but that's a guess."

"Based on what?"

"The shoes," he said. "The guy who came the previous night—assuming it was a guy—was wearing shoes that made a little ringing noise when he walked. This other guy didn't."

"Could have changed them."

"Yes, but the two attacks felt different. One came with these noisy shoes and ran away as soon as he heard me—till I jumped on him and got my clock cleaned, that is. The other came with all this stealth gear and a gun. Either it was a different person or he came with a very different agenda."

"He was white?"

"I think so," said Thomas.

"Could you say anything about his height, build?"

Thomas began to shake his head again and caught himself before the pain kicked in.

"I'm sorry," he said. "Medium, I guess. Not heavyset, probably athletic, maybe six foot or just under, but I couldn't be sure. A little smaller than me but at least as strong."

He had been confined to the Evanston hospital for two days. For the first he had been unconscious and had had surgery to remove the fragments of the .38-caliber bullet that had fractured his collarbone and then bounced around inside. They had drained his lungs of blood with a chest tube that was still in place and put him on a cocktail of IV fluids. The knife wound in his arm had been stitched and bandaged. Throughout, they had kept his recovery room under guard, as if he might still be a target. Or a suspect. Thomas wasn't sure which.

"So you believe me now?" he said to Polinski. "About Escolme? The Drake? The Shakespeare play?"

She smiled, a tiny quivering of one corner of her mouth.

"You know that Meat Loaf song," she said. " 'Two out of Three Ain't Bad'?"

"Not really a Meat Loaf fan," said Thomas. "Which two?"

"Let's just say it will be a while before I start quoting Shakespeare in a homicide report," she said.

Thomas grinned.

She cocked her head to one side.

"You think that's what he was looking for, don't you?" she said. "That lost play."

"It's the only thing that would connect two attacks at the same address in as many nights," said Thomas. "I just don't know why anyone thinks I have it. Unless they think Escolme gave it to me, then faked the theft."

"He faked other things," said Polinski. "But if it wasn't him crawling around your house with his night vision goggles and his personal armory, then he's attracted the attention of some people who won't be too happy when they find out that this priceless book . . ."

"Play," Thomas corrected.

"*Play*," Polinski repeated, "is lost or—more likely—never existed."

Thomas sighed.

"When can I go home?" he said.

"Not my department. But I'd think they'd want to keep you in another couple of days."

"Could someone contact the principal at Evanston Township? There are papers I could be grading."

"Your classes have already been reassigned," said Polinski.

"I'm perfectly capable of grading a few . . ."

"Relax," said Polinski. "You restaged the gunfight at the O.K. Corral in your living room and you got shot. Even a workaholic like you should realize that's grounds for taking a break."

"Till when?"

"Fall," she answered, smiling.

"Fall?" Thomas bellowed, sitting up in spite of his strapped shoulder, so that the word turned into a pained groan.

"The semester's virtually over." Polinski shrugged.

"It's my damn job!" said Thomas. "I've been with those kids all year . . ."

"Get over yourself," the cop said, standing. "Other teachers can get them through final exams."

She was right, of course, but the truth still smarted, and Thomas lay back down grumbling. He wondered if his students would miss him. They liked him, most of them. Part of it was that he had acquired a certain notoriety—something that would be fed by getting shot—and part of it was that he cared about his subject in ways that sometimes made them care too. Whether that made him good at his job, he couldn't say. Getting excited about a plot development in a Dickens novel or a phrase in Shakespeare had little to do with their SAT scores, after all.

"*I'm Thomas Knight,*" he said on the first day of class, "*and I love books.*"

It was supposed to be a bit of a joke, a familiar parody of AA meetings and twelve-step programs. He hoped that—by the end of his course—some of them would catch something of his enthusiasm. Thomas was just hopeful, old-fashioned, or naïve enough—he wasn't sure which—to think that mattered.

They had sent get-well cards through the principal, but it was hard to tell if they missed him. Thomas was surprised to find that he wanted them to.

That's maudlin, he thought, *and vain*.

"Just so you know," said Polinski, "we've been watching your house since the shooting."

"And?"

"Nothing. A couple of security companies came to scope the place out, give you an estimate. You'll find the paperwork waiting for you when you get home. Still," she added, "putting an alarm in now . . . Seems a bit like locking the barn door after the horse has . . ."

"Been shot?" Thomas completed for her. "Yes."

She laughed.

"Will you, you know, continue to watch the house after I go home?" Thomas asked, trying to sound like he didn't really care.

"For a few days at least, yes."

He nodded. She turned to leave.

"Did I hit him?" he said. "The intruder. I fired twice."

She gave him an odd look.

"Are you hoping you did?" she said.

The question, and the seriousness in her eyes, gave him pause. In the silence she just shook her head.

"You're going to have some work to do when you get home," she said. "We took a couple of nine-millimeter slugs out of the wall."

"Great."

"No gun, by the way," she added.

"What?"

"You said there were two guns, the one he shot you with and the one you redecorated the hallway with. We looked but we found neither."

"It should have been right there where I left it before I crawled into the kitchen. I could show you the spot . . ."

"It's not there," she said, and she looked serious again. "We figure he came back for it, probably before the ambulance arrived."

"While I was lying there unconscious?"

"Seems so."

The thought was strangely unsettling. Had the guy thought he was dead? If not, why had he left him alive?

"Bye, Thomas," said Polinski. "Try not to get into trouble."

Thomas considered the hospital room.

"Fat chance," he said.

CHAPTER 19

After she had gone, Thomas lay lost in thought for fifteen minutes. He had forgotten to mention to her the note he had left for Escolme. He wished he hadn't written it. It had been a momentary petulance, followed up on because he had felt manipulated and deceived. The funny thing was that even though the shooting made it doubly clear just how much trouble Escolme had put him in, it also suggested that unless his former student was the villain Polinski suspected him to be, then the kid—Thomas still thought of him in those terms— was probably in real danger. And if Blackstone's killer hadn't known Escolme's name before, there was a reasonable chance that Thomas's pissy little note had changed that.

He reached painfully for the phone and made a series of calls that eventually connected him with the concierge at the Drake. He gave a false name, said he was attached to the Evanston Police Department and was just checking something that had already been clarified.

"Shoot," said the concierge.

"I can't read my own writing," said Thomas. "Was Miss Daniella Blackstone staying in room 304 or 307?"

"In 304. Never had a chance to check out. Not till she— you know—*checked out*."

"Thanks," said Thomas. "That's what I figured."

He was about to hang up when another idea came to him.

"You couldn't connect me to the room of Randall Dagenhart, could you?" he asked.

There was a pause, and then the concierge said, "Mr. Dagenhart already checked out."

"What about Miss Julia . . ." He searched for the last name. "McBride."

"Hold on."

The phone rang three times before a woman's voice answered. She sounded rushed, and for a moment Thomas wasn't sure it was her.

"This is Thomas Knight," he said. "We met in the bar at the Drake."

"The recovering academic," she said, instantly composed. "I remember. I'm impressed."

"Why's that?"

"I didn't think I'd been obvious enough to encourage your call."

Thomas found himself blushing.

"Oh," he said. "Right. Well, I just wondered if I could ask you a question."

"And it's not going to be whether I'd like wine with dinner," she said, amused by his embarrassment. "Ah well. What's on your mind, Mr. Knight?"

"This lost Shakespeare play," he said, composing himself and adjusting his posture, trying to find a position that hurt less when he spoke. "*Love's Labour's Won*. You said it would be a big deal if it was found, but you didn't say whether you thought that likely."

"That it has been or could be?"

"Either."

"It's possible," she said.

"But do we even know it existed?"

"Debatable," she said, shedding her playfulness and turning professorial. "But almost certainly, yes."

"But it wasn't one of the plays published in the 1623 folio."

The First Folio was the first "collected" Shakespeare, compiled seven years after his death by members of the theater company for whom Shakespeare had worked. It contained thirty-six plays, half of which had not appeared in print before.

"No, it wasn't in the Folio," said McBride. "But then neither was *Pericles*, even though it had been published in quarto several times by then."

Quartos were small, cheap single-play editions.

"And it wasn't published in quarto either, right?" said Thomas.

"Well there's the rub," she said. "You've heard of Francis Meres?"

Thomas was about to say that he had never heard of him and then something came to him, something he remembered.

"A list," he said. "He wrote a list of which playwrights were famous and what for, right?" said Thomas.

"Meres wrote a book called *Palladis Tamia,* or *Wits Treasury*, in 1598," said the Shakespearean. "A tedious ramble through Meres's views on art, poetry, and pretty much everything else. 1598 was the midpoint of Shakespeare's career, pretty much. Meres lists six of his comedies, thereby providing good evidence for their dates of composition. They are *The Comedy of Errors, Two Gentlemen of Verona, A Midsummer Night's Dream, The Merchant of Venice, Love's Labour's Lost*, and . . ."

"*Love's Labour's Won*," Thomas completed for her, propping himself on his left elbow and wincing as he did so. "But . . . some of the plays have alternate titles, right? Like *Twelfth Night*, which is also called *What You Will*. So isn't it possible that Meres was just using a different name for one of the other plays that Shakespeare had written by 1598 but that isn't on the list? A play we already know?"

"Like *The Taming of the Shrew*?" she said. "A nasty, masculinist assumption, Mr. Knight. You surprise me."

"What do you mean?"

"*Shrew* should be on the list. It was definitely written by 1598, but Meres doesn't mention it. Some people think *Shrew* is *Love's Labour's Won. Love's Labour's Lost* is about men being deprived of their romantic conquests by death and politics. *The Taming of the Shrew* is about beating your wife into submission . . ."

"Well, I'm not sure I'd agree . . ."

"From a certain perspective," she inserted, amused, "it's about winning a woman by breaking her spirit. If that's *Love's Labour's Won,* then we're all in trouble. Anyway, your scholarship is out of date, Mr. Knight."

Thomas, who wasn't aware that anything he'd said so far could be called *scholarship* of any period, listened.

"In 1953, a fragment of manuscript was found inside the binding of a book. Turns out to be part of an inventory from a stationer's shop in Exeter. It listed what they were selling between the ninth and the seventeenth of August 1603. It included both *The Taming of a Shrew* and *Love's Labour's Won*. You can quibble over the *A Shrew/ The Shrew* discrepancy, if you like, but I think it pretty clear that *Love's Labour's Won* was a different play. And—more to the point— Mr. Knight, it was published."

"Then how could it get lost?"

"There are probably others," she said. "*Two Noble Kinsmen* was also left out of the first folio. By then, Shakespeare was dead and the Globe had burned down. Who knows how many other manuscripts were lost?"

"But you aren't talking about a handwritten manuscript," Thomas insisted. "You are talking about a play that was published in quarto, which means there must have been hundreds floating around. How could it get lost?"

"You know how many extant copies of the first quarto of *Titus Andronicus* there are?" said McBride. "One. Plays were penny-a-piece throwaways. They weren't high art, they weren't even poetry. We know that there's at least one other play Shakespeare wrote—*Cardenio*—that we don't have, though a manuscript might have survived till 1808 when the Covent Garden Theatre library burned.

"In the early seventeenth century Shakespeare wasn't the literary icon he is today. He was just a writer, a populist writer at that, who wrote entertainments for the stage. He was good at it and made a ton of money doing it, but the finest writer the world has ever seen, an artist whose every scribbling should be preserved like a sacred relic? Hardly."

"Then how could it have survived at all?" said Thomas, switching tack.

"There, Mr. Knight," she said, and the flirtation was back so that he thought she might be reclining, chocolate martini in hand, "you have me."

CHAPTER 20

Thomas spent two more days in his hospital bed, flipping through TV channels and periodically screaming at the stupidity of what he saw there till the pain in his shoulder made him sit back and shut up, and then he announced he was going home. The presiding physician, a hawkish, middle-aged man with keen eyes and a nasal voice, said he'd rather keep him in for a couple more days, but that going home now wouldn't kill him.

"Good enough," said Thomas. "There's only so much daytime TV a man can take."

"You could read a book," said the doctor. "People still do."

"My hordes of friends and well-wishers forgot to bring me one," said Thomas.

Other than the police he had had only one visitor, Peter the Principal from school, who had poked his head around the door looking embarrassed behind flowers and a large card signed by the kids. Thomas didn't have a lot of friends, but considering where he had been a little over a year ago, the drink, the loss of his job, and other, darker moments, he thought he was doing pretty well. He read through the names scribbled on the card and grinned.

He had called Kumi to say hello the previous day and had, somehow, and for reasons he couldn't clearly identify, said nothing about what had happened.

Don't want to worry her, he decided.

He had made the *Chicago Tribune* again—inevitable given his past notoriety—but she wouldn't see that, and no one else had thought to call her. So far as the police knew, he was still separated and had no next of kin.

On the phone, Kumi had talked about her ongoing struggle

not to be overly aggressive in her karate class and the need for similar restraint at work.

"I feel like I'm stuck in the middle somehow," she said. "Of everything. Not Japanese, but not quite American either. People don't quite know what to do with me. And I'm still tiptoeing around cultural protocols I don't completely get. Sometimes it feels like I'm trying to do my job in a space suit, or one of those diving helmets, which would be okay if the job had anything to do with space. Or diving. I'm getting better at it, but I'll never truly belong."

He smiled. It helped to hear her voice.

"So come home," he said. "Take a vacation. Apply for a stateside position."

"Let me master my sushi first," she said, referring to her cooking class. "I'm still too scared of preparing raw fish for anyone other than me. Let me get some *maguro maki* under my belt and then we'll see."

"Soon, I hope," he said. He put his left hand to his right shoulder and rubbed at the ache that wouldn't go away.

Why aren't you telling her? he wondered. *Why not just say it: Listen, Kumi, sorry about the sushi and all but I got shot . . .*

But he didn't. He didn't lie, but he dodged, and afterward he asked himself again. Why hadn't he told her?

Because, he decided, *if you told her and she didn't come, then that would mean she wasn't ready to throw out her job—however much she complains about it—to be with you, that she doesn't love you enough . . .*

Sometimes a little uncertainty was preferable to knowing for sure.

He thought of Julia McBride, the attractive Shakespearean who was also on the list of people he had not told about the shooting. He had not told her either, but he was aware that he hadn't, and that bothered him.

Careful there, Thomas, he reminded himself.

When he had been shot he'd been wearing a bathrobe that they had cut away to get at his wound, so he had nothing of his own but a pair of shorts the hospital had given him. He had asked Peter the Principal to bring him some jeans and a shirt from home, a request his boss seemed to find mortifying and baffling. Peter had shown up the following day with some clothes Thomas hadn't worn for years, which he must have gotten from the very back of his closet. Thomas concealed his exasperation and thanked him, but protested when the principal concurred with the police.

"No, Thomas," he said, patting his blanketed legs awkwardly. "We have all your classes covered. Rest up. Enjoy the summer."

After days in bed, Thomas fumed at the prospect of nothing to do even after he got out of the hospital, but for ten minutes after Peter left, he lay where he was, eyeing the ill-fitting clothes draped over the end of the bed. He snapped on the TV to distract himself and scrolled around till he found a *West Wing* rerun. He was watching it, still thinking vaguely about getting up, when the door opened again and a woman walked in. She was dressed in a businesslike gray pantsuit and her hair was quite unlike the way it had been when he saw her last, but there was no mistaking that unself-conscious giraffe gait. She strode in and put her hands on her hips, looming over him and staring like he'd just cut her off in traffic.

"You're just never happy unless you're getting shot at, are you?" said Deborah Miller.

CHAPTER 21

"Hello, Deborah," said Thomas. "What are you doing here?"

"In town for a meeting," she said. "Thought I'd look you up. Say hi, you know? Thought we might have a beer and reminisce about past near-death experiences. But you just keep right on having them, don't you? The school said you were here."

"They were right."

"If you were anyone else," she said, still scowling, "I'd assume you were involved in a mugging or were a bystander at some drive-by, but since it's you, I figure you've been sticking your nose where it isn't wanted."

He told her everything, partly because she was just the kind of person who didn't take evasion politely, and partly because their relationship—such as it was—had always been surrounded by intrigue, conspiracy, and men who wanted them dead. He hadn't spoken to her for six months, but it felt like they were picking up where they left off.

Deborah was a museum curator in Atlanta. Thomas had met her briefly in Italy, and they had been thrown together when their shared interest in archaeology had put them at the center of a particularly unpleasant murder case, a case tied to the death of Thomas's brother and to bigger, stranger things. After she had returned to the States, she had pressed her connections at the FBI in ways that had, he was sure, saved his life.

"A lost Shakespeare play, huh?" she said. "That's why you're full of holes?"

She had settled into the one armchair, her legs stretched out straight in front of her and crossed at the ankles. She seemed to fill the room, and made the chair look like it was made for a child.

Thomas nodded.

"One hole," he said. "One bullet."

"Because someone wants the play," she said, not even dignifying his remark with a nod, "or because they want to keep it secret?"

He shrugged.

"Maybe it contains Secret Knowledge about the Author," she said, grinning. "I think I read a book like that in college. It was about whether Shakespeare really wrote all those plays or whether it was someone else. The authorship question, they call it, right?"

"Right," said Thomas. He remembered it only dimly, but he had never met an academic who took the issue seriously, so he had never given it much thought.

"I took it to my English professor," she said, smiling at her own naïveté. "I think I was showing off a bit, trying to engage him in a discussion about Serious Things. He was pretty cute."

"And what did he say?"

"Let's just say that it did nothing for my credibility as a student. And I am now as sure as I can be that the plays of Shakespeare were written by a guy from Stratford called Shakespeare. Imagine that."

Thomas laughed.

On the TV Martin Sheen as President Bartlett was holding a press conference.

"This is a good episode," said Deborah, nodding toward it.

"Always nice to find something literate on the idiot's lantern," Thomas agreed.

"I think that guys who can't go a full year without getting shot at should be cautious with words like *idiot*."

"Maybe so," said Thomas. "So what's this meeting you're here for?"

"What are meetings always for?" she replied. "Money. The economy is faltering and when money's tight, all those high cultural bits and pieces that people think of as luxuries take it in the teeth. The museum, like every other museum in the country, is struggling, and we're forming a sort of consortium with a couple of others to share resources. The main one is the Archaeological Museum in Charlotte, North Carolina, but we're meeting here to discuss logistics and initiatives. Neutral ground."

"Not at the Drake?"

"The Drake?"

"It's a hotel."

"Oh," she said. "No. Nothing so grand. Back to Atlanta tomorrow, then frantic preparation for a trip to Mexico."

"Nice."

"Should be," she agreed, "but it's work. Fieldwork though—actual digging—not meetings with suits who want to *optimize earnings* by filling my museum with electronic dinosaurs."

Same old Deborah, he thought.

"Is Kumi in town?" she asked.

Thomas shifted.

"No. Still in Tokyo," he said. "Why?"

"Well, you being shot and all."

"Oh, you know how busy she is," Thomas fudged. "And I'll be out of here by the end of the day . . ."

"You haven't told her."

It wasn't a question. Thomas looked away, then said simply, "No."

Deborah shook her head and drew her knees up.

"I don't get you two," she said.

"You've never met her!" Thomas replied.

"How could I have?" she fired back. "You're never on the same continent, except of course when you are running from snipers. I'm surprised she's not in the next bed."

"I don't want her involved in this," said Thomas. He didn't want to talk about it.

"You're protecting her?" she said, smiling coolly. "From what I've heard, she doesn't need protecting."

"Maybe," Thomas conceded. "It's just . . . difficult."

He had told Deborah before about his uneven marriage, the miscarriage that had torn them apart, the trial separation that had slid into years of isolation, the bitter long-distance phone calls that had finally dried up, and the years of silence.

Deborah knew firsthand of the events last spring that had gone some way to healing the rift, but how do you properly fix a decade of mistrust and alienation when you were never together for more than a few days? Deborah was right: he and Kumi were almost never on the same continent.

"We're just not there yet," he said. "We're getting there, I think, but we're still very separate people. We've had a lot of time to get used to that. It's hard to change it. I don't want her to worry. I don't want her to *depend* on me," he said, finding the word. "We're not ready for that."

"Just don't leave it too late," she said. "Life is short. You of all people should know that."

CHAPTER 22

A half hour after Deborah left, promising to stay in touch, Thomas threw his few things into a bag and kicked it when it fell off the bed. His shoulder was still bound, if less tightly than before, and it ached when he moved. As he was completing his discharge paperwork, a hard-faced nurse brought him a large manila envelope.

"This came for you today," she said, apparently affronted. "Left at the front desk."

Thomas's name was written in careful block capitals. Inside was another, smaller envelope and a handwritten letter.

I'm sorry, Mr. Knight, it said. *It wasn't supposed to go like this.*

There was more, but Thomas's eyes dropped to the signature at the foot of the second page: *David Escolme.* Anger surged up in him like a rearing horse, and he wanted to tear the letter or ball it up and hurl it across the room. Instead he took a breath and read on.

When I heard Blackstone was looking for an agent I tried everything I could to get her to sign with me. I was a no-name agent working alone from his apartment, but it turns out that's what she wanted. She was a dreadful writer, but I figured her name would sell enough books to get me out of trouble. Fat chance.

But then she came to me with this harebrained Shakespeare thing. Claimed she had a lost play and wanted to get it published quickly so she could make a lot of money fast. That was why she didn't want to go through a big agency: too many people would see it. She was talking movie deals and an Arden edition, crowing about what a

star she was going to be. I thought it was nuts. Then I saw
what she had, and I changed my mind. It was the real
deal. I swear it. She wanted someone trustworthy to look
it over and I told her who I knew. She was leery of real
scholars because she thought they'd poach it. She chose
you. Sorry.

Then she disappeared. I figured she'd cut me out of the
deal and I decided she owed me. I thought it would be in
her hotel room because she hoarded all this crap wherever
she went: boxes of books and CDs and stuff. I was pretty
sure she hadn't spoken to you and I figured that you could
tell me what you thought of the manuscript. I mean, since
we were friends, sort of, I thought you'd be a safe person
to consult. I know that sounds sort of scummy and I'm
sorry. I faked the VFL page so you'd think I was legit.

Anyway, it wasn't there. When you came I was freaking out. Then I found out Daniella was dead and everything went to hell. I swear I had nothing to do with that.
I've not been a Boy Scout but I'm not a killer.

So, I'm hiding now, and not only from the police. The
only way I can get out of this is if someone produces that
damned play. I know what you did last year in Italy and
Japan. That stuff in the Philippines. The firefight on the
beach. Figuring out what happened to your brother. I read
about it. I know you can help me. Please, Mr. Knight. The
quest is worthy of Holmes himself. If there's money in it,
send me a finder's fee and keep the rest."

David Escolme

I'm sorry I ever got you involved in this, but now you
are the only person I can turn to. Meet me in Poets'
Corner at 4 P.M. on Thursday, June 12.

Poets' Corner?
The only Poets' Corner Thomas had heard of was in Westminster Abbey in London. Thomas stared into space, then
opened the other envelope. Inside was an open return ticket
to London Gatwick and five thousand dollars in cash.

"You have got to be kidding me," he said. He was getting angry, rereading the letter, his teeth set.

Escolme had lied to him, set him up, left him with a corpse at his back door, and then gotten him damn near killed in his own house. Now Thomas was supposed to put all the pieces together to save his neck? He could forget it.

Thomas remembered the note he had posted on the Drake's conference message board and figured he had done the right thing after all. He wanted nothing more to do with David Escolme. If he ever saw him again, it would be too soon, and if the guy wound up in jail for the rest of his life, that seemed no more than fair to Thomas. Escolme wasn't a kid anymore, which meant that Thomas hadn't been responsible for him in any way for a decade.

The phone rang. Thomas answered it.

"It's Polinski," said the cop. "You still planning to check out today?"

"I'm on my way out the door right now."

"Good. Can you come down to the beach at the end of Church Street?"

"Are we going to picnic to celebrate my discharge?"

"No," she said. "I need you to look at something."

Her tone was businesslike, clipped. Thomas felt a sudden chill.

"Something?" he said.

"I think we might have found David Escolme."

CHAPTER 23

"A couple who came down here to watch the sunrise over the lake found him," said Polinski.

He'd been in the water about six hours, they thought, and dead a little longer than that. He had been shot through the heart at close range with what looked to be a .38.

"The same gun?" asked Thomas.

"Too early to say," said Polinski, "but I wouldn't be surprised."

Thomas frowned. An hour ago he would have greeted Escolme with a volley of insults, maybe more if his temper got away from him. The guy had exploited him, made a fool of him, and put him in firing lines both metaphorical and literal. But looking at him now, half wrapped in a tarp, his boyish face pale, wet, and shrunken, Thomas could see only the bond that had connected them in the first place. Escolme was, after all, still a kid, and a screwed-up kid at that. He had done some stupid things, even some scummy things—the word floating up in Thomas's mind from the letter—but he didn't deserve this. Thomas's rage drifted away on the waters of the lake, and he felt unaccountably guilty, as if this is what he had wanted.

And then there was the note you left, the one including his name and LLW. There wasn't a Shakespearean in the world who wouldn't guess what those three letters stood for . . .

Thomas stared out over the water, his left hand stuffed into his pocket, his right in a simple sling to keep his wound from reopening. He was suddenly tired beyond words.

"Any chance it's self-inflicted?" he heard Polinski say to a man Thomas took to be the coroner or medical examiner.

The man muttered doubtfully in response.

"It's not suicide," said Thomas. "He wasn't ending anything. He was in the middle of it."

"And how would you know that?" said Polinski.

Thomas could feel the envelope with the ticket in his pocket, but he didn't draw it out.

"Just a hunch," he said. "Am I done here?"

"You're done."

"You need me around—in town, I mean?" said Thomas. "I'd like to get away."

Polinski considered him, her eyes narrow.

"Like where?"

"Don't know," Thomas shrugged. He avoided her eyes. "I just need to be . . . away. I'll check in."

"You're not a suspect," said Polinski, matter-of-fact. "You were under guard at the hospital when Escolme died." She sighed. "Yeah, you can go. Just make sure I can reach you."

Thomas nodded and turned, tramping wearily up the beach, then turned back to the cop.

"Polinski," he called back.

She turned, shading her eyes from the glare off the water.

"You know anything about where Blackstone had been before she came here?"

"Is there a reason I should tell you?" she said.

"No," said Thomas. "Just trying to help."

"Just take it easy, Mr. Knight. Rest up."

He nodded, but before he had a chance to turn away she seemed to think better of her decision.

"You know she was a Brit, right?"

"I figured that, yeah."

"Her passport says she flew here from Paris."

"Huh," said Thomas, thinking of the champagne bottles in the room he had thought was Escolme's.

"That mean anything to you?"

"Not yet," he said.

It could have been a mistake, that suggestion that it might mean something to him in the future, that he wasn't done with this case, and he caught a watchfulness in her face. She opened her mouth to say something and he pretended not to notice, raising a hand in farewell and turning up the beach. He walked purposefully away, his strapped shoulder aching, his right hand still clutching the airline ticket in his pocket.

PART II

When I have seen by Time's fell hand defaced
The rich proud cost of outworn buried age;
When sometime lofty towers I see down-razed
And brass eternal slave to mortal rage;
When I have seen the hungry ocean gain
Advantage on the kingdom of the shore,
And the firm soil win of the watery main,
Increasing store with loss and loss with store;
When I have seen such interchange of state,
Or state itself confounded to decay;
Ruin hath taught me thus to ruminate,
That Time will come and take my love away.
   This thought is as a death, which cannot choose
   But weep to have that which it fears to lose.

—Shakespeare, "Sonnet 64"

CHAPTER 24

Westminster Abbey was overwhelming. It wasn't the scale of the place—the vast, vaulted nave thronging with tourists—or even, strictly speaking, its age. It was the history that announced itself everywhere you looked. It was, Thomas thought, impressive to the point of being oppressive.

In this building every monarch of England had been crowned since William the Conqueror in 1066. The core of the building was actually older, a tenth-century Benedictine abbey for which King—later, Saint—Edward the Confessor had built a magnificent church. Edward's remains still lay here, as did the bodies of countless other monarchs including the giants of Shakespeare's day, Elizabeth I and James I. All this and a good deal more Thomas could learn from his guidebook, but the wealth of information—of history—made the abbey walls crowd in, so that visitors with an ounce of sensitivity to such things started to feel like the slender columns on which rested the tons of stone above. It was too much to take in.

Every inch of the place seemed to memorialize some long-dead dignitary or statesman, so that even the tombs of such colossi as Richard II and Henry V—both known to Thomas almost exclusively through Shakespeare's depictions of them—could produce little more than muted shock. The depth of the antiquity, the weight of it, was unlike anything Thomas had ever experienced. Here were buried the scientists Isaac Newton and Charles Darwin; the composer Handel; the actors David Garrick, Henry Irving, and Laurence Olivier; the writers Aphra Behn and Ben Jonson; the prime minister William Pitt; the engineer Thomas Telford . . . The list seemed endless.

Thomas drifted through Henry VII's chapel, where lay Elizabeth; her Catholic half-sister, "Bloody" Mary; her successor, James; and James's mother, Mary, Queen of Scots, whom Elizabeth had had beheaded for treason. He walked slowly, still bruised from the fight in Evanston, one arm still suspended at his waist in a sling. His invalid speed made everything about the place register more fully. As he exited the chapel he was confronted with the battered throne of Edward I, used in every coronation since 1309, now astonishingly disfigured by graffiti and carved initials, so that it could have been some forgotten chair at the back of any school hall.

Thomas stared at it, feeling the collision of the remarkable and the contemptibly familiar. How could anyone treat so revered an object with such casual disdain? But then how could anyone sustain a proper sense of awe in a place that strove to outdo each monument with something still grander, still more redolent of the distant and mythic past.

The abbey was a microcosm of the city itself, each corner of London stacked with a history so deep and layered that it dizzied the mind like vertigo. Maybe the whole country was like this, each square foot overwritten with the footprints of kings and writers, soldiers, politicians, artists, and heroes of all kinds, from the Saxons, Romans, and Vikings all the way through the Medieval and Renaissance periods through to more modern epics like the Second World War. On this spot, or close to it, had stood every Londoner for a thousand years: queens, princes, nobles, priests—first Catholic, then their Anglican equivalents—tradesmen, beggars, prostitutes, all seeking God or history, many of them tourists like himself. King George II. Oliver Cromwell. Winston Churchill. Jack the Ripper. Almost certainly.

And Shakespeare.

Thomas frowned.

David Escolme had planned to meet Thomas here, specifically in Poets' Corner, before he had been shot and dumped in the gray waters of Lake Michigan. Here were buried literary luminaries from Chaucer and Spenser to Charles Dickens and Thomas Hardy, but the place was also crowded with monuments to people buried elsewhere. Among these was an eighteenth-century statue of a slick-looking Shakespeare on the east wall. Thomas considered it and wondered, not for the first time, what in the name of God he was doing here.

Escolme was dead, so the idea of fulfilling the rendezvous was uselessly sentimental at best. On the plane over he had flirted with the idea that someone else would arrive in Escolme's place and lead him on some *Indiana Jones*–esque procession of revelations through the secret parts of the abbey, but this was pure fantasy. Thomas had arrived like all the other tourists and there was no one here to meet him or explain what he was supposed to do—or see—next. If Escolme had something in mind that he wanted to show him, Thomas would never find it alone, and it was more likely that his former student had chosen the place simply because it was a convenient location that smacked of art and seriousness: a fitting place to discuss the history of a lost and probably mythical Shakespeare manuscript.

All this he had known before, so the question of what he was doing here was a real one. He'd had no contact with Escolme for the best part of a decade, and when his former pupil had reentered his life it had been trailing a mesh of lies designed to ensnare him. That the kid had wound up dead was not Thomas's fault. He reminded himself that he owed Escolme nothing.

But here he was.

The fact was that Thomas was bound to David Escolme in life and now in death. There was, after all, the rash, childish note he had left for all to see, the scribbling that, perhaps, had given the killer Escolme's name . . . So yes, Thomas and his former student were bound together, and his old need to know the roots of things had been joined by something hard and chill, something in addition to the outrage, the need for closure and a sense of justice. Now it was mostly a sense of responsibility.

And before you get too high-minded about this quest, let's stop pretending that you don't think that discovering a long-lost Shakespeare play would be incredibly cool.

How could it not be? Shakespeare was woven into his life, had very nearly been the sole focus of his professional identity. Of course it was a part of him. To find a previously unknown play would be extraordinary. Escolme might have been interested in the money, but for Thomas the value of the thing would be in the words. To find it would make him the cultural hero of his age. He would be able to walk into those Shakespeare conferences, and the scholars—the very people who had said he couldn't be one of their esteemed number—would applaud and smile and honor him . . .

And you'd show that you really were as good as them after all? said the voice in his head with caustic amusement.

Thomas smiled bleakly.

"Okay," he muttered, "so I have some unresolved issues with academia."

Which was all very well, but standing here in this great shrine and mausoleum, Thomas had no idea where to start. He stared at the marble statue of Shakespeare, who was leaning in an improbable fashion on a stack of books but facing outward, one finger smugly indicating a handful of lines from *The Tempest*:

> *The Cloud capt Tow'rs,*
> *The Gorgeous Palaces,*
> *The Solemn Temples,*
> *The Great Globe itself,*
> *Yea all which it Inherit,*
> *Shall Dissolve;*
> *And like the baseless Fabrick of a Vision*
> *Leave not a wreck behind.*

The Great Globe itself was not simply the earth, of course, but the theater in which the lines had first been uttered. Otherwise, of course, the statue invoked Shakespeare the poet—the thinker with his books—rather than the man of the theater, though the posture of the figure was, perhaps, deliberately stagey.

"He's not buried here, of course," said a voice at Thomas's elbow.

He turned to find a man in a black cassock beside him, a verger of the abbey. He had pale, waxy skin and unfashionably long black hair that broke in waves about his shoulders. He wore wire-rimmed glasses. His voice was soft, reverential, and his face earnest. He considered Thomas's sling for a moment and then looked back to his face.

"Yes," said Thomas. "He was buried in Stratford, right?"

"At Holy Trinity church. Yes," said the verger. "This monument was erected in 1740."

"That would explain it," said Thomas.

"Yes, he is a bit of a dandy, isn't he?" said the verger, eyes on the statue. "Was there something in particular you were looking for? I couldn't help but notice you seemed to be drifting. Of course, I see a lot of that, and it's better than some of the alternatives."

"Alternatives?"

"Oh, we're on the *Da Vinci Code* tour now," he said, sighing.

"Really?" said Thomas.

"Oh yes. There's a scene in the book set at Isaac Newton's tomb. A spurious clue of some sort."

"Intentionally spurious?"

"You know," said the verger, perplexed, "I'm not sure. Fiction is fiction, of course, which is what makes it fun, but there's a point at which the pretense that fiction is really fact goes beyond marketing and becomes merely . . ." He sought for the word.

"Deception?" Thomas supplied.

The verger flashed a sudden and secret grin.

"You know, they wanted to use the abbey in the film version," he added.

"And did they?"

"Did we let them use a Christian church to make a movie about why Christianity was a lie?" said the verger, one eyebrow arched. "Astonishingly, no. I think they used Lincoln

Cathedral. God alone knows what the bishop was thinking— or at least I hope he does—though I think that the hundred thousand pounds for the church restoration fund was probably a factor. Ironic, wouldn't you say? Some might feel that repairing the roof at the expense of the foundations was a bit steep, but such is life in the twenty-first century. We have some leaflets about the mistakes in the book, if you'd like one. I don't think the theological errors are worth discussing, but one should at least get the facts right, don't you think?"

"I guess so," Thomas smiled.

"Still," said the verger, flashing that schoolboy grin again, "it was a cracking good read, and I was never a fan of Opus Dei."

"I was looking for a David Escolme," said Thomas, on impulse.

The verger's brow furrowed.

"Is he buried here?" said the verger, fishing a battered index from his robes.

"No," said Thomas, pleased by the man's eagerness to help. "I was supposed to meet him here, but . . . I think there's something here he wanted to show me."

The verger glanced at the stone floor beneath them, each polished stone flag engraved with a name and epitaph, each one resonating in Thomas's mind like distant bells: Alfred Lord Tennyson, George Eliot, Gerard Manley Hopkins, Dylan Thomas, Lewis Carroll of *Alice* . . .

"Ben Jonson, Shakespeare's friend and fellow dramatist, is buried here," said the verger. "He was allotted only eighteen inches of space, so they had to bury him standing up. He had killed a fellow actor, after all. There's a plaque here, but he's buried in the northern aisle of the nave . . ."

Thomas was nodding, but his heart wasn't in it and the verger could tell.

"I'm sorry," said Thomas. "As an American, I find this all a bit . . ."

"Undemocratic?"

"I was going to say *overwhelming*," said Thomas, smiling.

"Yes, I think most people feel that way, regardless of

where they are from. We have memorial stones to many famous Americans here too. Franklin Roosevelt, Martin Luther King Junior, Henry James, T. S. Eliot, though we've rather claimed him for the crown at this point." The verger smiled again.

"Are there people from other countries buried here?" said Thomas.

"In Poets' Corner? No. This is rather a monument to Britishness, I'm afraid," said the verger. "I think there's only one non-Englishman buried here, a Frenchman."

"A writer?"

"Yes," said the verger, "though I think *man of letters* might be a better description, and I think he is best known—in this country at least—for who he knew. Charles de St. Denis, an exiled lord from the court of Louis the Fourteenth. A friend of Moliere's, I believe. Hold on, it's here somewhere."

The verger steered him around, his head tipped up, till he found the plaque he was looking for.

"Ah," he said. "That's the one."

Thomas looked up out of politeness rather than curiosity and found a white marble tablet with a shield and flaming torches. The text was in Latin, the bold caps proclaiming the deceased's name as Carolus de St. Denis.

"Carolus is Charles, of course," said the verger. He gave Thomas a considering look. "Not what you were looking for, I fear."

"You've been most kind," said Thomas. "I wish I knew what it was I was looking for."

"Perhaps you'd prefer something less historical and more spiritual," said the verger.

"What do you mean?"

"I said you seemed lost, but I'm not sure it's the kind of *lost* you escape with a map and a guide book."

Thomas looked at the floor.

"I'm sorry," said the verger. "I didn't mean to pry."

"Don't worry about it," said Thomas. "I just kind of have to find something. For an old friend."

The verger's eyes said he knew there was more to it, but

he nodded and smiled seriously, even a little sadly, and Thomas was grateful for not having to say anything else.

There had to have been a reason Escolme had wanted to meet him here, something he had wanted Thomas to see. In so vast a place it was easily possible, even likely, that Thomas had missed whatever it was he was supposed to have found, but he was more troubled by the idea that he had in fact seen it and missed its significance. He would have to come back, but he had other questions to ask first.

CHAPTER 25

The tabloid headlines were a week old, but that didn't mute their shrillness. BRIT NOVELIST BUTCHERED IN STATES, screamed *The Sun*. MURDERED TALENT, said *The Daily Mail*. CRIME WRITER TURNS VICTIM, crowed *The People*. The stories themselves alternated between the sensational and the maudlin, though the papers had been unable to produce the obligatory grieving relatives, and within a couple of days the only sentiment they could muster was wrung from fans outraged that Daniella Blackstone would be writing no more books. There was also a grumbling undercurrent of anti-American feeling throughout, Thomas thought: if only she hadn't crossed the Atlantic, they seemed to say, none of this would have happened.

Thomas was scanning the stories on a computer at the British Library next to Saint Pancras, looking for anything of substance that would keep him informed as to how the case was progressing. He might be able to get a little out of Polinski if he called, but he would prefer not to announce to her that he was out of the country just yet. The Chicago papers had said little after the first announcement of the murder, but their English counterparts had seized on it as a matter of national importance. Or at least, they had tried to. No one had come forward to spill Daniella's secrets, her husband had died in a car accident ten years before, there were no bereaved children at her graveside, and Elsbeth Church, her erstwhile writing partner, was refusing to comment. Within a few days, the story's energy had stalled, and with no new revelations—about the case or the victim—the papers had moved on. A missing ten-year-old girl seemed to be stirring national outrage at present, particularly because she had vanished on vacation in Spain, and that seemed to generate rather more of what Thomas supposed was still called "human interest." It made his skin crawl.

There were two pieces of information on Blackstone that he didn't already know. The first concerned her family, and it was all about absence. Her parents were dead, her husband likewise, and she had no children, her only daughter having perished in what the papers called "a tragic fire" at the age of sixteen. One feature article used this information to sketch Blackstone as both tragic and faintly vampiric: a sinister figure (*those eyes!*) with a taste for the macabre—as manifested in her stories—who had lived under the shadow of death all her life, till it finally took her.

The second piece of information was a picture of a grand eighteenth-century house at the head of a gravel road through rough, green pasture. This was the house in which the novelist had lived. It was in Kenilworth, near Warwick, and though there was no address, it was "in sight of the castle." That, Thomas thought, should be good enough.

He took the underground—the tube—from King's Cross to Euston and a mainline train past the backs of houses and Warwickshire fields, to Coventry, followed by a bus to Kenilworth. The whole trip took less than two hours. If he had stayed on the bus, it would have taken him on to Warwick and then Stratford. Was it a coincidence that Blackstone had lived so close to Shakespeare's birthplace? Probably, but if *Love's Labour's Won* really existed, it made a kind of sense that it had found its way here. It could have been the author's own copy, given to someone local, or inherited and then forgotten . . .

And no one noticed it for four hundred years despite the fact that the entire region has become a virtual monument to Shakespeare? It's actually less likely that it would be found here.

Thomas scowled out of the bus window. He hadn't even told Kumi he was coming. He'd driven straight to O'Hare from the beach where he'd left Polinski and the body of David Escolme, pausing only to grab a bag of clothes and toiletries from home and load up his prescription pain meds at the CVS, as if he were on some urgent mission. Now he was a world away, his body bruised so that it was impossible to get comfortable in the bus seat—the flight had been a nightmare—in a place that was both familiar and strange. At least in Japan the absolute foreignness of the place had announced itself in everything. Here everything was only slightly unfamiliar— the voices and their language, the cars, the fields, the grown men in soccer shirts—as if the universe had twisted slightly on its axis and reality had distorted.

"You getting off 'ere, mate?"

The bus had stopped.

Thomas got out into the aisle, but he gave the driver a blank look. He could stay on, wait till the bus took him somewhere he could get a train back to London and take the first plane back to the States.

"Come on," said the driver. "You're 'olding up the line."

He sounded like someone doing Dick Van Dyke in *Mary Poppins*, but what might have been comic and quaint sounded brusque, hostile.

Thomas nodded, dragging his luggage with his left hand as he clambered down and out, moving, he knew, too slowly for the driver's satisfaction. With a pneumatic hiss, the door closed behind him and the bus rumbled away. The driver threw him a dark look as it passed and Thomas thought of the phrase *fish out of water* with its overtones not of being out of place, but of drowning in the air that everyone else breathed.

If he wasn't able to make some sense of this visit soon, he would go home, before he found himself flapping around on the sidewalk—what the Brits called the *pavement*—gasping for breath.

CHAPTER 26

Thomas checked in to the Castle Lodge hotel, which sat right at the access road to Kenilworth's most famous landmark. The hotel was a large brick house, perhaps once a grange or gatehouse for the castle itself, though he guessed it was only a couple of hundred years old. He had a sports bag crammed with clothes, a few toiletries, and a couple of books and was unpacked in under two minutes.

There was a rack of brochures and flyers for local attractions in the lobby. Thomas took a few that had area maps on them and wandered outside. It was overcast, a moist gray day that muted the greens of the clustered trees. He strolled down the road toward the castle, trying to put his finger on what made the English countryside so clearly different from the States. The fields were small and irregular, a million miles from the cornfields of the Midwest, hedged and fenced in ways they had probably been for centuries, edged with knots of un-recognizable trees and spotted with magpies and crows. There was no one around.

The parking lot was deserted, except for an English Heritage van and a utilitarian bicycle chained to a wooden perimeter fence. Thomas rotated several of the maps on the brochures until he had a sense of the land around the castle, bought his ticket and a guidebook in a shop stuffed with post-cards and plastic knights in armor, and entered the site via a broad path and a narrow bridge. There was a stream beneath, though a glance at the guidebook suggested that it might once have been a good deal grander. Indeed, much of the land around the castle—now low-lying fields scattered with desul-tory cows—had once been under water, so that the building on the hill had been a fortified island.

Thomas looked up from the guidebook and wandered in, between a pair of ruined round towers, above which the castle proper rose, a romantic straggle of broken walls with empty windows and ragged towers, all in the same warm russet and pink sandstone. It had been built in spurts over several hundred years beginning in the early twelfth century, besieged in the course of obscure medieval wars, and finally deliberately ruined during the English civil war by parliamentarian forces who feared it might prove a royalist stronghold. Compared to the Tower of London, or the castle down the road in Warwick, both meticulously preserved, this was the remnant of a forgotten past, now mysterious and heavy with atmosphere.

It was also a past saturated with Shakespeare. Thomas sat on the graffiti-carved stone foundation of some collapsed doorway, trying to orient himself, and the words leaped off the page, chiming with echoes of things he had once known. King John had once owned and developed the castle, as had Edward I and Edward II, who was forced to abdicate on this very spot before being gruesomely murdered elsewhere in a way immortalized by Shakespeare's contemporary, Christopher Marlowe. The core of the castle's remains was loaded with Shakespearean significance. Much of the major building had been done by John of Gaunt, duke of the house of Lancaster and the somber voice of impending collapse in Shakespeare's *Richard II*. Geoffrey Chaucer may have read aloud from his *Canterbury Tales* by the fireplace in the great hall . . .

He came from a city where anything over a century and a half was virtually prehistoric. No wonder he felt out of place.

This very house, said the book, was part of the land and property for which Henry Bollingbroke—Gaunt's son—had returned from exile in France in the final year of the fourteenth century. On his return, Bollingbroke became Henry IV, the first Lancastrian king and the subject of Shakespeare's most remarkable history plays. In them Henry's son, the young prince Hal, rioted in an Eastcheap tavern with Falstaff before beginning his studied redemption by defeating Hotspur and finally being crowned King Henry V, whom Shakespeare called—ironically or not, Thomas was never completely sure—the mirror of all Christian kings. A hundred yards or so to Thomas's left, Henry had received the insulting "ton of treasure"—tennis balls—sent to him by the French dauphin as better fitting his youth than the French crown he sought after.

Thomas marveled. He had always assumed the story was Shakespeare's invention. It was astounding that it had actually happened, and on this very spot. The insult had—somewhat conveniently—fueled Henry's march into France and his decisive and improbable victories, first at Harfleur—"Once more unto the breach, dear friends, once more . . ."—and then, still more improbably, at Agincourt: "We few, we happy few, we band of brothers . . ."

Thomas stared at the empty sandstone ruin, and he felt the weight of it all like a piece of his own past.

The best-preserved part of the castle had been built by Robert Dudley, Earl of Leicester and Elizabeth's most prominent favorite in the early part of her reign. Indeed, there were whispers that she might marry him, except that the strange death of his wife—she apparently fell down the stairs and broke her neck—raised such scandalous speculation that the politically savvy queen backed away from the possibility. Dudley entertained her here three times, and the festivities surrounding one of those visits may well have been witnessed by the boy Shakespeare in 1575. There was a good deal of pageantry, much of it cleverly but obviously aimed at persuading the queen to marry and settle down with the house's owner, and some of it seemed to stretch the royal amusement in the direction of irritation. She never returned to Kenilworth and, of course, never married.

But *A Midsummer Night's Dream* was sometimes thought to capture a memory of those showy entertainments in Oberon's reminiscence of Cupid firing his bow at a "fair vestal thronèd by the West." The arrow missed the "imperial votress" and fell on a flower that, when crushed on the eyes of a sleeper, makes them fall in love with whatever they next behold . . .

You should bring Kumi here, he thought.

She would like the age and the stillness of the place. She would like it the way he liked it and they would wander about in what those nineteenth-century authors called a "companionable silence." That was, perhaps, when they were happiest: not that they didn't like to talk, to debate, to spar, even. But there were times when they just clicked, and were content to be together, sharing not the same thoughts exactly but related thoughts, ideas, and feelings linked by analogy and bound by the constant awareness of each other. They might be reading separately by the fire, or bottling his inconsistent home brew, or preparing pasta with anchovy pesto while they listened to *Fresh Air* on the radio. They would move around each other easily, doing their own things, but somehow acting like a single organism, and from time to time they would catch each other's eye and smile, knowing. That was the best. That was how things had once been and—in the last twelve months, after years of chill silences and raging shouting matches—they had started to find those moments, those smiles, again. He imagined them together again in his kitchen, but he couldn't shake the memory of Daniella Blackstone's dead face against the window.

Thomas drifted slowly through the ruins, dwarfed by the associations of the place, reveling in it, disturbed only by the jackdaws that started squabbling up from the higher perches. He found his way to the western edge of the castle, where he could look out over the countryside. There, over the fields that had once been the submerged mere where Henry V had built a "pleasance," or summer house and garden, was a single building. It was nothing so large or ancient as any part of the castle, but it had a quiet Victorian dignity of its own and it was easily recognizable from the tabloid photograph he had seen. It was the house of the late Daniella Blackstone.

Thomas traced the walls down to where scaffolding braced a spot where what may have been a square tower or guardhouse had crumbled to almost nothing. He squeezed through, tripped down the embankment to the footpath that skirted the perimeter wall, and followed it to an unmarked road that pointed west toward the house. As he walked, he kept looking back, drawn to the ruins behind him as if he had been there once long before and had left something of himself behind.

Daniella had died at his house, he thought. Now he was visiting hers. Maybe, just maybe, he would leave with a piece of the puzzle.

CHAPTER 27

The house was sprawling and impressive. It had probably been a farm of sorts, but it had been gentrified and expanded, about a hundred years ago. The roof was steeply pitched and there was a kind of square turret in the middle. While he waited for someone to answer the doorbell, he considered the dark blue Jaguar with its yellow license plate that was parked on the gravel forecourt. Probably Daniella's.

The door was snatched open and a man appeared.

"Hi," said Thomas. "I'm Thomas Knight."

The man in the doorway—*a servant of some kind? Or a lawyer?*—waited for more and, when he didn't get it, said, "I'm sorry?" He spoke in clipped tones, his mouth barely moving, his eyes resting on the sling Thomas was still wearing.

"Thomas Knight. The journalist. . . ."

The door started to close.

"Not a *newspaper* journalist," Thomas inserted hurriedly. "I'm here for the story I'm doing on Miss Blackstone for the fanzine *Thrills*."

The threshold guardian paused, then shook his head.

"Her agent didn't tell you I was coming," said Thomas, as if just realizing the problem.

"I'm afraid not. I'm the steward of Miss Blackstone's estate for now. I'm afraid I can't let journalists in while the house is being inventoried."

"And this is probably a bad time," said Thomas. "It must be difficult for you."

The door, which had started to inch shut again, held. The man considered for a second and then returned his gaze to Thomas. He was perhaps fifty and balding. He wore a dark suit that made him look a little like a mourner at some nineteenth-century funeral, and though his eyes were a cloudy blue-gray, they were hard and skeptical.

"I did have an arrangement with her agent," Thomas pressed. "Actually it's part of a contractual obligation. Would you like to call to confirm it? I can wait."

"What was it that you were hoping to do?" said the steward, his jaw moving only the merest fraction as he spoke, as if he were practicing to be a ventriloquist.

"Just take a look around the place. You know, a bit of color. I wasn't even going to take pictures," he said. "Miss Blackstone was a favorite of our readers and she did a couple of interviews with us. I could come back, but I have to be back in London tomorrow and back in the States by the weekend."

"How long do you need?" said the steward, checking his watch.

"An hour ought to do it," said Thomas. "Maybe less."

"I'll need to come round with you, and I really don't have the time . . ."

"I'll be fine by myself," said Thomas. "Privacy would be great. I'd probably—you know—*absorb* more: the feel of the place, you know?"

"No doubt," said the steward. He had no intention of doing any such thing. "I can give you fifteen minutes," he said, stepping aside. "Let's get it over."

Thomas went inside. The hall was large and ornate, but gloomy. It smelled of wood polish.

"Miss Blackstone's living quarters comprise the living room, sitting room, dining room, and library downstairs and all the rooms upstairs. Please don't touch anything."

"Naturally," said Thomas.

Thomas had no handle on the man. He could have been a mere functionary, though why he wouldn't relax that persona after the death of his mistress, Thomas couldn't say. Perhaps he was privately grief stricken and dealt with it in this formal, businesslike fashion. The British weren't exactly renowned for their shows of passion. Perhaps he had been her lover and stood to inherit the whole place . . .

"Where would you like to begin?" said the steward.

Thomas looked around, and almost at once, a phone rang in another room. The steward shot him a look.

"Wait here, please," he said, and stalked off in the direction of the sound.

Thomas waited till he was out of sight and then moved down the hall as quickly as he could without making noise.

He began in the library. It seemed like the logical place, though he thought it unlikely that he'd find *Love's Labour's Won* shelved under *S* for *Shakespeare*. What he did find was a room with a single armchair, an end table, and floor-to-ceiling shelves. There was only one small window, which looked out of the back of the house over a field where cows grazed, and the room was dim. The chair looked worn and comfortable, and the oriental rug on which it sat was rubbed threadbare at its foot. Someone had spent a lot of time in here in this one spot, and—given the lack of furniture—had done so alone. A single reading lamp hovered over the back of the chair. Thomas switched it on, but even in daylight the room felt gloomy, and the lamp illuminated only the chair itself.

The bookcases would have been grand if they had been lined with leather-bound volumes of purpose and antiquity, but they were stuffed with beaten-up paperbacks of all shape and color. The only hardcovers he could see looked like her own, pushed off into a corner below the window where they sat, apparently unhandled. Thomas drew a couple out and flipped through them. The room was absolutely silent.

Blackstone and Church books were an odd hybrid combining the British equivalent of the police procedural mystery with the ghosts and vampires of horror. Stylistically they were flowery and overblown, full of purple prose and Dickensian grandiloquence but smart and atmospheric. Thomas selected *The Blood Rose* and thumbed through it. He remembered a scene in which the intrepid inspector had been cornered in a misty churchyard by a killer whose mortality was by no means assured. It had kept him up late into the night, and though he had smiled at it for much of the next day, the spectral murderess had stalked his dreams. He found the section of the book now and felt the hairs on his neck bristle, so that for a moment he forgot that the steward could return at any moment.

The rest of the books were in the same genre, or variants of it, most more firmly grounded on one side or other of the supernatural divide: P. D. James and Ruth Rendell over here, Stephen King and Ray Bradbury there. This, apparently, was where Daniella kept up with the competition. There was no Shakespeare here at all.

Thomas checked the hall, but there was no sign of the steward.

The other rooms downstairs were even less instructive. They were austere and a little fussy in a Victorian way: lots of dark oak and lace, a few family portraits in oil, only one of which was twentieth century. It hung over the stone fireplace in the sitting room and depicted a young man, blond, with what Thomas thought of as an Errol Flynn mustache. He was in some kind of khaki military uniform with brass buttons and cradled a flat peaked cap with a badge in one hand. A large pistol in a flapped leather holster was slung across his chest. He looked like an officer, though Thomas didn't know enough about such things to be sure, and it was only the apparent age of the painting and the stiffness of the pose that made him think it was First World War, not Second. The man himself looked cocky, self-assured, but whether it had been painted before, during, or after his military service, Thomas had no way of knowing.

He doubled back toward the kitchen and could hear the steward making occasional and inaudible remarks into the phone. Thomas tried the first door he saw. It opened into a stone staircase that descended into what was now a cellar with racks of wine and champagne—all bearing the Saint Evremond name. Thomas suspected the place had once been a coal house. The floor had been swept clean, but there was a persistent black sparkle in the walls where the coal had been heaped. He looked up and saw a hatch at one end of the room where light showed through the cracks.

Nothing here.

He retraced his steps to the main lobby, moving quietly,

listening, then climbed a slow half-spiral staircase, trailing his hand along a heavy oaken handrail polished slick with age and use till it was barely recognizable as wood. He wandered from room to room, finding more of the nineteenth-century fussiness, though here there were more concessions to modern comforts. The bed was an antique four-poster, but the mattress was new. The desk in the study was modern and solid and housed a state-of-the-art computer, while the antique writing desk in the corner looked like a museum piece and had seen about as much use. There were a few books, all modern, but—again—no Shakespeare of any vintage.

At one end of the landing a second flight of stairs doubled back and went up to a third level: the turret he had seen from the front. He went up, but the door at the top was heavy and locked shut. He felt above the lintel and found an old-fashioned key.

Sweet.

He was putting it into the lock, trying to work it with his clumsy left hand, when a voice behind him stopped him cold.

"What do you think you're doing?"

The steward was standing on the landing below, and his face was hard.

"What is in there?" said Thomas, trying to sound casual.

"That would be Miss Alice's room."

He said it as if this should be explanation enough.

"Could I have a look inside?" said Thomas.

Miss Alice?

"No. I told you to wait for me downstairs."

"Does Miss Alice still live there?" said Thomas, ignoring the man's hostility. Perhaps Blackstone had had what they used to call a "companion." Her husband was, after all, long dead.

"Miss Alice was her daughter," said the other, and his cloudy eyes flashed as if Thomas had said something offensive. "What magazine did you say you worked for?"

"I'm sorry," said Thomas. "I forgot. We always tried to stay out of Miss Blackstone's personal tragedy."

"And yet here you are."

There was a pause.

"The key, please," said the steward.

He extended his hand without taking a step, and Thomas had to come down to him. Thomas stretched out his left hand, twisting his body so that the pain in his shoulder flared. The steward noticed and his head cocked with interest, even amusement.

"Been in the wars, Mr. Knight?" he said.

"Walked into a door," said Thomas.

"And now you can walk out of one."

With the key in his fist, the steward turned and walked away, descending the stairs so quickly that Thomas had to jog to keep up.

He entered the office by the kitchen, where a wooden table sat beneath a rack of pans. The room was immaculate, but dim as the rest of the house and cool. There was a crate beside the table, its wood branded with the Saint Evremond crest. Above it was a board hung with keys. The steward hung the key in place and turned to Thomas. His face was still blank, but the muscles of his jaw were taut and his eyes were hard.

"Miss Blackstone liked her champagne," Thomas said, nodding at the crate.

It was the wrong thing to say.

"She liked many fine things in moderation," said the other, pointedly. Thomas could think of nothing to say.

"I'll see you out," said the steward.

At the door he added, "Oh, and Mr. Knight?"

"Yes?" said Thomas, turning to him.

"Don't come back, there's a good chap."

The steward's unblinking eyes held Thomas until the door swung heavily into place with a deep snap that resounded through the house.

CHAPTER 28

The University of Birmingham's Shakespeare Institute is located in Mason Croft, a sprawling two-story brick building on Church Street in Stratford that was once home to the novelist Marie Corelli. Located minutes from the properties most definitively associated with Shakespeare—his birthplace, the house he bought and lived in, the school he attended, and the church that housed his bones—it provided a unique focus for academic study and periodic conferences. It was here that Julia McBride, Randall Dagenhart, and a score of other Shakespeareans had gathered for a special week of seminars and lectures with their colleagues and students, a conference unshackled by the usual rules of the International Shakespeare Conference, which, as Julia had pointed out, did not permit graduate students to present. Thomas wondered if the professional Shakespeareans felt the aura of pilgrimage that haunted the place, or if—as scholars schooled in the posthumanism of current literary criticism—they were immune to such romantic mysticism.

Thomas knew that the kind of anonymity he had experienced at the Chicago conference was out of the question at the institute, Mason Croft being big for a house, but not for a conference center. Still, he was surprised to find the front door locked. There was an old-fashioned bell pull. He tugged it.

A moment later, the door opened.

"Can I help you?"

The woman was large and tough-looking, middle-aged rather than elderly by sheer force of character: a woman used to weeding out people who didn't belong. People like him.

"I was looking for the conference session," he said, trying to look like a confused delegate and not like an interloper.

"There's a guide to the institute with your registration materials. You are registered, I take it?"

In fact she didn't *take it* at all. She knew he wasn't, or she would be opening the door. Thomas opted for honesty.

"I'm not, actually," he said. "But there was to be a session on early comedy that I really wanted to attend. Randall Dagenhart is speaking . . ."

"I'm sorry," she said, crisp and patently not sorry, her back straightening. "The institute isn't open to the public."

"Yes, I realize that," he said, forcing himself to be patient. "I was wondering if I could register for that one session. A kind of day pass, as it were."

"I'm sorry," she said, "that's out of the question. The sessions are all fully booked."

"I can pay," he said.

"No doubt," she said, as if his offer had only proved his crassness, "but that really isn't the issue."

"Yes," he said, his smile hardening. "I can see how admitting one extra person might shake academia to its core. We wouldn't want to share the mysteries of literary scholarship with the great unwashed . . ."

"Good day," she said, stone-faced.

"Thank you so much," he said. "It's good to know knowledge is so well guarded."

"There's plenty of knowledge to be had elsewhere," she said. "And you can always go and look at the ducks."

Which should suit your brand of tourism, she added only with her eyes.

"Is there a problem, Thomas?"

He turned into the arch smile of Julia McBride.

"You know this gentleman?" said the battle-ax, with barely concealed astonishment.

"Tom Knight and I go way back," she said. "Mind if he sits in with me? He's been looking forward to this session."

"Not at all," said the woman, her eyes hard. "It would be a shame not to share the mysteries of literary scholarship with . . . all who show an interest."

She gave Thomas an icy stare and stalked away.

McBride giggled.

"That's Mrs. Covington," she said. "She's a kind of house-keeper and local historian. But she's also a self-appointed gatekeeper. She's very deferential to Shakespeareans, but a bit fierce with the general public."

"I spotted that," said Thomas.

He was irritated, by the old woman and the fact that Julia had had to rescue him.

"Thanks," he remembered to say. "I did want to hear this talk."

"What happened to you?" she said, noting his sling.

"Fell," he said. "No big deal."

"Come with me," she whispered, rolling her eyes. "If they try to throw you out, I'll hide you under my chair."

She took his left hand and led him, almost running, to the lecture. Her skin was soft and warm.

The room had been cozy once and still retained something of its former domesticity, but it still felt more like a Great Hall than a sitting room. There was a broad fireplace with a carved mantle painted white, and beside it a simple podium. The audience—Thomas counted twenty-three—were arranged on closely packed chairs. There were no vacant seats together and, with a moue of disappointment, McBride peeled off to the right while Thomas sat to the left, as close to the French windows at the back as he could get.

He sat between people he didn't know, torn between regret and relief at having been separated from Julia McBride. Both feelings made him want to call Kumi, who did not know he was in England, did not know he had been shot. He had become used to being alone in the years since she had left him, but since their reconciliation—or partial reconciliation, he wasn't yet sure what it was—they had talked at least once a week, usually more. He felt a crease of guilt for getting so preoccupied, and then wondered if she had missed his call or tried to reach him herself. If she was busy at work, she might not have noticed the silence. The thought bothered him, so he refocused his mind on what the lecture might be.

Cultural politics, probably. The nondiscovery—announced

with gleeful righteousness—that we are more insightful on
matters of gender, race, and class than Shakespeare was . . .
There was an annoying whisper of truth to it, which made
Thomas weary, confused, and disappointed. It sapped all the
color out of literature, all the life and excitement and nuance.
At least in the high school classroom the idea that literature
communicated with the present, that it enriched the reader,
was not obviously laughable.

The thought annoyed him as it had at the Drake conference, but before he could iron away the scowl on his face, the
lecture began.

The speaker was introduced as Alonso Petersohn, associ-
ate professor of literature at Stanford, and his talk was titled
"The virtue of your eye must break my oath: gendered
ethos/ethic and the post-Lacanian subject in *Love's Labour's
Lost*." Petersohn was young and confident, a smallish man
who dressed like a Hollywood studio executive—or at least,
as Thomas imagined they dressed—in an open-necked silk
shirt and some form of upmarket chinos with pleated fronts.
He wore brown leather sandal-like shoes, all straps and thongs
without socks, and a single earring with a bright blue stone.
He spoke fluently in a well-modulated, expertly paced tone
and was completely incomprehensible.

"The libidinal dynamism inherent in the Lacanian mirror
stage," Petersohn said, "is both a problematic as well as an
ontological structure of the human world . . ."

Thomas considered the rest of the room with an inward
sigh. He saw a few familiar faces, but other than McBride and
Dagenhart—still in tweed and armed with his laptop—none
he could put names to. Some—the very young—were obviously graduate students; a few—the very old—might have
been local residents, ex–high school teachers, perhaps. As the
talk continued, accumulating impenetrability, the young nodded seriously and made notes while the old looked blank or
worried. Thomas was merely irritated. After a couple of minutes he had begun to shift in his seat indiscreetly. After
twenty, he put his head in his hands.

Alonso Petersohn's argument wound its tortured way to

the three-quarter-hour mark and stopped with an uneven patter of applause. Thomas was far from clear what had been said, though he had to concede that Petersohn's rhetorical high-wire act had positively stunk of cleverness even though he had grasped little of it. Some of the old dears were clearly befuddled, but it was hard to get a sense of what people had thought, and Thomas had a glimpse of that Emperor's New Clothes dynamic again, in which to point and scream with laughter would only demonstrate his status as impostor. That he could neither talk the talk or walk the walk.

Thomas scowled at himself. He remembered the Drake conference all too well. However much he'd like to think of his flight from graduate school and the ivory towers beyond as a principled reconnection with all he thought valuable about books and teaching, he knew that the real reason had at least as much to do with the fear that he couldn't cut it as a scholar. Of course, any such sense of failure would vanish were he to emerge from this trip brandishing a long-lost Shakespeare play . . .

People were asking questions now, and Petersohn, smiling and nodding sagely, was fielding them as best he could. An older professor in horn-rims at the front had some grumpy quibbles, but all the rest who spoke up seemed to think that what Petersohn had said was insightful and dynamic, something they wanted to be seen to support. What it was they were supporting, Thomas had no idea. It came as something of a surprise even to himself, therefore, when he realized he had raised his left hand and that heads were turning toward him expectantly.

"Yes," he said. "This is all fascinating. I was just wondering what difference it would make to your argument if the play's sequel were available for study."

"The play's sequel?" said Petersohn, benign but bewildered.

"*Love's Labour's Won,*" said Thomas.

CHAPTER 29

Suddenly everyone in the room was smiling and shifting, some embarrassed, some enjoying what they took to be a joke.

"Is that likely?" said Petersohn, still smiling. "That *Love's Labour's Won* is going to be available for study?"

The audience relaxed, liking him more for his kindly treatment of the crank with his arm in a sling.

"Any day now," said Thomas, with complete composure.

"Well," said Petersohn, opting to spare Thomas the easy cruelty of ridicule, "won't that be exciting?"

And then another hand was raised urgently in the front row: Chad—Julia's eager and dour grad student—anxious to get back to serious matters. By the time Petersohn had fielded that one, it was time to break for tea.

"Like to make an entrance, don't you?" said Julia McBride, appearing beside him and whispering with delight. "Did you see their faces? Like polite people farting in an elevator. Wonderful!"

Everyone else was filing out, avoiding his eyes. Only one paused to join them. He recognized her regal bearing before he saw her face.

"For a high school teacher, you do like your Shakespeare conferences," said Katrina Barker, smiling.

"Just here to make trouble," he said, feeling suddenly stupid again.

"I think academic gatherings need all the trouble they can get," she said. And with another expansive smile she sailed off, parting the crowds before her.

"How on earth do you know Katy Barker?" said Julia. "She's colossal."

"Oh, we go way back," said Thomas. "I have a long history of making dumb remarks in her presence."

"Well, if it helps, she's a *nice person* as well as a genius," said Julia, "which really isn't fair."

"I thought genius meant you didn't have to be nice."

"She's the exception that proves the rule, I guess."

"Talking of genius," said Thomas, as Alonso Petersohn walked past.

"You didn't like his talk?"

"Did it make any sense to you?"

"Of course," she said. "I have my disagreements, and he really needs to define his terms, but yes . . ."

"He barely mentioned the play," said Thomas.

"What do you mean?"

"The quote in his title was about the only time he referred to the text at all!"

"This is the twenty-first century, Mr. Knight," she said. "You can hardly expect him to start analyzing image clusters and figuring out the ways they could be ambiguous."

"But I want to learn about the play, about what it means— or might mean—what makes it profound as literature, not about how it's a matrix for social energies and discourses . . ."

"Oh!" she shouted, with the kind of delight someone might muster on spotting a chipmunk. "You're a humanist!"

Thomas grimaced.

"You are!" she said, clapping her hands together.

"I'm a high school teacher who has to convince kids why these four-hundred-year-old plays are worth reading when they can be playing video games . . ."

"And joining street gangs," she said, still grinning.

"Some of them do."

"Well, I think it's sweet," she said. "Unfashionable and politically a bit suspect, but kind of sweet."

"There's nothing suspect about my politics," Thomas muttered. "I just want a little more literature and a little less theory."

"Aren't you a little young for the fogey club?"

"I'm not a fogey," said Thomas, offended.

"So there are things you stand for as well as things you stand against? Such as?"

"I love words," said Thomas, jutting his chin out. "Expressive nuance. Precision. I like implications and—yes—image clusters, themes, and tropes."

"Really?"

"Really," he said, warming to his theme. "I like getting my students to read critically—and therefore think critically—by exploring complex and sophisticated literature. They live in a visual culture, but without words . . . Language is about who we are, how we reason, even how we feel. Words make experience."

"Thank you, Wittgenstein," she said.

"I happen to think that literature has something to teach us, something . . ."

"Universal?" she inserted, delighted.

"No," said Thomas, avoiding what would damn him as a conservative. "Something that helps us reflect on who we are, on . . ."

"The human condition!" she giggled. She was enjoying his failure to dodge the mines of critical discourse far too much.

"I just don't think the sole purpose of literature," said Thomas, pushing through her amusement, "is to expose social hierarchy."

"Neither does Petersohn," she replied.

"Who the hell knows what he thinks?" said Thomas. "I didn't understand a word of it."

"So you're mad," she said. "That's understandable. But this isn't a talk at the local library for whoever happens to walk in. This is a seminar for professional Shakespeareans to talk to other professional Shakespeareans about the things that interest them in the terms they understand."

"I'd just like to hear something about the *play*," Thomas huffed. "I thought that was why we were here."

"No, you didn't," she said. "This was exactly what you thought it would be and you came to complain as much as those kiddies in the front came to applaud. Which is fine. But let's be honest about it, shall we?"

Thomas frowned. The room was now empty except for them.

"Tea?" she said, taking his left arm and propelling him out.

"Okay," he said. "But don't expect me to enjoy it."

"Heaven forfend."

As they stepped out into the hallway where the attendees were still chatting in huddles, Thomas caught two sets of eyes fixed on him, both cautious and attentive: thoughtful eyes, wary eyes. One set belonged to Alonso Petersohn, who was staring past the admiring graduate students clustered around him, fixing Thomas with a stare that was quite unlike the genial charm he had displayed in the lecture room. The other set of eyes belonged to Randall Dagenhart, Thomas's former advisor, and though they shared Petersohn's unnerving focus there was something else to them, something very like rage.

CHAPTER 30

"What are you doing here, Knight?" snapped Dagenhart.

He had waited only for McBride to take a step away from Thomas's side before closing on him like a mastiff. His bloodhound face was flushed and his wet eyes were hard and bright.

"I'm a tourist," said Thomas. "Just here to take in the sights . . ."

"You're a liar," said Dagenhart, his voice close to a snarl. "First Chicago, now here. Why? What are you up to, and what was all that nonsense about"—he lowered his voice—"*Love's Labour's Won?*"

"Just a bit of fun," said Thomas. "Petersohn was annoying me so . . ."

"You're a damned liar," said Dagenhart again. "And an amateur. Stay out of things you don't understand, Knight. Go back to your *schoolroom.*"

He said it as one might say *gutter*, or *prison*.

"I'll stay till I'm ready to leave," said Thomas.

"You couldn't cut it as a student, Thomas, remember?" said Dagenhart, pressing in so that their noses almost touched. Despite his age, he was a big, imposing presence. "You can pretend you opted out as some kind of protest," he said, "but the truth is you just couldn't do it. Now you are trying to prove that you are somehow better than the rest of us, better than the profession that rejected you. You can't. You aren't."

Then he turned on his heel, his laptop bag swinging, and strode away, barging past an elderly woman who spilled her tea and peered after him with a wounded look. Thomas flushed with sudden anger and embarrassment, scanned the crowd quickly to see if anyone had seen, and as he did so, shrugged painfully out of the sling and looked for a trash can.

Over in the corner, still the center of attention, was Petersohn, whose eyes returned to the group as Thomas met them. And over by the door from the ladies' room, moving slowly in his direction and looking more thoughtful and less amused than usual, was Julia McBride. Thomas wasn't sure she'd seen, but she accelerated as she found his eyes on her, and her smile broadened.

"Having fun?" she said, pleased with herself.

"Not particularly."

"At an academic conference?" she said with mock amazement. "Let me introduce you to another of my graduate students."

She turned, beckoning, and a mousy-looking girl with wide, astonished brown eyes hustled over with quick, embarrassed steps.

"This is Angela Sorenson," said Julia. "One of the best and brightest."

"Hi," said Angela, waving self-parodically. "Do you really think *Love's Labour's Won* will be found?"

"It's at the Birthplace," said Thomas, rallying but still red-faced. He had to tear his eyes away from the door where Dagenhart had stormed out. "Slipped down the back of the couch. You'd think someone would clean that place out once a century, wouldn't you."

Angela looked unsure.

"Mr. Knight is teasing," said Julia, "which is very naughty of him."

The graduate student smiled and nodded to show she got the joke.

"Still," she said. "It would be exciting, wouldn't it? To find a lost Shakespeare play, I mean."

"Someone certainly thinks so," said Thomas, considering the sling he had bunched up in his left hand.

As the girl's face blanked again, Julia made a playful, dismissive noise and waved his comment away.

"What school are you at?" said Angela, filling the silence.

"Evanston Township," he said, defiantly misunderstanding.

"Oh," she said, uncertain. "I don't know that one."

He took a breath and relented.

"I'm afraid I never made it out of graduate school," said Thomas. "Made a tactical withdrawal ABD. I teach high school now."

"Right," said the student, relieved. "That must be so rewarding."

"Must it?" said Thomas. "Yes, I suppose it must. Sorry. Yes, it is. It dignifies being a failed academic."

"Oh, come now, Thomas," Julia inserted. "There are plenty of *failed* academics who are also quite *successful* academics, if you see what I mean. Depends what you mean by success. And I'm sure no one thinks that you couldn't hack it."

"Randall Dagenhart thinks exactly that," said Thomas. "He just said so."

"He's just a grumpy old man who knows the profession is starting to pass him by."

"Maybe, but he's probably right about me. I quit because I knew I couldn't do it."

"I don't believe that for a second . . . ," she began.

"That's because you don't know anything about me," Thomas returned, his irritation getting the better of him. "You've never seen my writing, heard me teach, and you sure as hell have no idea what I was going to write my doctoral dissertation on because I couldn't figure that out myself. You don't know me at all, Julia."

Angela flushed and looked away.

"Well now," said Julia, switching gears and smiling her feline smile, "*that* we can fix."

"I think I'm going to go," said Thomas.

She turned to look full at him then, and her face was unnervingly frank and appraising, as if she was deciding what to do or say next. Angela was forgotten. It was Thomas's turn to look away.

"Okay," said Julia. "You have a local phone number?"

He faltered.

"I'm just . . . I'm going to go," he said again. "Thanks for getting me in. To the lecture, I mean."

"Anytime," she said. She smiled once, a tiny crinkling of one side of her mouth. "See you next time."

Thomas made for the front door. He was almost out when a voice behind him called.

"Thomas?"

He turned. There was a man hovering a few yards away. He was pale and earnest looking, perhaps a few years Thomas's junior. It took only a moment before full recognition dawned.

"Taylor?" said Thomas. "No way!"

"It's been a while," said Taylor.

"A decade?"

"Something like."

"What are you doing here?" said Thomas.

"Other than watching you throw grenades in conferences?"

"God, you were in there?" said Thomas. "Sorry. I just . . ."

"Wanted to screw with that smug son of a bitch," Taylor completed. "Good for you."

Taylor Bradley had been in graduate school at BU with Thomas. They had even shared a cramped office on Bay State Road for a semester or two, and had grown acquainted while complaining about the students in their freshman composition classes. Later they had both been in a Renaissance drama seminar together. Thomas hadn't thought of him in years.

"You still at BU?" he said.

"God, no," said Bradley. "I got a job."

"Doing what?"

For a moment Bradley looked confused.

"I finished," he said. The utterance seemed to embarrass him or, more likely, he feared it embarrassed Thomas. "I mean, I got my dissertation done and went on the job market. Took me a couple of shots but I got a position."

"Tenure track?"

"Yep," said Bradley, unable to keep the pride from his

voice. "I think they assumed I was related to A.C. Small college, heavy teaching load, but still . . ."

"That's fantastic," said Thomas, taking his hand and shaking it.

"Listen," he said, as if the idea had just struck him, "how long are you in town? I need to get back in there, but maybe we could get a drink or something?"

"Sure," said Thomas. "That would be great. Tonight?"

"I'm going to see a matinee of *King Lear* at the Courtyard, but we could get together after."

"Sounds good. Where?"

"The Dirty Duck," said Bradley. "Say, six?"

"So long as I have time to get the bus back to my B and B."

"You're staying in town?"

"In Kenilworth."

Bradley looked quizzical, but Thomas just shook his head and smiled: *Don't ask* . . .

"See you later," he said.

Thomas walked away wondering about them all, wondering most about Randall Dagenhart, who had been, he supposed, as much a mentor to him as Thomas had been to David Escolme, wondering also about the old professor's bitter outburst and what might have motivated it. As he passed a trash can in the hall, he tossed the balled-up sling away.

CHAPTER 31

"Hi, Kumi," said Thomas.

He had found a public phone booth and was using a phone card he'd bought at a newsstand in the high street. The time difference to Japan was actually more manageable from the U.K., and he figured that—given the absurd hours she put in—she would have just gotten home from work. He wanted to talk to her about his days in graduate school, about Dagenhart's accusation that he had never had what it took . . .

"Tom?" she said.

Then it started. She was angry and upset. Where the hell had he been? She had called his school when he hadn't phoned, and the principal had told her he'd been *shot*! She hadn't believed it at first. She just knew he would have called her. There must have been some mistake. But Peter had insisted, and then she had reached the hospital and they said Thomas *had* been shot but that he was okay now and had *discharged himself*. So she had called his house a thousand times, left a thousand messages, and nothing. Had she even crossed his mind or was he too busy solving mysteries . . . ?

"And now you call me like nothing has happened and tell me you're in England . . . !?"

"Sorry," he said. "I kind of lost track of time."

But that wasn't going to cut it. She said he was selfish. That she had thought they were past this, but that he clearly wasn't thinking about her or what she might be going through . . .

He couldn't think of anything to say, couldn't even really remember why he hadn't told her about the shooting.

The call lasted two minutes and thirty-seven seconds, and Thomas emerged into the too-bright afternoon light as if he had been holding his breath. Or his tongue. She had a right to be upset and indignant, but there was a fury in her voice he couldn't fathom, a hurt deeper than the things she had said.

. . . what she might be going through . . .

What did that mean? He wondered if there was something she hadn't said, something beyond her concern for him. After all, the hospital had told her he was okay. She was probably just feeling humiliated that he hadn't kept her informed, but still, it was not like her . . .

"I didn't want to worry you," he had said.

"Nice going, Tom," she said, with the kind of sarcasm her Japanese colleagues found baffling. "Another study in your communicative genius."

And she had hung up on him.

He couldn't really blame her. It might have been better if he'd anticipated her knowing about the shooting, but the truth was that he had had no intention of mentioning it when he called her, so he'd been doubly unprepared. By the end, he had suspected she was biting back tears. The idea bothered him. Kumi did not cry easily.

He wandered down to the canal and watched the narrow boats going through the lock, wondering whether to call her back, but decided to leave it for another day. Right now she wouldn't answer, or would eat up his phone card with long angry silences.

Let her be mad, he thought. *She has a right to be. Call tomorrow and talk properly.*

He wasn't sure about the strategy, but once the decision was made, he didn't reevaluate it. Even so, her anger bothered him.

Maybe there's something else. Something she didn't say.

"I'll call her tomorrow," he said aloud.

He fished in his wallet for Polinski's card and called the Evanston Police Department. It took a moment for the lieutenant to get on the line, and she was cool with him.

"How long do you plan to be out of the country?" she said.

"I'm not sure. I'm still not a suspect, right?"

She seemed to consider that for a second, before saying

that he wasn't, that they didn't have a suspect yet, and—in answer to his question—that the half brick that had killed Daniella Blackstone had revealed nothing conclusive.

"What about you?" she said. "You doing okay, not getting shot?"

"I'm fine," he said. "Not making much headway."

"On what?" she said, suspicious again.

"Oh, you know," said Thomas, backpedaling. "Research. Work stuff."

"Don't interfere in police matters, Mr. Knight."

"Right," he said.

"But if you find anything useful . . . ," she added.

"I'll let you know," he said.

Since he had learned nothing so far, it was an easy—if dispiriting—promise to make.

CHAPTER 32

Thomas spent the afternoon seeing the sights, or some of them. The town was thick with tourists, and though it was quaint, something about its carefully preserved medieval and Renaissance buildings felt almost implausibly picturesque, so that he thought he'd wandered into some kind of theme park. Shakespeare's birthplace was a picture-postcard timbered house with an exquisite garden almost too perfectly right for the man who penned *A Midsummer Night's Dream*, *Much Ado About Nothing*, and *As You Like It*. Inside was a useful exhibition, and helpful people in every room were keen to inform about the market town Stratford had been, the living conditions in the house itself, its structural alterations over time, and—of course—the kind of environment that had shaped its most famous resident. No one wore faux-Elizabethan costume, quoted Shakespeare, or—thank God—affected to actually be four-hundred-year-old residents of the town, quipping about modern technology and scattering *forsooth*s at the end of every other sentence. In other words, it was not nearly as bad as he had feared, so Thomas was at a loss to see why he felt so unmoved by the place. Perhaps it was the throng of tourists, many of whom would know less about Shakespeare than they did neuroscience. Perhaps it was that air of Colonial Williamsburg—everything a bit too cute and studied—history made shiny, like something you might find in a snow globe. Or perhaps it was that he preferred his history and culture like he preferred his religion: private, and reflective, the still, silent air echoing with uncertainties. More likely it was a residual grumpiness for which he was blaming the town when it was really more to do with his failed call to Kumi.

Down by the Memorial Theatre—currently half demol-
ished and framed with scaffolding and plastic sheets that
flapped in the breeze—he ate fish and chips with a dollop of
luminous green stuff they said were "mushy peas." He tasted
it cautiously and liked it. He was eating his well-vinegared
chips and looking across the Stratford to Birmingham Canal
when he became aware of a huddle of tourists to his left,
gathered around a smiling elderly man in a worn gray suit
that looked like it was made of felt. He was small and balding, but he had a big voice and Thomas could hear isolated
phrases: "Love me? Why, it must be requited. I hear how I
am censured. They say I will bear myself proudly: happy are
they that can hear their detractions and can put them to
mending . . ."

One of the tourists shouted "Romeo!" but the old man
continued as if he had not heard her. Another shouted "Petru-
chio," but with the same result.

"Benedick," Thomas whispered to himself.

". . . and wise but for loving me; by my troth, it is no addition to her wit, nor no great argument of her folly . . ."

"What's his name from *Much Ado*?" said a large woman
in a flowered dress. "Benedick!"

The old man bowed low, and there was a little scattered
cheering, but by the time he had straightened up, he had
started again.

"Look what is done cannot be now amended," he said.
"Men shall deal unadvisedly sometimes, which after hours
gives leisure to repent . . ."

Some of the crowd stayed, but many had had enough of
the game and drifted away. Others replaced them, and
Thomas stood and started walking over as someone called
"Lady Macbeth." Again the old man continued as if he had
not heard her.

"If I have killed the issue of your womb," the old man was
intoning, "to quicken your increase I will beget mine issue of
your blood upon your daughter."

"Richard the Third," said Thomas.

Some in the crowd turned toward him, and the old man's

eyes briefly met his, but then he was bowing, and straightening, and starting again.

"What's he that wishes so?" he demanded. "My cousin Westmoreland? No, my fair cousin. If we are marked to die, we are enough to do our country loss, and if to live . . ."

"Henry the Fifth," said Thomas.

Again the old man bowed, and again he came up talking.

"Anon he finds him striking too short at Greeks . . ."

Thomas nodded and smiled, and turned away. Some of the tourists watched him, impressed, and Thomas felt absurdly pleased with himself.

See, said a voice in his head. *Dagenhart was right. You're trying to prove that leaving grad school was a choice, not a failure, that you're better than all of them.*

That's not true.

That's why you want to be the one producing Love's Labour's Won *out of your hat like some Vegas magician. So they'll applaud and say you are The Best Among Them . . .*

Not true. Surely not.

He kept walking. Behind him he could still hear the constant stream of the old man's quotations as he walked across the green. For some reason, the sound bothered him.

The church where Shakespeare was buried was more to his taste, if only because the aura of sanctity about the place shut everyone up. He did what he always liked to do in such places, sitting alone and absorbing the weight of age and seriousness from the carved tombs and airy vaulted chancel. Outside he wandered among the graves through heavy, ancient trees, feeling like a mote on the breezes of time and mortality.

Julia was right, he thought. *You are an old humanist.*

Maybe so. There were worse things to be. And as if to celebrate the point he wandered down to the river and sat under the lengthening shadows of an old willow to watch the water, thinking vaguely of lines written by a man who could have been recalling this very spot when he wrote them.

> *I know a bank where the wild thyme blows*
> *Where oxlips and the nodding violet grows*

Quite overcanopied with luscious woodbine
With sweet muskroses and with eglantine . . .

And so thinking he lay and napped in the sun for an hour, as the swans and ducks dabbled at the shore as they had done for centuries unnumbered.

CHAPTER 33

The Dirty Duck was a Stratford institution. Its official name was The Black Swan—or at least that was the name of its restaurant—and it had been an actor hangout since the days of David Garrick, if his guidebook was to be believed. Thomas was skeptical. Surely, Stratford hadn't been a theater town in the days of Garrick? Still, the place looked old enough. It overlooked Waterside and the Avon beyond, a brick-and-timbered building like a hundred others he had seen in rural England already, but lit by a Bohemian aura of expectation. Maybe he'd bump into Ian McKellen or Judi Dench having what they might call "a swift half" after the show, or sit where Richard Harris, Peter O'Toole, and Richard Burton had drunk each other under the table . . .

Thomas arrived early and ordered a pint of Old Speckled Hen. He paid with a ten-pound note and received a handful of heavy pound coins as change. His pockets were already full of them as if he was collecting them. He had been spending nothing but notes because they were easier to read, because fumbling with unfamiliar coins made him feel like a tourist, and because everything was so damned expensive that trying to use single pounds seemed pointless.

The place was quiet—a couple of big guys on the patio, and a near-silent family of four in one corner—though the barman assured him it would fill up as soon as the matinee got out.

"You must have seen some famous faces over the years in here," said Thomas. "You could probably write a book."

"I probably could," said the barman in a tone that said he never would. He was drying a glass with a white towel, but his eyes were on Thomas.

"American?"

"That's right."

The barman nodded as if that couldn't be helped.

"Shakespeare professor?"

"No," said Thomas.

"Not just a tourist, though, right? Not here by yourself at this time."

"Meeting a friend," said Thomas. He added on a whim, "Actually I'm from Chicago, looking into the death of Daniella Blackstone, the novelist."

The barman stopped polishing the glass and his eyes grew wide and interested.

"That right?" he said.

"I suppose this was a bit far from Kenilworth to be her local," said Thomas.

"She did come in, once or twice," said the barman, pleased not to be talking about actors, "but I don't think she was a *local* type. Wasn't around much anyway. Book tours and celebrity appearances all around the world."

He said it with a roll of his eyes, his voice gruff and a little sour. Thomas just nodded.

"Still," he said. "I expect she had her reasons."

"For what?"

"The fame, the glamour. Filling a void, as it were."

He used the phrase as if he'd heard it on the radio, or read it somewhere.

"Alice, you mean," said Thomas. "Her daughter."

"Maybe," said the barman, nodding significantly as if unwilling to be drawn. "I mean, tragedy makes people do strange things."

"What exactly happened?" said Thomas, emphasizing the word *exactly* as if he knew all but the details.

The barman leaned in.

"She was sixteen," he said. "Imagine that. Fancy losing your daughter at that age. Tragic," he said. "Bloody tragic."

"It was a road accident or something, right?" said Thomas.

"A fire," the barman corrected him. "At the secondary school. Five girls were in the school hall one evening after classes. All local girls—students at the school—apart from one. There was a fire and they couldn't get out. All killed. Worst incident of its kind since the war. I remember the television pictures. Well, after that . . . I mean, who knows what something like that does to a mother?"

"How did the fire start?"

"There'd been a what-d'ya-call-it . . . a *spate* of them. Empty buildings. Three or four over the previous few months. Vandals. Delinquents. Bored kids with nothing to do. Schools are always a target for yobs like that. 'Cept this time, there were kids inside. They weren't supposed to be there. No one knew. They only found out when they found the bodies. Like I said, tragic."

Thomas nodded and stared at his beer, unable to think of anything to say.

"Someone die?" said Taylor Bradley, brightly.

The barman shot him a cool look and Thomas rallied.

"Hey," he said. "How was the show?"

"I'm not sure," said Taylor. "Generally good, I think, but I need to let it sit. There were some really wonderful moments, and the Lear himself was terrific a lot of the time, but there were parts of the play the show wasn't that interested in."

The barman rolled his eyes again and moved off. Taylor didn't notice.

"I hated the Fool," he said, "though it's a tough role. Liked Cordelia: spunky, you know? More personality than you often see. At the beginning she was clearly in love with Burgundy, so marrying France was hard. Nice touch."

Thomas had forgotten that Taylor Bradley was a performance person. He remembered how he would trudge into that dusty, overheated university office on the ground floor of the BU English department, ranting or rhapsodizing about what he had seen at the American Repertory Theatre or the Huntington. When he talked about theater he came alive. His customary diffidence fell away and his eyes brightened. A good production filled him with excitement, a bad one with vitriol. Thomas prompted him now as he had done then, enjoying the way he relished those grace notes of a performance most audiences barely notice, and railed at the things he despised.

Thomas smiled and sipped his beer.

"Don't tell me you *liked* it?" said an amused voice behind them.

Julia McBride was easing through the suddenly crowded bar, looking sardonic.

"Didn't see it," said Thomas. "Taylor did. You know Taylor, right?"

"You're at the institute, yes?" she said. "Enthusiasm for productions like this could get you barred."

Taylor laughed.

"You didn't like it, I gather," said Thomas.

"It was ghastly," she said. "I wonder sometimes if these directors have read a single word of scholarship. How do you misread the power politics of a play like *Lear* that badly?"

"I was just saying," said Taylor, "that it seemed a more *domestic* version of the play."

"If cursing your daughters with sterility—a moment, incidentally, that they completely misplayed—is your idea of domesticity, remind me never to settle down with you. I'm Julia McBride, by the way. Is this seat taken?"

"I think you're being sought for," said Thomas.

Alonso Petersohn was pushing his way through the crowd, cradling what looked like a gin and tonic in one hand and a murky cocktail in the other.

"Over here, Al," she waved.

Petersohn nodded and pressed on, struggling to part the crowd with a constant muttering of "Excuse me, please." He wasn't making much headway. Suddenly the people parted and Thomas saw Angela and a scowling Chad, Julia's attendant graduate students. Chad pushed his way through, his pint held high, and Petersohn followed in his wake. Taylor met Thomas's gaze and pulled a face.

"It seems everyone is here," said Thomas.

"Doesn't it," said Julia. Her smile at him was a little rueful, or was intended to seem that way. Her eyes had the familiar amused sparkle, so that the look—like every other—seemed ironic, playful. Thomas wondered how she would respond if he made a pass at her overtly, then dismissed the thought.

Petersohn was shaking hands with Taylor.

"I think I saw you in Chicago," he was saying.

"You were at the Drake?" said Thomas to Taylor. "Why didn't you look me up?"

"Didn't know you were there," he shrugged. "And we have kind of grown apart."

"True," said Thomas, raising his glass. "Here's to catching up."

They clinked pints and drank.

Chad was watching, a slight sneer on his face. Julia was watching too, amused, but just as interested. Thomas caught her eye, smiled, and then realized he was fiddling with his wedding ring. He looked at it and stilled his fingers. When he looked up, Julia had turned her attention to Petersohn, who was leaning into Taylor, midstream:

". . . well, obviously if you think the purpose of the plays is to *communicate*," he said, as if no one could be that stupid, "or if you think the speaker is a *character* rather than a discursive nexus generated out of the energies of class and language . . ."

Thomas opened his mouth to say something, but chose to drink his beer instead. Taylor could not keep quiet.

"You think Cordelia is a *discursive nexus*?" he said with baffled disbelief. "What the hell is that? She's a daughter, a princess, a fiancée, a sister . . ."

Petersohn just laughed.

"That's just a romantic projection onto a textual intersection," he said.

"What are you talking about?" said Taylor, shrill. He turned to Thomas. "What is he talking about?"

Thomas just smiled and held up his hands. *Hey*, they said, *I'm not one of you.*

"I'm saying that to treat Cordelia as if she is a person is to misread the nature of the early modern dramatic text," said Petersohn.

"But she's right there on the stage," said Taylor, spiking the table with his index finger as if the whole show were playing out in miniature before them. "She's a thinking, feeling person . . ."

"But of course," supplied Julia, "on the early modern stage, she wouldn't have even been a woman. Just some boy in a dress . . ."

"So what?" Taylor protested. "That changes nothing . . ."

And so it went on. Thomas sat back and watched and listened as they railed at each other, feeling half envious and half relieved that he was not expected to contribute. The discussion left him behind quickly, and though he got the gist of some points, he was in the dark for a lot of it. He watched Chad, realizing how much anxiety there was under the surliness, realizing that for graduate students and junior faculty, these gatherings were little more than interviews with beer. They were unlikely to be the basis of your career, but they could certainly help or hinder. Being here in Stratford, finding himself surrounded by the same faces he had seen at the Drake in Chicago, reminded him of just how tightly focused the academic community was. Everyone knew everyone. If not enough people knew you, you were no one.

Probably why Taylor is going toe to toe with some of the biggest names in his field, even though he knows he's branding himself as a reactionary.

At least they'll remember him. Thomas wasn't sure the strategy would work. If they thought he was stuck in the nineteenth century, if they deemed him wedded to those outmoded ideas Julia lumped together as "humanism," then this kind of outburst could do him more harm than good, however engaging he was as he did it. Maybe he had had too much to drink.

"Thomas, what are you having?" said Taylor, on cue.

"Same again, please."

"Julia?" said Taylor.

"Oh no, I should be getting back."

"Nonsense," said Taylor with an expansive gesture. He was a little flushed from the beer and was determined to be the life of the party. "Come now, dearest chuck," he said, "another chocolate kiss?"

Thomas thought Julia hesitated a second, and there was something frosty in her gaze, as if she didn't like being pushed, or thought he was being too familiar.

"Come on, Julia," said Petersohn. "One more won't kill you."

"Very well," she said.

Taylor cheered, and Thomas thought her eyes lingered on him, thoughtful.

"Just one more," she said.

"Dost thou think because thou art virtuous," Taylor demanded half joking, "there shall be no more cakes and ale?"

She laughed at the quotation, but she looked away almost immediately, as if to catch her breath, or compose her thoughts, and Thomas felt sure something had passed between them that no one else understood. Only Chad seemed to notice, and he glowered from one to the other, till Angela put her tiny hand on his arm and pulled him back into the conversation.

Thomas thought the girl looked troubled, even afraid.

CHAPTER 34

It was dark by the time Thomas boarded the Warwick bus, but that was okay. All he had to do was wait for the last stop before changing for Kenilworth. He rode on the top deck, for the sake of novelty, but it was too dark to see anything, though going up the stairs as the bus leaned around corners was, he decided, adventure enough for one evening.

He wouldn't have noticed the two men if the Kenilworth bus had been on time. As it was, he had four minutes to kill waiting for the doors to open, and that gave him ample time to recognize the two heavyset men who had been sitting on the patio at the Dirty Duck. They had probably been on the lower deck of the Stratford bus, but Thomas only saw them now, and really only paid attention because one of them was smoking, contrary to the signs all over the bus station.

They had similar looks, though one was completely bald and wore an earring that sparkled. The other—the smoker—had a florid face and a flattened nose like a prizefighter. They were dressed well, in square-cut suits that made their shoulders wide enough to block doors, and wore trench coats over the top. They had the look of ex-sportsmen run very slightly to seed, but what really struck Thomas was that sense that they did not belong in those clothes and in this place, where the poor and drunk made their way home to bed. They didn't talk to each other, they never seemed to make eye contact with anyone, and their movements were small and easy. The bald guy had a rolled-up newspaper. The other had an umbrella.

Thomas didn't like it.

He had some small hope that when the bus doors opened

they would stay where they were, waiting for another, and for a moment he seemed to have gotten his wish. He had taken his seat at the back as the loud kids and a couple of old ladies had filed dutifully on, but there was no sign of the two men, till the engine started to turn over. Then they had gotten on, moving with animal nonchalance, paying, and sitting midway down the bus so that Thomas could see the backs of their heads. They never looked at him, never spoke, but Thomas's heart had begun to race.

He watched the lights of the town slipping away, becoming patchy as they hit the outskirts of Warwick and then merged into Kenilworth. The two men had still not said a word to each other, and Thomas felt a gathering weight in the pit of his stomach, though he tried to will it away. Surely he was overreacting. It was a coincidence, and not a particularly remarkable one, that the two men had been in Stratford's most celebrated pub and were now on their way home. He stared hard into the darkness outside as trees flashed green and close in the light from the bus windows. It was almost his stop.

He thought quickly. The bus stop was maybe a quarter-mile walk from the hotel, and he could remember little of the route: a house or two? A lot of trees, certainly, and a quiet road: at this time, close to deserted. He could make to get off, and if they rose too, could pretend to change his mind and stay on, though where he would go from there, he had no idea. He could speak to the driver, but what he would say that wouldn't sound pathetic—even crazy—he couldn't imagine.

An old woman with shopping bags up front reached up and pushed a button. A bell rang. Moments later, the bus began to slow and she began gathering her belongings together in a ponderous manner. Thomas glanced out the window, then leaped to his feet.

He was past the woman in three long strides, then off the bus as the two men—surprised—hurried after him, their way blocked for a moment by the woman's groceries.

Thomas didn't look back. He sensed the commotion, but

he peeled off across the road at a run, keeping out of the glow from the bus windows, hitting his stride as he turned into the wooded and gravelly road with the sign to the parking lot of Kenilworth Castle.

CHAPTER 35

He knew now he should have stayed on the bus, knew it the moment they had given chase. He should have simply faced them down or suggested that the driver radio for the police. At worst, he would have looked stupid.

Too late now.

He ran.

More accurately, he loped, his right arm clasped to his stomach as if he were still wearing the sling. It was too much to hope that they wouldn't realize which way he had come. They would be after him, maybe only a hundred yards behind. But Thomas was prepared to bet that his visit to the ruins earlier meant that he knew the layout of the castle better than his pursuers. He also knew that, apart from a strand of chain looping across the gateway, there would be nothing substantial that would stop him from getting in.

So he ran, pounding the gravel road even more awkwardly than usual, listening for sounds of pursuit but not pausing to look back, his pockets full of change jingling with each step. A moment later he was crossing the bridge and passing between the two ruined round towers that guarded the entrance proper.

Now what?

It was dark, the kind of darkness a city boy like Thomas was unused to. There was a soft glow in the sky to the north and east, where the town nestled, but the ruins themselves were mere silhouettes against it, and even as his eyes adjusted, the castle itself was a black labyrinth of stone. There was heavy cloud cover overhead and no moon. Thomas spun around to get his bearings and felt a wave of panic. The site with which he had gotten reasonably familiar had been a picturesque monument of rosy stone against a sharp blue sky: this tumbled-down maze of jagged black rock was a different place entirely. Then he heard voices and running footsteps.

They're coming.

He surged up the grassy rise toward the inner court, trying to remember what he had seen. The keep loomed to his right, blank and imposing. It was too dark to see, but he had an idea there was only one way in from this side, that he could get trapped if he went in there. But to turn left—toward Leicester's building—took him back toward his pursuers. If they had seen him enter the courtyard, he could run right into them as he doubled back . . .

The inner court was covered with close-cropped turf, and Thomas's shoes made no sound as he dashed across, hands in pockets to silence the coins. He ducked through a doorway and, for the first time since getting off the bus, stopped running. He flattened himself up against the stone door frame, stared back into the inner court, and sucked the air into his lungs. He couldn't keep this pace up. The pain in his shoulder was spreading into his chest. He needed a strategy. He had been thinking no more than five seconds when two things happened at once.

First, two figures appeared no more than a hundred yards away, shadows revealed only by their movement against the hard face of the keep. They entered at a run, but then stuttered to a halt, spitting words at each other that rebounded meaninglessly to where Thomas stood gripping the stone. One of them shrugged out of his coat and let it fall where he stood. They barked orders at each other, and then, as Thomas was starting to lose them in the gloom, they began to move again, surging apart with a professional urgency like hunting dogs corralling their prey. One went toward the keep and vanished, probably inside. The second came directly toward where Thomas was standing, loping across the grass, his posture low and spread, ready to fight. Something flashed in his right hand. A blade of some kind.

The second thing that happened was that with a sudden steady patter, it began to rain.

CHAPTER 36

Thomas thought fast. One of them was coming right at him, but they couldn't have seen him or they would both have come. If he could get past this one, he could get out while the other searched the keep. He looked east, the way he would go to get to the outer court and back the way he had come, and tried to remember where exactly he was. He was turned around, and he couldn't make sense of his memories. It was the dark and the panic of pursuit. It wouldn't let him recall anything useful.

Stop.

He closed his eyes, breathing as slowly as he could, and tried to picture the place as it had been in daylight.

Think.

Any moment they might see him.

Wait. One more second.

He opened his eyes and looked around him.

He was in the oriel, he thought, the entrance to the state apartments and great chambers. If he went east, he would reach Leicester's building, but that was part of the castle's latest construction and it was comparatively well preserved. Though the floors were gone and many of the walls were ragged around the tops, they were far too high to get over.

So, no way out in that direction.

He struggled to remember more, even picturing the guide-book floor plan, then he ducked back against the far wall and looked around. Behind him rose a thin tower, a shard of masonry that rose up like a chimney, and below it, more wall with fractured window traces high above the ground.

No way out there.

He could cut west through the apartments and great chamber toward the Saintlowe Tower. From there, he figured, he could move through John of Gaunt's great hall, then down to the perimeter wall, and out by the ruined Swan Tower. Then he could find the road back to Daniella Blackstone's manor house and safety. If he could lose them in the castle, they'd never track him beyond it.

If they were still running, he thought, *they'd be here by now. They're stalking you.*

He hugged a lump of broken wall and listened. The rain was falling hard now, bouncing off the weedy, fractured pavement, making the russet stone black and slick so that the castle seemed to fade into the night. What light there had been had dropped to almost nothing. He kept still, but he knew that he might neither see nor hear them till they were on top of him.

The rain surged harder still, drumming the ground. It cooled him, which was all to the good. His heart was thumping in his chest, the ache in his shoulder had become a constant throbbing, and his breathing was heavy. Maybe the downpour would make him harder to spot. He moved deeper into the shadows, his eyes on the tops of the walls ahead to keep himself oriented. He could see the jutting bay window of the great hall ahead and, to his left, the taller ruin of the Saintlowe Tower. A few more yards that way, he thought, and he'd be through to the great hall, then down to the wall and out toward the Blackstone house before his pursuer knew where he was.

He stood still another moment, straining to hear, peering back into the dark and irregular hollow of the chamber behind him.

Still nothing.

He took another step, still looking back the way he had come. Then another. He tried one more but bumped up against something solid and cold. He turned quickly and found a wall.

No, he thought. *There has to be a way through . . .*

Fear gripped him as he scanned the stone for a door or window through to the structures ahead, but there was none.

The great chamber might once have connected to the Saint-lowe Tower, but it did so on the second floor, which was now gone. At the ground-floor level, there was no passage.

Thomas turned, his back to the wall. Any moment now his pursuer, finding no way out through Leicester's building, would round the corner. He kicked off his left shoe, pulled off his sock, and reached into his pockets.

He was straightening up from his task when he found the man standing there. It was the bald one with the earring, and even in the darkness Thomas could see that his face was hard and impassive. The blade in his hand was short and curved so that it traced three quarters of a circle, ending in a cruel point: a lino cutter. He stood his ground, arms spread, and then he tilted his head very slightly, his eyes still on Thomas, and called over his shoulder,

"Here!"

Thomas took a breath.

"Look," he said, forcing his fury and terror down into his gut, "I don't know what you want . . ."

This was a lie. He knew what they wanted, and it didn't involve conversation. He had hoped that pretending to misrecognize the situation would make the bald man lower his guard, but it seemed to do the opposite. He tensed, the lino cutter rising a couple of inches, but he took no step and Thomas knew he was waiting for the other guy to join them.

"I have money," said Thomas, taking a step forward and turning his right shoulder toward the knife man as if reaching for a wallet, trying to sound weak and apologetic. The other responded as expected, sweeping the blade across Thomas's stomach.

Two inches closer and it would have opened him up. As it was, Thomas was ready for it. He pivoted to his right, catching his attacker's knife hand in his right and pushing it away from him. It took all the strength he had just to deflect the weapon, and his shoulder screamed its protest. In the same instant he brought his left hand with its sockful of heavy coins down hard on the bald head like a mace. The first swipe stunned him, but he didn't go down, so Thomas—

rage pulsing through him like adrenaline—hit him again, harder, catching him just above his right temple. There was a dull thump as the blow connected. The lino cutter fell from the man's hand as his legs buckled, and he fell like a tree.

The other would be coming, and who knew what he would be armed with. Thomas picked up the lino cutter, but he didn't like the brutal feel of it. He pushed it into his pocket and looked around. If he went back, the other guy would see him, maybe meet him. He turned back to the wall, slipped his bare left foot back into his shoe, and started looking for somewhere to climb.

There was a place in the corner. The chamber wall was no lower, but there was a heap of what looked like rubble but was actually the masonry remains of some great buttress. Thomas looked for handholds and began to climb.

The stone was slick with the rain, but it didn't crumble in his grasp, and he was able to kick his shoes into crevices just deep enough to bear his weight. He hauled himself up a foot at a time, doing all the work with his left side, till he reached the uneven lip and found himself looking into the shadowy shell of the great hall where Henry V had vowed to turn the dauphin's tennis balls to gunstones . . .

"For many a thousand widows shall this his mock mock out of their dear husbands, mock mothers from their sons, mock castles down . . ."

Back where he had come from he heard a shouted curse. Thomas's other pursuer had found his companion. For a second Thomas crouched motionless beside the fractured bay window of the hall, gazing back and down through the rain like some medieval gargoyle, glaring through the darkness.

He slung one leg over the wall and lowered himself down, hanging for a second and dropping the last two feet into a silent crouch. Then he moved quickly and lightly, straight through the hall cellars toward the inner court, slowing to a halt before making a break from the shadows. He could feel the lino cutter in his pocket and the weight of the coins dangling from his left hand. He was angry, outraged by the attack still, but he didn't want to fight if he could avoid it, and not only because he might lose.

The great hall was above him, open to the sky and the driving rain. The building had long windows down the sides so that the structure felt little more than a stone frame, narrow columns of rock and great revealing spaces. He felt vulnerable, but the thought of making a break for it, of dashing into the openness of the courtyard, was terrifying. Again he tried to remember what he had seen when he had visited in daylight.

There were towers and a complex of rooms to the left of the entrance to the hall cellars, but he knew he had exited the castle over there when he had been in daylight. Somewhere. There was a doorway, small, hard to see, that led down the embankment to the perimeter wall. He was sure of it. He leaned fractionally out, and there was his other pursuer, only yards away.

He was turning very slowly on the spot, his hands splayed. One of them grasped what looked like a nightstick or a piece of pipe. He seemed disoriented, but he was being calm, professional . . .

Thomas flattened himself inside the stone alcove at the entrance and waited to see which way he went. After a moment, he risked another look, shifting fractionally, his cheek mashed hard against the stone.

The man with the stick was nowhere to be seen.

Thomas leaned out farther and looked all around, including up. If he could climb, so could they. Then he looked left and saw the doorway into one of the towers. The Strong Tower. Suddenly, he was sure. Down there, he remembered was a long spiral to a storeroom that felt like a dungeon. But farther back, lost in the shadows of the chambers above it, was the almost invisible exit he had been looking for.

He gambled. The door into the tower was more obvious, and if his pursuer had gone in there he had a moment, but probably no more than that.

He ran, as lightly as his driving and uneven gait would let him, past the Strong Tower, under the second and third stories of the hall, and through the narrow door that led to the rolling mounds of the outer courtyard and the curtain wall. The rain was falling harder than ever, and he was moving on memory now, skirting north, past the window with the iron grill that looked out over the fields that had once been the mere. Then to the Swan Tower, and the tumble of stone he vaulted like a country stile, and he was out.

There was no sign of pursuit.

CHAPTER 37

Thomas sat on the edge of his bed and removed the dressing from his shoulder. It had started to bleed again. He swabbed at it with cotton doused with an antiseptic called Dettol that his wary landlady had given him, and then retaped it as best he could. He took double his usual pain medication, then lay on his back, trying not to move. It took him twenty minutes to fall asleep, twenty minutes of staring blankly at the dark ceiling, mapping the contours of its plaster in his mind, and he was still in the same position when he woke the following day, having slept through breakfast.

The landlady scowled, but cooked him a fat sausage, fried egg, mushrooms, and—for reasons he couldn't quite grasp—baked beans, telling him he needed to build up his strength. He hadn't told her what had caused the wound in his shoulder or what had happened to him the night before, so he figured he just looked like hell. Her scowl deepened when he asked her for directions to the local police station.

Thomas fished in his pocket and drew out a clear plastic bag containing the lino cutter with its almost circular hook of a blade.

"Nasty little weapon," said the policeman.

"I thought you could check it for prints," said Thomas.

"An excellent idea, sir, thank you."

The policeman was so deadpan that Thomas wasn't absolutely sure if he was being sarcastic. The whole exchange had been like this since he had showed up at the station. Everyone was businesslike and formal, but there was an edge of humor to everything they said, a slightly ironic dryness that Thomas found disorienting. While he had been waiting to give the details of his attack, he had heard the beginning of an exchange between a cop and some guy who had come in to pay a traffic ticket. The police officer had checked the details and remarked,

"Good morning, wing commander. Couldn't quite reach takeoff speed, could we?"

The other guy had shrugged and smiled in a sheepish fashion before drifting after him to pay his fine.

The policeman assigned to Thomas's case—a Constable Robson—had responded with similar witty detachment.

"And you led these men into the castle because you figured you could dump boiling oil on them or shut the portcullis on their horses, did you, sir?"

"Well, no," said Thomas, bewildered and responding as if that had been a real question, "it was just close by and I had been there recently, so I figured I might know it better than the guys who were after me."

"It was close by," the constable repeated. "Handy, even."

"Right."

"Well, that's good, isn't it?" the policeman said, smiling amiably. "I mean, it's not often that you can hide from muggers in a castle, is it? I'll bet they built it with you in mind."

"Are you saying you don't believe me?" said Thomas, genuinely unsure.

"Certainly not, sir," said the constable, still cheery. "I'm just remarking on the handiness of the castle's locale in relation to that of your pursuit and subsequent assault."

"I could give you a description of the two men," said Thomas.

"Absolutely," shrugged the genial cop, "why not? They weren't wearing armor or carrying some sort of battering ram, were they? Only that might make them easier to spot in the high street."

"I'm afraid not," said Thomas, trying to decide if he was irritated or amused.

"Well that's a pity. We get so few bands of medieval marauders these days up for a weekend's pillaging, that they would have stood right out. As it is . . ."

"There's probably not much you can do," said Thomas.

"It's a question of man-hours," said Constable Robson. "You weren't robbed. You weren't injured. You may have been scared, but that's a tough thing to devote resources to. I mean, I'm scared of Angelina Jolie. And Cliff Richard, actually. Gives me the willies. Never been able to explain it. Anyway, you see my problem."

"Yes," said Thomas, smiling now.

"But I thank you for the lino cutter. I was planning to remodel my kitchen and this will come in right handy. Only kidding, sir. We'll get this checked out, and give you a bell if anything comes up."

"Sightings of marauders, for instance," said Thomas.

"Vikings, perhaps," the cop agreed. "We haven't seen any round here for centuries, so they're due for a rampage."

CHAPTER 38

Back on the high street, Thomas asked a suited man where he could find a liquor store and got a blank stare.

"A place to buy wine," he tried.

"A pub or a bar?"

"To take home."

"Oh," said the man, light dawning, "you mean an off license."

"Okay," Thomas shrugged.

"There's a Threshers on the Warwick Road," said the man, pointing. "Nice not to have to work, eh? Have one for me."

Thomas wasn't sure if this was friendly banter or mockery for being jobless, so he just smiled, thanked him, and followed his pointing finger.

After last night, he was ready for a drink, but had no intention of buying except, he told himself, for research purposes. He located the so-called off license and paced the aisles of wine racks till he located the champagne selection. It was, unlike the standard American supermarket selection, all French except for a bottle or two of Italian spumantes and an English brand called Nyetimber Classic Cuvée. There was Moët Hennessy, Taittinger, and Louis Roederer. No Saint Evremond.

"Help you find something, sir?"

The man was portly and wearing a green apron. He had a clipboard in one hand and carried his head to one side like a solicitous chicken.

"A friend of mine recommended a champagne house to me, but I can't find it anywhere," Thomas lied. "Saint Evremond."

"No, I'm afraid we don't stock that, sir," said the proprietor. "Saint Evremond, you said? I'm not familiar with the name. Hang on a sec and I'll look it up."

He waddled away and returned with a hefty and well-thumbed tome with a torn dust jacket sporting the title *A Companion to Wine*. He flipped it open and started riffling through, running one fat index finger down the entries repeating the name under his breath.

"Here we go, sir," he announced. "Saint Evremond Brut. Oh, it's a Taittinger brand. 'A blend of several crus from vineyards in the Champagne region around Reims and Epernay. It is made up of thirty percent Chardonnay and sixty percent Pinot Noir and Pinot Meunier as well as a selection of reserve wines as prescribed by the seventeenth-century French exile Charles de Saint Denis, Lord of Saint Evremond.' "

Thomas nodded, none the wiser, thanked him, and was considering buying something to show his gratitude when something chimed in his memory.

"Can I see that again?" he said.

He leaned in and stared at the entry till he found the name. A moment later he was in the street, scanning the sidewalk for a pay phone and fumbling in his pocket for his wallet.

It took him five minutes to find a public phone, and another six to get through to Westminster Abbey.

"I'm sorry," he said, "I'm trying to reach a particular verger. I don't know his name but he was on duty two days ago. Small man, longish jet-black hair and wire-rimmed glasses . . ."

"That's Mr. Hazlehurst," said a woman with a cut-glass accent. "You wish to speak to him?"

"If that is possible."

"I'm sure it's *possible*," she said, as if he had asked if Mr. Hazlehurst swam the backstroke, "though it may take a few moments to locate him. Can I tell him what it is you wish to discuss?"

Thomas told her that they had chatted in Poets' Corner and he wanted to check on one of the monuments, or rather on the person commemorated by the monument . . .

"Hold the line, please," she said, crisp as a January breeze.

The phone went silent for seven minutes. Thomas watched the display, anxious that his card was about expire.

"Hello? This is Ron Hazlehurst."

The voice sounded uncertain.

"I'm sorry to bother you," said Thomas, talking fast. "We met at the abbey two days ago in Poets' Corner. We talked about *The Da Vinci Code*."

"Did we?"

"And . . . I don't know, Britishness and tourists and . . ."

"You were the lost gentleman who wasn't sure what he was looking for," said the verger, pleased with the memory.

"That's right."

"And did you find it?"

"I'm not sure," said Thomas. "Perhaps."

"But you need some help."

"Just a little. Would you mind?"

"So long as it doesn't involve the Knights Templar, I'm at your disposal," said the verger.

Thomas could almost hear his mischievous grin.

CHAPTER 39

Thomas took the bus into Stratford and walked down to the river past the Gower Memorial, where a bronze Shakespeare stood surrounded by statues of his creations: Falstaff, Lady Macbeth, Prince Hal, and Hamlet. There was a scattering of tourists taking pictures, and behind them, wearing the same suit he had been wearing last time, the old man who rattled off lengthy quotes from the Bard. Thomas caught his eye and nodded, but the man was in midstream—Puck, it sounded like—and did not respond. Thomas didn't mind. There was something about the game that depressed him a little even as it pleased him to identify the speeches. Maybe it was the man himself. There was something about him, or rather something *absent* from him.

Thomas shrugged the feeling off and returned to the riverbank and the quiet spot under the willow where he had dozed before. He got comfortable and then reread *Love's Labour's Lost*. He had not looked at it since graduate school and then somewhat cursorily, and his memory of even the story was sketchy. He read the whole play in an unbroken two-hour sitting.

The main plot was simple enough; the King of Navarre forms a kind of academy with his friends Longueville, Dumaine, and Berowne, their purpose to study and reflect for three years, mortifying their flesh by avoiding banquets, drinking, the company of women, and anything that might distract them from their philosophical labors. The pact lasts until the ambassadorial visit of the Princess of France and her ladies, Rosaline, Maria, and Katherine. The men fall for the women, abandon their academy, and pursue them with various romantic inventions, pageantry, and verbal pyrotechnics. All seems to be going well, moving toward something like the multiple weddings that occur at the end of *A Midsummer Night's Dream,* until something remarkable happens. At the very end of the play, a messenger arrives announcing the death of the French king, the princess's father, whereupon the ladies prepare to leave. The men try to get words of love from their respective women—presumably, promises of marriage—but the mood has shifted drastically. All the witticisms and conventions of romance that the men have used to date are now dismissed as courtly games by the women, who will promise to be theirs only if the men can endure a year of isolation and hardship. But then the play ends.

There was more to it, of course, much of it involving the Spanish braggart Don Armado and the pedant Holofernes, but the play was light on plot, and the delight for the original audience must have been primarily in the sentence-level banter, the verbal posturing, and those puns to which Samuel Johnson thought Shakespeare morbidly addicted. It was an early play, according to the introduction in his edition, though scholars seemed to disagree as to how early it came in Shakespeare's career: no later than 1595 or so, but possibly as early as the late 1580s, which would make it among the playwright's very first attempts. Even if pushed back to 1595 it would still be earlier than any of Shakespeare's comedies except for *The Comedy of Errors, Two Gentlemen of Verona, The Taming of the Shrew*, and, at a push, *A Midsummer Night's Dream*. Whether or not it could be considered evidence for dating the text, Thomas thought the play's language and characterization was different from any of these, particularly *Errors*, which was all plot, and *Dream*, which seemed an altogether richer and more imaginative piece. *Love's Labour's Lost*, with its expressly courtly setting and themes, felt like a clever variation on a familiar theme—courtly love—though that cleverness went beyond the repartee and extended images and finally raised serious questions about the validity of the whole enterprise.

The ending was, after all, truly amazing in its unexpected darkening and lack of closure. Thomas couldn't think of another romantic comedy from any period in which the central couple or couples so pointedly failed to get together. The princess's remark that they had received the gentlemen's wooing merely "like a merriment," something that had passed the time but was of no real value and had nothing to do with actual love, was extraordinary. It was as if, on the death of her father, she and her ladies moved into another genre entirely and the men just didn't know how to adjust. It wasn't as if the goalposts had been moved so much as that the light had shifted and it became clear that there never had been any goalposts at all. The king and his friends were utterly thwarted in that which, in romantic comedy, is usually given so easily at the end: the promise of a relationship the audience would never see.

"Now, at the latest minute of the hour," says the King of Navarre, still not hearing how his suit has been weighed, and with the French court packing to leave all around him, "grant us your loves."

The princess answers,

> *A time, methinks, too short*
> *To make a world-without-end bargain in.*

And that was it. The end.

Except, of course, that it might not be. Thomas found it impossible to read the ending without imagining what might happen in *Love's Labour's Won*, the romantic conclusion it must surely bring that the earlier play resisted. Never, since the idea had first been mentioned to him, had he been more sure that there had indeed once been such a sequel, and believing that, he thought, was more than half the way to believing that it still existed.

But even as he felt the excitement of the thought, he wondered if the play was not better with the darker inconclusion of *Love's Labour's Lost*, less romantically conventional though it was.

Less conventional, more like life, he thought, thinking briefly of his most recent squabble with Kumi. *Which is less a squabble and more a stage in a longer tactical engagement the end of which might yet be closer to* Love's Labour's Lost *than any more hopeful sequel . . .*

Thomas looked up and saw, on the other side of the river, a couple in earnest conversation. He probably wouldn't have given them another thought, but the woman, who looked at least sixty, suddenly shouted "No!" with surprising ferocity. She had long, unkempt black hair slashed with gray and her eyes, though dark, were wide and staring. As he watched her, she started to rant, gesticulating and pointing at the man, who had his back to Thomas and the river, though it was impossible to hear what she was saying. The excess of her fury was alarming. Some of it was measured and even rhythmical so that Thomas would have thought they were doing a scene from a play if the woman had not seemed so out of control. She waved her hands and pointed at the man—a long stab with her bony finger—and Thomas thought she was calling him names, long hyphenated insults.

"Bunch-backed toad . . . !" he thought she yelled.

Or perhaps he imagined that, because the line seemed right, old Margaret screaming her venom at Richard III.

The man seemed to take it without response, or with muttered words that didn't carry across the Avon. His hands flitted a little, as if in calming gestures, but they were small, dwarfed by the woman's rage.

Then, quite suddenly, it was over. The woman marched away and the man, hunched-shouldered and wilted, turned quickly toward the water before walking slowly back toward the scaffolding surrounding the Memorial Theatre.

Thomas blinked. It was his former professor, Randall Dagenhart.

CHAPTER 40

Thomas called Kumi twice before she answered. He had been putting it off because he had begun to enjoy himself, playing sleuth and academic in this quirky and history-laden place, and a part of him didn't want her irritation with him to spoil that. He wanted to tell her all about what he was doing, share it with her, but he thought there would be some awkwardness first so he had delayed. Normally, when he sensed a problem he dealt with it as directly as possible, but with Kumi he knew she sometimes needed time. If he forced the issue, the reconciliation would take longer in coming.

Because she's almost as stubborn as you.

She sounded weary and distant, though the line itself was clear. He said he was sorry for not calling before and she said it was fine, that she was sorry she had been so upset. He should have been glad, but she sounded so tired, so lacking in emotion that even the apology didn't sit quite right. He asked about work and her classes and she answered briefly, that same blankness in her voice, so he told her what had happened since they last spoke, including the episode in the castle ruins. That, he hoped, would kindle a little sympathy.

"But you're okay?" she asked.

"Right as rain, as they say here. Do we say that too? I'm losing track."

"I think so," she said.

She sounded distracted still and her concern for his welfare, the root of her anger when last they spoke, was perfunctory at best.

"You okay?" said Thomas.

"Sure. Just tired."

"Should I leave you to it?"

"To what?"

"I don't know," said Thomas. "Work. Rest. Whatever."

"Maybe."

"Is there something on your mind?"

"Not really," she said. "I'm just . . . I don't know. Can we talk about it later?"

"You aren't in danger, are you?" he asked.

It sounded like a line from a bad movie, and as soon as he said it he wished he hadn't, though in the circumstances it wasn't an unreasonable question. She had been in danger because of him before. But he wasn't ready for her response, which was a whispering, breathless laugh like a series of sighs, which gradually turned into something else. He realized with a start that she was crying.

"I have cancer, Tom," she said. "Breast cancer. They found a lump a couple of weeks ago. I didn't think it was anything. A cyst maybe. I would have mentioned it last time but I was mad at you for not calling, and I really didn't think it was anything. But they biopsied it . . ."

"Wait," said Thomas. "What? Cancer? How can you have cancer? I don't understand."

And he didn't. There was nothing she could say that would change that, so he just listened.

Cancer?

She told him not to come, that it would do neither of them any good, that she trusted her doctors and felt she was in good hands. She would know more soon about what they planned to do and when. Thomas stood there, his teeth clamped together to lock the sound in, nodding like an idiot. Then she repeated it all again, and wept, and he listened, nodding, until his phone card ran out and the line went dead.

CHAPTER 41

Thomas drifted around Stratford as if wrapped in a fog. He had been like this since the phone call, since he'd heard that word, and he had spent the evening shut up in his room, pacing, or sitting in silence for hours at a time. He slept in the armchair, fading in and out, dreaming dreams he forgot immediately but that left the impression of panic and apprehension like footprints under his window. The only one he remembered was the last, Daniella Blackstone, her strange, mismatched eyes vacant and her head bloody, tapping against his Evanston kitchen window and mouthing Kumi's name. When he woke this morning it was waiting for him, like some taloned beast nestled in the corner.

Cancer.

So he walked, and when he had done that for a couple of hours he called Deborah Miller on her cell phone, staring blankly through the call box window while she picked up.

"No, tragically you didn't wake me," she said. "I had to come in to Valladolid to help with the lab. If you'd called later—you know, at a decent time when I could be expected to be out of bed—I'd be on site where you only get a signal if you climb above the jungle via a specially built four hundred foot tower. Made of wood."

Thomas, who had forgotten she would be in Mexico, interrupted, speaking gently but insistently. He told her simply. She was quiet for a while, and he thought she might be crying. When she spoke, it was to ask the question he had known she would get to eventually.

"Are you going to go to Japan?"

"She said not to," Thomas said. "I don't know. She seems

to want to just . . . you know . . . carry on, as if everything is the same. But maybe I should just go. Be with her."

"For her, or for you?"

"Both, I guess. Does it matter?"

"Maybe not," said Deborah. Thomas had never heard her so quiet. "Maybe she needs normalcy."

"And I'm not part of that," said Thomas.

"Thomas," she said, and now she was back to her usual assured self, "this isn't the time to feel sorry for yourself. Not while you are dealing with her, at least. You have to do and say the things she needs from you. If you think that what she really needs is for you to go to her, then hang up and go. If you want to go so that you can feel better, feel like you're doing something, forget it. A neighbor of my mother's had terminal cancer twice."

"Is that a joke?" said Thomas.

"Kind of," said Deborah, "but it's true. And she kept going because she didn't have time to stop. She refused to. I'm not giving you some new-age mind-over-matter crap, Thomas, but from what I've heard, attitude is important when you have cancer."

He nodded, wincing slightly at the word.

"You've not been part of her life for the last few years," she said. "Not the day-to-day, work, meals, sleep kind of life anyway. If you go out there now, it's not normal. It all becomes a big deal."

"A big deal . . . ?"

"I know it *is* a big deal, but she can't think of it like that. She needs to work right through it. Stay on task. Isn't that the Kumi you know?"

Thomas hesitated.

"You don't think I should go," he said.

"I think she's being honest when she says she doesn't want you to. Not now. Not yet. Don't take it personally. It's not about you."

* * *

Thomas took the bus into Stratford and joined the sprawl of Shakespeareans taking tea and smoking on the steps of the institute. Anything to focus his mind. He nodded to Taylor Bradley but made no move to speak to him, and as soon as the group began to return inside for the eleven o'clock session, he lowered his head and pushed through before anyone could close the door on him.

He sat at the back of the seminar room, which was full. He didn't care who was speaking, or about what. It was just something to do so that he could think. Or not think.

It was, it turned out, the Julia McBride show. There she was, sitting at a table, flanked by her graduate students, Angela on her right, Chad on her left. The moderator—a hawkish-looking Scottish woman with a defiantly thick accent, introduced them, and the graduate students tried not to look proud and terrified as their meager accomplishments were cited, while Julia, serene, sipped bottled water from a glass. The panel was titled "More Early Modern Bodies."

Thomas didn't really listen. From time to time a phrase caught his ear, a quotation usually, but though he understood the words, he didn't grasp what the papers meant. Chad's— which used the twin Dromios in *Comedy of Errors* to say something about how Renaissance (or, as he preferred to say, Early Modern) identity was shaped by clothing—was the least professional of the three, though it seemed workmanlike enough. But whereas his sounded like it was reinventing the wheel a bit and substituting fervor for deep knowledge, Angela's was clearly the coming-out party. She talked about clothing buttons: their manufacture in the period, the various styles, how they signified rank and allegiance, and the way they "served as gateways between the public and the private." A part of Thomas wanted to laugh, but the more she talked, the more compelling her case became, and when she segued into a discussion of key "button moments" in the plays, ending with Lear's dying "pray you, sir, undo this button. Thank you," he was convinced. It reminded him of what he had loved about scholarly research, when some unnoticed little detail became a fulcrum on which the entire work seemed to pivot, shifting it so that it seemed new and revelatory. For a moment, Angela's paper concentrated his mind on history and literature and the significance of the body, rather than its disease.

Julia McBride was obviously the headline act, but it was tough to follow Angela, and Julia seemed more nervous than he had ever seen her. The paper seemed solid enough and was warmly received, but she seemed out of sorts, and when Chad fielded a question about clothing and started talking about servants' attire in general, she cut him off irritably. When it was all over, she spent an age fiddling with her sheaf of notes, and Thomas was sure she was avoiding having to talk to anyone. That might have been as well, because it was Angela who had gathered the telltale huddle of admirers.

"Interesting panel," said a woman beside him.

Thomas found himself standing next to Katrina Barker.

Time to wheel out further evidence of my unbelonging.

"Yes," he managed. "Who knew buttons could produce so much material?"

She started to nod, then picked up the pun and began to laugh.

"Excellent," she said, wagging a finger as she sailed through the crowd like the *Queen Mary*.

Thomas slipped out of the room, down the hall, and out the front door before he had really decided to leave. His hesitation outside cost him, and when he turned to go back in, he found Mrs. Covington looming.

"If you intend to come in, you will need to have registered," she said, intoning the words like some high church minister.

Thomas just turned and was walking away when someone fell into step beside him. Chad.

"Good paper," said Thomas.

"Could have been better," he said.

He didn't look at Thomas, so there was no gratitude for the politeness even in his face.

"Not staying for requests from editors to submit to their journals?" said Thomas.

"Right," said Chad. "No, I'm running errands for Professor McBride. As befits my stature."

"I'm sure she was very proud of your work."

"Yeah?" said Chad, with a quick, sneering glance. "What would you know about it?"

"You know," said Thomas, rounding on him, "I'm really not in the mood to be condescended to by a jumped-up little nothing like you, so just take the compliment and shut up, all right?"

It was like he'd slapped him. The boy withered, lost at least a decade, and flushed. He opened his mouth but couldn't think of anything to say.

"I'm sorry," said Thomas. "I've just had some not-so-great news and . . ."

"It's okay," said Chad, lowering his eyes. The boyish humility was already morphing back into surly adolescence.

"She obviously values you, is all I'm saying," Thomas offered. "Julia, I mean."

"Yeah, when she needs someone to go buy her a jump drive she values me," Chad said, scowling. "But when it comes to answering questions about my work—*my* work—that's another story."

"I'm sure she wouldn't have set up the panel if she didn't respect your work."

"Oh, she respects it all right," he muttered. "Maybe a little too much."

"What does that mean?"

The boy colored again and looked down: a kid caught talking in church.

"Nothing," he said. "Forget it. Look, I'm going this way. I'll see you later."

And he peeled off down a side street at a jog. Thomas wasn't sure if it was just the result of the boy's professional anxieties combined with Thomas's putdown, but he was sure that Chad was retreating, kicking himself for whatever he thought he had revealed.

CHAPTER 42

Back at the hotel the landlady was hovering with a slightly affronted look.

"A Constable Robson wants you to call him," she said.

He thanked her but offered no explanation while she loitered restraining herself from telling him that this was a respectable guest house, and that if he was going to bring it into disrepute he should pack his bags . . .

"Could I make a long-distance call first?" said Thomas.

She was a muscular woman, with bobbed, graying hair and bright dark eyes.

"Where to?" she said. She seemed to ask out of surprise. He couldn't imagine his answer would make any difference, which actually took the pressure off.

"Japan," he said.

She didn't actually stagger, but something flitted through her eyes.

"I'm afraid we have no way of charging guests for overseas calls," she said, polite.

"It's important," said Thomas. "You can time it and guess. Or charge me when you get the phone bill."

"We're just not set up for this kind of thing," she said, as if he had suggested something improper.

"I'll pay in advance," he said, fishing pound coins from his pocket and spilling them onto the telephone table. "And you can bill me if you don't think it's enough. It doesn't matter how much it is. I really don't care."

She considered the money, then him in the dim light of the hall, and he could tell that she was interested in people's stories.

"You mind using this one?"

"That's fine."

She checked her watch. Thomas turned away and dialed. By the time Kumi answered, the landlady had retreated to the kitchen.

His wife sounded tired, but glad to hear from him.

"The surgery is tomorrow," she said.

"Tomorrow!?"

"They didn't want to wait, just in case. It has been a few days since they got the biopsy results . . ."

"I'm sorry I didn't call earlier."

"It's okay, Tom. Really. But yes, they're going to operate tomorrow. I can't eat tonight and have to be up at five so I'm going to bed now . . ."

"You want me to come?" he cut in. "I could come. I could go to the airport right now."

"And I'll be unconscious when you get here," she said, and he thought he could hear her smile. "No, Tom. Not yet. Give me your phone number there and I'll pass it on to Tasha Collins at the consulate here. One way or another they'll get word to you the moment it's over. You'll probably know something before I do."

"How's that?"

"I'll be sleeping."

"Right."

"And Tom?"

"Yes?"

"If it is bad news," she said. "If they can't get it out, or it's bigger than they thought, or it's obviously spread already . . ."

"Yes?" he said, quickly, to stop her from saying any more.

"Then I'd like you to come. Please."

"Okay."

Thomas warned the landlady that he had given her number to Kumi and, when the woman started to look indignant, told her why. She blinked, then nodded tightly.

"I'll get you the portable," she said. "You can keep it in your room. For privacy."

"Right," said Thomas. "Thanks."

"You want something for lunch? I could do you a sandwich."

"That would be great," said Thomas, grateful as much for the consideration as for the food.

"Ham and cucumber, all right?"

"Perfect. Thank you, Mrs. . . ."

"Hughes."

"Thank you, Mrs. Hughes."

"I'll have it out to you in a moment," she said. "And you can call that policeman."

He thanked her again, took a steadying breath, and then dialed the station, squinting at the landlady's handwriting in the low light of the hallway.

"Ah, Mr. Knight," said Robson. "I was hoping I might hear from you. I've been checking up on your marauders. On their fingerprints, specifically."

"And?"

"And nothing, which is odd," said the policeman. "You said they were in their thirties or more, right?"

"Right."

"So for petty villains to have evaded the national fingerprint registry for that amount of time means one of two things. Either they are upstanding citizens who turned to crime because there was something about you that did not strike their fancy . . ."

"Or?"

"Or they are very good at staying out of trouble, which would suggest the opposite."

"The opposite being . . . ?"

"That these are very serious men who know what they are doing. If they were paid to follow you, to attack you, then they may do so again. You see, Mr. Knight, I don't know how it is where you are from, but over here we find that most criminals are petty and not very bright. Criminal masterminds are strictly the stuff of fiction."

"Why do I sense a 'however' coming?"

"Well, I did say 'most.' There are a few who are both

clever and dedicated. If what they do is harass people, threaten them, perhaps even kill them, then they will have a reputation to live up to."

"You think these guys were hit men?"

"I think that, psychologically speaking, ordinary men of their years and grooming do not pursue someone arbitrarily through ancient monuments. Furthermore, I think that their ability to have eluded fingerprinting over years of nefarious activity suggests a certain professionalism. Such professionals do not like to leave tasks for which they were employed uncompleted. It looks bad to future employers."

"So you're saying I should watch my back?" said Thomas.

"Do you need to be in Kenilworth right now, Mr. Knight?"

"Not really. Why?"

"Then if I were you, I would give serious consideration to shaking the dust of our humble settlement from your feet on your way out."

"You think I should leave town?"

"*Stand not upon the order of your going*," said the policeman, sounding pleased with himself, "*but go at once*. That's Shakespeare, that is."

CHAPTER 43

Thomas sat up through the evening and into the early morning, reading absently from Shakespeare's sonnets, waiting for the phone. From time to time he looked up and stared into the middle distance, thought turning uncertainly into prayer. A few weeks ago when a Jehovah's Witness had showed up at his Sycamore Street door, he had referred to himself as a "borderline agnostic Catholic," a phrase that had baffled the earnest young black man and sent him on his way. Thomas wondered about it now, wondered if he was angry at God, as people seemed to be when faced with tragedy, and decided that he wasn't. Since Kumi's announcement, he didn't think God had entered his head till this moment. Was that because his faith wasn't strong enough in the first place, or was it just that his version of God didn't interfere in the natural order of things? He thought of the words from that XTC song that had caused all that furor on college radio in the late eighties, that stuff about whether God made diamonds and disease, whether God had made us or the other way around. "Dear God," it was called. He hadn't thought of it in years. It was off that album that reeked of the English countryside, every song coming out of the small towns and pastoral landscapes that lay all around him.

At twelve minutes past three, the phone rang. He pounced on it and heard an unfamiliar American woman's voice.

"Hello, is that Thomas?"

"That's right."

"This is Tasha Collins?" she said. It wasn't a question, but she had one of those voices that raised the pitch at the end of each sentence so they sounded like questions. "Kumi's friend at the consulate?"

"Right. Yes. How is she?"

"She's good. Resting. The surgery went well? They removed the tumor and I spoke to the surgeon after. He said the tumor was small—grade two—but he thinks they got it all." It sounded like she was reading. "The margins were good and there's no sign of it spreading? They took some lymph nodes to be sure, but it looks good. They got it early."

"And she's okay?"

"So far. Like I said, she's resting. They'll release her from the hospital in a few hours? She'll be home by evening our time."

"Thank you," he said.

Thomas slept for two hours, left a note for Mrs. Hughes, packed his bag, and ordered a cab to the railway station. He stood there on the platform, waiting for the first train to London, feeling the chill of the morning and breathing in the air as if for the first time in weeks. He would call her from London. But for now . . . For now everything was if not good, then at least better than it had been, and the difference was extraordinary.

Once in the city he called Westminster Abbey and left a message for the verger, who, he was assured, would be arriving shortly. He took the tube to Westminster, and though it was packed with silent commuters who kept their eyes to their newspapers or their iPods, he smiled all the way.

At the abbey, Thomas checked with a marshal and found the verger in the cloistered walk on the south side of the abbey proper.

"Mr. Knight. I have some news for you," said Hazlehurst, his gait bobbing with pleasure.

Thomas shook the little man's hand and fell into step beside him as he reported his findings with bookish glee.

"The grave in Poets' Corner does indeed belong to Charles de Saint Denis, Lord of Saint Evremond. He was an exile from the court of Louis the Fourteenth over some political impropriety, and though the matter was later resolved and his relationship with the French crown was reinstated, he never returned to France. He lived in London, a poet, essayist, and dramatist, known for his epicurean habits and the sophisticated company he kept. He was a master of the quotable bon mot—a sort of seventeenth-century Noel Coward—and celebrated the flesh at every available opportunity, a religion to which he ascribed his long life. He wrote a play called *Sir Politick Would-Be* that was supposedly in the English style, corresponded with some prominent ladies—philosophers, hedonists, and society types—maintained at least one lengthy affair with a considerably younger woman, was on very good terms with the English monarchy, particularly Charles the Second, lived to be over ninety—which is extraordinary for the period—and was buried in the south transept."

"And the champagne?"

"Well, this is where it gets interesting," said the verger. "Did you know that champagne wasn't originally sparkling? No, I didn't either. Anyway, this Saint Evremond chap was from the Champagne region, though its wine was little valued in those days. The popular wines were much heavier and sweeter. Anyway, it was he who introduced champagne to England, and though there seems to be some disagreement on the subject, it was also he who effectively created the sparkling stuff we know today."

"How did he do that?"

"By bringing it to London," said the verger. "Everything gets fizzier here."

Thomas laughed.

"I don't really understand the science of it," Hazlehurst continued, "but it seems that the time taken to transport the wine to England allowed a secondary fermentation that produced carbon dioxide. If the cork was kept tight—lashed in place with string or wire—the gas produced was harnessed and made the wine sparkle. The fashionable English salons that Saint Evremond favored were most enamored of the wine's effervescence, and the method was re-exported to France, where it found its way into mainstream champagne production."

"So the English invented champagne?" Thomas grinned.

"Delightful, isn't it?" said the verger. "An exaggeration, perhaps, maybe even a distortion, but an amusing one nonetheless. And now it's time for you to answer me a question."

Thomas had sensed this coming, but he didn't mind.

"Go on," he said.

"Why do you care? You are interested in this long-dead French nobleman, but know nothing about him, so . . . ?"

He let the question trail off, eyebrows raised, an ironically Gallic expression.

Thomas told him about the lost Shakespeare play, Daniella Blackstone's curious passion for an obscure brand of champagne, and David Escolme's planned meeting with Thomas in Poets' Corner. To his surprise, the verger's excitement wilted.

"It's not much to go on, is it?" he said. "I mean, these might be completely unrelated items. You may be on the wrong track entirely."

"I know," Thomas admitted, "but think about it. A man of letters and culture who embodies a kind of Anglo-French accord, if you will, who had ties to French theater and wrote plays himself 'in the English style.' The man knew English drama and lived in London only a few decades after the last reported copy of *Love's Labour's Won* was on sale. Is it not at least possible that he acquired a copy—perhaps the only copy—of this English play about French royalty? A play that—if *Love's Labour's Lost* is anything to go by—celebrates verbal wit and the triumph of love and pleasure over restraint. If my sense of the lost play is even close to being right, I can't think of anything better suited to a French hedonist, socialite, and man of letters. Effervescent you said, right?"

"I was talking about the champagne."

"Well, that's probably the best word to describe what I imagine *Love's Labour's Won* to be. Effervescent. Right up Saint Evremond's alley."

"So, if we make the leap of faith and say he did own a

copy of the play," said the verger, "what happened to it? His library has been cataloged, and he is—in some circles—quite well known. If he still had the play when he died in 1703, it would have come to light."

"Perhaps he gave it away."

"If there is no textual record of the play postdating that 1603 bookshop inventory," the verger mused, "it must surely have been something of a prize possession already: a curiosity, at the very least. A man of Saint Evremond's tastes and learning would not give it away lightly."

"You said he maintained various correspondences and kept a mistress or two," said Thomas. "Maybe he gave it to one of them."

"These were fairly prominent people," said Hazlehurst. "Wouldn't their libraries have been researched and documented? Let me see who I can talk to. I have an acquaintance at the Sorbonne who might be able to connect me with someone who knows more."

On his way out, Thomas found a quiet spot to sit where he could ignore the tourists. He had been so pleased that the surgery had gone well that the full enormity of the disease had paled for a few hours. Now, in this place, loaded as it was with mortality, it all started coming back. Surgery, after all, was only the beginning.

Maybe he should go to her no matter what she said she wanted, no matter what Deborah said, abandon all this aimless investigating and get back to what mattered. But Kumi was still used to being alone. If things had gone badly, he would have gone. As they were, Deborah was right: she would be in her usual crisis-management mode, and if he went out there now he would be in the way, particularly if he moped. She was, he thought, stronger than him. Always had been. Let her find her strength. Then he would go.

He looked up at the vast space above him and the great stone arcs of the ceiling buttresses and he mouthed the word *cancer* to himself over and over, as if trying to mute the terror it held. It didn't work, but he sat there a while longer, quite still, thinking of nothing at all, trying to shut out what might happen next. Eventually he lit a candle in a corner of the abbey where a marshal was reprimanding a brash tourist for shooting video without a permit.

CHAPTER 44

Thomas spent an hour in one of the packed and silent reading rooms at the British library by the Saint Pancras station. In the main exhibit hall were remarkable literary relics, including the Beowulf manuscript and hand-corrected pages from Thomas's favorite translation by Seamus Heaney. He had had to tear himself away and descend into the bowels of the building. It had taken him almost another hour to get his library card and figure out the system, because he wasn't permitted to get his own books. So much of the massive collection was rare or ancient that the handling and shelving was done by the staff. When they had located the books Thomas had requested, a light came on at his desk in the reading room, and he went to collect them. No one spoke, and the entire business felt secretive and protected.

Unlike the precious tomes being gingerly handled by the white-gloved woman at the desk next to him, Thomas's selections were fairly mundane: an atlas and a couple of books on European history. He had read the character prefix "King of Navarre" a hundred times in *Love's Labour's Lost*, but none of the footnotes told him where Navarre was and he had never heard of it outside the confines of the play. It took him only minutes to see why.

He returned his books and checked out, first from the library and then from his hotel. He took the underground from Kings Cross to the Waterloo station and then called the abbey and asked for Ron Hazlehurst again, to share his discovery. The verger had news of his own, and the two discoveries meshed significantly.

"My contact at the Sorbonne says that Saint Evremond

made a habit of bestowing books on his friends," said Hazlehurst. "She knows of no reference to *Love's Labour's Won* in
his letters, but she does recall a reference to a gift of books to
the King of France himself in the course of their reconciliation. In a letter to an elderly dowager he mentions one book
in particular that was in English but that celebrates—hold on,
let me get this right—'the royal seat of the receiver.' She took
that to be the King of France himself. Now, I know the King
of France isn't in *Love's Labour's Lost*, except that he dies
offstage at the end, and that *Love's Labour's Won* would presumably not involve a King of France at all, since the princess
would be queen . . ."

"That's what I was calling to tell you," said Thomas. "The
Kingdom of Navarre was in the Basque region of the Pyre-
nees, occupying parts of what are today France and Spain
and centered on Pamplona. The southern part was absorbed
by Castille and became part of Spain in 1513, but the northern part joined with France in 1589 when King Henry of
Navarre became king of France. When Shakespeare wrote
the *Love's Labour's* plays, the two countries were effectively
the same and were formally joined in 1620. The last Queen
of Navarre—a title they continued to use—was Marie An-
toinette!"

"Indeed!" said the verger. "A story celebrating that union
would be a perfect gift from an estranged subject to his royal
master, wouldn't you say?"

"My thoughts exactly."

"Which leaves you where?"

Thomas glanced toward the sleek train that would take
him south and under the English Channel.

"En route to France," he said.

Before he boarded the train, he called Kumi at home in Tokyo
from a phone box. She was drowsy, but upbeat, and as she repeated what Tasha Collins had already told him about the surgery, he let her talk.

"What happens next?" he asked.

"More tests over the next few days, then they'll want to start radiation," she said. "Once that begins, I won't be able to travel for six weeks."

"I can come out," said Thomas.

"Actually," she said, "I was thinking I might come to you. In England. Just for a couple of days. I'd like to see you and it would be nice to be somewhere new, somewhere pleasant but unfamiliar."

Thomas told her of his plans.

"How long do you expect to be in France?" she asked.

"No more than a couple of days," he said. He told her what he was doing, the questions he wanted answered, the trail he was trying to follow.

"Good," she said. "I'll look into some flights."

"I can meet you in London."

"You know, I think Stratford sounds more my speed right now," she said. "Call me in a couple of days, okay?"

"Okay."

"And Tom?" she said. "Don't worry. We'll beat this."

PART III

No, Time, thou shalt not boast that I do change.
Thy pyramids built up with newer might
To me are nothing novel, nothing strange;
They are but dressings of a former sight.
Our dates are brief, and therefore we admire
What thou dost foist upon us that is old,
And rather make them born to our desire
Than think that we before have heard them told.
Thy registers and thee I both defy,
Not wondering at the present nor the past,
For thy records and what we see doth lie,
Made more or less by thy continual haste.
　　This I do vow and this shall ever be;
　　I will be true, despite thy scythe and thee.

—Shakespeare, "Sonnet 123"

CHAPTER 45

Whatever someone else thought he knew, Thomas didn't feel he had made much progress in Stratford. He was no nearer to determining where the lost play might be, but he did have an idea as to where it might have gone. Perhaps in tracing its past, he would discover its present. Still, for all that "the game's afoot" stuff he had done with the verger, he had found the journey dull and dispiriting. His mind constantly strayed back to Kumi. He wished he could think about something else, but long-lost plays and murder seemed too sensational, even disrespectful.

Blasphemous, he thought, echoing a man he had once known.

Thomas disembarked the Eurostar in Calais. He had studied rail maps and decided that because he didn't really know where he was going, he was better off with a rental car.

Moments later he was walking through a French town less than twenty-five miles from the English coast, and a totally different world. Calais was said to be the most English bit of France and had been a crucial British foothold throughout the Hundred Years' War. To the south were the battlefields of Crecy, where King Edward the Third used massed longbows and cannon to decimate a much larger and better equipped French force, and Agincourt, where Henry V delivered the *coup de grâce* and—briefly—claimed the French throne, thus ending the campaign that had begun with the tennis balls incident at Kenilworth castle.

Kind of, he thought.

It was rather more complicated than tennis balls, as Shakespeare suggested, with his hints about domestic troubles, the curtailment of church power, and the plots of old enemies who had reason to doubt Henry's claim to the throne. For all its talk of heroism, the play was clear-sighted about the brutalities of war.

The town itself seemed to further undermine the heraldic myths of the ancient war, with its looming petrochemical works and the cranes that huddled along the dockside. The roads were jammed with container trucks, and there was a gray functionality to the place that made it hard to imagine why Elizabeth's sister Mary had been so distressed when Calais finally slipped from English control. Now it thronged with returning English shoppers towing shopping and kids.

Now I am in Arden, he thought. *The more fool I . . .*

It took him ten minutes to find a pay phone and twice that to get the necessary card that would let him use it. Ron Hazlehurst had obviously been waiting by his phone with news from his contact at the Sorbonne, and he was excited.

"There is a story that there was a Shakespeare Second Folio in the Versailles collection," he said, "which supports the idea of the French royalty taking an interest in English drama. The evidence isn't conclusive and no one seems to know where it is now, but I still thought it rather extraordinary, don't you? I can find no sign of the Missing Play, however."

Thomas smiled at the verger's term, selected—apparently—in case their call was being monitored. Hazlehurst was clearly enjoying the intrigue.

"That said, a lot of stuff went missing when the revolution started pounding on the palace gates. Some stuff was looted, some stuff was smuggled out, and some stuff was destroyed."

"If it was looted," said Thomas, "it could be anywhere or nowhere."

"So you have to assume it was smuggled out or reclaimed by the original owner."

"What do you mean?"

"Well, if someone dies in possession of property that was given to them by someone else, that property might revert to the giver."

"But Saint Evremond died long before the revolution."

"But his family retained interests in the Champagne region," said Hazelhurst, who had clearly been thinking this through, "and there's a brand of champagne named after him. Wouldn't it make sense that his property reverted to the house?"

Thomas supposed so, if only because he could think of no other options.

"Where is it?" he asked.

"The Taittinger champagne house—the one that produces the Saint Evremond brand—is in Reims on the Place Saint Nicaise. It's just under a mile southeast of the cathedral."

"Impressive," said Thomas, still smiling. "Thanks."

"I Googled it," said the verger, pleased with himself.

CHAPTER 46

Thomas found a Hertz rental stand and selected a boxy maroon Peugeot from a man with a salt-and-pepper mustache as wide as his mouth who steamrolled Thomas's faltering, schoolboy French with a stream of clipped English and a laconic stare that hardened when Thomas asked for an automatic.

"No automatics," he said. "These you have to book in advance." He pronounced the last word "hadvance" with the kind of authority that seemed to critique others for lazily dropping the *h*. Thomas shrugged, signed, and took the keys, privately remarking—not for the first time—how little his dollars seemed to buy him.

He took a minute to get used to the little Peugeot's controls, moving the stick around into each gear as the man with the mustache watched with frank disdain from the window. When he started it up, the car lurched forward, but Thomas stared ahead, aiming at the slip road to the rotary and the A26 toward Reims.

Once on the highway and heading south, Thomas was startled by road signs echoing wars fought more recently than the campaign of Henry V. The Second World War had, of course, figured prominently throughout the region, and he was moving now through a corridor dividing the land conquered shortly after D-Day from the Ardennes to the east, where the Allied push had almost stalled in the Battle of the Bulge. But it wasn't the Second World War that whispered back from the road signs he passed. It was the First.

Arras, Vimy, the Somme, Bapaume, Cambrai, the river Marne . . . The names chilled Thomas, but they were only ominous words evoking vague images: countless casualties for a handful of yards of ground, and the unspeakable horrors of trench warfare. Like most Americans, Thomas knew little of the First World War. It didn't stamp the national consciousness like the Civil War before it and the Second World War after it. Maybe that was because the States had entered the war late, that its losses had been comparatively few, and that the war's emblematic stamp of futility and devastation had somehow been trumped by the bleakness of later conflicts, particularly in Vietnam. Or perhaps people had just forgotten. So far as Thomas knew, his school didn't teach what used to be called The Great War in its history classes, and history as a subject was being steadily eroded by subjects such as economics that the powers that be thought more obviously useful.

Thomas found himself thinking about Ben Williams again, who had made speeches from *Julius Caesar* in his class six years ago, and had died in uniform in Iraq. In the States, war always seemed so remote, so easily turned into the subject of glamour and heroism. He wondered if the French ever thought in those terms, here where the ground had been soaked with blood every forty years or so since long before any of them had ever heard the name of America.

It was a hundred and forty miles to Reims, and Thomas cursed himself for not staying on the train as far as Lille. But long as it was, the drive was easy and even picturesque, the countryside opening up the farther he went, till he was passing through great open fields considerably larger and more obviously farmed than the irregular pastures he had seen in England. Sometimes the crop—rapeseed, he thought—was an almost unbelievably vivid shade of yellow-green. Elsewhere fields of grain or some long, nameless grass stretched hundreds of yards back from the road, dotted with immense bales like the wheels of some colossal cart.

Reims itself was—a little disappointingly—newer than he had expected, and more industrial, and Thomas doubted that much of it predated the Second World War. He parked in the rue de l'Université, a hundred yards or so from the cathedral where in 1429—and in Shakespeare's *Henry VI, part 1*—the dauphin had been crowned Charles VII, in defiance of England, by Joan of Arc: Saint Joan for George Bernard Shaw, the enigmatic and unsettling "La Pucelle" for Shakespeare. Thomas didn't remember the play well, and hadn't especially liked it.

He parked and slid out of the car. The drive had stiffened up his shoulder, but he couldn't stretch for fear of reopening the wound. He pressed it with his left hand and rolled it a few times, but didn't dare do more than that.

He walked up toward the cathedral first, not because he wanted to see it, but because he knew there'd be guidebooks to the region in English in the stores that clustered the surrounding square. He found a shop nestled between a patisserie and a bank. He bought a *Rough Guide* to France without comparing it to the others, and a *pain au chocolat* at the patisserie next door, and then he walked back to the car, munching, thinking about his wife, who loved good pastry.

He hung a left and then walked briskly down the Boulevard Victor Hugo till he reached the Taittinger headquarters, an oddly triangular, modern building with its main door in the apex and the walls crowded with windows. Inside was an imposing model of the equally imposing Saint Nicaise Abbey, which had sat on this spot since the Middle Ages but was now gone, destroyed, not—as Thomas had assumed—during one of the world wars, but by the French Revolution. Again he found himself struck by the density and violence of the region's history. It was no wonder Americans felt so rootless by comparison that they craved a historical dimension to their lives and families. In Europe that history was everywhere, stacked deep like piles of well-cut stones, many of them bloody.

He paid a seven-euro admission fee to an appropriately bubbly hostess who suggested that he "feel free to wander inside" and descended into the cellars, passing phalanxes of empty bottles bearing the Taittinger name and stacked wooden barrels. The bottles were racked at steep diagonals, base end up, like banks of dusty rocket launchers. As he went down he entered the past and, at least in some places, the distant past.

As the displays made clear, Taittinger had bought the remains of the abbey and its cellars comparatively recently, returning them to the purpose to which the monks had dedicated them. It was chilly, and the air felt slightly moist, and Thomas—who had never liked dark, enclosed spaces, felt a tremor of unease.

CHAPTER 47

Champagne requires storage for years underground as it matures, the bottles being periodically tipped and rotated to clear the sediment that collects in the neck. When ready, the bottle is dipped into icy brine, then uncorked, and the frozen plug of sediment is deftly removed. A little sugar is added to the bottle and it is resealed. The method, a time-consuming, skilled, and labor-intensive one, was still performed in the traditional manner to this day, said a guide, when he asked. A man in a sharp stone-colored suit snorted dismissively, and the guide shot him a look.

"These cellars date from Roman times," said the guide, redirecting the attention of those who were still watching the suited man. "They were cut out of the chalk in the fourth century, around the time that Attila the Hun was battling the Roman legions to the north . . ."

Thomas turned to the man and gave him a quizzical look.

"They all say that," said the man, clearly an American, "but these days it's BS. It's picturesque, you know, this everything-hand-done-as-it-was-back-in-the-day. Quaint. Makes for good footage: nice long dolly shots of some old dear turning the bottles in soft light. But if it were true, it would be wasted time and money. These days everyone does it mechanically. It's faster and more efficient and you don't lose anything in terms of flavor. The flavor is all about the grape blend, additives, yeast, and such. The disgorgement process doesn't matter a damn. They just like to pretend they still do it that way to keep the tourists happy."

He grumbled the entire speech, but Thomas found his iconoclasm amusing.

"They say they do it the traditional way," he remarked.

"They would," said the American. "But what do you see here: a few thousand bottles at most? These guys must be producing in the order of six or seven million units of product a year. Maybe more. You think they've got some guy who walks the cellars with a candle in his hand like some medieval monk in a docudrama, twisting each bottle a few inches, one at a time? They'd have to be nuts."

"Sounds like you know your subject," Thomas smiled.

"Let's just say I'm in the trade," he said, with a private grin. "But we should probably keep that to ourselves. You?"

"Teacher," said Thomas. "Kind of a vacation. You done many of these tours?"

"Oh yeah," he said, ticking them off on his fingers with a mixture of bravado and boredom. "Martel, Piper-Heidsieck, Mumm, Pommery, Veuve Clicquot-Ponsardin, Lanson. And those are just the ones here in Reims. I did Bollinger in Ay, and tomorrow I'll be in Epernay: Mercier, Perrier Jouet, Castellane and Moët et Chandon. Anything you need to know about making fizzy wine, I'm your guy."

Thomas thought the guide was listening in discreetly and that she scowled at that reference to fizzy wine. Maybe it was the cool, softly lit alcoves in the pale stone, the hushed air of seriousness in the tourists, or some holdover from the place's monastic origins, but it felt oddly like being in church, a house of eternal mysteries not reducible to fizzy wine. The American grinned, enjoying himself.

He was middle aged and slim faced, with a strong, sinewy build. His hair was thinning on top and he had a habit of running his fingers through it, as if estimating the day's loss, but there was a brassy confidence to the man that Thomas found appealing.

They moved off together, drifting from display to display, admiring the vaulted arches with their stone ribbing and the endless side passages of racked and crated champagne.

"The locals will tell you it's the squid fossils in the chalk beneath the vineyards that make the flavor," said the American, unimpressed. "Or the climate. Or the pruning techniques. Or the centuries of tradition and the way the grapes have evolved. More BS so far as I can tell."

"So what is it?" said Thomas, taking the bait.

"Depends which 'it' you mean. I'm not talking about flavor, nose, bubble distribution, and all that stuff because I think you can simulate that stuff in a lot of places. I'm talking about what makes champagne *champagne*."

"I don't think I follow," said Thomas.

"To call it champagne, according to international law, it has to come from here, did you know that?"

"I think I'd heard it."

"Champagne is defined by the region," said the American, overtly scornful now, and loud enough that Thomas was aware of those around watching them. "Make the same product anywhere else and it's just sparkling wine made according to 'the method champenoise.' That's all you can call it. The champagne method. God forbid you should call the stuff in the bottles *champagne* unless you are one of the grand old U.S. companies who managed to get themselves a loophole in the law."

He snorted again as if to punctuate the remark.

"You work for a U.S. wine company?" said Thomas.

"A U.S. *champagne* company," he replied, pointedly.

"Right," said Thomas. "A new one?"

The man nodded, but looked away as if he didn't want to say more. He might have been fifty, though he moved like a younger man. His voice—a wine-soaked cannon, rich, dry, and loud—breezed with style and a command that seemed habitual. Only this almost-question about who he worked for seemed to silence him.

"I don't know anything about champagne," said Thomas, backing off.

"Do you like it?"

"Sure," said Thomas, shrugging.

"Then you know enough."

"But how do you tell the really great ones from the . . . less so?"

"Oh, they're all pretty much the same," he said, and this time he looked away so that the confidence sounded like bluster. "Is this the only cellar you are visiting?" he added.

"Not sure yet," said Thomas.

"Looking for something in particular?"

Thomas immediately felt himself tighten.

"Not really," he said. "Why?"

"Weird," said the winemaker. "Someone who doesn't drink champagne vacationing around here and touring cellars. Seems like a—what's the word—a blind? Yeah. Like one of those things you hunt in. No?"

"Just a tourist," said Thomas, conscious that he was withdrawing, conscious that the other man's brash and opinionated persona didn't quite square with the careful eyes that now held his. "What would I be looking for here if not wine?"

The other man paused for a second or two, his gaze level, and then the smile snapped back into place and he threw open his arms expansively, bellowing, "Search me." He laughed then, too loudly, back in character.

Thomas wasn't sure about this man, with his easy dismissals of champagne and his facility with a language that sounded more akin to TV and film than it did the wine industry. What the hell was a dolly shot or, for that matter, a docudrama?

"So, if it's all a shell game," he said, "a ruse, this myth of French champagne's greatness, what are you here for?"

The man smiled and looked away.

"Oh, I'm just here to see what I can learn," he said. "Maybe grease the transatlantic gears a bit, you know? See if we can strike up a first-look deal on some import-export, maybe."

First-look deal, thought Thomas. *More movie-speak.*

"But," the man in the suit concluded with a last panoramic gaze around the stone arches, "I've seen enough. Have fun, mister teacher. Don't drink too much."

Thomas gave him a nod, but he was already striding out, moving quickly, the side buckles on his shoes ringing slightly in the stone hall. Thomas wasn't sure if it was the abruptness

of the parting, but he considered following him out, just to
see where he went. He didn't, but over the next few minutes
he kept checking over his shoulder to make sure the guy had
really gone.

Thomas approached the guide. She was a pretty girl, no
more than twenty, with pale skin and blue eyes that turned
frosty when she realized who was speaking to her.

"I said, I was wondering if I could ask a question," he repeated.

"Of course," she said, unsmiling.

"Well, it's not about the champagne method or anything
like that. I wanted to find out about a particular account."

"An account?"

"Yes. Taittinger has a relationship with a friend of mine
and I need to ask some questions about it."

The blue eyes grew harder still.

"If anyone could tell you that, I do not think they would,"
she said. "It is confidential, no?"

Her English, superb when she was comfortable, seemed
to have slipped fractionally. She was suspicious.

"Could you, perhaps, ask someone?" he said, smiling.

She bit her lip, her eyes never leaving his, then said, "Wait
here," and walked quickly away. As she was about to climb
the stairs up to the lobby, she turned.

"That man you were with," she said. "The American. Is he
a friend of yours? A business colleague, perhaps?"

"I'd never met him before he spoke to me a few minutes
ago," said Thomas.

She gave him a long, hard look, then turned and went up
the stairs without comment. She didn't believe him.
Stranger still was Thomas's nagging sense that she might be
right not to.

CHAPTER 48

Thomas was just starting to get used to the scale of the cellars. He had assumed that such places would occupy roughly the size of the building above them, but he was way off. The cellars were actually a network of tunnels and passages, stacked on top of each other and reaching far out into the chalk and limestone like serpentine burrows. The major champagne houses had literally miles of such cellars.

Good place to hide something you wanted people to forget about, he thought. Could that be what the man in the stone-colored suit had been hinting at? Surely not. But there had been something about the man, something almost familiar that Thomas couldn't quite place . . .

"Sir?" It was the girl with the ice-blue eyes.

"Yes?"

"If you go back to the lobby, one of the officials is waiting for you."

Thomas wasn't sure what she meant by "officials," and though he assumed it was an inaccurate translation, he thought there was a touch of pink to her cheeks, and both the smile she gave him and the way she turned away seemed hurried and deliberate. He felt immediately cautious.

The man at the top of the stairs who was so conspicuously doing nothing seemed similarly wary.

"You had a question, monsieur?"

He was a young man, businesslike and slick in his immaculate, stylishly slim-fitting suit, but Thomas couldn't help feeling that his casual manner was feigned.

"A couple, actually," said Thomas, opting to lead with the one that sounded more like general research. "The Taittinger house makes a Saint Evremond brand, named after Charles de Saint Denis, the marquis of Saint Evremond who was exiled from the court of . . ."

"Le Roi Soleil," inserted the other. "Louis the Fourteenth."

"Right. I was wondering what the connection was and if the house possesses any of Saint Evremond's books and papers."

"The Saint Evremond champagne is made by the Irroy company, which we own. It is made according to Saint Evremond's own principles, with thirty percent Chardonnay grapes, sixty percent Pinot Noir, with Meunier and others for balance. It is aged for three years . . ."

"Pinot Noir?" said Thomas. "But that's red."

"Did you not read the display in the cellar?" said the other with a touch of hauteur. "Many kinds of champagne are made with a blend of grapes, including red, but the skins are separated from the juice. It is the skins that make red wine red."

"I see," said Thomas, looking suitably humbled. "But other than following the recipe of Saint Evremond . . . ?"

"There is no connection," he shrugged. "It is a tradition that we are proud to hold."

"Is it true that the English invented modern champagne?"

"Of course not," he said, as if nothing could be more ignorant. "No one invented champagne by themselves, not even the monk Dom Perignon, no matter what they tell you at Moët et Chandon. Saint Evremond, like Dom Perignon, was important in blending grape varieties, but his contribution to the drink came from popularizing it in sophisticated society. What the English contributed was a market that enjoyed champagne as a sparkling wine, and the bottles to store it."

"The bottles?"

"Many champagne producers—including Dom Perignon— tried to prevent champagne from being gassy. They tried many things to stop the second fermentation. People who liked it gassy did the opposite, but when the wine moved from cask to bottle, and the sugar was added, the fermentation was so . . . what? So *fierce* that the bottles would burst. It was common to lose two-thirds of the champagne in storage for this reason. The English, who are primarily a beer-drinking nation, were used to this problem and developed a stronger bottle, and a method of wiring on the cork so that the gas was trapped inside. It is important, but it is not the invention of champagne. Champagne is French."

"My other question is about an account of yours," said Thomas, moving on. For all the young man's languid good humor, this debate seemed close to rekindling the Hundred Years' War. "An English lady. She receives crates of your Saint Evremond brand periodically."

"A single woman? Not a company?" he shrugged, the smile now genuinely confused. "I don't understand."

"I'm acting on her behalf," Thomas improvised. "Or rather, on behalf of her estate."

The young man's brow creased as he considered the word.

"She died," Thomas inserted. "I'm just trying to clear up some details of her arrangements."

"Certainly. Come this way, please."

Thomas followed him through the lobby to an imposing door that opened into offices of a less public kind. They passed several, wordlessly, until they came to what seemed to be the rear of the building. The young man took a seat at an immaculate desk and tapped his fingers on a computer keyboard, nodding to Thomas to sit. After a moment, he asked for the name on the account and Thomas spelled Blackstone's name. The Frenchman typed some more and then grunted with puzzlement.

"What?" said Thomas.

"Daniella Blackstone," the other read off the screen. "One crate, per year."

"For how long?"

"Life," said the man at the computer.

"Would that be expensive?"

"Not for her. She has never been charged."

"Is that common?" asked Thomas.

"Not at all. I have never seen such a thing."

"How long has she been receiving the champagne?"

"It does not go to her precisely," said the young man, turning to Thomas. "It goes to her family. It has done so since 1945."

"Do you know why?"

The other shook his head.

"There is no information in the file and we have no paper records that go back so far."

"Why 1945? Something to do with the end of the war?"

"Indirectly," he said. "The deal, I suspect, goes back further in time. It begins in 1945 for Taittinger because that was when we bought up certain smaller champagne houses in Epernay. The arrangement with the Blackstone family seems to have come from one of those houses: Demier."

Thomas walked past where he had parked and up to the cathedral. It had been one of the most extraordinary medieval churches in Europe, a rough counterpart to Westminster Abbey in terms of royal coronations and age, but it was brutally shelled during the First World War and had been heavily restored. Even so, much of the statuary around the outside was headless or otherwise fractured, and Thomas could only imagine the hell that must have been unleashed when the building had been hit by—according to his guidebook—285 shells. It was said that of the forty thousand houses that had surrounded the cathedral, only forty survived the devastation.

In many ways it was a very different kind of place from Westminster. It was sparer inside, uncluttered by monuments, so the overall impression was of air and vast stone, and flashes of color from the windows. It was also quieter. Thomas wandered its cool, massive transept, admiring the immense columns with their decorative vine-leaf carvings, then sat staring at the deep cobalt blues of the Chagall stained glass. It was like being under deep water and looking up toward the sun, a shifting and vivid color that seemed to extend into infinity. The more he gazed at it, the more he felt himself floating on undulating currents, drifting like a spirit cut free from the body.

He remembered the lines from the XTC song about God making disease and the diamond blue . . .

He had to force himself to get up and return to the world,

which seemed darker by comparison. He lit a candle in a rack for Kumi and walked back to the car. It was cold outside now, breezy and on the point of rain. He felt reflective. What sense of progress he had had was dulled even when he imagined scooping a lost Shakespeare play from some crumbling and forgotten cellar under Epernay. In this reflective mood he was surprised to notice the man at all.

He had been behind Thomas in the cathedral, a young man with close-cropped hair and a long, drab coat, and Thomas suspected he had seen him before that as well, perhaps in the Taittinger cellars. He had been walking briskly only a few yards behind Thomas when he reached the Peugeot, but had faltered as Thomas paused to fish for his keys. The young man had turned to a shop window as if arrested by something he'd seen there. As Thomas pulled away from the curb, the man in the long coat turned back to the road and stuck out his arm as if hailing a cab. Thomas watched in his rearview mirror as a green, low-slung sedan—a Citroen, he thought—that had been idling at the corner sped up, and the man got quickly in. He couldn't be sure, of course, but Thomas was prepared to bet that the sedan was no taxi.

CHAPTER 49

Thomas took the N51 south to Epernay, through broad flat expanses of fields and vineyards in meticulous array on the sides of low chalk hills. He came off the highway and took at least one wrong turn that took him through quaint villages of antique farmhouses, markets, and war memorials, some Napoleonic, some First or Second World War. One, where he got out to check a road sign masked by a heavy plane tree, was located in what seemed like the middle of nowhere. He assumed it had been a battlefield of some sort and climbed the few steps to the monument with its faded French flag, brick obelisk, and surrounding slabs covered with names. Flowers had been laid recently. It was only when he considered the inscription and saw how many of the surnames repeated that he began to wonder if there had once been a village here that the war—in this case, the First World War— had overtaken and destroyed. Many of the names were women. Was it possible that whole villages could have been wiped out, their buildings and people eradicated in the entrenched four-year horror that had been the War to End All Wars? He checked the map in his guidebook and decided that it *was* possible. Epernay sat squarely on the river Marne, the site of major battles at the beginning and end of the war. In the meantime, the land around the river had shifted from Allied to German control, and the region had been utterly decimated.

He stood at the top of the steps and looked back along the road he had come. There was nothing more than fields and the curious round towers with slated, conical tops that might have been silos, and a few isolated trees. There was no sign of the green Citroën he had thought was following him when he left Reims, and he couldn't be sure he had even seen it on the highway once he was out of the city.

Getting paranoid, Thomas, he thought. *Not a good sign.*

He got back into the car and turned it around.

Epernay, once he found his way, was a picturesque town of tree-lined avenues and large, square-fronted buildings with steeply pitched tiled roofs. It was getting dark fast and Thomas was tired. He found a small, anonymous hotel where he dined on a rich venison stew and an assortment of local, Brie-like cheeses and then went up to his spartan room. The bed was hard and narrow, but Thomas fell quickly asleep, waking only once before it was completely light. He did not remember his dreams, but woke anxious, sure there was something he was supposed to do that he could not remember.

Thomas thanked his slightly officious landlady for his breakfast of bread, cheese, and café au lait; studied a map of the town center; and decided to leave the car at the hotel.

Epernay seemed almost wholly geared to champagne, and one broad street was lined on both sides with the gated mansions of the famous houses: Perrier Jouet, Mercier, and, of course, Moët et Chandon, with the statue of the monk after whom their most famous label was named, Dom Perignon. There were other, smaller houses, all backing onto vineyards that rose above the town, and among them, close to the end of the street, Thomas found Demier.

It was not as impressive as the other champagne houses, less elegant, resembling something between an overgrown farmhouse and a small and poorly maintained château. But as with many of its neighbors, there was a gravel drive behind ornate wrought-iron railings, painted black and trimmed with gold. The gate itself was open and a sign welcomed the public to its cellar tour. Halfway down the block, a green Citroën was parked by the curb, empty. Thomas strolled casually by it and into a *tabac* on the corner, but couldn't be sure the car was the one he had seen in Reims. In the shop he bought a small plastic flashlight, which he stuck in his pocket before returning to Demier.

Again, Thomas bought his tour ticket—twelve euros this

time—and browsed the lobby materials as he waited. Unlike Taittinger's fairly casual arrangement, Demier's tour was regulated and—he learned—automated. He had assumed Demier to be a minor producer, hardly worth the attention of tourists spoiled by the delights higher up the road, but the place was full of people, almost all of them French. Demier was indeed a small champagne house with a tiny output compared to juggernauts like Moët et Chandon, but it produced what was regarded, at least domestically, as champagne of excellent quality. The company owned less than forty acres of vineyard and produced only a few hundred thousand bottles per year, but—they claimed—they were alone in adhering absolutely to traditional methods of champagne production, and their prices reflected as much. Thomas strolled through their extensive store and didn't see a single bottle priced at less than one hundred fifty dollars U.S., with many reaching several times that. Thomas wondered if people could really tell the difference, if they could really like—really *want*—something so outrageously expensive—a thousand dollars a bottle? Two thousand? Five?—or if it was all a ruse to lure those with more money than sense.

As the tour group was herded into a pair of stainless-steel elevators by three attendants, Thomas scanned the crowd and saw two familiar faces. One was the suited American he had seen in Reims; the other was the young man in the coat who had followed him in the green Citroën. The driver was probably there too, but Thomas hadn't gotten a good look at him.

"Step inside, please, sir," said the attendant.

Thomas gave the huddle in the elevator a worried look and said,

"I'll wait for the next one."

He turned away as the door began to close, unsure if his pursuer had seen him, but pretty sure the American had not. The attendant, a hard-faced woman with streaks of gray in her black braided hair, gave him a polite nod that didn't bother to mask her displeasure.

Tourists, she was thinking. Or—worse—*Americans*.

Thomas bobbed his head apologetically and smiled. She

didn't thaw, but stood there clicking her fingernails together as she waited for the second elevator. As soon as it arrived, she motioned him in and began the speech her colleagues had done for the larger group as they descended.

"When we reach the bottom, please proceed to the train on your right . . ."

"Train?"

She stared at him.

"Yes. It is not a *real* train. It is . . . joined-up electric cars. When you get there, move to the right and take a seat. The train is guided by lasers, so if you take flash pictures, please shoot them to the sides, not directly ahead, or this can confuse the directional controls and produce an accident."

Thomas, unable to stop himself, grinned. The attendant glared. The elevator slowed and stopped.

It was cold in the stone passage, and almost all vestiges of the modernity and luxury of the lobby were gone. Here were only tunnels carved out of the rock, dimly lit by softly glowing strip lights that ran overhead. The train—more like a sequence of square golf carts—was waiting. He took a seat at the very back, two empty rows behind the last passengers, and sat as low as he could. No one in front turned, their attention on the guide. She was sitting at the front of the train on a raised, rear-facing seat. No one was driving and she couldn't see where they were going: hence the laser guidance system, visible as pinpricks of red light in the tunnels ahead.

The woman who had escorted Thomas down gave a nod to the guide and returned to the elevator. The guide brightly gave final safety notes in a very English English—all long *a*'s and precise little final *t*'s—and set the train in motion. It moved with a faint electric *whir*, gliding down the passage and snaking around the corner past a dozen arched alcoves of bottle racks. The guide talked constantly in her practiced, lilting way, presenting the obligatory facts on soil conditions, the properties of chalk, an abbreviated history of champagne before the seventeenth century. Then came biographies of the monk Dom Perignon and his fruitless attempt to rid the wine of gas, and the Veuve Clicquot, the widow who industrialized nineteenth-century champagne production and perfected the riddling rack by which the yeast plugs were collected and disgorged. Thomas had heard or read most of it before, but there was something pleasingly cryptlike about the cellars, and their sheer scale was impressive enough to keep his old claustrophobia at bay. The place was a maze of interconnected tunnels, each both a storage area in its own right and a way of getting somewhere else.

"There are six miles of tunnels," said the guide, "mostly on the same level, though some have not been reopened since the last war."

It was, Thomas thought, something between an underground town and a great pale mine. That some parts were closed suggested structural instability, but he decided not to think about that. That was why the train made sense for tourists, he thought. It kept them contained and made the trip fun—slightly comic, even—like they were on some Disneyland ride. Without it, the great network of passages could quickly get daunting, even scary, and that was before anyone started using phrases like *structural instability*.

He was still grinning at his own insight when, without warning, the train stopped and all the lights went out.

CHAPTER 50

The panic took a few moments to blossom. For a second every-one sat there, polite tourists still, as the guide brayed calming suggestions into her dead microphone, waiting for something to happen. But when nothing did, when the darkness contin-ued, and the silence—untouched by all the humming electron-ics no one had noticed till they disappeared—deepened, things got quickly out of hand.

"What's happening?" shouted someone.

"Is this supposed to be funny?"

"Put the lights back on. I can't sit here in the dark!"

"Why are there no emergency lamps?"

"Who touched me?"

Then they were moving, though they couldn't see where they were going, spilling off the train as if afraid it might lurch suddenly into wild motion and kill them all. Indeed, with all the movement and feverish talking, and the guide's shrill pleas for restraint, Thomas wasn't sure how he knew that at least one person had left the train and moved quickly away. He sensed it, a movement that was unlike all the chaos around them: pur-poseful, deliberate. He thought he heard measured footsteps receding to his right, brisk, confident strides. Someone who knew where he was going.

Thomas slid out of his seat, arms spread against the dark-ness, and began to follow those receding footsteps, fumbling in his pocket for his flashlight. He was almost into the per-pendicular tunnel when there was a flare of yellow light back at the train. Someone had struck a match. As the shadows leaped, the guide's voice rang out.

"Stay on the train, please! Sir? Sir!"

He kept walking, snapping the flashlight on and breaking

into a padding run, his ears straining for sounds of whoever it was who had left the group first. Someone saw his light and called after him, "Over here!" as if they had been at sea for weeks, waiting for rescue. He made a hard left to get out of sight and picked up the pace.

He didn't know where he was going, and once out of sight of the train he stopped, trying to hone his senses. He shut his eyes, held his breath, and listened.

There were three levels of sound. First, and most obvious, was the garbled panic of the tourists back the way he had come. They were no more than a hundred yards or so away, but the caves bounced and distorted their indignant bluster so that it seemed to drift at him, ghostlike, from all sides. Second, lower but at least as insistent, was the throbbing of his own heart. He had to reach for the third sound, stretching out with his mind as if only imagining it would allow him to hear, but there it was: brisk footfalls. He rotated, eyes still shut, tracking the sound until he felt he had its bearing, and began to walk.

He was breathing again, but his mind was holding on to the footfalls so that the other sounds faded away, screened out by his concentration. The footsteps were hard and rang slightly on the stone, not with the *clack* of a woman's high heel, but with the solid *thud* of hard leather soles, and something else, another sound he couldn't place. A man, he thought, still walking, who knows where he's going. He tried to identify the other sound, and thought it was a thin and high-pitched metallic clink that punctuated each step.

Remember that sound? he thought.

He did, and the memory made him pick up the pace.

The flashlight was inadequate, its beam yellowish and hazy, and trying to keep up with the footsteps was making Thomas reckless. If there was a rack of bottles in the center of the tunnel, instead of in the alcoves to the side, he might run right into it before he saw it. He slowed for a second, caught the insistent stride of his quarry, and sped up again.

Each length of passage was virtually identical to the one before it, and as he moved, the limited reach of the flashlight repeated the same shapes in the pale stone arches above, the same dark alcoves and tunnel mouths to the sides. Thomas felt like he was burrowing deep into the hill, and realized that his jaws were clamped. He was also starting to sweat. Neither was from exertion or anticipation of what might happen if he ran into the man he was pursuing. It was the place itself that was starting to get to him: the tunnels, the darkness, the colossal weight of stone overhead. With each step he took away from the parts the tourists saw, the ceilings seemed to get lower, the limestone more cracked and irregular. He was running now with his head dipped, ducking still farther as the rock kicked down and in.

Keep breathing, he told himself.

He sucked in the air, and it felt dank in his throat and lungs. The ache in his shoulder was starting to spread again. He could smell the stone that crowded in on him from all sides.

. . . structural instability, he recalled.

The flashlight flickered, and he shook it, still running. It came back on full, but Thomas felt a mounting dread. If he lost the light and the power wasn't reconnected, how long would it take him to blunder out to the elevators? If they got the tourists out and there were no voices to guide him back, he could be down in this antique labyrinth for days, weeks . . .

The footsteps seemed to have faded, but quite suddenly they grew louder, as if their owner had rounded a corner somewhere. Thomas hesitated, sure now that the rhythmic pounding of the footfalls was counterpointed by a tiny, shrill ringing like a bell.

He thought back to when he had heard that sound last time, and the memory slowed him for a second. For a moment he was back in a different darkness, on the porch in Evanston, listening to those footsteps down the side of the house, as someone crept into his yard . . .

And don't forget what happened next.

No chance of that. And almost immediately he remembered the side buckles on the shoes of the American in the suit, the man who had claimed to be a winemaker but who talked like a studio executive.

Not for the first time on this trip, Thomas felt manipulated and abused, and he suddenly wanted to find this man in his fancy shoes and pay him back for their encounter on Sycamore Street.

The thought drove away his rising discomfort, and he made another turn toward the sound, running as quietly as he could, trying to match the other man's strides so that their footfalls came together.

But then there was something else: another set of footfalls from over to his right. Thomas stopped and spun around. For a second he thought he had imagined it, but then, in between the jangling steps of the winemaker, he heard them again. They were cautious, stealthy.

Thomas felt his skin go cold, and the hairs on his arms bristled.

Someone else was down there with them in the dark. Someone new who didn't want to be heard.

Thomas started to walk again, faster than ever now, trying to fasten again on those distant, jangling footfalls. He made a left, then a right, then went straight for another hundred yards, and then he heard something different and stopped, shutting off the flashlight. He felt his eyes widening, in spite of the darkness, as he tried to home in on the new sound.

Running feet. A lot of them. Coming from behind him.

CHAPTER 51

There were voices now. Not the whining and demanding voices of tourists, but terse and guttural shouts. They seemed to be coming down several passages at once, calling to each other in what Thomas took to be French, though he couldn't catch the words in the vaulted and echoing passages. The running sounded purposeful, organized, like soldiers.

They're hunting, he thought.

It was a controlled and rapid sweep of the tunnels, and it sounded both urgent and brutal.

Ignoring the swelling pain in his shoulder and chest, Thomas ran. He was used to running in his lumbering buffalo fashion, but he was no forty-yard sprinter even when he was healthy. The exertion was getting to him, and even in the clammy air of the cellars he was starting to feel hot and breathless. He looked behind him, saw the strobing white splash of a halogen flashlight as it bounced through some archway, and forced himself to go faster. He could no longer hear the man he was pursuing, or those other, stealthy footfalls, but that hardly seemed important. This was no rescue party rounding up stray tourists.

He played his light off to the sides, looking for somewhere to hide, but saw only tunnels.

The voices were getting louder.

He made a right, still swinging his flashlight's sorry glow over the walls, then stuttered to a halt. What he had taken to be a tunnel was actually a large open area filled with stacked wooden casks, the walls hung with ancient iron implements. He had no time to think. He decided.

Thomas ducked among the barrels, forcing his way through to the center, and squatted, listening. His heart was beating so hard and fast that his bullet wound ached in time with it, and his breathing was ragged and hungry. He forced himself to breathe as deeply as he could, resting his forehead against the metal-strapped timber of the barrels, trying to hear past the panic in the blood pulsing through his shoulder.

He could still hear them. They sounded like they were everywhere, their harsh voices calling from the dark mouth of every tunnel. And then there was one set of footsteps closer than the rest and slower.

It wasn't the man in the buckled shoes. It could have been the other, the careful walker, but Thomas doubted it. This man had a slow, cautious step, but his shoes dragged slightly on the ground as he moved. It was one of the hunters, and he had a hunch that Thomas was here.

Thomas clicked the flashlight off and kept very still.

The footsteps entered the storage area from the tunnel Thomas had come down, and then they stopped. A light flared, a hard-edged white beam flashed over the tops of the casks, and then there was a new sound: a metallic *ting*, as if one of those metal implements had been taken down from the wall. It was probably something like a poker, but it scraped the stone and rang like a sword.

The man was stalking him now, his feet soundless as he crept around the perimeter. Thomas didn't breathe. His fingers were splayed against the stone floor for balance. A trickle of sweat ran into his right eye and he blinked it away. He could hear the other man moving: not his footsteps, but the shifting of the fabric he wore. He was very close now.

There was a moment of total silence, and then, quite suddenly, he was moving away again.

Thomas stayed where he was for a full minute, counting the seconds silently to himself as he listened. Then the man was gone.

Cautiously, waking each muscle one at a time, Thomas began to move. First he straightened his neck, which had been bowed, feeling the cool air on the sweaty patch where his forehead had been pressed to the cask. Then he flexed his fingers and, when they felt suitably braced against the ground, began to straighten his elbows till his back was stiff. He could see over the barrels now. There was no light. No sign of movement. He flexed the muscles in his thighs and started to stand up. He thought the sounds of pursuit had faded some.

He looked around, risking the flashlight, trying to gauge which way he had come, which way he might still be able to get out. He was no longer sure of his bearings. He knew which tunnel had brought him to the barrels, but which direction he needed to take after that, he wasn't sure.

He crept out of his hiding place and took a couple of silent steps up the tunnel and then froze. Someone was there. He had stepped out from a side passage, and he was carrying a flashlight in one hand and a pokerlike implement in the other.

So, not gone after all.

It took a moment for Thomas to realize that the flashlight was not directed at him. It was facing the opposite end of the passage, as was the man holding it.

With excruciating slowness, Thomas stepped out of his shoes. Eyes still on the back of the man with the light, he took a step backward. Then another. The third and fourth were faster, lighter. Then he was around the corner and running again, feeling the cold stone through the soles of his socks, sure he had made it away unheard.

He kept moving, pleased with his stealth, wondering if he might go back to hunting the man in the suit.

Only when you're sure they've given up looking for you, he thought.

Back near the casks, he heard a cough, then voices and noisy footfalls. Then, unmistakably, two words bellowed like a hunting cry:

"Ses chaussures!"

They had found his shoes.

CHAPTER 52

Thomas ran another twenty yards flat out, turned right, dashed for the next turn, threw himself around the corner, and slammed into something solid, something that shuddered and crashed in an explosion of glass and liquid.

Thomas fell hard among the shattered bottles. For a second he lay there, pain flaring in his wounded shoulder and in the knee that had made the most contact with the wooden rack, just long enough to catch the yeasty scent of the foaming champagne. Then he heard the renewed shouts of his pursuers and knew they were coming.

He seized the flashlight he had dropped and shook it, but it was lifeless. He began to clamber over the ruined bottle rack, and another bottle fell and burst. Thomas pushed through the wreckage, but then the walls leaped and shrank with the sudden blue-white of a large flashlight ahead. He turned back the way he had come, but someone was there too, a big man in overalls with a heavy mustache and a heavier pickax. There was a shifting in the shadows behind him—at least two more of them—and then they started coming toward him.

Thomas turned back toward the light source, lowered his head, and charged. There were at least two of them, but only one at the front. Thomas hit him hard with his left shoulder, and the man staggered back, leaving a dark hole behind him. Thomas rushed it, felt the whistle of a blow that missed the side of his head by inches, and was almost past them. He took another two sprawling strides and turned sideways into another tunnel. There was at least one at his heels. Maybe a lot more.

Without his flashlight he could see only what they lit from behind him, and the surging, frenzied shadows made it almost as bad as darkness. Then two more strides and—without any warning—the darkness was gone. The lights came on, rippling through the tunnels like falling dominoes. Thomas shielded his eyes and his heart leaped. But then, just as suddenly, it failed him completely.

Slumped against the wall no more than thirty feet away was a man. Everything about him—the angles of his limbs and the twist of his head—looked wrong. But it was the color that was so paralyzing, the crimson that daubed the suddenly dazzling walls.

Even without being able to see his face, Thomas knew it was the American winemaker he had met in Reims. The body was half sitting, half lying, limbs splayed and head lolling unnaturally back so that the wound in his throat was horridly exposed. He was quite still and the blood was still pooling wet around those shoes with the buckles that rang like bells.

Thomas stuttered to a halt, immediately raising his hands to his face and bending at the waist. For the briefest moment he forgot the men at his back, and when he remembered them, it was too late.

He turned into the blow. His weak right arm rose ineffectually and the ax handle hit him hard on the side of his head. The lights became momentarily dazzling and then faded completely.

CHAPTER 53

Thomas dreamed of tunnels and darkness, and then there were snatches of French and a graying of the dark, until he realized he was awake. He shifted and his head throbbed where he had been hit, so that for a moment he felt nauseated. He kept his eyes closed and his body still until the feeling passed, and then cautiously he looked around him.

He was lying on a metal-framed bed with a thin mattress that smelled of vinegar, in a vaulted stone room carved out of the ground. He was not where he had been when he was attacked, but he had clearly been moved only to some other part of the cellars. The air was chill and the light low. He was still shoeless and his watch was gone. His right wrist was handcuffed to the bed frame.

He moved his hand, testing the cuffs, but they were tight and secure. He sat up, swung his legs around and down so that he was sitting on the edge of bed, and put his left hand to the back of his head. There was a hard and painful lump behind his ear, but his hand came away clean and he could feel no break in the skin. What they might do to him now, however, he preferred not to consider.

Tough not to in the circumstances.

He checked his pockets with his free hand. Empty. Which meant they had his wallet and knew who he was. That wouldn't help the situation. He checked his shoulder. It was painful, but no blood showed through his shirt.

There was a single metal door. The room was bigger than he imagined a cell would be, and there were a couple of barrels sitting in one corner, but otherwise it would do the job just fine. There was no window and the door looked solid. He wouldn't have been going anywhere, even if he wasn't chained to the bed.

So he waited, replaying what had happened in the tunnels, gingerly approaching the memory of the dead winemaker—or whatever he had been—as if walking slowly up to the corpse again. He felt no great sadness for the man he had not known, only confusion and horror at the manner of his death, and a certain dread about what it meant for Thomas himself. After all, whoever had done that to the man in the buckled shoes might be about to do the same to him.

Except, of course, that they could have already done it.

He considered this, and could come up with two explanations. If the men who had hit him had also killed the other American, then they wanted him alive for a reason, and it probably had something to do with what he had to say when his captors eventually showed up.

If they hadn't killed him, then there had indeed been someone else skulking around those cellars.

Thomas was baffled by the dead winemaker. If this had been the man who had been in his yard the night after the murder of Daniella Blackstone, then what was the link between them? He thought of the man as he had met him in Reims, wondering if the other had been sizing him up, testing to see if he recognized him from that dark passageway in Evanston. It must have amused him that Thomas had had no idea that they had met—and fought—before. The idea was maddening and reinforced that sense that Thomas had no business being here, that he knew nothing, and that he had merely blundered from one disaster to another.

This one might get you killed.

So he waited, wondering how to prepare for whatever the inevitable interview would bring, wondering how long he had been out and, because he had no watch, how long he had been awake. Five minutes? Ten? He wasn't sure.

The more time passed, the less sure he became, and it was only the lack of serious hunger or the need to go to the bathroom that told him that what felt like four hours had probably

been only one. From time to time he thought he heard distant
rumblings or movement in the tunnels and once was sure he
had heard voices, but he got no response to his shouts of bad
French and didn't know what to call out anyway. Anyone who
could hear him, he figured, already knew he was here.

Once the lights flickered. Thomas stared at them, willing
them to stay on, swallowing back the bitter panic that had
risen like acid in his throat. They settled again, low but steady,
and Thomas watched for a full five minutes until he was sure
they would stay on without his attention, and looked away.

As he sat there, the pointlessness and stupidity of the
whole thing weighed on him. He was an amateur, blundering
around as corpses accumulated in his wake. He thought of
David Escolme. What he should have done was leave well
enough alone. Where he should have gone was Tokyo. What
the hell did Deborah know about what Kumi needed? She
had never even met her.

The surgery had gone well and radiation was scheduled.
Was that what made people's hair fall out? Or was that
chemotherapy? He knew, he was startled to realize, nothing
whatsoever about cancer. It was one of those words he had
fled from all his life, as if ignoring it would make it disap-
pear. That it might be real, that it might stalk people of his
age, of *Kumi's* age, had never seriously occurred to him. She
was still in her thirties and had no family history of the disease. He knew it was possible, of course—intellectually—but
understanding it with his gut, grasping it like you might grasp
the tumor itself, hard and expanding so fast you could almost
feel it . . . ? No. How could you? How could you go on knowing how quickly it could all be taken away by your own body
turning on itself . . .

Stop.

Yes. No more of that.

The footsteps, when they came, began abruptly and close, as
if their owner had been waiting only a corridor away. There
were two of them, sinewy men in overalls dusted with chalk

and dirt, their eyes dark and mournful. One had an ax handle in both hands, the other a large and ancient-looking black revolver. Neither spoke. The gunman stood by the door, the weapon trained lazily on Thomas's midsection as the other unlocked the cuffs. Once free, Thomas was nudged toward the door with the butt of the ax handle, and out. The gunman followed.

They walked straight for a hundred yards or so, then another couple of jabs steered Thomas right and down to the doors of a service elevator, all scraped and dented iron, a far cry from the polished, elegant thing the tourists used. Thomas got in, standing silently between them, wondering vaguely where they were going and whether he should make a grab for the gun.

Ah yes, he thought. *A survival plan based on your extensive experience of watching James Bond movies. You could stun them with your exploding shirt buttons . . .*

He smiled to himself, and the guy with the ax handle gave him a sharp look.

The elevator rose clanking but fast. It was one of those old-fashioned affairs with the grille that closed inside the door so you could see the floors streaking past. Except that here were no floors, only a few dozen feet of stone, then a battered steel door and, one level above it, something quite different.

The door was a lacquered exotic wood with a pronounced striping in the grain. It was trimmed with polished brass.

As his companion dragged the metal grille aside, the gunman stepped back and motioned for Thomas to lead the way. It felt strange, as if some curious shift in the tone of the day was happening, but in ways he couldn't understand. He pushed the wooden door open and glanced down, half expecting to be thrust out into nothingness like the kid stepping into the floorless tower room in Stephenson's *Kidnapped*. There was a plush crimson carpet trimmed with gold. Thomas stepped out, but his escorts did not follow. They closed the grille behind him, their eyes unaltered and blank, as the door closed, and the elevator whirred into life.

Thomas was in an elegant hallway hung with oil paintings in ornate gilt frames: landscapes and portraits from, he guessed, the eighteenth and nineteenth centuries. At one end of the hall was a pair of the same wood paneled doors, closed. At the other end a pair of identical doors stood open, inviting him into a broad and sunny sitting room of chaise longues and formal armchairs. Everything was royal blue and gold leaf. Chamber music was playing, recorded, Thomas assumed, though he would have been only mildly surprised to round a corner and see violinists in powdered wigs. There was a solitary figure standing near the window, a man in his sixties, small and frail-looking, dressed in a well-cut suit of pin-striped gray flannel. He wore a white carnation in his buttonhole.

"Come in, Mr. Knight," he said. His voice was rich, distinctly French in accent, but perfectly clear. "Have a seat."

CHAPTER 54

"Why am I being held here?" said Thomas, still standing.

"Please," said the man, gesturing to an armchair. He had white hair, heavy eyebrows, and eyes so blue and bright that they shone across the room. They were unnerving, almost unnaturally vivid, like the blue of the Chagall windows Thomas had seen in Reims. They projected an extraordinary intelligence and an energy belied by his birdlike frame. On an end table beside an armchair were Thomas's wallet, his watch, and the contents of his pockets. His shoes sat on the floor like slippers awaiting his arrival. Thomas stepped into them with as much dignity as he could manage, then sat.

"Mr. Thomas Knight," said the man. "A high school teacher. Among other things."

He smiled, and Thomas wasn't sure if there was a question there.

"And you are?" he said. He was trying to throw the other man off, derail his aura of ease and control. It didn't work.

"I am Monsieur Arnaud Tivary," he said, smiling. "I own this house, the Demier factory, and the cellars beneath it. Perhaps you would like to tell me what you and your friend were doing down there."

"I came on a public tour. Alone," said Thomas.

Tivary, still smiling, went back to looking out the window.

"This will be a good deal easier, more—pleasant—if you tell me the truth, Mr. Knight. You entered on a public tour, but then you left it and did a little exploring of your own."

"The power went out," said Thomas. "I was disoriented."

"So it would seem," Tivary replied, and now he fixed Thomas with a long look and the smile drained. "But the power did not simply go out, did it? Someone used a spade to cut through the main power line. Was that you, Mr. Knight?"

"Don't be absurd."

"Perhaps it was your friend?"

"I told you," said Thomas. "I came alone. I had no friend here."

"Who do you work for, Mr. Knight?"

"I'm a high school teacher, as you said."

"And your friend?"

"For the last time, I came alone. If you are referring to the man your people butchered in the cellars, I met him once in Reims. We chatted a little, but I did not know him."

"And he worked for . . . ?"

"He said he worked for a winemaking company in the States, but I don't know which. No doubt the police can find out for you, if you are curious."

The smile came back.

"No doubt," he said.

"Is that why you killed him?" Thomas ventured. "Because he was snooping around your facility looking for . . . what? Industrial secrets he could take back to Napa Valley?"

"You sneer," said Tivary, "but it is not so unlikely. Industrial espionage is part of the world we live in. Mechanization has meant that most champagne brands use essentially the same processes. What makes them different is the grape blend, the yeast, and any other additives, including types and amounts of sugar. These are what make the wines different."

"So?"

"*So?*" echoed Tivary, incredulous. "You may be a barbarian, Mr. Knight, but surely even you understand that the difference between brands is what separates their values. If a house that produces champagne for thirty euros a bottle can make the kind of adjustment that will allow them to sell it for three hundred, what would they not do to get that information? What if they could sell a single bottle for three thousand euros? They could increase the value of their production by a hundred times simply by learning the secrets of another house and implementing them."

"So you slit a man's throat to keep his bubbles uneven."

Tivary's smile split wide.

"So you are not a complete barbarian, Mr. Knight," he said. "You know a little about the bubbles. But it's really about taste. To find the right ingredient, or the right amount of that ingredient . . . some people will stop at nothing."

"Apparently."

"Not me. Not anyone at Demier."

"Taittinger then."

"This is ridiculous, what you say," said Tivary, with a dismissive Gallic wave.

"Because you are all fine, upstanding citizens, though your men came armed to catch me, beat me, and imprison me."

Tivary shrugged.

"Some precautions are necessary," he said. "We do not work in the light of the streets where the police patrol. We work deep in the earth, in the shadows of the stone underground. The rules are a little different down there. We have to protect our work. It is what we love and it is our livelihood. But this does not make us monsters."

"And you can prove this, I take it."

"No," said Tivary. "As far as I am concerned, you found the body of the American while being pursued—lawfully—by my workers. Gresham was his name. Miles Gresham. The police know about the unfortunate victim, though they do not know about you. To tell them that we were pursuing another American at the time this Gresham died . . . It makes things, *untidy*, does it not?"

"I'm sure it would," said Thomas. "But they will find out I was here."

"Probably," Tivary agreed. "In time. But by then they will be on the trail of the murderer, and your involvement will be an irrelevance. But you still seem to be suggesting that I—or people I employ—killed this man and that you are also in danger. Nothing could be further from the truth."

"But you've just explained why you would want Gresham dead."

"No. I explained why we would not want a rival winemaker

snooping—that is the word, *snooping*?—snooping around our cellars. But this Gresham was not a winemaker."

"He told me he was," said Thomas, surprised out of his defiance.

"Yes," said Tivary. "It is interesting, is it not? He pretended to be the one thing that would draw the greatest attention. But, according to the police, he was not a winemaker. Not even a wine dealer."

"So he was killed by mistake?"

"I do not think so," said Tivary. He was half smiling and considering, as if sampling an intriguing glass of wine. "I think he was probably killed for what he was, not for what he pretended to be."

"What was he?"

"The police say Gresham was indeed from California, but he was not involved in the wine industry. He was involved in another business entirely, one in which California is second to none in the world."

"Movies," said Thomas, becoming very still. "He was a producer."

"*Précisément*," said Tivary.

CHAPTER 55

Blackstone had talked to someone in movies about *Love's Labour's Won*. Escolme had said so. She had been looking for ways to make the most possible profit off the newly revealed play, and films had obviously figured large: this despite the relative failure of Kenneth Branagh's film version of *Love's Labour's Lost*, which was widely considered the low point of his career. But a new film of an old play was one thing, and the first film of a newly discovered play was something entirely different. It would market itself into the record books.

So Blackstone had talked to Gresham. Perhaps she had revealed something about the provenance of the original manuscript as a way of attesting to its authenticity. He had come looking for it. On his own? Because someone at his studio wanted proof that the script was genuine before they made a commitment to another Shakespeare film? Perhaps. He doubted there would be many script doctors in Hollywood who could reliably say whether something was or was not Shakespeare based solely on a handwritten copy. Whatever she had shown him was clearly not enough. He was looking for the original.

"Please," said Tivary. He offered Thomas a flute of pale golden champagne.

"I'm not really a champagne drinker."

"Please," said Tivary again.

Thomas shrugged, took it, and sipped. It was dry and intoxicating, alive with flickers of festivity and celebration.

"Yes?" said Tivary, smiling broadly, his eyes on Thomas's.

Thomas swallowed and couldn't help returning something of the old man's smile.

"Yes," he said.

Tivary gave a little cough of a laugh and gestured with his index finger triumphantly.

"Good," he said, as if Thomas had conceded some point in an important debate. "Now, this Gresham," said Tivary, "is not the first to go wandering my cellars with no good reason. Only the first to die. Most of the spies come from other houses we know, and most of them are not so rude or clumsy to go wandering the caves like that. I had word about this Gresham—and yourself—from my colleagues at Taittinger in Reims because I have been looking out for such people. In the last few months there have been several. So I ask myself: what are they looking for? I think you know, Mr. Knight. I think you know because you are also looking for this thing, are you not?"

Thomas considered the man seriously, but said nothing.

"Come this way, please."

The old Frenchman's gait was stiff, his strides short, and he strutted a little like a bantam rooster. Still, he moved quickly and Thomas, his physical opposite in many ways, had to jog to catch up, thudding through the delicately furnished room like the proverbial china-shop bull.

They left the room and went back the way Thomas had come, past the elevator, to the double doors at the far end of the hall. Tivary unlocked them with a tiny brass key from his waistcoat and trotted inside. He waited for Thomas, then shut and locked the door behind him.

The room was the architectural mirror of the one they had just left, though this was red instead of blue, and the furnishings seemed less designed for sunny and elegant entertainment. It was darker, more lived in, and the desks were heaped with papers and other clutter. The walls were hung with paintings—more portraits—and the credenza and bookcases were laden with framed photographs, mostly black and white, many sepia with age. Thomas glanced at them politely as Tivary turned his back to the room in order to fiddle with the dial of a safe.

"I asked you if you knew what they were looking for, these others," said Tivary.

"Perhaps," Thomas conceded, staring at the elderly man's back.

"Very good," said Tivary, turning, pleased to face him. "And for your honesty you will be rewarded."

He leaned on the handle of the safe and the door opened.

CHAPTER 56

"Mister Knight," said Tivary, "are you familiar with Charles de St. Denis, Marquis de Saint Evremond?"

Thomas stared as the little French man stood up. He was beaming, his disarming blue eyes bright with amused excitement. In his hand was a stained leather folder bound with ancient scarlet ribbon. Thomas's breath had caught. He nodded but could think of nothing to say.

"Voilà," said Tivary, reverently laying the folder on the desk, considering it for a moment, and then busying his clever fingers with the bow. In a second the two ends fell untied. Tivary gave Thomas an expectant look.

"Be my guest," he said.

Thomas smiled, suddenly nervous, and stooped to the leather folder. Gingerly, holding only the edge between thumb and forefinger, he opened it.

The folder contained two pouches. The one on the left contained what looked to be a letter in fine and florid script. The other contained a small book about the size of a paperback, but much slimmer. An old book. Instantly, Thomas knew he was looking at a late sixteenth- or early seventeenth-century quarto, or a damn good forgery.

"Is it . . . ?" he faltered.

"A play," said Tivary. "Yes."

"By Shakespeare?"

Tivary's eyes fluttered and something complex passed through his mind.

"No," he said. "See for yourself."

Thomas hesitated, momentarily crushed with disappointment, but then his fingers gently prized the quarto from the leather folder and he was able to read the cover.

Volpone, he mouthed. "Ben Jonson's *Volpone?*"

He opened the little book to the first page.

"To the most noble and most equal sisters," he read aloud, "the two famous universities, for their love and acceptance shown to his poem in the presentation, Ben Jonson, the grateful acknowledger, dedicates both it and himself."

He stared at it.

"Sixteen oh seven," said Tivary, almost chuckling with delight at Thomas's reaction. "Purchased by Saint Evremond, used as a source for his own play, *Sir Politick Would-Be,* and sent as a gift to his lord the King of France and Navarre. You see the letter?"

Thomas looked up. Tivary had removed the single piece of parchment from the other pouch and unfolded it. Thomas, half-dazed, looked from the letter to the pouch, aware of Tivary watching him closely.

The folder's two pouches were both empty, but that only made the way they both bulged in the exact same way the more striking. Though the left one had held only a single sheet of paper, it was stretched into an outline perfectly matching that which had held the quarto. Unless Jonson's play had been routinely moved from one side of the folder to the other over the intervening three-hundred-plus years . . .

"There was something else in here," said Thomas. "Another play."

"Quite," said Tivary. "The letter to the king suggests as much. See?" he said, tapping the letter with his finger. " '*Les livres,*' plural. There was another book in the folder."

"So where is it now?" said Thomas, fighting back the urge to scream the question.

"Alas," said Tivary with a shrug that lasted at least three seconds, "we do not know. We think it came here from Versailles with the folder, but then . . . *pouf!*"

He gestured: *into thin air.*

Thomas felt his whole body sag as if some great pressure that had been holding him upright had suddenly been released.

"We have no details of what the folder contained," said

Tivary. "So we cannot say if the other book disappeared after it reached us, or before."

Thomas looked for a chair and sank into it.

"More champagne, I think," said Tivary, frowning. "Or perhaps, cognac would be more appropriate. You have had a minor shock. A . . . what? A *letdown*, no?"

"No," said Thomas, trying to be polite. "A little. I had hoped . . ."

"That there was a Shakespeare play here," he said. "So I see. But why?"

"I had thought . . . well, I don't know. I guess it doesn't matter."

"You thought Saint Evremond had a play by Shakespeare," said Tivary, apparently thinking aloud. "That would be valuable. But the Jonson quarto is also valuable, though perhaps not worth so much. Yet you clearly have no interest in the *Volpone*. So it is not simply about the value of an old book. Also, others have come looking for this missing play, so there is something special about it. What?"

"I thought—and others apparently thought—that there may be a play by Shakespeare that has otherwise been lost."

"A new play by Shakespeare?" said Tivary, his eyes flashing again.

"New to us, yes," said Thomas. He glanced around the room, not wanting to reveal the disappointment in his eyes. "But I guess not. Or if it ever was here, it has somehow . . . subsequently . . ."

Thomas stopped, his eyes fixed.

"Monsieur?" prompted Tivary, turning to see what Thomas was staring at.

On the edge of the credenza were a pair of yellowed photographs in a hinged silver frame.

"Who is that?" Thomas said.

"*Mon grand-père*," said Tivary, smiling at the image of the slender man with the archaic mustache and the fat cigarette. "My grandfather. Etienne Tivary. He died before I was born . . ."

"No," said Thomas. "The other man. The one in uniform."

The man was tall. The uniform that of a First World War British officer.

"I do not know," said Tivary. "A friend of my grandfather's, I suppose. Probably stationed here during the war. There were barracks all over this region and soldiers used the cellars as places to get away from the . . . the bombs?"

"Shells?"

"Yes, the shells. There were trenches cut all through this area. For almost the whole war there was fighting here. Almost continuous. And the line between German and Allies moved. There were two battles of the Marne—the river—in 1914 and 1918. The Germans moved very quickly at first and took much of this region, but after the first battle, they were pushed back, just not far enough to stop them from shelling the area. For most of the war, my family lived in the cellars."

"But this man is in two pictures with your grandfather and he looks different in each. They both do." Thomas pointed. "In this one his hair is longer, and this one he has no mustache. So they knew each other for some time."

"Why else would my family have kept his picture?"

As Tivary spoke, he was considering the back of the frame.

"Would you?" he said, offering it to Thomas. "My fingers are not as strong or steady as they were."

Thomas twisted a pair of clasps and popped the black-velvet-covered back off the frame. One of the pictures was unmarked on the back, but the other had a simple inscription in faded pencil: *Monsieur Etienne Tivary avec son ami, Captain Jeremy Blackstone, Janvier 1918*.

Thomas reconsidered the smiling Englishman in the picture, the same face he had seen staring down at him from an oil painting over the fireplace in Daniella Blackstone's sitting room. So now he knew the story of the missing play book, how it had found its way to France and then, three hundred years later, back to England. The circle was closed at last.

CHAPTER 57

He couldn't be sure, he supposed, but Thomas felt he had an edge on the competition now, including those who had beaten him to the Demier cellars, because they still thought the book was there. He had no idea how Daniella's grandfather had first seen the lost play or how he had come to take it back to his family in England. Was it a gift from the Tivary family, the returning of a work of English literature to its homeland in the hands of a man they had come to like and trust? Or had the English officer stumbled on the play in one of his many visits to the château, perhaps when the rightful owners had been moved off by the imminence of the fighting? Had he simply stolen it? Thomas couldn't say, and with everyone from that increasingly remote period dead, he doubted he would ever know for sure.

He called Kumi from an ivory-colored phone in Tivary's office, to let her know he was going back to England and that, yes, she should plan to join him there, if she felt up to the journey.

"I can sleep on the plane," she said. "I'm actually quite looking forward to it. A glass of wine. Quiet. A dumb movie or three. I'll be fine."

"I can meet you at the airport," Thomas said.

"I have a connection to Birmingham," she said. "Let me get you the details."

After he had hung up, Thomas gave the contact information for his Kenilworth guest house to Tivary, and then returned to his hotel. The local police might want to speak to him at some point, but thus far they did not have his name and because Thomas had nothing material to tell them, he hoped that he could be back in England before they started asking about him. He called Polinski and left the short version of what had happened on her voice mail, glad he didn't have to listen to her skepticism.

Thomas wasn't sure about Tivary. He seemed both trustworthy and trusting, something that would have been inconceivable only an hour or two before. Too trusting? Thomas, Tivary had said, had been tracked down and cornered on suspicion of industrial espionage, but his being pursued by Tivary's men had also given him an alibi for Gresham's murder, so once it became clear that Thomas was no spy, the champagne house had no further interest in him.

And they probably don't want to complicate the murder of one American with accounts of assaulting another . . .

That too. Thomas figured he should tell the local police what he knew, but he felt too driven to get back to Kenilworth to bear the idea of sitting around in some local police station trying to explain stories of lost plays and a pair of Chicago murders in wooden French. He'd talk to the British police, and doubtless Polinski would want to yell at him, but he would deal with that later. Now he was racing, his mind turning almost as fast as the wheels of the rented Peugeot that bore him back to Calais and the Chunnel. Thomas thought of Tivary as he drove: those bright, intelligent eyes, the easy, old world charm, and he hoped the old man was what he seemed. The presentation of the half-empty folder could have been merely a show designed to send him on his way, the lost Shakespeare play still sitting in the safe where it had been left.

But then why show him the folder at all? Tivary had nothing to gain by producing more evidence that the play had actually been in his family's possession. If it did not turn up elsewhere, that folder would inevitably bring Thomas—or someone—back to the château. Unless it was just about buying time, and Tivary knew that he would be able to cash in on his secret before Thomas came back . . .

Unless, unless, unless.

The ideas turned over in Thomas's head, questions chasing each other, branching off into new questions like the tunnels of the Demier cellars. But he never let his pressure off

the gas pedal because in his gut he felt sure that the play had
left the land of its fictional characters and returned to the
home of its author. Daniella Blackstone had been many things,
but she would have to have been a special kind of fool to have
claimed ownership of a book whose whereabouts she did not
know exactly. Her grandfather had brought it home. He must
have.

The place-names flashed through his mind as he drove,
and whenever he strayed from the autoroute he saw war memorials. They were everywhere. He knew of the fields of
stone crosses and stars, but these local memorials were almost as potent, at least when you got used to how many there
were. In the first battle of the Marne, the famous Anglo-
French victory that stopped the German advance short of
Paris (thanks, in part, to the commissioning of six hundred
Parisian taxicabs that shuttled thousands of reinforcements
to the front), more than five hundred thousand men were
killed, almost ten times as many as the United States lost in
the entire Vietnam War. And mind-eluding though such a
number was, it was really only the beginning, because the
Marne victory was so exhausting for both sides that all they
could do was dig in and shell each other for the next four
years up and down the largely static front. The troops sat for
months in rat- and disease-infested trenches, often half submerged in water, waiting for the enemy to blow poison gas at
them or pin them down with thousands of high-explosive
shells. Then the trench raids would come, the soldiers pouring
over the top with gas masks and bayonets as the machine
guns opened up. It was as good an approximation of hell as
Thomas could imagine.

He thought of Henry V moving among his troops in dis-
guise on the eve of Agincourt, and the bitter truths the king
overhears from his soldiers as they consider their fate. If their
cause is just, they say, then even their deaths have value. "But
if the cause be not good," says one, "the king himself hath a
heavy reckoning to make, when all those legs and arms and
heads, chopped off in battle, shall join together at the latter
day and cry all 'We died at such a place;' some swearing,

some crying for a surgeon, some upon their wives left poor behind them, some upon the debts they owe, some upon their children rawly left . . ."

It was a harrowing speech.

He thought again of Ben Williams, who had wanted to be a teacher, and felt an urge to lay flowers in his memory at one of the monuments to soldiers fallen before him.

He didn't. He kept driving.

Because the thing burning hottest in his mind was Thomas's flashbulb memory of Gresham's blood-splashed corpse in the tunnels and the unsettling conviction that being cornered by Tivary's men had saved him from the same fate. Someone had been stalking those stone passages, someone who had been on the same trail as Thomas, someone ready to kill to get the play.

Or to keep it secret.

It was an odd thought that had been floating at the back of his mind for several days. Thomas had been acting on the assumption that the killer—or killers—was trying to recover *Love's Labour's Won*, something that—however brutal—made a kind of sense. Someone wanted to find the lost play because publicizing the discovery would somehow make them rich or important: the book was of massive cultural, historical, and financial value, and if its pages could also make careers, turn the finder into a luminary of his or her field, then that value became almost incalculable. But now, anyone who produced the play would immediately become the prime suspect of three murders. So perhaps it wasn't simply someone trying to do what Blackstone had planned . . .

Thomas kept his eyes on the road and headed north.

Keep it secret . . .

The thought lodged and the world shifted as if he had walked into a hall of mirrors or—more unsettlingly—as if he had just left one. Someone didn't want the play found. Someone wanted it hidden and not because they already had it.

So, why? What could make someone see past the wealth and fame the lost manuscript would bring and make them want to keep it dark? Because the only reason Thomas could think of to keep such a treasure buried was because of what the text itself said. But what could a Shakespeare play say that was unsettling enough that someone would kill to keep it silent?

CHAPTER 58

He pressed one hand to his free ear to drown out the noise of the Calais traffic.

"It's Thomas Knight," he said into the phone. "Are you busy?"

"I'm leading students around Chitchen Itza," said Deborah. "Frankly I could use a break. How are things?"

He told her about the surgery, that—so far—things were looking up.

"Good," she said simply.

"But I wanted to ask you something."

"Shoot."

"You told me that you had an argument with your Shakespeare professor years ago about the authorship question," said Thomas. "What was the gist of the argument? Can you remember?"

"I can, but there are a lot of people better qualified than me to explain it."

"Let's just say I'm not sure I can trust those people right now," he said. "Every Shakespearean in the world has something to gain or lose where this missing play is concerned. Just tell me what you remember."

"Okay. But this is my Shakespearean party piece: the thing I wheel out to impress people at cocktail parties. Take it with a grain of salt and remember that I'm kind of ventrilo-quizing my old professor."

"Go ahead," said Thomas, shouting as a semi rolled by, honking.

"The book I read was about the seventeenth Earl of Ox-ford," said Deborah. "Edward de Vere. Of the various people who might have written Shakespeare's plays, he's the front-runner these days. His supporters call themselves the Oxfordians."

"Right," said Thomas.

"You're a fan of *The West Wing*, right?" she said.

"What?" he shouted.

"*The West Wing*. Martin Sheen. You had it on in your hospital room."

"Right. Sure."

"And what if I told you that the person who supposedly created and wrote most of the show . . ."

"Aaron Sorkin . . ." inserted Thomas.

"Aaron Sorkin," Deborah agreed, "could not possibly have invented the show because he never worked in or near the White House and had no experience in law or politics? What if, more to the point, I could show you that numerous episodes he supposedly wrote contain characters modeled expressly on people Sorkin could not possibly know, people specifically from Richard Nixon's administration?"

Thomas pressed the phone harder to his ear.

"So who are you saying wrote them?" he asked.

"The only person with the contacts, the knowledge of how government works, the intimate knowledge of the people sketched in the show," said Deborah, "was former President Richard Nixon, himself."

"Wait," said Thomas. "Nixon was dead by the time the show aired."

"That's the genius of it," said Deborah. "Nixon couldn't be seen to be writing for television, particularly if he was revealing things about his former colleagues in the show, so it had to be done secretly. He was paid up front, but the contract clearly specified that the shows couldn't be aired till after his death."

"But . . ." Thomas shook his head. "I'm sorry. That's crazy."

"Right," said Deborah. "It is. But it's a pretty good approximation of the Oxfordian argument about Shakespeare. It's bad history, bad textual scholarship, snobbery, conspiracy theory nonsense, and self-promotion. I don't think there's a scrap of good sense in it and I don't think one new play could possibly alter that."

"This is what your Shakespeare professor said?"

"He used a different analogy, but the gist is the same."

"It's good," said Thomas, surprised at how much sense it made to him.

"I've had years of museum fund-raisers to perfect it," she said.

"Thanks," he said. "That helps. Look, sorry, but I've got to go."

"Keep me up to speed," she said. "On the other thing, I mean."

"I will. I'm going to see her in England. She's flying out. Her choice."

"Good. Okay. Wish me luck."

"On what?"

"This dig. Today's is my last day playing tour guide. Tomorrow we have to finish the surveying of the site and then we start digging. Real soon after that we'll find out if I know what I'm doing."

"You'll be great."

"Let's hope so. Okay. Bye. And Thomas?"

"What?"

"Look after yourself, okay?"

"Okay."

Thomas hung up and drove to the station, only to find that there had been some unexplained delay with an earlier train, resulting in several cancellations. Unless he was prepared to wait a day, he would have to take the ferry to Dover and a train to London from there. Thomas cursed and blustered but the attendants were unmoved and uninterested.

"Monsieur, I cannot change this. So you must make the choice. Delay or ferry. Which do you wish?"

He chose the ferry.

It was a clear day and the water was calm enough that he barely sensed the movement of the boat. He had expected something small, but these were the big roll-on, roll-off car ferries, and there were hundreds of people aboard. There were kids everywhere, running around and clustering around arcade games that beeped and flashed. Hoards of sun-pinked English people weighed down with bags of wine and cheese waited in lines for the duty-free shops. The boat felt like something halfway between a dilapidated cruise ship and a low-end mall. Thomas, tired and increasingly irritable, fled, climbing the metal stairs and pushing through heavy doors until he found himself on deck.

He sucked in the sea air, steadied himself, and walked toward the prow. There was no one out here. Gulls wheeled, screeching, overhead, riding surprisingly strong gusts of wind, and Thomas could taste the salt in the air. It was a little cold, but he couldn't imagine why anyone would stay belowdecks. They had barely left the harbor behind, but he could already see the white cliffs of the English coast rising up in the distance. Their journey would be a little over twenty miles.

Strange, he thought, that so small a distance could generate such difference in language and custom, such separateness. For an American, for whom considerably larger distances generated difference usually only in nuance, it was doubly strange. He thought of the little American towns spreading over the Midwest and South, with their strip malls, their Wal-Marts, their McDonald's, and wondered how long it would be before everywhere became the same. At least in Europe the generic urban sprawl had to go around the castles and ancient churches. In the States it felt like a disease spreading across the country, contaminating everywhere, eating up whatever had been there before like . . .

Like cancer?

The wind blew the thought away, and as he turned his face from it, he saw a single figure inching along the rail. It was Julia McBride.

CHAPTER 59

She hadn't seen him. He was fairly sure of that. But that was about all he could say. He moved quickly around the deck and ducked into the first door he found.

"I'm sorry, sir, this is the club lounge. Do you have your pass with you?"

For a second he ignored the attendant, watching through the porthole window as Julia walked past without looking in.

"I must have left it in my car," he said.

"I'm afraid you can't stay here without it," said the woman. She was English, perhaps thirty, with hard, combative eyes. She wore a garish uniform, "tan" makeup leaning to orange that made her look like a store mannequin, and black hair streaked with gold.

"Right," he said. "Can you give me a second? I feel a little seasick."

She gave him a revolted look, as if he had already thrown up on her shoes.

"Perhaps you should go to the bathroom," she suggested.

"Perhaps you should give me a moment," said Thomas. He was stalling, but couldn't suppress a sense of indignation at the way she was treating him. After all, he thought, she didn't know he wasn't really sick.

"I'm sorry, sir," she said, the politeness brittle now, "but if you don't have your pass . . ."

"I can't enter Valhalla," said Thomas. "I get it. I'm going. In a second. I just have to be sure I can walk without . . ." He clutched his stomach.

"You can have a minute," she said, backing away with a grimace. "But I don't have a mop in here. If you're going to puke, you should go outside."

"You are the heart of generosity and compassion," he said, walking away, still peering through the windows. Julia McBride was nowhere to be seen.

And now Thomas had a new question. Could the footsteps he had heard in the cellars, the cautious pacing that had interspersed Gresham's purposeful jangling steps, have been a woman's?

CHAPTER 60

He did not see Julia again, not on deck, not in the boat's cattle-car restaurant, not at the *bureau de change* or in the lines that began forming for the car deck twenty minutes before they docked. She didn't appear at the railway transfer point, nor at the Hertz car rental stand. She was gone.

Thomas didn't know what he would have said to her if she had seen him, or what he would say when they next met. It could be a coincidence, but he didn't like it, and all the possible explanations he thought of were, in varying degrees, troubling.

He hated the idea that he was dependent on buses and trains again. England might be small, but it was densely populated, and getting from A to B could be extremely difficult if neither were major towns. So he rented another car, only realizing the strangeness of what this would be like when he tried the driver's door and found he was on the passenger side.

Driving on the left, he thought. *How hard could it be?*

Pretty hard. He had ridden a bicycle in Japan, where they also drove on the left, but the Japanese driving test had a famously difficult writing component that effectively (some said deliberately) prohibited foreigners from driving. He had to check himself at every junction, doubly so at those numerous and maddening "roundabouts"—rotaries—where everyone else seemed to know exactly where they were going and shifted from lane to lane with a discreet flash of their turn signals. Thomas went around two or three times before picking his exit, and people blared their horns at him as he cut across the traffic to get out.

The car was small but the lanes still felt narrow, and he had to concentrate hard to keep the little vehicle out of the way of the trucks and coaches that roared past him with only a couple of inches between their side-view mirrors. After twenty minutes he was stiff with tension and had drifted into the left lane to try to stay clear of the worst of it. Still, he was constantly in the way of people trying to get off the highway, so he moved into the middle lane, tried to keep steady, and put his foot down.

He got off the M25 and headed north on the M40. At Oxford he found what was ambiguously signposted as "Services," and pulled in to eat, use the bathroom, and make a phone call.

"Constable Robson."

"This is Thomas Knight. I spoke to you after I was attacked in the castle ruins."

"Ah, yes," said the policeman. "The siege of Kenilworth Castle. How could I forget?"

"I told you a little about what I was doing here," Thomas said. "I'd like to tell you a little more."

"Okay," said Robson. "Is this going to take a while, because I was hoping to get a bite to eat soon . . ."

"Order a pizza," said Thomas.

He told Robson about his visit to the Demier cellars and what had happened there. He gave him Polinski's contact information in Chicago and suggested that they go through Interpol, or whatever they did, so that they could cooperate with the French police.

"Okay," said Robson, deadpan. "Look, Mr. Knight, this story of yours is pretty bizarre."

"Why don't you order that pizza and I'll call you back later," Thomas suggested. "In the meantime, you might make a few calls of your own."

"Fair enough," said Robson.

The calls he would make were, they both knew, to check up on Thomas's story and make sure the policeman wasn't dealing with a certifiable lunatic.

Thomas bought an apple and a block of white cheddar. The English, it turned out, knew their cheese. He told the cashier as much.

"It's a place, you know," she said, "not far from here."

"What is?"

"The Cheddar Gorge. Where the cheese comes from."

"Oh," said Thomas, who had never thought of Cheddar as a place. "Good cheese there, is there?"

"S'pose," said the girl, shrugging. "I don't eat cheese. Makes me gassy."

Thomas called Robson back a half hour later, and though the policeman's voice was the same, he sensed a different level of seriousness in the way he listened. Clearly he had confirmed the events in Epernay. Thomas begged one piece of information in return for what he gave: the home address of Daniella Blackstone's erstwhile writing partner, Elsbeth Church.

With that in his pocket, Thomas promised to meet with Robson when he got back to Kenilworth. Then he bought a new map, and returned to his car.

Elsbeth Church's home was south of Stratford, just off the M4 between Newbury and Hungerford in what was now the county of Oxfordshire but was referred to as the Berkshire Downs. She lived well, but not ostentatiously, on the edge of a village called Hamstead Marshall in the kind of country cottage only England could produce with a straight face: stone, hung with creepers, and tiled with slate, its garden rustic to the point of wildness but dotted with colorful flowers. The house had small, leaded windows, and the walls bulged out of true in ways that could have been ramshackle but were merely quaint. Behind it were meadows running down to a brook, with a massive sycamore tree where some sort of large dove or pigeon called. It was a house off a postcard or a chocolate box.

Robson said she had divorced her brute of a husband the moment she became financially self-sufficient. She had no children and—unlike Daniella with her steward—lived alone.

No one answered the door when he rang. He waited and tried again, but with no better luck. The closest house sat back from the road a couple of hundred yards away. Thomas took one look and saw a net curtain twitch in an upstairs window. Someone was watching him. He considered going over there but guessed that this was not a part of the world where people volunteered news of their neighbors to strangers. He drove into the village and, heading north to the motorway, found a pub called The Green Man.

It was clouding over and the fine day was cooling fast. He went inside, hugging his light jacket to him, took his place at the bar, and ordered a pint of best bitter.

Unlike Stratford or Kenilworth, the pub was unused to Americans, and he was soon engaged in a playful discussion with the bartender about the various merits of cricket versus baseball, and the American "buggering up" of the word "football."

"I mean, you don't even use your feet, do you?" he was saying, genuinely bemused. "What's all that about? And the constant stopping and starting so you can wheel these half-ton monsters onto the field. I mean to say: come on! Those blokes wouldn't last five minutes in a rugby match—or in a real football match for that matter, when they don't get to sit down and have a drink on the sidelines every thirty seconds. Taking oxygen between plays. *Oxygen?!* I mean, if there's not enough in the air, there's something wrong, isn't there . . ."

And so it went on. Thomas endured with a grin and a shrug and the occasional obligatory remarks about zero-zero ties in soccer, the impenetrability of cricket, and England's failure to qualify for the European cup, which was then dominating the sports pages. It was good-natured enough, an excuse for a little verbal sparring rather than an actual disagreement. The barman was a lean, middle-aged man who tended to look off to the side when he talked and whose smile at his own wit was so light you might miss it. Eventually the talk moved on to other things: what the area was like to live in, and why the bartender secretly hoped one day to move to Florida. There was nothing around here, he said. The kids were all migrating away to the city. The farms were dying. Even the tourists didn't come here.

All of which led neatly into inquiries about what Thomas was doing there and a slightly retooled version of his journalist's feature on Daniella Blackstone.

"I had made an appointment to meet with Elsbeth Church, but I guess something got screwed up because she wasn't home."

"She probably got the wrong day," said the bartender. "She gets a little confused."

"Really? I thought she was the brains behind that writing team."

"That's what people say," he confided, "but she was always a bit batty if you ask me, and she's getting worse. Good at making stuff up, you know—stories—but even with all that cash rolling in can't seem to keep her life from going pear-shaped. Not that she cares. What time is it?" he checked his watch. "She'll be at the old house," he said. "If she's in town, and it's not raining. Bound to be."

"The old house?"

"Hamstead Marshall Park Manor."

"Can you direct me?"

"Having lived here all my life I might just be able to manage it," he said, with that sand-dry smile of his. Then, with a shrug and a roll of his eyes that he didn't explain, he added, "Your funeral, mate."

CHAPTER 61

Thomas turned the napkin the bartender had written on, but he couldn't make any sense of it. He'd driven to where the house should be, but there was nothing. The road rolled through open fields and scattered trees. There was a church and an occasional farm building, but nothing that merited the grand title of Hamstead Marshall Park Manor. It wasn't raining yet, but it would soon, and the light was dropping steadily. If he didn't find it soon, he would miss the chance.

He drove the stretch of road twice, then stopped and got out. It was cold and a stiff wind was blowing. He was, he realized, looking for something like the Blackstone place—an imposing stately home in expansive grounds. There was nothing of the kind around.

He parked beside the church, a small stone building with a square tower, probably medieval in origin but tinkered with over the years. He walked through the churchyard, hoping that someone might be working there who could point him in the right direction. No one was there.

He walked around the ancient graveyard with its lurching, weathered headstones, looking out over the fields for a sign of the great house, and it was then that he saw something strange. Standing in the middle of the rough and tussocky field was a pair of tall brick pillars with inset niches, surmounted with stone vases. Weeds sprouted from the very brickwork and blew in tangled masses from the urns on top. They looked for all the world like gateposts, but there were no gates, no walls outside the posts, and nothing he could see inside.

Thomas walked toward the pillars.

On the ground was a yellow flower. He took it to be growing there, but its stem was cut as if it had been dropped there. A few feet away was another. He couldn't say why, but the flowers bothered him.

Thomas walked carefully over the uneven ground, feeling the first raindrop fall from the gray sky and streak down his cheek. When he got close to them, he was even more convinced that they were gateposts, but in this completely open space, they seemed surreal and unearthly, like the monoliths of an ancient stone circle, growing out of the earth itself. He looked around him. The rain was falling steadily now, and the place felt strange and isolated. He entered the gates—insofar as there was anything to enter—and looked about him again, as if expecting a building to suddenly appear before him, like some spectral structure in a fairy tale or a ghost story. There was nothing, and with the cold rain falling harder, he began to think that he should go back to the car. He was clearly in the wrong location. There were more flowers here too, cut and strewn at random or blown about the field, some fresh, some faded, some dried to nothing, but none of them native to this spot.

There was something about the place, something old and elemental. Thomas shivered.

And then he saw her. She was squatting on the ground about two hundred yards away, motionless, her head turned slightly away from him. She might have been a half-submerged rock, but even though she was still, he was surprised how long it had taken him to see her. She was elderly, he thought, frail-looking, her hair long and blowing wildly. He moved closer. She wore a dark overcoat fastened tight. There were flowers all around her. Cut flowers.

CHAPTER 62

What are you, Thomas thought, suddenly feeling like Macbeth stumbling upon the weird sisters on the blasted heath, *that look not like the inhabitants of the earth and yet are on it . . . ?*

He took a step toward her. Then another. She knew he was there. He would bet his life on it. There was a tension to her, an alertness, like a rabbit in open country.

"Miss Church?" he said. "My name's Thomas Knight. I was hoping I might talk to you . . ."

And suddenly she turned and he thought, *Oh my God. It's Margaret!*

It was the woman he'd seen by the river in Stratford, the woman who had cursed Randall Dagenhart with such fury that she had reminded him of Margaret of Anjou in Shakespeare's early histories. The shock stopped him cold, and he stood there in the rain with his mouth open.

The fury he had seen in her then was gone, and her face, though distant, was quite composed. When she spoke, her voice was low but clear, despite the wind and rain.

"What do you want?"

"I'm looking into the death of Daniella Blackstone," he said, the truth spilling out unforeseen, "or rather, I'm looking into the death of a friend of mine, David Escolme, who represented her and was murdered shortly after she died."

"I don't know anything about that," she said in a voice that was almost dreamily uninterested.

She turned away, staring blankly into the rain.

"I just wanted to ask you a question or two," he repeated.

She sat quite still, unanswering.

"Miss Church," he said. "I'm sorry if this is a bad time, but I'm over from the States and I can't stay too long . . ."

She sat motionless as one of the monolithic gateposts, as if she did not even know he was there.

"Daniella was a friend of yours," Thomas ventured. "You worked together for years. What did you fall out over?"

The woman didn't look at him and said nothing.

"I found her body," he said, suddenly angry. "I found her in my yard. I never asked to get involved in this. I didn't want to."

"Did she die quickly?" said Church, still not looking at him.

"I think so," he replied.

"Well," she said, "I suppose that's something."

She stood up abruptly, and Thomas saw that she wasn't as old as she had first seemed. She moved slowly but with control. She walked toward him, and Thomas remembered just enough of her fury with Dagenhart that he had to stop himself from taking a step backward.

"I didn't kill her, Mr. Knight," she said. "We disagreed over a lot of things—ultimately, of course, money—but I did not kill her. I did not want her dead. We disagreed, but there was a lot we had in common."

"Can we get out of the rain and talk a little? I could take you to the pub. Chat a little. Have a drink."

"I have a bicycle."

"You could put it in the trunk. Get you out of the rain."

She considered him with wide, frank eyes, and Thomas had to force himself not to look away. It was like being close to a bull or a fox, her black eyes full of an unknowable instinct, a sense of self so foreign it barely seemed human.

"You can drive me home," she said.

She walked past him, and for a moment he was left standing in that unearthly space inside the gateposts, alone in the elements, surrounded by cut flowers.

CHAPTER 63

"What was that place?" he asked, as soon as they pulled away. He had to be cautious in his questioning and thought this might be a sufficiently indirect starting point. He could feel her presence beside him in the passenger seat, a little too close, smelling of rain-sodden clothes and earth.

"It was a great country house. It burned down in the eighteenth century."

"Why do you like it?" he asked. There was something about her voice he found unnerving, a distant, reflective quality that sounded like an old recording echoing through time and static. It was like she wasn't really there.

Like Margaret, he thought.

Shakespeare's vengeful French queen who first appeared in *Henry VI, part I* was still hissing curses three plays later in *Richard III*, during events that occurred long after the historical Margaret had died. She stayed around by the sheer force of her vengeance and malice like a ghost out of Seneca.

"I like the quiet," she said.

It wasn't true. He was almost sure it wasn't, but it was all she was going to say.

"You and Daniella fought over money?"

"Daniella was always better at the public stuff," she said, still reflective but more immediate now, more there, "the interviews and book signings and TV appearances. They loved her in the States, with her cut-glass accent and ancestral home. I didn't mind. I preferred to be out of the spotlight. But the weight of the touring, getting up in the night to do live interviews for stations six time zones away, the constant smiling for cameras, it all got too much for her. Or rather she began to feel it more than she had. She felt she was doing the lion's share of the work."

"But you were the one actually writing the books!" said Thomas.

Elsbeth Church laughed softly, and Thomas felt the hair on the back of his neck stand up. It was a knowing, bestial chuckle that came from deep in her throat.

"Yes, but writing is only part of what makes a bestseller, particularly when you have a celebrity writer," she said. "Daniella felt that her public profile was actually more important to our sales than the contents of the books. She had a point. Many of the best books make no one any money, but put a star's picture on the cover, some ghostwritten memoir by a former talk-show host, sportsman, or politico, and you can rake in millions. Daniella's face—those strange, remarkable eyes—painted a thousand words and rather more than that in pounds."

Thomas had almost forgotten Daniella's eyes, one green, one uncannily violet. Even in death they had been unsettling. He could only imagine what they had looked like when she had been alive.

"But you disagreed," he said, shoving the memory away with a shudder.

"It was what you might call a leap of faith or principle. I knew that in real terms, in what they call *market* terms, she was probably right. But I still felt that a book should be about what's in it, the sentence-level stuff, not how it's sold."

"So you separated and she couldn't sell another book."

"Ironic, isn't it? The market loved her, but they also loved that double-barreled author: Blackstone and Church. The publishers thronged to her, but when they saw what she had written, they pulled back, cut her adrift. 'Too risky,' they said, particularly since she expected a colossal advance. Sad. When I first heard she was dead, I thought she must have killed herself. Daniella so wanted to succeed."

She still sounded distant, like a sleepwalker or someone under hypnosis, but she seemed less strange and alien to him now. Maybe it was just being in the car instead of that strange, desolate place. Maybe he was just getting used to her.

"Was Daniella fond of Shakespeare?" said Thomas.

Church hesitated, staring at the rain-swept road ahead.

"Not especially. Why?"

"I just thought, you know, a writer living so close to Stratford . . ."

Thomas let the statement trail off, but she didn't say anything.

"Have you ever heard of *Love's Labour's Won*?" he said.

"It's lost," she said.

"What do you mean?" he demanded, excited.

"It's *Love's Labour's* Lost, not *Love's Labour's Won*."

"Oh," said Thomas. "My mistake."

"We're here," she said, as the stone cottage hove into bleary, rain-streaked view. "I won't invite you in."

She offered no explanation for that, and Thomas couldn't think of a reason to argue.

"Another time, perhaps."

"Perhaps. Could you open the boot, please?"

Thomas gave her a blank look.

"The boot," she repeated, her dark eyes flashing again. "My bicycle."

"Oh," said Thomas. "The trunk. Right."

He fumbled for the release lever and heard the trunk pop open. He started to get out but she grasped his wrist with one strong, thin hand. He flinched, then became quite still as she gripped his arm and stared into his face.

"I can manage," she said. "I'm a very capable woman."

"I don't doubt it," he said.

"Stay out of the rain."

She turned to get out of the car, and her wild, wet hair brushed his face. He caught again that musky, animal scent of hers, and thought it again:

What are you, that look not like the inhabitants of the earth and yet are on it?

CHAPTER 64

Thomas bought a set of bolt cutters from a hangarlike DIY superstore on the Warwick Road, then drove to the Castle Lodge and the best night's sleep he had had since leaving the States.

The following morning he feasted on Mrs. Hughes's obligatory "full English breakfast" and checked Kumi's arrival time. He had more than enough time to do this one thing in town before heading out to the airport to meet her. The bolt cutters were still in the car. With luck he wouldn't need them, but at least he was prepared.

From the road Daniella Blackstone's house looked the same as before. The castle in the distance seemed to brood a little more, though whether that was the gray day or the memory of his last visit, Thomas wasn't sure. There was no sign of the steward's car. Thomas drove back around to the castle lot and parked there.

He trekked back to the house, the bolt cutters swinging heavily in the store's flimsy plastic bag so that he had to actually hold the handles to stop them from tearing through. A hundred yards from the drive up to the house he clambered over a stone wall and jogged through trees and across the lawn to the back of the building. A cluster of brick chimneys marked the kitchen, and over to their right he saw a small wooden shutter, painted a gloss green: the coal hatch. It was, as expected, padlocked, but the lock was rusted and immobile. He doubted that even the key opened it now.

The bolt cutters chewed the steel loop through in two squeezes. Thomas reset the cutters and did the same to the other side. He glanced around before opening the hatch. He had moved, he knew, from the inquisitive, even rude, to the downright criminal.

You had better be right about this, he thought.

Which overstated the case somewhat. It wasn't like he just needed a bit of evidence to prove a theory. He had no theory. He had only a gut-level hunch that amounted to little more than the sure knowledge that he had missed something important.

The hatch creaked open. It was dark inside and smelled musty, damp. The little door was at ground level outside, but was at least six feet off the cellar floor within. Thomas backed in, lowered himself as far as he could, doing his best to pull the shutters almost closed behind him, then dropped, leaving the bolt cutters outside.

He rubbed the coal dust from his hands and stared up at the telltale crack between the shutters. If anyone who knew the house came around the back, they'd see they were open. He looked around for something he could use to pull them shut, decided he wouldn't be able to do it properly without locking them from the outside, and went up the stone stairs to the kitchen hallway.

The office door was unlocked, and Thomas was unaccountably glad he didn't have to break in, as if this made his crime less. On the wall was a board of keys on hooks. They were not labeled, but he knew which one he needed. It was, like most of the others, a large, old-fashioned key, but it had tarnished from disuse.

Miss Alice's room, he thought, in the steward's voice.

He paused in front of the portrait of Jeremy Blackstone wearing his First World War uniform in the sitting room, that confident smile looking, Thomas now thought, defiantly optimistic. Then he moved quickly up the two flights of stairs to the tower room that had been locked during his last visit.

The key was stiff, but it turned. He stepped inside, and closed it behind him.

He wasn't sure what he had expected, some Miss Havisham–esque shrine of dust and cobwebs, perhaps, but this was not it.

This was bright, airy, and dustless, with windows on three sides looking out over fields from a significant height, and though it was effectively a kind of turret befitting some nineteenth-century folly, it was also the room of a teenager, circa 1982. There was an England soccer shirt in shiny white fabric, its shoulders trimmed with blue and red tacked over the door. There was a flyer for an "End the War" rally to take place May eighteenth in Reading. There were other political notices: "Thatcher Out," and one adorned with peace symbols and the acronym CND: Campaign for Nuclear Disarmament. The war in question, judging by an article cut from the *Guardian* dating from June of that year, and celebrating its end, was the Falklands conflict.

The place was like a time capsule. Another newspaper from July tenth reported a break-in at Buckingham Palace by an unemployed Irishman who had managed to find his way to the queen's bedroom and sat talking to her for ten minutes before the alarm was raised. In pride of place over the girl's bed was a poster-sized copy of XTC's *English Settlement* album cover, the disjointed but somehow cursive sketch of an animal (a horse?), stark white against flat green. Thomas stared at it, remembering Escolme's interest in the band and the copy of the disc he had seen in what he had taken to be Escolme's hotel room.

But it hadn't been Escolme's room, it had been Blackstone's, and the CD was almost certainly hers: a memento of her daughter carried with her wherever she went. Thomas found himself moving quietly, not because he was listening for sounds of the returning steward, but out of respect. The ordinariness of the room—its stuffed animals on the bed, its outmoded fashions hanging in the open closet, its heaps of childish jewelry on the dresser—made him feel more like an intruder than he had when he cut the lock off the coal hatch door.

There was one further violation to be committed, however. He had seen it as soon as he came in, but he considered the rest of the room first, as if hoping that what he learned from the walls would make the other thing unnecessary. He leaned into a photograph stuck above the desk: five girls together. The one in the middle was, almost certainly, Alice Blackstone. She had her mother's uncanny violet eyes, though hers matched. There was a trace of the hauteur as well, a faintly aristocratic profile that could have been cold and hard, but wasn't. She was laughing, her arms around the other girls. Thomas wondered how much longer she had had to live when that was taken.

For a moment he saw the girl—and perhaps those with her in the picture—trying to get out as the school hall filled with stifling smoke, and then he pushed the image away and, in the same instant, stooped to the diary that rested by the bed.

He took a deep breath, eyes closed.

"Sorry," he whispered.

Then he opened it and began to read.

CHAPTER 65

Thomas put the book down after reading thirty days of entries from the first six months of the year and then all of the June entries, which ended abruptly on the sixteenth. The rest of the book was empty. He sat in the girl's desk chair in silence, and by the end he felt only absence—hers—and failure—his.

There was nothing of value in the diary. It was a catalog of trivia: who was on *Top of the Pops*, what movies were on TV, who was going out with whom, what clothes she was buying or hoping to buy, an occasional glimpse of political feeling. It was a series of snapshots of the life of an ordinary sixteen-year-old middle-class English girl. Occasionally there were flashes of intellectualism—little tentative references to books she was reading (everything from James Herriot to Dickens), expressed with the teenager's uneasy mixture of pretentious bluster and excited discovery so familiar to Thomas from his own students. At the same age, his jottings would have been much the same, he thought—a good deal less clothes, and correspondingly more sport—but otherwise about the same. She agonized more about her body, her hair, but probably less than most girls her age, though Thomas didn't know what would have been normal in England then.

Alice wrote in a fat, open cursive full of flourishes, and all her dots—both periods and those above her *i*'s—were tiny circles. Her vocabulary was bland and slang-ridden, all things falling into three categories: the "total crap," the "alright" (much of this), and the rarer but more fully expounded "ace," "magic," or "excellent." A lot of things were "a doss," which seemed to mean both easy and fun (watching movies with her friends was "an ace doss"), and less-satisfying experiences were marked with the deadpan "O Tragedy."

Despite these minimal hints of personality, what really came off the page was the sense of community: a core group of high school girls whose names, or nicknames, appeared even on days Alice didn't see them. "Didn't get to see Pippa today," she wrote. "Had a good laugh with the gang, but Liz was having her hair done and couldn't come property shopping."

Property shopping!

What would that have been? Records? Clothes? The pretension of shopping for "property" was ridiculous and touching. They were just kids playing at being grown-ups.

"Debs and Nicki spent the whole day at Bruno's: when me and Pippa came out of the pictures they were still there and had only bought two cups of coffee between them!" "Went scouring the horse with Pippa which was ace, but Liz, Debs and Nicki couldn't get away. Their loss. It was brilliant. Beyond brilliant."

And so it went on. The name that cropped up the most was Pippa. She was Alice's best friend, the person who most clearly shared her politics and, more important, her taste in music. They went record shopping together and spent hours listening to their albums and singles: Depeche Mode, Duran Duran, Yazoo, Elvis Costello, Dexy's Midnight Runners, Madness, Spandau Ballet, Blondie, Haircut 100, and New Order. Top of the list, of course, were XTC, who were edgy, clever, and local. Much of the diary was dominated by the extraordinary trajectory of the band's career: the massive success of *English Settlement* and the appearance of their anthemic "Senses Working Overtime" single, followed by rumors that something had gone badly wrong with their foreign tour.

Alice had clearly picked over the music papers with a fan's devotion, trying to build a clear sense of what was happening with what was supposed to be XTC's world-conquering tour. This was to be, it seemed, their time. They had built a core audience over their previous albums, particularly *Drums and Wires* and *Black Sea*, and were the darlings of the music press. In March, her confidence seemed to stall a little, and a week into April it was clear that something terrible had happened. "They say Andy has stage fright," she wrote. "How can Andy Partridge—one of the great performers in pop music today—have stage fright?" But she never found a satisfactory answer, and though she plaintively hoped that the cancellation of the tour was only a temporary problem, she seemed to recognize that the beloved local boys would never get the glory they deserved.

Thomas found himself smiling with nostalgia. If she had lived, Alice would have been about his age, and though her taste was, perhaps, eclectic to a fault, they shared a lot of common ground. Many of her favorite bands he had known and loved, and utterly forgotten. He liked her better for it, and because that faulty eclecticism gave the lie to some of her snooty pontificating about books and politics. She was smart, and the arguments she had with her friends about which was The Jam's finest song, or whether Adam Ant was doing anything different from the New Romantics, and whether either amounted to a new kind of music, were serious discussions based on actual thought, albeit spiced with the mania of fandom. In these opinionated rants he heard her real voice, not the faintly moralistic posturing she inhabited when she talked literature and Labour Party politics. In the end she was just an ordinary kid as he had been, brighter than most, perhaps, more serious, but otherwise a typical teenager. It was hard to think of her dying at this age, harder still to think that the girls she talked about—the gang—were as likely as not to be those who had perished with her.

He was about to replace the book when it fell open and he realized that the diary went from mid-June—Alice's last entry—to the end of July. An entire month had been razored out of the journal, and with them had gone any sense of what Alice had been doing in the weeks leading up to her death.

Thomas was considering this when he heard footsteps on the stairs outside.

CHAPTER 66

There was nowhere to hide. The box spring of the bed barely cleared the carpet, and the closet was too full of boxes. He scanned the walls quickly, but all he saw were windows.

They were old fashioned, with metal frames and wrought-iron hand latches. One of the three was all diamond panes in a lead lattice. Thomas crossed to it, opened it, and—pulse racing—was halfway out when he heard the footsteps at the door stop. He threw both legs out and lowered himself gingerly onto the ledge below, pushing the window shut behind him. He heard the rattle of the handle, then the creak of the door, but by then he was out.

The problem was that there was nowhere to go. He was standing on a ribbon of stone trim that ran around the sides of the turret. Thomas inched toward the corner to avoid blocking the sunlight as it filtered in through the window, but there was only the irregular stone and thin frame of the window frame itself to hold on to. He had pushed the window closed as calmly as he could, but he couldn't latch it from the outside. For five seconds he stood out there in space, holding his breath, waiting for the window to kick open, sending him falling to his death as it did so.

He heard movement inside, then silence.

Thomas had half expected an ornamental balcony or a venerable old drainpipe that he could shin down, but there was nothing. In front of him was the long drive through fields and hedgerows, then the jagged, rust-colored fragments of Kenilworth Castle. He risked a look down and saw only the sheer sides of the turret, then the gravel forecourt.

Thirty-five, maybe forty feet, he thought. *Broken legs at the very least if you try to jump. Or fall.*

A breeze whipped suddenly over his face, and he pressed his back into the building, flattening himself against the tower.

This could end very badly . . .

Thomas had never been good with heights.

Should have tried to talk your way out, he thought. *Or just hit him and run.*

Both of which could have led to his being arrested.

Right, he thought dryly, *and this lunatic high-wire act is way better . . .*

He glanced down at the ledge again. It was maybe four inches wide. At a push he might edge his way around the tower, find his way onto the roof of the house proper, but one misstep—or one bad gust—and he'd be off and down. There was still no sound from inside. Thomas used his right hand to grip the thin metal frame above the window, and tried to get some purchase on the stone with the splayed fingers of his left. Slowly, with absolute caution and feeling the stone digging into his back, he turned his head toward the window and craned his neck.

The glass was beveled and cloudy, but he could make out a human shape, sitting on the bed, his back to the window. A man, he thought, though he couldn't be sure. He was quite still. Thomas shifted fractionally, and a new leaded diamond of glass presented itself. This one was clearer in the center.

It was the steward, and he was reading Alice's journal.

Then he was up, moving swiftly, turning. Thomas snapped his head away from the window. The action almost threw him off balance, and for a dizzying second he seemed to be leaning out into nothingness.

At the same moment, the window opened.

Thomas shrank flat against the wall and held his breath. He could see the steward's pale hand on the window latch. If he leaned out and turned a little, he would see Thomas and then . . .

God knows what then.

He was still thinking this when the window closed suddenly. A moment later the latch snapped shut. Then came the muffled creak and click of the door closing. Thomas twisted his head again and found the pane of glass he had used as a peephole.

The steward was gone, and he had taken Alice's journal with him.

Thomas pressed his right hand to the window, but it didn't give. He might be able to punch out a pane or two with his elbow, but the leading was so tight that he would still never get his hand in to free the latch without tearing out half the panes. Even if he could do that without falling, it would make one hell of a noise. If the steward caught him in the act, any kind of scuffle would send Thomas falling to his death.

Better work your way around the turret to where it joins the roof, he thought.

He swallowed hard, staring fixedly off toward the castle remains, then took a single inching sidestep toward his left. Doing so stretched his right arm—still gripping the window frame—as far as it would go. He turned his head to look to the corner. A right angle. He couldn't get around that with his face out. He'd never make it. The only way was to turn around so his face was against the stone, and to do that, he was going to have to let go of the window.

CHAPTER 67

It sounded easy, turning around to face the wall, but faced with the logistics of actually doing it on a four-inch ledge forty feet in the air, it suddenly seemed impossible. He began by turning his left foot, pivoting on his heel till he got his foot pointing toward the corner, all the while keeping his left palm flat to the wall. He was still gripping the metal edge of the window frame with the thumb and first two fingers of his right hand. There wasn't much to hold so it was more a stabilizing influence than something that gave him real purchase. If he started to fall, he would not be able to stop.

Next he started to rotate his hips counterclockwise very slowly, keeping flush to the wall. As his shoulders began to follow the movement, rolling around to his left, he felt his arm twist along its length. His right shoulder was leaning out now, well over the ledge, and he felt the sickening sensation of the ground swimming up to meet him. His injured shoulder groaned, then shrieked with pain.

You can't do it.

He unwound back to his former position, spine to the wall, and caught his breath. He waited, counting silently to ten. Then began the process again.

This time, when he reached the point where his left shoulder was against the wall, he began to walk the fingers of his left hand in toward his body. He had to get his arm between his side and the turret. That meant creating a space between his body and the house that was wide enough to pass his arm through.

In other words, you have to lean away from the house.

He had started to sweat. He could feel the skin of his face

cold in the wind. He took a deep breath, then counted down from three.

Two.

One.

He let go of the window, swung his aching right arm through the empty air as he leaned out and pulled his left arm through. He pivoted onto his toes, his right hand reaching for the corner as his left stabbed blindly for the window frame.

For a terrible moment he thought he'd missed it. There was just nothing there. Then his slashing, desperate fingers found that edge of metal trim and he seized it like Dumbo's feather.

Except that Dumbo didn't really need his feather, did he? So it's a bad analogy. Because without your feather, you're a stain on the flagstone forty feet below.

Always helpful.

Still, he almost laughed. His face was mashed against the chill stone and he was still balanced precariously on a four-inch ledge, but it seemed like a triumph. A second later he began to inch toward the corner, which meant letting go of the window.

He suspected that holding on was not really helping his actual balance much at all. It was in his mind, that sense of stability through contact. Letting go wouldn't make that much difference.

Okay, Dumbo, let's see it . . .

He got a grip on the corner with his right hand, and that helped. As he started to negotiate his way around, he was struck again by the rightness of what he had done. There was no way he could have done this with his back to the wall. Once around he could see his goal, a glorious ten feet away: the roof, tiled with ancient mossy slate and a row of chimneys. He was nearly there. Then—surely—he'd find that missing drainpipe. Or maybe some *Romeo and Juliet*–style ivy that, if old enough, would be as good as a ladder . . .

There was a bang from below.

Thomas winced, and the wobble nearly killed him. He stilled himself, then looked down. He was right over the front door. The steward had just come out through it and slammed it shut. If Thomas fell now, he'd land right on him.

He froze. Then, gripped by an urgent thought, he looked down the drive for the steward's car. If it was facing the house, the steward would turn toward the turret to get in and Thomas would be caught.

There was a dark blue Jaguar parked nose first against the front wall of the house.

Knowing he had only seconds before the steward would see him from the driver's seat, Thomas moved quickly—recklessly—along the edge. He launched himself onto the steeply raked slates and scrabbled up without looking back. As he reached the apex of the roof where the cluster of chimneys were and slung one leg over, a fragment of stone, dislodged by his crawling, skittered down the roof, bounced off the gutter, and pinged off the windshield of the car below.

Thomas threw himself over the top and hugged the slates, shrinking down behind the first brick chimneystack with its clay-colored smoke pot. But he was not the first to take refuge up there today. With a great croaking squall, a crow rose up, flapping madly, its black beak and talons scything the air, its whirling feathers in Thomas's face as it took off.

Thomas shrank away, face into his chest in case the bird came at him. Below, the steward looked from the stone that had clicked off his windshield, up to where the crow wheeled overhead, and shouted "Get out of it!"

Then, with Thomas crouched gargoyle-like above him, he was in the Jag and driving away.

CHAPTER 68

It took Thomas no more than two minutes to scout out his best way down, which turned out to be the kitchen chimney. It was a stepped brick affair that ran down the side of the wall and was handily flanked by a cast-iron downspout. He flattened his entire body against the roof and crawled over the slates till he got there, then clambered carefully down. Compared to his apelike fooling about on the turret ledge, his final descent was child's play.

He recovered the bolt cutters and trudged back over the fields to the castle parking lot, picking the moss and cobweb off his clothes as he clambered into the rental car. He was hot and sweaty and covered with dust and grit. He hadn't noticed it till now, but his palms and fingers stung from the way he had gripped the metal and stone of the tower. He had scrapes on his arms and bruises on his knees from his final clamber over the roof, but he was down, safe and undetected. The ground felt good beneath his feet.

He checked his watch. He needed to get ready to meet Kumi at the airport.

The landlady of the Castle Lodge hotel met him in the hall as he was coming in. Her eyes slid slowly over his grimy clothes and smeared face, and Thomas made some vague brushing gesture that made no difference whatsoever.

"You have a visitor," she said. "In the sitting room. In future you might want to make sure you're around when people come calling. She's been here almost an hour."

She?

"Sorry," said Thomas. "I wasn't expecting anyone."

"And yet here she is," said the landlady. It was a reproof,

though Thomas wasn't sure what for. She turned to go. "Will you be wanting tea?"

"I'm not sure," said Thomas. "Depends who's come to see me."

"Your wife," said Kumi, from the sitting room doorway. "My plane from Japan got in early. I made the morning connection from Gatwick . . ."

Thomas went to her, enfolding her in a crushing bear hug and hiding his face in her hair.

"Yes, Mrs. Hughes," Kumi managed. "Tea would be very nice."

"I'm sorry I told you not to come," she said. "You couldn't have helped and I was—you know—angry and confused."

"Of course," said Thomas. "You had been diagnosed with—I mean—you were sick and . . ."

"Cancer," she said. "You have to be able to say it."

Thomas nodded, but said nothing.

"Anyway," she said, "I just had to tough it out alone for a bit. Sorry. It was stupid. And selfish."

"That's crazy," he answered. "And I wouldn't have been any use anyway. Too—I don't know—anxious."

"Still," she said, "it would have been nice to have you there. But you know me, Tom: self-sufficient to a fault."

"So where are we?" he said.

He wondered at his use of the word *we* as soon as he said it. It sounded wrong, flippant, but she didn't seem to notice.

"I'm lucky that they caught it so early," she said, and for a moment there was a haunted look in her eyes, a wild terror that peeped through and then went back under. Thomas saw it and recognized it. "It was just luck, really," she continued. "They have me on these hormone-suppressant drugs and I'll start radiation on Monday when I get back. No chemo, we think."

"Which means what?"

"It's good, Tom. It means things are going well. The chemo is what makes you really sick, so I'm glad I don't have to do that, but my oncologist is sure we don't need it right now. They'll reassess after the radiation in about six weeks. They removed a couple of lymph nodes during the surgery, to be on the safe side, and I have to wear this sleeve thing on the plane; something to do with embolism. I didn't completely understand all of it. That's what having you there would have been good for. There's so much information. I'm not sure I processed all of it."

She was starting to race, her voice rising in pitch, volume, and speed.

"And they have me all marked up for the radiation. Little stickers and magic marker lines. I look like a nautical chart. They said they wanted to tattoo me, but I said no. They said that if I am really careful about how I wash, so that I don't erase the lines or lose the little sticky . . . things . . . then it should be okay, but I have to be mapped for the radiation, and I don't really know what it will be like, but they say there can be some burning and it's just all so much to take in . . ."

He held her again then, gripping as tightly as he had to the stone of Daniella Blackstone's turret, holding on as if he might fall or—worse—as if *she* might.

They lay on his bed all afternoon. She asked him if he wanted to see the scar under the dressing, and he said yes because he guessed she wanted him to see it, so he stared at it as if he were really looking and said it didn't look so bad, though his knuckles were white where he gripped the bed frame.

He asked her if she wanted to go out. Drive into Stratford and have a pint in the Dirty Duck, maybe meet up with Taylor Bradley.

"How is he?" she asked.

"Good, I think. Has a tenure-track position at some little college in Ohio. Still staging plays. Still struggling to get much written and less published, but he has a job."

"He's not married, right?"

"No."

"Girlfriend?"

"No one serious, I don't think. He hasn't mentioned any-one," said Thomas. "But it's been a long time. We've lost touch over the last ten years."

"That long?"

"That long," said Thomas. For a moment he said nothing, then added, "We've wasted so much time."

"Plenty more to come," she said.

He gave her a desperate, questioning look, and she stared him down till he nodded.

"You remember when Taylor did that show?" she said. "What was it called?"

"*Gammer Gurton's Needle*," said Thomas, laughing. "Maybe the stupidest play I've ever seen."

"Funny though," she said. "In parts."

"In parts," he agreed.

"You want to get something to eat?" she said.

"You aren't going to make sushi?"

"I thought we'd work on my karate."

"I think I'll pass," he said.

"I had been wondering about dropping that class—what with being *too aggressive* and all—and I'll have to take a break from it for a while what with . . . everything . . . but now I think I'll keep it up."

"Yeah?"

"Yeah. If I'm going to be spending any time around you, I'll probably need it," she said. "Just try not to get shot till I have my black belt, okay?"

"Okay."

They couldn't make love without condoms—because of the hormone treatment and upcoming radiation, which would be lethal to a pregnancy—and Thomas didn't have any. He couldn't imagine going looking for any, particularly after that talk of doomed pregnancies, and neither of them felt the need for that kind of intimacy anyway.

A part of him was glad when they decided to just lie there, because he felt the scar of her surgery like a knife in his own groin, and there was a voice in his head that was shrieking with anger against her body. Having sex would be like saying it was all okay, this love wrapped in flesh and bone. But it wasn't okay. Because flesh failed. Always, inevitably, it failed, and so he resolved to hate it.

She read his thoughts, or seemed to, and smiled at him with her sad, worried eyes, and kissed away his tears, till he felt guilty about making it about him, even as he knew that somehow made it easier.

They drove into Kenilworth at her insistence and had dinner at a tandoori restaurant, where they split two big bottles of Kingfisher and gorged themselves on popadoms and paratha with mango chutney so that by the time their main courses arrived, they were full. They boxed up their chicken and naan to take back to the hotel, even though they had no fridge.

"Midnight snack, maybe," said Kumi.

"Maybe," Thomas said, taking her hand.

Back in his room, they watched soccer on TV, then moved between championship darts, some oppressively serious world news, and an inane game show. Thomas supplied ironic commentary because it made her laugh, and whenever he started drifting back toward her health, she shushed him pleasantly.

"Let's just watch," she said.

Then he would nod, too emphatically, and push it all from his mind as best he could, which usually meant merely not talking about it. She held his hand, and rested her head against his shoulder, and they lay there till it began to get light and Thomas realized that she had fallen asleep.

After breakfast they went walking through the castle ruins, talking about what she called his "case." Thomas went over everything he knew and suspected, and she listened and nodded, occasionally asking questions to show she was paying attention.

"When it's all done," she said. "Perhaps you could come to see me in Tokyo."

"I'll come back with you right now . . . ," he began.

"No," she said, flat. "You have something to do here. It's important. You aren't responsible for David Escolme's death, whatever you think, but if you can help bring his killer to justice, that's a good thing. And you have to find that play."

"I could come to the airport and see if there's a seat on the plane . . ."

"I'll be back at work, Tom," she said. "The radiation only takes about twenty minutes a day and I'm scheduled to do it before I go to the office. If you came out now you'd be sitting in my tiny apartment ministering to me—unnecessarily—and going crazy. In two days you'd be ranting about Japanese politics, protectionism, xenophobia, and the denial of World War Two atrocities. In the end, I'd have to kill you."

He smiled.

"And besides," she added, "you want to find that play."

"It's not the play that's important . . ."

"Sure it is, Tom," she said. "From the moment you first mentioned it, I could hear it in your voice. If the play is out there, you want to be the one to find it. I don't blame you. It would be a great thing to do."

"It seems sort of stupid now."

"No," she said. "It's not. I love to see you excited about something, especially now. And the world needs all the comedy it can get."

"Even Shakespearean comedy?"

"Especially that," she said. "Especially now. So."

After that she packed her single bag and Thomas drove her to the railway station.

"Soon," he said. "I'll see you soon."

"Don't come to the platform," she said. "That's just too hard. I'm going to go now. I'll call you when I get back."

"I'll see you soon," he said, again. "And we won't waste any more time apart."

"It'll be okay, Tom," she said. "They say that if you're going to get cancer these days, breast cancer is the one to get."

"Yes," said Thomas. "You really won the lottery on that one."

She laughed then, a real laugh.

"Bye, Tom," she said.

After she had gone, and he was negotiating the tight Kenilworth streets with their maddening one-way system, he switched on the radio to drown out his own thoughts. Paul Simon was singing about taking two bodies and twirling them into one, hearts and bones binding together. Inseparable.

The words of the song—the anguished, joyous, tragic, almost Shakespearean phrase—bounced around in Thomas's head so that he had to pull over and sit with his head down, until he could see to drive.

CHAPTER 69

Thomas had been planning to enter the Shakespeare Institute through the French windows at the back, but he was lucky, for once. A senior scholar was exiting just as he crossed the street. Thomas called to him to hold the door and dashed over.

He had been inside no more then twenty seconds when she arrived, bearing down on him like an elderly vulture in pince-nez and a floral print dress. Mrs. Covington, local historian and guardian of the institute's hallowed halls. For a moment he pretended he hadn't seen her and studied a sign-up sheet for a minibus trip to the neighboring Warwick Castle. Among the names of the conference delegates on the list were Katrina Barker and Randall Dagenhart.

"May I help . . . ?" Mrs. Covington began. "Ah," she concluded, recognizing him.

"Hi," said Thomas, inadequately.

"The American gentleman who suggested that I did not wish to share the *mysteries of literary scholarship with the great unwashed.*"

"You remembered," he said, beaming. "I'm flattered."

"You shouldn't be," she said, staring down her beaklike nose at him from heavily lidded eyes. "That excursion is for conference delegates only."

A few days earlier, Thomas would have found this maddening, but Kumi's visit had eased his mind or—at the very least—reset his priorities.

"Yes, I see that," Thomas said, "and I'd hate to negatively impact your day, so let's get through this as quickly as possible, shall we?"

"The castle tour is out of the question, I'm afraid, and if

you want to sit in on a seminar, you'll need a pass or a *friend* who will chaperone you."

"Because not having a pass means I'm probably here to torch the place," Thomas said, still smiling.

"People who use *impact* as a verb are capable of anything," she remarked. "And the word is naturally trochaic, not iambic: IMpact, not imPACT."

He laughed then, because it was the kind of thing he might have said in class.

"That's good, Mrs. Covington," he said. "But here's the thing. I don't actually need to get into the institute, and I'm all castled out."

Her face clouded.

"Then what are you doing here? I'm not running messages to your acquaintances like some lackey . . ."

"No," he said. "Of course not. I actually came to see you."

That stopped her. She stared at him, her mouth open, speechless, and for the briefest of moments she looked like a completely different person.

"Me?" she said.

"How long have you worked here, Mrs. Covington?"

"Thirty-five years in October," she said, proud of the fact.

"Could I buy you a cup of tea?" Thomas said. "I'd like to ask you a couple of questions. Think of it as local history."

Stratford was crawling with tearooms. Mrs. Covington selected Benson's on Bard Walk and stalked there. She was tall and angular and there was something mechanical about her movements, but the woman had a sharpness and vigor that Thomas couldn't help liking. Even so, he sensed that she felt at sea in this new relationship, and there was a wariness about her that she was clearly unused to.

"I'm not a gossip, Mr. Knight," she said, as soon as she had ordered her pot of Earl Grey and a scone.

"I never thought you would be," Thomas answered, honestly. "And besides, my first question is about the distant past, not the recent."

She eyed him, saying nothing.

"Hamstead Marshall House," he said. "It was a little south of here in west Berkshire, near Newberry."

"Hamstead Marshall *Park*," she said. "Yes, I know it. Burned down in 1718, I believe. It was actually a series of houses. One of the latest incarnations was a Tudor manor built for Thomas Parry that was probably destroyed during the civil war, like Kenilworth Castle. Another house was built on the estate in the late seventeenth century by the Earl of Craven. He modeled it on Heidelberg Castle as a gift for the exiled Queen of Bohemia, Elizabeth, with whom he had fallen in love, but she died before the house was built. It burned down shortly thereafter. The family moved to Benham Park, and the Hamstead Marshall site has been derelict ever since."

Thomas gazed at her. The woman was an encyclopedia.

"Mrs. Covington," he said, "you're a marvel."

She colored, muttering about having had an "interest in such things since girlhood."

"But to be able to carry all that around in your head!" Thomas exclaimed. "Most academics would kill for that kind of memory."

"You sound like Professor Dagenhart," she said, waving the compliment away. "I've been telling him stories like this for thirty years and he never stops treating me like the Delphic oracle. When you live in a place all your life, you know it, and that's all there is to it. And reading, of course. One doesn't have to be a professor to like books."

"I was a student of Dagenhart's," said Thomas. "In Boston."

"Were you indeed?" she said, looking him up and down as if she had never seen him before.

"I didn't know him well, and he was constantly disappearing to come here."

"Every summer," she nodded. "He's become something of an institution himself. First person I ever knew with a laptop computer. He has a newer model now, but he leaves it in the institute's reading room constantly, usually switched on.

Doesn't seem to worry about it being stolen. I can't decide if I think him admirably principled or woefully misguided. I hate to say it, and I know it sounds like mindless sentimentality, but I think the world as a whole is a sight more wicked than it was when I was young."

"How does Professor Dagenhart know Elsbeth Church?"

For a second she looked baffled. Then it came to her.

"Oh, the novelist! Yes, he would, wouldn't he? Through Daniella, I suppose."

"Blackstone?" said Thomas, surprised.

"Oh, yes," she said breezily. "They knew each other for years."

"Intimately?"

"Mr. Knight, I told you I was no gossip. I thought you wanted to hear about Hamstead Marshall Park."

"Yes," said Thomas, adjusting. "Could the place be considered a *shrine* of some kind?"

"In what sense?" she said, brisk and hawklike again.

"I don't know," said Thomas, trying to find the words. "Is there something about its history that might inspire—I don't know—nostalgia, devotion, strong personal feeling of some kind?"

"I suppose the story of the earl and his love might be that," she said, "and there is the legend about the Tudor house, though there's probably nothing to it."

"What legend?"

"It's completely unverifiable, and is probably a local version of a story from elsewhere . . ."

"Your interest in historical accuracy has been duly noted," said Thomas. "What's the legend?"

CHAPTER 70

Mrs. Covington leaned forward and her eyes grew brighter. It wasn't just that she was flattered by his interest, she was thrilled by the prospect of telling the story itself.

"I said that the Tudor manor was built for Thomas Parry," she began. "It is said that the gift of the estate was made by Queen Elizabeth herself and was, perhaps, a very particular kind of reward. Elizabeth, as you know, made much of her status as the Virgin Queen. It was a useful political image that drew on Greek and Roman mythology—Artemis and Diana, goddesses of the moon—and, most importantly, on the iconography of Catholicism. The country was nominally Protestant, but that was a very recent change, and even for those who embraced the new religion there was a lot about the old that they missed. So Elizabeth made herself a kind of royal Virgin Mary. In doing so she neatly tied her secular authority to the divine in a way that protected her from a lot of complaints from subjects who would prefer to be ruled by a man.

"Of course, the issue of her virginity was also very much about her refusal to give up England to a foreign power. If she married, the kingdom would become property of her husband, and with England at war with every Catholic power in Europe, that could spell disaster. So you can imagine how much damage could have been done if it got out that she was not actually a virgin at all, that she had, in fact, already had a child."

Thomas stared at her, feeling the tension and excitement of her narrative.

"Now Hamstead Marshall Park had been given to Elizabeth by her brother Edward the Sixth in 1550. When her

Catholic sister Mary was on the throne, Elizabeth was kept under house arrest at Hatfield House and at Bisham Abbey—close to Hamstead Marshall—where Thomas Hoby, the great translator, lived. This was in the mid-1550s. The story goes that one night, an elderly midwife was woken from her bed in London, put in a coach, and driven out to Hamstead Marshall. There she was instructed by a mysterious lord to minister to a young gentlewoman who was in labor. A fire was built in the hearth, and the midwife was supplied with the tools of her trade and commanded to ensure that nothing befell the mother. You must recall, of course, how many women died in childbirth in those days, often because of some hemorrhage that those attending could not stop. But in this case, the young woman came through her ordeal satisfactorily and the midwife was pleased to deliver a healthy baby girl."

Mrs. Covington then leaned in, and her eyes widened.

"It was at this point that the midwife was ordered by the nameless lord to hurl the infant into the fire!"

Thomas listened, his eyes on the old woman's.

"Did she?" he asked.

"She had no choice. Weeping, she allowed the child to be burned before her eyes. When it was done, she was given a goblet of wine to steady her nerves, and sent back to London, charged to say nothing to anyone. A few days later, she was dead—poisoned, of course—but not before she had whispered to others that the young mother had been none other than the Princess Elizabeth."

She held Thomas's eyes, then sat back again and sipped her tea, gratified by his response.

"But you think it's not true?" he said, breaking the tension.

"There are problems with the dates," she said, clinical again. "If Elizabeth got pregnant before she ascended the throne, the father was most likely High Admiral Sir Thomas Seymour, uncle to the boy king Edward. This was rumored extensively, and there are documents to suggest that the matter was seriously investigated and that there was at the very least some truth to the stories. But Seymour had fallen from grace and was executed in 1549. So if the story is true, it must have taken place *before* Elizabeth was given the house, before she was placed under guard at her sister's orders. It's not out of the question, because the house had belonged to her step-mother, Catherine Parr, so she could have stayed there, but I fear we will never know. Still," she added, leaning forward again and grinning so broadly that her entire face was glee-fully altered, "it's a *scrumptious* story, wouldn't you say?"

"I would," said Thomas, thoughtful now. "I would indeed."

Thomas walked her back to the institute and they hesitated outside.

"Thank you for tea," said Mrs. Covington.

"My pleasure," said Thomas.

"I'm afraid I may have misjudged you, Mr. Knight," she said.

"That happens." He smiled.

Mrs. Covington turned her key in the lock and pushed the door open. Two men were talking just inside the doorway.

"Five o' clock tomorrow, Professor," said one of them. "Don't keep me waiting."

The other man turned on his heel, head down, and moving fast. Mrs. Covington adjusted awkwardly and Thomas reached up to steady her, but even so they were nearly sent sprawling down the steps as the man pushed past.

He did not apologize or pause to look back, but they had already seen his ashen face as he barreled through, and even if they hadn't, Thomas would have recognized the incongru-ous pairing of tweed suit and laptop case.

"Perhaps Professor Dagenhart senses I was talking about him," she remarked ruefully, watching his back.

"Maybe he just heard a paper by an Oxfordian," Thomas replied.

"Excuse me," said the other man as he also tried to get by.

Thomas and Mrs. Covington stepped aside, and the man passed between them, turning to give Thomas a level, unread-able look. It was Daniella Blackstone's steward.

CHAPTER 71

As soon as Mrs. Covington left, Thomas returned his gaze to where the steward had been. He was still watching him walk calmly away when someone beside him forced a cough. Thomas turned to find Julia's scowling graduate student loitering beside him, looking nervous.

"You have a moment?" said Chad.

Thomas considered him. He seemed abashed, surly as ever, but chastened somehow.

"What's on your mind?" said Thomas.

"I just wanted to clear up what I said before."

"About Julia respecting your work too much?"

He winced at the words.

"Yeah. I didn't mean anything by it."

"So you said."

"I just didn't want you to think . . ."

"What?"

"That, I don't know . . ."

"Chad, when we first met at the Drake in Chicago, you were polishing a paper you were going to deliver the following day."

"Yeah. So?"

"Julia—Professor McBride . . ."

"I call her Julia too."

"Right. Of course. So Julia was overseeing your revisions. What form did those revisions take?"

"Just polishing," he said, cagey. "It was too long. Stuff had to come out."

"What stuff?"

"Some stuff on early modern servant clothing. Livery and stuff."

"Why that specifically?"

He hesitated.

"It just didn't fit."

"You'd been researching that subject with her? Under her guidance, I mean?"

"Yeah," he said, switching tack and coloring a little. "But that was really her work. I was just a kind of assistant. I shouldn't have been putting that stuff in my own paper."

"Right. I see."

"So," he said. "Let's just forget it, all right?"

"All right."

The graduate student was sloping off when Thomas stopped him.

"Chad?"

"What?"

"Does Angela know about this?"

Chad's face clouded and he took a step up to Thomas.

"Yes, but I don't want you to talk about it with her."

"Why not?"

"She and I are . . . it's complicated. We're close, all right? Angela really respects Julia's work, but . . ."

"But what?"

"Angela is just a bit protective of me sometimes. Okay? That's all."

"Okay," said Thomas.

"Okay."

Chad smiled, but there was still something hunted in his eyes, and Thomas could tell that things were far from okay.

CHAPTER 72

Thomas walked down to the river again to think, but he couldn't come to any hard conclusions about Chad or about why Daniella Blackstone's steward was meeting with Randall Dagenhart. He had ideas about both, but they were vague and based on little more than instinct. His thoughts got no clearer as he walked, and he found the town distracting.

He couldn't decide what he thought of Stratford. It was quaint, and its famous son guaranteed a cultural and intellectual life disproportionate to a town of its size, but there were times when it felt a bit like Epcot. If you sat by the Gower Memorial, you could watch the tourists, bused in on luxury coaches for their allotted half day, snapping digital pictures of thatched cottages and swans under the willows. Few of them made it inside the theaters, and though they processed around the Birthplace and Holy Trinity, he wondered if they were secretly wishing they were in the Rock and Roll Hall of Fame. At least then the carefully preserved artifacts, the history enshrined therein, would mean something, would connect to things they knew, things that mattered to their lives.

Snob, he thought.

But that wasn't what he meant. He wasn't saying Shakespeare was beyond them, or was necessarily better than the Beatles or XTC. Popular art probably had more in common with what Shakespeare had meant in his own time than all this carefully preserved history with its high-culture gloss. But it was odd, these people filing dutifully through, instinctively bowing their heads to an idea of literature and theater that was probably quite alien to their own experience. He imagined that Stratford was, for them, a bit like being in church, where only the fanatics don't shift between contented faith and doubtful unease, where your energy goes not into communing with the divine but into standing up at the right time, remembering the right words and not yelling at the idiotic sermon.

But then you don't really know that, do you? You don't know what goes on in the heads of the other worshippers, and you don't know what connection to Shakespeare these hordes of camera-wielding tourists have. They might be teachers like you, spending their carefully monitored savings for this pilgrimage. They might be community theater types, or—for that matter—lawyers, laborers, or lobbyists who love literature, or theater. They might carry Shakespeare around in their heads, dimly remembered from high school years ago when their class had put on some scenes from Julius Caesar, *led by a National Guardsman . . .*

Okay, Thomas thought. *Enough.*

He turned to shake off the idea and found himself looking into the face of the old man in the felt suit.

"Good morrow, cousin," said the old man, smiling.

"Is the day so young?" said Thomas, reflexively.

"But new struck nine," said the old man.

Thomas smiled appreciatively, but he couldn't remember any more.

"I don't know how you remember all those lines," he said. "The tourists must love it."

"To be or not to be, that is the question," said the old man, nodding thoughtfully. "Whether 'tis nobler in the mind . . ."

"Do you have to memorize them deliberately, or did you just, you know, *absorb* them over the years?" Thomas said.

"And my poor Fool is hanged," said the old man, and now the smile was gone. "No, no, no, life. Why should a dog, a horse, a rat have life, and thou no breath at all?"

"Yes," said Thomas, wanting to be gone. "*King Lear*. Did you see the show at . . . ?"

"I am dying, Egypt, dying. Only I here importune death awhile, until of many thousand kisses the poor last I lay upon thy lips."

Thomas said nothing. The old man barely seemed to see

him. He was staring through him, his eyes full of tears, and Thomas knew that what he had taken for a routine to please the tourists was in fact a kind of madness.

"I'm going to go now," he said.

"So out went the candle and we were left darkling."

"Okay," Thomas said, backing away. "Sorry. Bye."

"Here's the smell of blood still. All the perfumes of Arabia will not sweeten this little hand."

Thomas fled.

He walked straight up Waterside to the Warwick Road, moving briskly, trying to get as far from the old man, the tourists, and the theaters as possible. When he reached St. Gregory's Road, he stopped on the corner and stood quite still, his eyes closed.

He needed to go home. He would like to solve it all, of course, but mostly he would like to go home and find Kumi waiting for him there. He no longer cared if he ever found the stupid play, and the idea that it might find its way into the crazy ramblings of the old man in the memorial gardens lodged like a stone in his gut.

CHAPTER 73

Back at his hotel, Thomas found a phone message waiting for him. "Have a spare ticket for *Twelfth Night* tonight. Join me? Taylor."

They met a half hour before curtain outside the Courtyard Theatre, which was the RSC's main space while the Memorial Theatre was being rebuilt. It was a nondescript warehouse of a building on the outside but lavish enough within, with a deep and broad thrust stage that pushed the action right into the audience.

It was a beautiful production, full of melancholy yearning and frustrated desire. Viola got her Orsino in the end, and Olivia got Sebastian, but both seemed a little uncertain as to how things would go from there. Antonio was abandoned, Sir Andrew rejected, and Malvolio left to fume about future vengeances. Sir Toby married Maria resignedly, and she him out of a desperate impulse to improve her social station. In doing so she cast off Feste, the fool, who lamented the way of the world in his final song, a bleak and haunting rendition of "The rain it raineth every day."

The audience leaped to their feet at the end, the applause shaking the Courtyard's rafters, and Thomas stood with them.

"You okay, man?" said Taylor.

They were in the Dirty Duck again, this time huddled in a quiet corner.

Thomas nodded and reached for his pint.

"It was a good show," said Taylor. "Happy and sad at the same time. Poignant." He was thinking aloud, organizing his ideas by speaking them. "I wonder what the conference crowd will make of it. If they come in here, Petersohn and company. I mean, can we get out of here? If he starts talking Lacan and Derrida, I swear I'll hit him. You ever think these people make lousy audiences? That they are so invested in seeing their *reading* of the play up there on stage that they don't understand theater as well as regular people? Lacan and Derrida! God help us. You sure you're okay?"

"Kumi has breast cancer," said Thomas.

Taylor stared at him, his mouth open.

"Kumi?"

"Cancer," Thomas said. It was still an effort to say the word, like he had to get it out it before it could turn, snapping at him, but Kumi said he had to say it, that the only way to get past it was to use the word like you might say *table* or *Shakespeare*. Then you weren't afraid of it.

"I'm sorry," said Taylor. "Is she . . . How is she doing?"

"Pretty good, considering. She's had the surgery. Seemed to go okay. Next is radiation."

Taylor was still staring at him.

"She was just here. I told her I'd seen you and she asked about you," said Thomas. "Talked about *Gammer Gurton's Needle*. Remember that?"

"Ah yes," said Taylor. "The joys of academic drama . . . You okay?"

"Sorry," said Thomas. "I guess that show, *Twelfth Night*, I mean . . . Love and death, right? That's what Shakespeare is always about. And time. Which amounts to the same thing."

"Loss," said Taylor, the word sounding like a bell in his mouth. "I think it's about loss. Loss, and the fear of loss, which is almost as bad."

For a moment they sat there in silence, staring at their drinks.

"You look like a study for a Rodin sculpture," said a woman looming over them.

"I'm sorry?" said Thomas, looking up.

"*The Thinker*, double version," said Katrina Barker.

"You have a knack for catching me unawares," said Thomas.

"It's my one true skill," she said, smiling.

"I think a lot of people in this town would think otherwise. You know Taylor Bradley? We were in graduate school together."

She shook his hand and nodded. Taylor looked like he was being introduced to the queen, all self-consciousness, admiration, and a little terror.

"And where are you now, Taylor?"

"Oh, I teach at Hattie Jacobs College in Ohio," he said. "Small liberal arts school."

Barker nodded, but clearly didn't know it.

"You just came from the show?" she said. "You look like you did. I thought it was marvelous, didn't you?"

"Yes," said Thomas, pleased by her response. "I did. We were just saying how much we liked it."

"Well, *liked* isn't really the word, is it?" Taylor inserted. "How much we were struck by it. I thought they executed the power dynamics of the households particularly well, didn't you? Olivia's house was quite the little panopticon, with Malvolio modeling the kind of authority he didn't really have."

Thomas gave him a look. Taylor was trying too hard.

"I loved those curtains," she said. "All that rich blue swag. Marvelous."

Thomas nodded.

"I thought they offered a commentary on logocentricism and masculinity," said Taylor.

Katrina Barker looked at him, trying to unpack this baffling remark, and Thomas cut in.

"Care to join us?"

"Thank you," she said, sitting. "But only for a moment. I'm waiting for some friends."

Taylor was gazing at her, flushed.

"I just had the most remarkable encounter," she said. "There's an old gentleman in Stratford, a former scholar, I believe, and something of a prodigy in his day. He suffered a stroke quite early in life and now has a kind of aphasia. He speaks solely in quotations from Shakespeare."

"I met him," said Thomas, unnerved by the memory.

"I've seen him around before," she said. "Heard about

him. But today was the first time I actually spoke to him. It was really rather distressing. I spent half the afternoon wandering around town to get it out of my head."

Thomas nodded. Suddenly she seemed quite upset.

"It's a terrible thing," she said. "Like Alzheimer's, I suppose. Loss of memory, of a sense of who you are, reduced to babbling someone else's words like that. Really terrible. And scary. I mean, what if that happens to me? What if it's already happened?"

"Already happened?" said Taylor.

He was inserting himself into the conversation to remind her he was still there, but he also looked uncomfortable, like he needed to go to the bathroom but didn't want to leave.

"Sometimes I feel like it has. That I know what I want to say—in my writing, I mean—but I have to say it through him: Will. For me, it's probably not Will himself, but the words of the field we've built around him. I wonder about our profession sometimes. Do you feel sorry not to be in it, or do you think you escaped, before it sucked you in, force-fed you with its words?"

"Both, I guess," said Thomas.

Taylor got up.

"Excuse me a moment," he said. As he walked away, he looked back at Thomas and mouthed, *Keep her here*.

Barker seemed to sense the gesture and turned to watch him go.

"An earnest young man," she pronounced.

"A little intimidated by you, probably," said Thomas.

"Unlike you."

"No, I am intimidated by your intelligence and your work, but I'm not an academic, so it doesn't matter if I make a fool of myself."

" 'Those wits, that think they have thee, do very oft prove fools,' " she said, quoting from *Twelfth Night*, " 'and I, that am sure I lack thee, may pass for a wise man.' Do you think that old gentleman is saying something when he quotes like that, that he's expressing himself somehow? Or is it just words? Sounds he learned by rote?"

"I'm not sure."

"I don't know which would be worse. If he was just babbling or if there was a method . . ."

". . . to his madness," Thomas completed.

"God," she said. "I'm doing it already. So are you."

"I feel like I've been doing it constantly for weeks," said Thomas. "Every second thought I have seems to come as a quotation from Shakespeare. At first it was fun. I thought it made me sophisticated and profound. Now it's annoying and—I don't know—limiting, depressing, like every idea I've had has been had before. Not too long ago I was running for my life through the ruins of Kenilworth Castle, and all I could think about were lines from Henry the goddamned Fifth."

She raised her eyebrows, then leaned into him suddenly and her penetrating eyes fixed him.

"What were you thinking about before?" she said. "There's something going on with you," she said, giving him a shrewd look. "I'm not sure what, but you don't quite fit in, and not because you aren't a college professor. I saw you talking to Mrs. Covington, which is a triumph of itself. Most of the Shakespeareans walk right past her, assuming, wrongly as it turns out, that she is somehow beneath them."

"Professor Barker . . . ," he began.

"Katy."

"Katy," said Thomas.

"Just don't call me that in front of your friend. He may have a heart attack."

"Did you know Daniella Blackstone?" said Thomas.

"Ah," she said. She sat back then and looked at him. "I wondered if that was it. Randall has been positively jumpy ever since he saw you in Chicago. I met her once or twice, but no, I didn't know her, and I really don't know much about her. She had strange eyes: different colors, I mean. One was almost purple. It was quite unnerving to look at her, though I think some people—men—found it . . . arresting."

"Did you know Randall's—Professor Dagenhart's—wife?"

"Not well," she said. "No one did. I hate to speak ill of the dead, but she was a difficult woman. Randall said it was the illness. Maybe it was. But she was a bitter person. One of those invalids who resent the healthy. Randall danced attendance on her every moment of every day for almost ten years, but all he got from her was scorn. It was painful to see. When she was finally so sick that she couldn't leave the house, I think everyone who knew them breathed a sigh of relief. Terrible really, but there it is. It was just too awful to see her and the way she treated him. You felt for her, of course. How could you not? But she was relentlessly cruel. And it was more than the sickness. It was as if she had secret knowledge about him that she used to keep him in line, a kind of constant emotional blackmail."

"About his relationship with Daniella?"

"Perhaps, though I always suspected there was something else. She loved to make dark hints in public around him. It was her only pleasure. By the time she died—about six years ago—Randall was so broken by the endless servitude and humiliation that he never recovered."

"And you've no idea what it was that she held over him?"

She shook her head slowly.

"We're not that close outside professional gatherings. If you want my hunch, I'd say that it involved Daniella Blackstone and that it went back a long way."

"Hundreds of years," said Thomas, "or about a quarter century?"

"I'm not sure, but Randall and she were connected on some deep level, the kind of level that only time can build. History, Mr. Knight. That's what it is about. But what time builds it also destroys."

"Cormorant devouring time," Thomas quoted reflexively from *Love's Labour's Lost*.

"See," she said. "You're doing it too."

CHAPTER 74

First thing the following morning, Thomas called Kumi, then Constable Robson from his hotel. Kumi was back in Tokyo and looking forward to a night's rest before beginning radiation first thing the following day. She would then, contrary to Thomas's protests, go to work.

"If it's too tiring or painful," she said, "I won't go. But I have work to do. So."

"You should rest," Thomas said.

"See, Tom," she said, not unkindly, "this is why you shouldn't come. What I need right now is something like normalcy."

"That's what Deborah said," he said.

They talked about her flight, and the *Twelfth Night* production he had seen.

"I wish I could have been there with you," she said, as he struggled to convey why he had liked it.

"Me too," he said.

An hour later Thomas was sitting with Constable Robson in the Kenilworth police station, a worn manila file on the desk between them.

"You think someone wants to keep the play buried because of something in it?" Robson said. "Like what?"

"I've no idea."

"Something big, right? Something that would turn scholarship on its head. So what are the options?"

"Well, there are a lot of controversies tied to Shakespeare's biography, like whether he was a Catholic, whether he was gay—or whatever the sixteenth-century equivalent was—the extent to which he supported the monarchy, and so on. Any of them could be a big deal in academic circles if they were proved, but I find it hard to believe that the play could do that: not definitively, not enough to kill for."

"But if some scholar was really invested in the idea that Shakespeare was a Catholic, say, wouldn't the wheels come off his career if a new play proved he wasn't? Or what if someone didn't like queer . . ." He caught himself. "*Homosexuals*. But the play proved Shakespeare was one. If you're crazy enough, isn't that a motive to keep it hidden away, so the image of the writer doesn't get . . . you know . . . *tarnished*?"

"But that's the thing, isn't it?" said Thomas. "I don't see how a single play could prove that, when the rest of his plays don't. Even if it was a strong statement one way or the other, it would still be just one piece of evidence to be weighed with the rest. I can't imagine any one play putting any of those controversies to bed completely."

"What if it proved that your man Shakespeare wasn't the author at all?" said Robson. "I read something in the paper about some actor saying that the plays were probably written by some lord . . ."

Thomas remembered Deborah's *West Wing* analogy and shook his head.

"Even if that were true," he said, "it wouldn't explain why an academic was trying to keep that information secret. Fifty years ago, Shakespeareans might have been card-carrying establishment types, but not anymore. Most academics think they're countercultural progressives socially, politically. Most Shakespeareans have little invested in the man from Stratford. Some of them don't even like his works that much. More would embrace any hard evidence challenging his identity as the playwright without batting an eyelid. It hasn't happened because there's no real evidence that William Shakespeare of Stratford didn't write the plays credited to him in his lifetime. I don't think the kind of evidence we'd get in a new play would change that at all."

Robson scowled.

"I don't know," he said. "If it turned out that all them plays were really written by the queen or something, I'd think that was a big deal."

"Maybe," Thomas conceded without really believing it. He wanted to change the subject. "What were the names of the girls who died in the fire with Alice Blackstone?" he asked.

Robson picked up the file on the desk and flipped it open.

"That I can tell you," he said. "The evidence room is full of boxes from this case. CID went over them a dozen times but got nothing they could use. From time to time someone starts poking around again, but they never get anywhere. If it happened now, we'd have CCTV and such, but then . . . Anyway, I don't think we'll ever throw the evidence away."

He paused and then said,

"Okay, Alice Blackstone, Philippa Adams, Elizabeth Jenkins, Deborah St. Clair, and Nicola Rogers," he read.

Pippa, Liz, Debs, and Nicki. The girls from the journal. The girls from the picture.

Thomas frowned and drummed his fingers on the table top.

"What exactly happened?" he said.

"It was the twentieth of July, 1982. The girls were in the school hall. It was six o'clock and everyone else was gone. They were working on some project or other. They had a slot in an upcoming school concert: a dance routine or something. We never found out the details. They used to meet in an old-fashioned coffeehouse called Bruno's. It's gone now: part of a dry cleaner's. Anyway, they usually went to Bruno's after school, but they were practicing this dance, or whatever it was, and stayed in the school hall. The fire started at the back of the building. We found accelerants—petrol, specifically—that had been used to start it. Some sort of Molotov cocktail, they thought: a bottle of petrol with a burning rag stuffed in the neck. We think it was thrown in through a window.

"The girls were all found in what they called a green room behind the main stage. We think they didn't know the building was on fire till it was completely ablaze, by which time, they couldn't get out."

"Was the main door to the school hall locked?"

"No," said Robson. "That was the maddening thing. If they had looked out a few minutes earlier and smelled the smoke, they would have been able to walk right out without a scratch. I mean, *a burn*, I suppose."

Robson, usually so amused and separate, looked rattled. He was remembering it all.

"There had been a few fires like this in the town earlier in the summer. All in abandoned buildings. Kids, we figured, with nothing better to do, getting their kicks. There weren't drugs in those days, you know? There was drunkenness and vandalism and random beatings, but . . . I don't know. Random destruction of property wasn't exactly common, but we kind of understood it, and if the truth were told, we probably weren't that good at providing kids with things to do. Still, the school fire was different."

"No one was hurt in the other fires?"

"Nope. And after this one, they stopped."

"You think it was the same arsonist in each case?"

"Well, there's the question," said Robson. "The first fires weren't considered as closely as they probably should have been, so the evidence was patchy, but I know some of the blokes who were on the case, and they thought no, it was different. For one thing, this was the only large, public building, the only one where there was even a possibility of people being inside."

"Was it considered deliberate," said Thomas, "I mean the deaths of the girls?"

"I don't see why it would have been. I don't even think whoever set the fire knew they were inside. And if he had wanted them dead, he would have locked them in. It was pure chance that they didn't step out—go to the bathroom or something—and see the fire while they could still, you know . . ."

"Get out," Thomas completed for him.

"Right."

"Were there any suspects?"

"No serious ones. We brought in the caretaker a few times because he should have been at work by the time the fire started, but the general feeling was that his only crime was laziness."

"Is he still in the area?"

"In a manner of speaking," said Robson. "He's buried here. Died about ten years ago. Poor bastard spent the rest of his life drunk. Felt guilty for not being around to get them out, I suppose. But no one ever thought he had set the fire."

"Can I see those names again?"

Robson showed him the list and he copied it down, feeling again the frustration he had when he had first heard them. He had been almost sure, but now . . .

Suddenly he got to his feet.

"Where's the nearest bookstore?" he said.

"There's a place called Browsers on Talisman Square."

By the time Robson had finished giving him the directions, Thomas was already on his way.

Thomas raced through the store, scanning the signs for MYSTERY, ROMANCE, and CRIME FICTION. He found them under THRILLER and snatched the first Blackstone and Church book he saw from the shelf. He tore open the cover and found the copyright page. In tiny print, under the phalanx of addresses and publisher information, he saw the © symbol. Beside it were the names of Daniella Blackstone and Elsbeth Adams.

Pippa Adams, he thought, his heart thumping.

Elsbeth Church wrote under a pen name that she had made official. Her real name was Adams and her daughter had burned to death with Alice Blackstone.

CHAPTER 75

Thomas called the Shakespeare Institute and got Mrs. Covington on the second double ring.

"Is Randall Dagenhart still signed up for that Warwick Castle trip?" he asked.

"He is," she said, "though I can't imagine why. It's become rather tacky of late."

"What time are they due back?"

"They aren't going till after lunch—two o'clock—so . . . Let me see," she said. "Yes, the minibus leaves the castle at six. Why?"

"Just curious," said Thomas.

He considered tailing the minibus in his car, but because he knew where they were going, that seemed pointless. Instead, he drove over to Warwick, parked in the castle lot, and paid the fairly exorbitant admission all before the scholars from the institute were due to leave. Thomas walked down the well-maintained path through lawns and shrubberies to the drawbridge and gatehouse, and into the castle proper.

Warwick Castle was about as different from the ruins of Kenilworth as could be imagined. There were no crumbling remains here, no patchy foundations and tumbled-down walls. The building had been fully restored, largely in the last century and a half, and though its walls and towers were impressive and showed what a medieval fortress may have actually looked like, Thomas preferred Kenilworth's romantic devastation. It didn't help that the castle was run by the Tussaud's waxwork group who, as well as pumping millions of dollars' worth of restoration funding into the castle, had also turned it into a theme park, complete with lifelike effigies of knights and squires, atmospheric sounds, and movie screenings. Souvenirs of one sort or another—plastic swords, catapult pencil sharpeners, and the like—were on sale everywhere he looked. There were people in costume herding tourists into the "ghost tower" (at an extra cost), and various displays were scheduled: jousting and archery, birds of prey, and the firing of a trebuchet across the river. Not surprisingly, the place was packed, particularly with school parties, many of them uniformed, all of them screaming.

Thomas was glad to have a reason not to do the tour, and found his way to what was called Guy's Tower—a fourteenth-century, five-story guard post north of the main entrance, accessed by a staircase from the battlements. He climbed the stairs up from the top of the walls slowly and, once at the top, stayed there.

The tower was massive, unassailable, a twelve-sided lookout that gave him an excellent vantage over both the inner courtyard and the grounds outside the walls. When the Shakespearean party arrived, he'd be able to watch them all the way down to the gatehouse.

They appeared a little before two thirty. There were eight or nine of them. He saw Dagenhart first, but Katy Barker was there too, as was Alonso Petersohn. There was no sign of Julia, but he was alarmed to see Taylor Bradley trailing the group, trying to be part of it. Thomas didn't want to be seen. Anyone in the group might recognize him, he supposed, particularly after his antics on the first day, but he would have to steer particularly clear of Taylor, who would spot him a mile away.

Thomas sat beneath the crenellated tower wall, braced against a chimney stack, and wondered whether he should go down. If any of them came up here, they would see him, but there was a lot to do in the castle, and the top of Guy's Tower was quite a stair climb. Taylor might be the only member of the group under forty.

Stay where you are, he decided.

So he did, and the time passed slowly. The group moved

as a unit, which made them a good deal easier to track. By three thirty they had seen the dungeon, what was (somewhat arbitrarily) called Caesar's Tower, and a film exhibit called "The Dream of Battle." They then moved on to the main block on the south side of the castle: the chapel, great hall, and staterooms. Thomas was getting restless. After forty minutes, he started to worry that he'd lost them, but at four thirty-five, they emerged and collected in a pool on the central lawn, as if mulling their options.

Five o'clock, the steward had said. Thomas watched, ignoring the kids who came clambering and shouting up the stairs, shooting imaginary arrows at their friends, turning away only when Katy Barker seemed to scan along the walls and then, as if walking the tower stairs with her eyes, moved up to his face at the top.

He ducked back and waited a minute, but when he checked back down, they were all still loitering there, talking. Petersohn was pointing, lecturing. Dagenhart checked his watch.

If he's meeting the steward somewhere in the castle, where would they go?

Somewhere quiet, private, away from the mass of tourists but a legitimate part of the site that wouldn't get them into trouble if they were caught there. Thomas checked his map, considered the possibilities, then looked back down.

The group had broken up.

He could just see Katy Barker entering a gift shop with a couple of the others—including, unsurprisingly, Taylor—in tow. Two graduate students were walking toward the "ghost tower," but the others were gone.

Thomas leaned over and looked hurriedly around the courtyard, but there was no sign of Randall Dagenhart. He turned to the curtain wall below and to his right and saw Alonso Petersohn coming up the steps toward him.

CHAPTER 76

Thomas thought fast. Petersohn might just stroll the walls, but having made the bulk of the climb, he would probably come the rest of the way, if only for the view. Thomas descended as quickly as he could. He burst out from the tower, down the external stairs, and onto the wall with his head lowered. Petersohn was ten yards ahead of him, still on the stairs to the courtyard, his eyes down on the worn stone steps.

To Thomas's right was a squared bulge in the battlements, an alcove giving vantage over attackers at the foot of the walls outside. Thomas stepped hurriedly into it, turned his back to Petersohn, and bent low as if peering through the great crossbow slit in the parapet.

He sensed Petersohn, wheezing slightly, behind him, but the scholar didn't pause and moved to the tower stairs. Thomas turned and descended quickly to the courtyard.

He was now at a significant disadvantage. The group had split, he didn't know where Dagenhart was, and any of them could see him as he hunted about. He doubted being seen would put him in any real danger, but it would certainly draw suspicion and would hamstring any attempt to learn anything from Dagenhart's proposed meeting.

The group had split in a little starburst and Dagenhart hadn't been with them, which meant he had gone in a different direction. Thomas gambled that he wouldn't have returned to a portion of the castle they had already seen, because that would look conspicuous, and that reduced the options to one: he had gone out, back through the gatehouse, and over the bridge.

Thomas began to trot, still with his head down, still close to the walls. Outside, by the ditch surrounding the castle's east face, a crowd of tourists had gathered to watch an archery display. Thomas scanned their faces then looked at his watch: ten minutes to five. The path snaked north, up to the main entrance, and south—by the sound of it—to the river. He turned south, furious with himself for having lost Dagenhart, knowing that he didn't know what was on this side of the building at all and that that could cost him.

The path dropped through trees, skirting the walls and Caesar's Tower, emerging suddenly beside the river Avon, broad and even farther downstream, but here tight and fast. Fragments of an ancient stone bridge lurched out of the river like the arches of a sea serpent, covered with grass and overhung with ivy. Downstream was a weir, and beside it a square Gothic building butting into the castle's lower embankment, where an iron waterwheel turned rapidly. The path led there.

Thomas stopped jogging and walked down to the building via a railed ramp that ran down to the water's edge and the great churning wheel. There was no one around. Thomas moved into the arched stone doorway and tried to hear above the sound of the mill mechanism. He could hear voices, one low and calm, the other loud and angry: Dagenhart. At first he couldn't make out the words, but then he heard the old professor quite clearly.

"Or what?" he shouted.

The other man—surely, the steward—responded, but Thomas couldn't catch any of it. He dared not lean in any closer. The sound of the mill and the echoing stone made it impossible to tell how close they were.

"I don't have that kind of money!" Dagenhart shouted.

The steward's response was louder, but no less clear.

For a moment there seemed to be silence, and then a different kind of sound, a scuffling, grunting, physical noise like a struggle.

Thomas stepped inside and followed the sound, past informational displays, whirring pumps, and other pieces of machinery. Part of the floor was cut away in one room so that the huge sprockets of the system were revealed. Thomas kept his distance. If there was to be some sort of confrontation, he didn't want to find himself falling into those grinding gears.

And then, quite suddenly, the sounds of fighting had stopped and he could hear voices again, low and breathless. Then footsteps, coming his way.

Thomas turned and ducked behind a great blue-green mechanism with a huge belt-driven wheel that looked like a generator. He squatted down, flattening himself against the mechanism, as first one set of feet, then another stormed past and out: first the steward, stuffing paper into his pockets distractedly, then Dagenhart, slower, winded. Thomas waited for a second and then started to follow but stopped himself.

He moved to the room they had just left, which opened into a re-creation of the mill manager's office, complete with a stuffed and mounted fish and an archaic telephone. The mill might once have been for grinding grain, but more recently it had clearly been converted into a power generator.

On the floor in the corner was something that did not belong: a scrap of torn and crumpled paper. Thomas picked it up. It had words written on it in ballpoint pen: "shouldn't practice at . . ."

The words meant nothing, but he knew that writing, particularly the little circle over the *i* of *practice*: Alice Blackstone's diary, and though he couldn't be sure, he was prepared to bet that this fragment came from a page that had been cut from the rest of the journal.

That was what Dagenhart and the steward had been fighting over.

Thomas headed out the way he had come. Outside, he paused by the massive waterwheel to think, leaning against the rail beside a spoked iron ring that might control a valve somewhere. If he went after the steward now—assuming the steward still had the pages he had razored out of the journal—he would have to take them from him by force, something that would certainly land him in jail.

The thought had barely gone through his head when he realized what he was looking at. Below him, wet and clinging to a grate only inches from the waterwheel, was a page of closely written paper. He had no doubt what it was, or how the steward had dropped it as he stormed away.

He looked about him. The castle was ready to close and there was no one about. He threw one leg over the wooden barrier and dropped to the grate. He shrunk to his left to keep clear of the great metal wheel as it spun, turning the water in a fine spray. There was only a single wooden beam between him and the foaming river below.

Thomas crouched down and peeled the journal page off the timber and tried to read it. The ink had not bled much, but the paper itself was translucent and fragile. He bent to it, studying it, and only then became aware of a presence behind him, some movement half heard. Someone was there, standing behind him. He started to turn, but the kick still caught him off guard and off balance.

He fell forward through the square of light below the wooden rail and into the churning Avon.

CHAPTER 77

The kick had been little more than a push, so Thomas never lost consciousness, but the shock of hitting the water—the surprising cold of it—was so disorienting that it took a second for him to realize the true danger.

The wheel!

He felt the water turn him toward it, pulling him down. He fought it, but as he struck out with his arms, he felt the metal blades crash against his injured right shoulder. The pain was so violent, so intense, that he started to cry out, and his mouth filled with the musty coolness of the river. He tried to blow it out, but a second blade, then a third hit him, and he was being sucked down with the motion of the wheel, driven toward the riverbed.

He rolled against it, trying to surface, and the wheel edge slapped hard against his forehead, tipping him backward. For a moment everything was black, and then he was aware enough to feel his whole body stuck on the wheel as it rotated him deeper, chest and groin curved to the edge of the wheel as it turned him down. He was just awake enough to know that if there were rocks less than a couple of feet below it, he would be split upon them . . .

There weren't.

The wheel shoved him down and he pulled his arms in tight instinctively. If he got a hand or foot between the wheel and a support bracket, the force would slice it right off. So he went still, letting the mechanism drive him deeper and then kick him out the other side.

But a second later he was yanked out of the water and revolving up. His belt was snagged on a blade of the wheel. He looked up. Above was only sky, but if the wheel could take him up, it would take him over, and he remembered the bracing beam with the valve controller at the top. If he didn't get off, he was dead.

Belching water, he slammed both hands to his waist and fought to free himself. The wheel spun him higher. His fingers clawed at his belt buckle.

He was almost at the top, less than a second away . . .

The belt came free and he was falling back into the river. He tried to turn, to put his arms back to protect his head, but it all happened too fast. He landed with a heavy splash, sank deep enough for his left foot to graze a submerged rock, and then was up again in air and daylight.

As soon as he broke the surface, he twisted around to see the platform by the mill wheel, but whoever had kicked him was gone.

For a second he drifted out of sheer relief, and then swam to a reedy island where the river divided. He hauled himself onto a jagged stone, spat the last of the river from his mouth, and breathed. Then he sat up and opened his palm.

The page had torn some, but there was enough left to prove that he hadn't imagined what he had read.

"Third rehearsal and Debs still doesn't understand her lines . . ."

Thomas sat there, soaked and freezing, and didn't know whether to laugh or cry. The girls had not been preparing to do some dance routine. They may have been obsessed with pop music, but they considered themselves thinkers, sophisticates.

"*Didn't get to see Pippa today,*" Alice Blackstone had written. "*Had a good laugh with the gang, but Liz was having her hair done and couldn't come property shopping.*"

He had assumed that reference to "property" was adolescent pretension, a slang supposed to make their petty purchases mature. He was wrong. There was a little pretension there, perhaps, but only in the sense that they used the full word and not its more common abbreviation. They weren't buying property, they were buying *props*.

Alice and her best friend Pippa, along with Liz and Nicki

and Debs, had been rehearsing a play—a play with obscure wording—that Alice had found among her dead great-grandfather's things, a play by the world's foremost writer that no one had seen on stage for almost four hundred years.

CHAPTER 78

Thomas drove back to his hotel, his clothes sopping, his shoes sliding on his wet feet. He showered and changed. His right shoulder would bruise badly where the waterwheel had hit him, but the wound had not reopened. He had a matching bruise over his right eye, but things could have been much worse. He took more painkillers, replaced his sodden loafers with running shoes, and went straight back out to the car.

He wasn't happy about returning to Hamstead Marshall Park, but he knew that he was close now. He could sense it.

The weather was better than it had been the last time he had visited the absent manor house and there was no sign of Elsbeth Church skulking among the ruins, but the place still unnerved him. He parked by the church and wandered around through the graves before straying out into the ragged meadow that had once been the grounds of the great house. It was sunny, but the air was cold and there was dew in the grass, and an edge to the wind. It might rain yet.

He entered through the gateposts—a strange and unnecessary choice, given the openness of the land—and walked slowly toward the spot where he had seen the novelist at her most unearthly. There were still fragments of cut flowers, brown and faded in the grass, and Thomas couldn't help but think of Ophelia distributing herbs to the Danish court in her madness: *"There's rosemary. That's for remembrance . . ."*

It was a fitting enough association, he supposed, though Elsbeth Church was mourning her daughter, not her father. And Thomas was convinced that flowers weren't the only memorial Elsbeth tended here. There was something else. Something buried.

But there was no sign of recently dug earth. If the play had been interred here, the site had not been disturbed in a long time, and there was no way he was going to light on it by chance. Thomas muttered to himself as he combed the wild patch of ground, but there was nothing to see and the area within the vanished walls of the estate was just too large.

It was only a hunch to begin with, he reminded himself.

A part of Elsbeth saw the loss of her daughter in that (surely apocryphal) tale of Elizabeth's incinerated newborn, but now that he was here he doubted that this was the place where she and Daniella Blackstone would have chosen to hide the play their daughters had been rehearsing. Daniella had been extremely level-headed, and he doubted even Elsbeth would have seen this as a fitting place for the play. After all, Elsbeth's association with the old house had come about after—indeed because of—her daughter's death. It would have meant nothing to Pippa herself, and less to Alice, who did not live close by.

Then where?

Thomas stood there, listening to the rooks cawing in a distant oak, and he had no idea. If it had been put into some conventional storage—a safe-deposit box, say—official representatives of the Blackstone estate would surely have uncovered it. If so, the steward would have it. But that seemed impossible. And besides, other people were looking for it, and—if the episode in the Demier cellars was anything to go by—in pretty unconventional places. Thomas wasn't the only one who thought the little quarto had been concealed where someone else might find it.

But there was something else that made him think that the play wasn't simply in a locked drawer somewhere. The two novelists had fallen out immediately before Daniella had started whispering about the play to other people. Elsbeth now claimed no knowledge of the play, but the two women had worked together for years after the fire, intimately bound by loss and grief.

What could have disrupted that closeness?

Elsbeth said it was about money, but that seemed unlikely, unless money was only part of a larger issue. Blackstone had certainly been looking to profit from the play once it was clear that her solo career was going nowhere. Could that have been it from the start, the source of the tension between them? Had Daniella wanted to cash in on the value of the play and found Elsbeth defiantly adamant? If so, perhaps the original intent had been to keep the play secret as a kind of private memorial to their dead daughters.

Yes, thought Thomas, his stride quickening.

If they had pledged to keep the surviving manuscript to themselves in memory of their daughters, then Daniella's desire to go public with the text might have seemed like a violation of that promise and, by extension, a cheapening of Alice and Pippa's deaths. If so, the play would have been hidden somewhere symbolically fitting not to their deaths, but to their lives. The play would have been concealed somewhere the girls had valued, not somewhere linked by vague historical association to their deaths in the fire. He didn't know where it was, but Thomas was sure that he would never find *Love's Labour's Won* on the grounds of Hamstead Marshall Park, even with a fleet of industrial excavators at his disposal. He tried to remember what he had read in the diary, the places they had gone together, the things they had done, but all he could remember was a bunch of references to concert venues and something about "scouring" a horse. Perhaps Pippa's family owned a stable.

He stood quite still and looked out over the empty plot where the manor had once been, and he felt a sudden and unexpected sadness that made his breath catch. He thought of Elsbeth Church's pilgrimage to this spot, made almost daily for years, wondering how long after Pippa's death it had begun. He and Kumi had had only one viable pregnancy, which had failed to produce a child. The miscarriage had scarred them for life, had—for a time, at least—sent fissures through the base of their marriage till they had not been able to live on the same continent as each other. What the loss of a teenaged daughter would do to a person, he couldn't begin to imagine.

What about the loss of a wife?

The thought came gusting out of the chill air. It stopped him.

"She'll be okay," he countered, aloud.

He looked down at the earth with the cut and drying blossoms, and the thought he had been holding back since she had first told him about the treatment options finally broke through.

Yes, she could beat it. Lots of people do. But if not this, then something else. Sooner or later. Everything dies.

It was beyond obvious, but the fact was that he hadn't known till now. Not really. Not even when he had been lying on his kitchen floor with a bullet in his shoulder and his lungs filling with fluid. Not even then.

When she had first told him, something had started buzzing in his ears, something terrible and ordinary. For the first time, he knew what it was. It was the sound of a clock ticking off their remaining time together.

Love's not time's fool, he thought, *though rosy lips and cheeks within his bending sickle's compass come . . .*

But that wasn't true, was it? And when things die, everything about them is lost. They become unimaginable, as if they never really existed.

That was the worst.

"She'll be okay," he said.

He rubbed his bruised forehead, then took a breath of the cold air and felt it sear his lungs. He began stalking back toward the car, eyes focused like a blinkered horse, convinced he had to get out of this place, as if the air were infected.

CHAPTER 79

After the episode at Blackstone's, Thomas hardly needed to remind himself of the dangers of breaking and entering, but he was in no mood to play it safe as he pulled up in front of Elsbeth Church's stone cottage. Somewhere, in some dark, unreasoning place in his mind, something that worked by an obscure system of symbolic association instead of actual logic, he thought that if he could solve the mystery into which David Escolme had propelled him, it would somehow make other things better. He didn't dare think of Kumi's name in this context, because to make the vague assumption even that specific would make it absurd, but he thought it anyway.

But as a kid Thomas had dreamed up all kinds of absurd superstitions: that it would be a good day if he did not look back until he reached the bus stop, that three cardinals in the tree outside his house meant that his parents would get home early, that avoiding cracks in the sidewalk really kept his mother's back from breaking . . . or something. It was usually vague, privately gleeful, something he never discussed because he knew that to put it into words would make it stupid. Now a small, unreasoning part of him clung to the childish certainty that if he could get these wholly unconnected things *right*, then other things would follow suit. Unravel one set of knots—Escolme, Shakespeare, champagne—and the one he couldn't untie—Kumi—would somehow resolve itself. Stupid, he knew, but still . . .

So he rang Elsbeth Church's front door hoping that she would not be in.

She wasn't, which was a relief of several kinds, and he was able to move quickly around the back, looking for an open window, or a flimsy door. A coal hatch was too much to hope for, but there was no sign of an alarm system. The house across the street looked quiet and the curtains didn't twitch when he looked at it.

Now or never.

Thomas checked his wallet and fished out an expired MasterCard. He worked the corner of the plastic into the crack between the jamb and the back door. He had never tried this before, and wasn't sure what he was doing, but he pressed the card hard against the latch and was amazed at how easily it snapped free. He opened the door, heard no beeping or barking, and stepped inside.

He smelled it instantly, that aroma of damp earth and leaves, and something muskier underneath it, something animal. It made the hairs on the back of his neck prickle.

He was in a stone-flagged kitchen that looked like it hadn't been upgraded since the turn of the last century. It was clean but spartan, boasting no implement that postdated the Second World War. Ancient iron cookware and heavy knives were laid out on a scrubbed stone counter. Thomas turned and flinched as he brushed up against something that shifted, something that seemed to generate that outdoors scent, but underwritten with a darker note: blood.

He flinched away before realizing what it was.

From a ceiling rack hung two gutted rabbits, head, eyes, and fur intact.

Thomas backed away from them, steadying his nerves with an effort.

He moved quickly from room to room, and the smell followed him. Every room was the same, swept and dustless spaces without character. They were like those rooms in castles, uneven plaster walls and open wood or stone floors with a few hulking pieces of rough-hewn furniture. There were no pictures on the walls, no drapes, no paint other than the default whitewash, no TV, no couch, no shades on the lightbulbs, no carpet, no sound system of any kind. It could have been a house from four hundred years ago, except that Thomas would have expected the period to somehow stamp itself on the place: a piece of tapestry, an obsolete tool, an inkwell . . . Something. This place had no period, no context. It was a space in time.

All but two rooms.

One was where Elsbeth wrote. It was still spare but there was an absolutely modern computer sitting silently on the desk, and there was a *Concise English Dictionary* beside it. On a pine shelf was a complete Shakespeare and a set of her own books. Nothing by anyone else.

The other fully furnished room was upstairs. It was unlocked. As soon as he stepped inside, Thomas was sure that this was Pippa Church's—or rather Pippa Adams's—room, but it couldn't have been further from Alice Blackstone's. The shock of it rooted Thomas to the spot. For a long moment, all he could do was stare, gazing around the walls in horror.

The room was papered with details of the school fire. There were newspaper cuttings circled and underlined in red. There were grainy, faded pictures of the funeral, stoic mourners in black and stunned locals with out-of-fashion raincoats and umbrellas. There was a photocopied blueprint of the school hall, with red felt-pen arrows indicating, Thomas assumed, the path of the flames. There were evidence memos tacked up, crime scene pictures, even a pathology report that talked in terrible, clinical terms about "smoke inhalation" and "extensive postmortem burns." Only one thing tied the room to Alice's. Over the coverless bed was the same XTC album cover, the white horse outlined against green.

Thomas left.

In thirty seconds, he was down the stairs, through the rancid kitchen, and out, sucking in the cool, misty air and fighting the impulse to throw up.

But standing out there beneath a vast horse chestnut, Thomas knew he had seen something, that the visit hadn't merely been a violation of Church's terrible monument to her daughter's death. The pictures of the funeral had shown the childless parents as a confused huddle, as if segregated from the others by grief. At the edge of that group, not quite of it, but somehow in it, was a quarter-century-younger Randall Dagenhart.

He felt a rush of exultation. His hunch had been right, and he had managed to prove it without climbing out windows and over rooftops like some overgrown chimp . . .

Thomas started to turn exactly as the hand clapped his shoulder. He flinched, but the hand was heavy and its grip was firm. He heard the voice before he saw the man:

"All right there, son?"

He was a large man—his shoulders looked a yard apart—and he had short red hair and pale eyes. He was wearing a black jersey and a peaked cap with a black-and-white diced band around the headband.

A policeman. There was another behind him.

"What?" said Thomas, half feigned innocence, half genuine surprise.

"Neighbor reported a strange car," said the policeman. "Is that your house, sir?"

"Er, no," said Thomas, looking past them to the house over the road where the net curtains were now being held open.

"Can you tell me what you're doing here?"

"I was just . . ."

Thomas's mind went blank.

"I was passing," he said.

"Were you passing *through* the house?" said the policeman. "Only I just saw you come out."

"Sorry," said Thomas, "I was hoping Miss Church would be in, but . . ."

"I'm afraid you're nicked, mate," he said, smiling as if at a private joke.

"I'm sorry," Thomas began. "*Nicked* . . . ?"

But the policeman cut him off in measured, no-nonsense terms, and he wasn't smiling anymore.

"I'm arresting you for suspected burglary. You do not have to say anything, but it may harm your defense if you do not mention, when questioned, something that you later rely on in court. Anything you do say may be given in evidence. Please step this way."

PART IV

When I consider every thing that grows
Holds in perfection but a little moment,
That this huge stage presenteth nought but shows
Whereon the stars in secret influence comment;
When I perceive that men as plants increase,
Cheered and checked even by the self-same sky,
Vaunt in their youthful sap, at height decrease,
And wear their brave state out of memory;
Then the conceit of this inconstant stay
Sets you most rich in youth before my sight,
Where wasteful Time debateth with Decay,
To change your day of youth to sullied night;
    And all in war with Time for love of you,
    As he takes from you, I engraft you new.

—Shakespeare, "Sonnet 15"

CHAPTER 80

Thomas was walked to an inappropriately cheery "panda" car—white with borders of blue and white checks but slashed with luminous yellow and red—handcuffed to the second officer, and given a seat in the back. It was a small car, a toy by American standards, but the situation more than made up for that. Thomas was in trouble.

As they drove the rural roads to the Newbury police station, Thomas tried to figure out just how much trouble. In any circumstances, an arrest was bad news, but in a foreign country, he thought, it could be devastating. He knew he wouldn't be tortured or beaten in an English cell, or thrown into prison indefinitely, but he suspected he had just walked into difficulties of another kind, difficulties that were likely to cost him money and dignity at the very least.

And time. How long would it take to straighten this all out? Days? Weeks?

God, he thought, *what a screwup.*

"Listen," he said, "I really didn't do anything. I know Miss Church. I talked to her just the other day. This is crazy . . ."

But the two policemen said nothing, and though a part of him wanted to laugh off the absurdity of the thing, the surreal feel of it all was starting to settle like lead in his gut. As they approached the station—a nondescript brick building as unassuming as the car—and the road swelled with houses, shops, and traffic, Thomas found himself huddling lower in the seat, staring ahead to avoid the eyes of the people they passed. A woman with a blue plastic stroller gave them a long look as they stopped at a traffic light, and Thomas looked down, feeling stupid and humiliated.

Inside, the custody sergeant listened to the account of the arrest, then asked for his name.

"What was that, sir?"

"Knight," said Thomas, conscious that he was muttering. "Thomas Knight."

"And I'll need some form of identification."

Thomas fished in his pockets and drew out wallet and passport.

"A visitor from overseas?" said the sergeant, pleasantly, as if Thomas were clearing customs at Gatwick. The red-haired officer who had arrested him gave him a long look.

"If you will just empty your pockets," said the custody sergeant, "remove all jewelry, your belt, and your shoelaces, then you can step through there."

Thomas stared at him.

"I really didn't do anything," he said. "I just wanted to see if . . ."

"Your belt, please, sir."

Thomas was in a daze. His fingers didn't work properly. He had to focus on them as they unfastened the belt buckle, watching them as if they belonged to someone else.

"And your shoelaces, please, sir."

"That really isn't necessary," Thomas began.

"I'm afraid it is, sir."

Thomas's gaze faltered and shifted.

This can't be happening.

"I'm going to check your pockets now, sir."

He did so.

"You are entitled to call your consulate prior to your interview if you wish."

Thomas shook his head quickly. He wasn't sure why, but he didn't want to talk to anyone about what had happened, and he certainly didn't want to draw attention from home to his idiocy. If nothing else, it could cost him his job, though in truth he wasn't being that practical right now. He just couldn't stand the idea of admitting what he'd done to some official to whom it would be a stupid inconvenience.

"And you understand why you have been detained?"

He nodded.

"Burglary," he said. "I didn't take anything, but, yes."

"Burglary doesn't necessarily involve theft," said the custody sergeant. "But it is a Crown court indictment punishable with up to fourteen years' jail time."

Thomas, who had lowered his eyes, looked up again.

"Sure you don't want to talk to your consulate?" said the sergeant.

Thomas thought, then shook his head again, slower this time.

Fourteen years . . . ?

His eyes closed.

He was photographed and fingerprinted, each finger individually rolled, then the palms of both hands. He washed his hands but couldn't rinse off the ink. The sergeant gave him a cloth impregnated with methylated spirit, which got the ink out from everywhere but under his nails but left a sharp, alcoholic stench that he couldn't get rid of, even with more washing. He was searched. He was shown to what the duty sergeant called—sarcastically or not, he couldn't tell—the "custodial suite." It was a small room, perhaps ten feet by twelve with a single narrow window—barred and with unusually heavy glass—above head height: a cell.

He stepped inside, and was about to say something—what, he didn't know, just something—when the heavy metal door swung clanging shut behind him.

A spy hole in the door slid open and the sergeant said,

"I'll be by to check on you."

Then he was gone.

The room was brick, but painted with a thick gloss paint the color of mantling cream. The floor was concrete. There was a long solid structure against one wall that was obviously supposed to be a bed, though it was really a brick platform—part of the structure of the room—on which lay a stained mattress

covered with rubberized plastic. There was a toilet in an alcove, which was flushed remotely from outside. Suddenly
Thomas found he wanted to use it, but couldn't bring himself
to do so. He considered calling for assistance, but couldn't
bear the idea of speaking to anyone.

CHAPTER 81

They came for him about a half hour later.

"This way, please, sir," said the sergeant.

Thomas smiled weakly at their politeness, then looked down as he followed them. He still felt stunned, drained of energy, of fight, by a sense of guilt and stupidity. He thought of Kumi and shrugged the image away, barely holding in a groan of horror and shame.

They took him to another room, this one with a large silver tape recorder labeled Neal Interview Recorder 7000 Series. It contained two sets of spools. There was a mirror on one wall and a camera in the corner on a ceiling bracket. There was a table with four chairs of thin tubular steel with wooden seats and backs, almost exactly the kind of chairs he had in his Evanston classroom.

A young man in shirtsleeves was already inside. Thomas was motioned into the chair next to him. He shot Thomas a quick look and then returned his gaze to a sheet of paper. The sergeant didn't sit, but stood by the door like a guard.

The officer who had arrested him produced two reels of tape.

"Please confirm that these are sealed," he said, looking at Thomas.

"What?"

"The tape reels. Can you confirm that they are sealed?"

Thomas looked at them and then at the officer, as if he had been asked to perform some complex conjuring trick.

"I guess so," he said.

The policeman turned on the recorder.

"This interview is being recorded and is taking place in an interview room at Newbury Police Station," he said, in the flat monotone of someone who has said the same thing a thousand times before. "If your case is brought to trial, this recording may be given in evidence. At the end of the interview I shall give you a notice explaining what will happen to the tapes and how you can obtain a copy. The time by my watch is five thirty-five P.M. and the date is the twenty-first of June, 2008. I am Sergeant Jeff Hodges, the arresting officer. I am accompanied by the Custody Sergeant Harry Philips. Since the suspect is not a British citizen, a solicitor—Mr. Devan Cummings—has been provided for him. If this is not acceptable, the suspect can request other counsel."

He gave Thomas an expectant look. Thomas, belatedly, shook his head.

"The suspect has signified in the negative by shaking his head."

Thomas just looked at him. The whole thing was surreal, like he was in a TV show.

"For the benefit of the tape," Hodges went on, "could you please state your name, age, and address."

"Thomas Knight, age thirty-eight, 1247 Sycamore Street, Evanston, Illinois."

"That's in the United States of America, is it, sir?"

"Yes, that's right."

"Could you please speak up a little, sir. For the tape."

"Right. Sorry."

"Do you agree that the people whose names I just gave are the only people in the room?"

"Yes."

"A little louder, please, sir."

"Yes. They are the only people in the room."

"The sheet of paper I am giving you now is the notice to persons being interviewed. Please review that now. If you have questions, the interview will be delayed until we have answered them to your satisfaction."

Thomas stared at the form but his mind could not take it in. He looked at Hodges.

"May I proceed?" said the policeman.

"Yes."

"Mr. Knight, you were arrested because you were seen coming out of a house that you do not own. Would you mind telling us what you were doing there?"

Thomas had known since he had been picked up that this is where they would start, but he could still think of nothing to say. How was he supposed to explain that he was looking into the death of a child twenty-six years ago as a way of tracking two more recent killings and a lost Shakespeare play. It would seem absurd. No, worse than that. It *would* be absurd.

I know not seems, he thought.

For the first time since Escolme had called him, it all seemed completely preposterous, and the prospect of telling the story made him feel even more humbled.

But tell it he did, slowly, haltingly, doubling back to clarify points, speaking in a hushed monotone, while the others sat in silence, listening. He gave them the names of Polinski in Evanston and Robson in Kenilworth, as if merely knowing officers of the law would help somehow, and he insisted that he had not taken anything from Elsbeth Church's house, that he had merely looked and left.

"Was the back door open?" said Hodges.

Thomas hesitated, knowing that he had dodged this point before, that it was a fork in the road that would determine a great deal. If he admitted forcing the door, he would surely be charged. If he lied and said the door was open, he might walk, but he also might find himself in considerably deeper waters when Church swore she'd locked it behind her.

"I tried it, and it opened," he said.

"Did 'trying it' involve the use of this?" said Hodges.

He produced a clear plastic bag containing Thomas's out-of-date MasterCard.

"I mention it because it seems scratched," said Hodges, pretending to discover the damage for the first time. "And see there? There's a notch in the bottom edge, as if someone forced it . . ."

"Yes, I used the credit card," said Thomas.

Hodges sat back in his chair, considering him. For a moment he didn't speak.

"Your passport says you're a teacher," he said. "That right?"

"Yes."

"I'm sorry, you'll need to speak up a bit."

"I said yes, that's right," said Thomas, raising his head.

"And this detective thing you're doing, that's like a summer holiday, is it? A bit of a lark before you go back for the autumn—sorry, the *fall*—term."

He used the word like it was something shiny he had just picked up.

Thomas shrugged.

"I was trying to help," he said. It sounded pathetically inadequate. "I wanted to clear Escolme's name, to prove that what he had said was true. He was my student . . ."

Silence.

"And you didn't remove anything from Miss Church's property?"

"Nothing," said Thomas. "You saw me as soon as I came out. You have my things."

"Nasty bruise you're getting there," said Hodges, peering at Thomas's forehead.

Thomas rubbed it self-consciously.

"I had a bit of a fall. By the watermill at Warwick Castle."

"And you carry your shoulder funny," said Hodges. "That a fall too?"

"No. I got shot. In Chicago. You can check with Polinski."

"Quite a life you lead, isn't it, Mr. Knight? I mean, for a teacher."

"I don't know what you want me to say to that," said Thomas.

"Did you find what you were looking for, at Miss Church's?"

"Not sure what I was looking for," he said. "No, I don't think so. I now know that Dagenhart—an old professor of mine—knew Daniella Blackstone at the time of the fire, but I pretty much knew that already."

"So just your arrest to show for the day's work," said

Hodges. "I hope the rest of your holiday—sorry, *vacation*—goes better."

"Is it likely to?"

"Well, let's see," said Hodges, looking over a sheet of notes. "We have you on suspected burglary . . ."

"I told you," Thomas inserted. "I didn't take anything!"

"Burglary is a complex crime," said Hodges. "You don't have to have stolen anything. Section nine, subsections one A and B of the Theft Act say that burglary has various possible ingredients, which include theft, but also might include rape, grievous bodily harm, or unlawful damage."

"I didn't do any of those things."

"You don't need to have actually committed any of those offenses if the intent to commit them was part of your unlawful entrance."

"Why would I be looking to attack Elsbeth Church or smash her property?"

"I can't say, can I?" said Hodges. "But I can tell you this. You could be charged with various crimes pending consultation with the homeowner. At the very least, civil trespass. Or we could go back to the venerable English common law—a law preserved not through statute but practice from time immemorial—and charge you with conduct likely to cause a breach of the peace. Or we can get really creative, and charge you with being found on enclosed premises for unlawful purposes, as per the 1824 Vagrancy Act. But we'd have to clear you of burglary before we started trying those, and we're a long way from having done that, aren't we? So no, Mr. Knight, to answer your question: I don't see your vacation getting any better."

CHAPTER 82

Hodges asked if he thought English law didn't apply to him. He wondered aloud if Thomas was relying on his citizenship to save him from trouble and if as an American he was used to thinking that he was somehow above the law and custom of other countries, that his own interests and desires—however frivolous or absurd—somehow trumped all other concerns. If he did, said the policeman, he was sorely misled.

Thomas said little, merely shaking his head and periodically saying, "No, sir, I don't think that."

The policemen were being studiously polite and methodical, but Thomas couldn't help wondering if he had touched a nerve. He had seen enough of the U.K. papers to catch a recurrent preoccupation with American high-handedness on the global stage, a tendency to act on their self-declared moral authority regardless of what the rest of the world thought. He knew this rankled a lot of Europeans. They didn't think much of that America-as-policeman-of-the-world stuff. They probably weren't too keen on Americans playing world private investigator either . . .

The last thing Hodges said to him was a cliché, offered halfway between explanation and defiance:

"You ever hear the phrase, 'An Englishman's home is his castle'?"

Thomas said he had.

"Well," said the policeman. "There you are then."

Thomas was taken back down the hallway, escorted by a tall black officer who watched him impassively, as Hodges and the sergeant continued their conversation elsewhere.

Thomas was allowed to call the American consulate, but whatever he expected that to produce, he got only frosty acknowledgments and a reminder that a U.S. citizen charged with a crime on foreign soil was subject to the laws and systems of punishment of the local authorities, not his native country. He considered mentioning Kumi's name as a contact in the State Department, however irrelevant her area and function, but he couldn't bring himself to do it.

Not that he had a choice. As soon as he hung up with the consulate he realized he had just used his phone call. He needed to call her, not to tell her what had happened, but to see how she was doing. That was more important.

"Can I make another call?" he said. "I'll pay for it."

"Who to?" said the sergeant.

Thomas checked his watch. It would be late in Tokyo. The prospect of waking Kumi to tell her this was too much. He hated to hide it from her, but she had said she wanted normalcy.

"Never mind," he said.

"Perhaps tomorrow," said the sergeant.

Thomas was nodding when he realized what he had just heard.

"You're keeping me in overnight?"

It wasn't outrage so much as weariness and something close to despair.

"Pending further enquiries," said the sergeant.

"About what?" said Thomas, flaring up. "What else is there to find out?"

"When you were brought in, before you admitted entering the house illegally," the sergeant explained, "we set about trying to locate the householder to inquire about the condition of the back door when she left it."

"But I already admitted that I forced it. Why do you need her to corroborate that?"

"We don't *now*," said the sergeant. "But we didn't know that at the time, did we? But in looking into Miss Church's whereabouts we found something that rather complicates your predicament."

"Which is what?" said Thomas.

"We can't find her," said the sergeant. "And if we continue

not to find her, as it were, your poking around her place starts to look like more than a public-order offense now, doesn't it?"

Thomas stared at him.

"You can't think that I . . . that I'm somehow responsible for . . . whatever . . ."

"Step this way, please, sir," said the sergeant.

"Where are we going?"

"I'm going to have to ask you to change into this, please."

He produced a package wrapped in plastic and shook it open. It contained a white jumpsuit made of what looked like paper.

"I'll need your clothes, please, sir."

"What for?" Thomas asked.

"Forensic examination."

CHAPTER 83

It wasn't the first time he'd been locked up, he reminded himself, thinking back to his holding cell in the Demier cellars. He had been afraid for his life, then. He had been running with a gang of pickax-wielding men at his heels and had walked into the body of the movie producer, Gresham, so he had had good reason to fear for his own safety when he woke up cuffed to the bed.

In this little cell, by contrast, he was safe. He would not be beaten, tortured, or killed, trussed up, and dumped in some abandoned French quarry . . .

So why does this feel worse?

He felt no imminent danger, but this sense of humiliation and failure was deadening. Again he thought of Kumi and, again, pushed the thought away.

He lay on the mattress facing the wall, not turning around when he heard the spy hole in the door slide open, which it seemed to do about every half hour. The mattress smelled of rubber and disinfectant. He tried to sleep, not because he was tired but because he wanted to stop thinking about the situation, but the more he tried, the more alert he felt. The zip-up paper suit crinkled as he shifted, and he had to keep his eyes closed so that the look of it—his body laid out like an astronaut or a skier—could be forgotten.

He had no watch and nothing to occupy his mind but his own thoughts. After some time—perhaps two hours, though he had no way of knowing for sure—he heard shouting, a man's drunken bellows, so distorted by dialect that Thomas caught only about one word in five, every one an expletive. That lasted about ten minutes, then went away. After that, nothing for at least another hour. Not having his watch was infuriating. Then he heard one of those heavy doors clang shut. Then silence again, till the next time the spy hole in the door slid open. The ceiling light dimmed a little. And then, finally, he slept, albeit shallowly.

He woke feeling sick to his stomach, but he knew that was more mind than body. When an Indian or Pakistani policewoman offered him breakfast on a plastic plate, he turned it down. He was taken to the bathroom, then returned to the interview room, where Hodges and the custody sergeant joined him. Moments later, the duty solicitor arrived, a foam cup of coffee in one hand, apologizing for being late and talking about traffic in the town center. The smell of the coffee turned Thomas's stomach, but he said nothing.

"So, Mr. Knight," said Hodges once the recorder was running and the introductions had been made. "Anything you'd like to add to your statement from yesterday? Now that you've had chance to sleep on it, like."

"Have you found Elsbeth Church?" said Thomas.

The question seemed to surprise Hodges.

"Why?" he said.

"I want to make sure she's okay," said Thomas, shrugging.

He felt different this morning. He was used to the idea of his arrest, and however bad things might still become, he had resolved to meet them head on. He had never been especially good at self-pity. It had also occurred to him that if this had happened in the States, he was pretty sure he would have been screaming for lawyers, shouting about his rights, and fighting them on every point. He was rarely cowed by authority.

So it struck him as strange that he had felt so small and defeated. It was, he thought, something to do with being here, away from what he knew, in an environment that was strange if not actually hostile.

No home field advantage here, he thought, imagining the Cubs on the road in Philadelphia or—worse—New York.

But it was more than that. He was drained, and had things on his mind that had nothing to do with lost Shakespeare plays, and wasn't making much headway on those things that did.

But he was done feeling embarrassed by his stupid little indiscretion. Could they make life hard for him? Sure. Here and back home, probably. But he had done nothing very wrong, and morally, he had decided, he may yet be in the right. It was, after all, a small thing to force someone's door, if it led to exposing a murderer.

So he switched into righteous mode, choosing to ignore the fact that he was no closer to exposing a murderer. The mind has to shape reality, he thought.

There is nothing either good or bad, he thought, *but thinking makes it so.*

And Hamlet should know. If ever man made perception reality, it was Hamlet. That such perception led to a stack of bodies, Hamlet's included, Thomas chose to ignore. Instead, he came out swinging, at least rhetorically.

He told Hodges he was being treated in a way grossly disproportionate to his alleged crime, that he was being victimized by a xenophobic campaign of intimidation, and that the station should expect to hear from the consulate any moment. Hodges, who had doubtless faced weightier allegations over the years, chose not to respond directly, but calmly answered Thomas's original question.

"Elsbeth Church was located in Stratford, alive and well," he said. "The custody officer will explain what happens next."

"Am I free to go?" said Thomas, not bothering to conceal how badly he wanted to get out.

Hodges frowned, looking at him, then nodded. "We're releasing you on Part Four Bail," he said, "pending the determination of charges in accordance with section thirty-seven of the Police and Criminal Evidence Act of 1984 as modified by Schedule Two of the Criminal Justice Act of 2003. Since you are of no fixed abode in the United Kingdom, you will report to this police station every third day, and your passport will be held as surety of bond. If you fail to abide by these conditions, you will be committing an offense for which you could be fined, imprisoned, or both. Within two weeks, probably sooner, determination of charges will be made and submitted to the Crown Prosecution Service, after which trial specifics, if appropriate, will be set. Do you have any questions, Mr. Knight?"

"Do I have to pay—for bail, I mean?"

"That's not how we do things here, Mr. Knight," said Hodges. "Any other questions?"

Thomas shook his head.

"Your clothes and personal effects—minus the passport— will be returned to you. When you have changed, an officer will return you to your car. I look forward to seeing you again on Wednesday."

CHAPTER 84

Thomas bought another phone card and caught Kumi at home in Tokyo. He didn't tell her about his arrest or the incident at Warwick Castle, and kept the conversation focused on her. He felt no guilt or doubt about withholding the facts this time. It was, he was sure, the right thing to do. She was, she said, doing well. The radiation was tiring, but not as bad as she had feared. All things considered, things were as good as they could be.

Thomas drove back to Hamstead Marshall, not so much because he wanted to go there, but because he didn't know what else to do. He had eaten almost nothing since being arrested and was suddenly very hungry. He pressed on through the village and then spotted The Green Man near the motorway. He parked, went inside, and sat at the bar. It was late for lunch and the place was deserted, but the barman consulted his wife, Doris, and declared they could "rustle something up." Thomas studied the menu with its now familiar dozen or so pub standards, and ordered the steak and mushroom pie and chips, along with a pint of Fuller's. When the pub's background music dried up, Thomas asked the barman if he had any XTC.

"Now there's a blast from the past," said the barman. "Haven't listened to them in years. Hold on, let's see what we've got."

He emerged a moment later with a stack of discs and read off their titles.

"*The Big Express, Mummer, Skylarking, English Settlement . . .*"

"*English Settlement*," said Thomas.

"They're local, you know."

"Yes, I heard that."

"Never really made any money, the way I heard it," said the barman. "Screwed by the label and a dodgy manager. One minute they were touring with the Police and Talking Heads, next, vanished. Still recording and all—even the odd hit—but never what you'd call stars. I suppose that's the way it goes. Course, they did stop touring. That probably hurt."

"I guess so."

He sat and listened as the familiar songs played, waiting for his food. American radio played little more than the bewildered and angry "Dear God" and the joyfully lightweight "Mayor of Simpleton," so it was good to hear these songs again. They took him back, as only music can do, to specific moments, long ago. The exuberance of "Yacht Dance," the plaintive introspection of "All of a Sudden (It's Too Late)" . . .

Just what I need, thought Thomas. *More rumination on time and mortality.*

His food arrived, courtesy of Doris, a round, pink woman with a kindly smile. Thomas thanked her and dived into the pie, which was rich with a flaky crust, and fat chips that he doused with vinegar. He felt like he hadn't eaten in days.

As he sat there eating and listening to the music, Thomas replayed those questions about what might be in the play that was so troubling that people would kill to keep it hidden, considering Robson's speculations about the authorship question or Shakespeare's religious and sexual orientation. What secret might *Love's Labour's Won* reveal about the man who wrote it that someone wanted kept quiet?

The conclusion he came to was really his old gut instinct kicking in. There was nothing in the lost play, he decided; no great secret, no coded truth about life, the universe, or the author. No cipher about religion, no world-changing biographical details. He just didn't believe it.

As a teacher, as a graduate student, as a reader he had always resisted the notion that art and literature could be boiled down to some single truth, what his students called a "message" or "hidden meaning" and what the publishing world had come to call a "code" or "secret." Any book that could be reduced to such a single meaning wasn't worth reading. He had always felt so, and the current fashion for novels and movies that found clues in paintings or statues, maps on the Declaration of Independence, and so on, had only confirmed his instinct. Art was layered, complex, susceptible to a thousand different readings, the source of questions and ruminations, not tidy solutions. Literature was as multifaceted as history itself, which shifts with the light of perspective, and the idea that literature used its stories and characters merely as a vehicle to point up some hidden truth reduced all text to the thinnest of allegories. It was absurd, and if some art did do that, that only diminished it in Thomas's mind. He would not believe Shakespeare capable of such a thing, and if that made him an old humanist, so be it. Shakespeare did not treat his plays as fields in which to bury treasure. He couldn't— wouldn't—believe it.

The idea that someone else might believe it, however, was an entirely different question. Thomas didn't believe that *Love's Labour's Won* contained some new, startling insight that would alter academia fundamentally, but he was increasingly sure that someone else did.

Before he switched the disc, the barman played "Senses Working Overtime" again. At the end Thomas could hear the cawing of rooks and crows on the backing track, and it struck him how local the sound really was, how British. No wonder the kids around here had loved them. He thought of Alice and Pippa listening to these same songs, talking about them to each other as they went about their lives.

The barman had put on another disc.

"This them too?" asked Thomas.

"Yep."

He skipped a few songs to get to the one he wanted and then went back to the bar. Thomas listened. It was slow and dreamy with an odd pattering keyboard in the background. It was a very different sound, but the lyrics had that same playful quirkiness. Something about being a dark horse . . .

"Did Elsbeth Church ever own a stable?" he asked the barman as he was clearing his plate.

"No, though lots of folk around here do. Famous horse-breeding country, this. Why?"

"Nothing," he said. He was thinking aloud. "I read something about 'scouring' a horse. I figured it was some Britishism for grooming or something. I thought Pippa Adams might have been in a pony club. Her friend never talked about riding, but there was this reference to scouring the horse and . . . What?"

The barman was giving him an odd look. It was both quizzical and amused, as if he thought Thomas might be pulling his leg.

"Scouring a horse?" he repeated.

"Yes," said Thomas. "What?"

"Scouring *a* horse," said the barman, "or scouring *the* horse?"

"Oh. *The* horse, I guess. Why?"

"Go down that hallway."

He pointed, an arcing gesture, full of energy. He was grinning, and it was Thomas's turn to wonder if he was being kidded. "And take this," he added, handing Thomas the green CD case.

"What . . . ?"

"Seriously," said the barman. "Go."

So Thomas went.

"Well?" called the barman.

"I don't know what I'm looking for," said Thomas.

"The pictures on the wall," said the barman as if this should be obvious. "Show him, Doris."

"Show him what?" Doris returned, wiping her hands as she squeezed down the hallway toward him.

"The horse!" returned her husband.

"Oh," she called back. "Tough to miss, that is."

Thomas turned, baffled, and then saw a large framed photograph. It was taken from the air, it seemed, and the background was a deep and vivid green: a hillside. On top of it was a white outline seemingly cut into the earth, a massive, stylized horse, hundreds of feet across, galloping across the countryside.

"Famous, is that," said Doris. "The Uffington white horse. Very old. Ancient like . . . You all right?"

"Yes," said Thomas. But he wasn't. His sense of the puzzle had shifted and the pieces were reordering themselves in his head. "Where is this?"

"Couple of miles that way," said Doris, orienting herself toward the kitchen and pointing.

"They put that picture on one of them records you were listening to before," she said. "Local group. You won't know them, being American and such."

"XTC," said Thomas, still gazing at the picture but raising the CD.

"Now, how'd you know them?" asked the landlady.

Thomas couldn't take his eyes off the photograph of the white figure on the green hill, the source of the *English Settlement* cover art that both Alice Blackstone and Pippa Adams had pinned up in their rooms.

"A friend of mine was a fan," he said.

CHAPTER 85

The scouring of the white horse, the barman told him, was once a significant local festivity. Every few years—seven, he thought—the people from the surrounding countryside would gather to cut back the encroaching turf to keep the horse clear. No one knew how long it had been going on, as they didn't really know how old the horse itself was or what its original purpose had been. Some said it was an Iron Age advert for a local horse trading market, but most scholars thought it much older, about three thousand years old, and was more likely to have roots in some fertility cult or animal worship. What the barman referred to as the "Stonehenge nutjobs" used the fact that the best view of the horse was from the air to claim that it was some sort of marker created by or for visiting aliens. This last developed a kind of truth during the Second World War, when local people had been obliged to lay turf over the horse to prevent its being used as a navigation aid by German bombers.

"What's the name of this song?" asked Thomas.

The barman had replaced the disc with one of XTC's later albums. The song had a lilting, hauntingly dreamy melody over a backdrop of climbing arpeggios.

"Chalkhills and Children," said the barman.

"I have to go," said Thomas, picking up the disc. "Can I borrow this? I'll be back."

Thomas parked in a dusty and empty lot and followed a wooden sign that pointed right to something called "Wayland's Smithy via the Ridgeway," and to the left to the white horse. The Ridgeway path was hedged on both sides in the

English country fashion, rambling tangles of bushes and little trees, with grass, nettles, and wildflowers at their feet. Turning toward the horse took him through a gate and into sloping pasture, the path unmarked except by a flattening of the turf. It climbed toward the ridge and then swept off, less distinctly, toward the crown of the hill, and the circular base—now merely a shape in the earth—of what had been an Iron Age fortress.

Halfway up, the breeze stiff and fresh in his face, Thomas was startled by a sudden movement off to his left. A rabbit, he thought first, but it was too big for a rabbit, and as it lolloped off into the longer grass, flailing hindquarters stirring up a spray of dew, he realized with a rush of delight that it was a hare. There would have been hares here thousands of years ago, he thought, and they were woven into the fabric of Celtic and Anglo-Saxon culture and mythology. For a moment he paused and scanned the surrounding hills with their patchwork of green fields and could see no sign of anything or anyone that would have been out of place three thousand years ago. Perhaps there had been more forest then, but up here he guessed the downs were largely unchanged.

Somewhere on the way up he lost a clear sense of the path and wondered if he had gone too far. The hill crest was still to his left and he was starting to skirt it, so he cut across the field till he came to a single-strand wire fence that was marked with a lightning bolt sign. He had no idea if it was actually electrified and could see no sign of whatever animal—sheep, presumably—it was designed to keep in or out.

Still, he thought, *a little caution won't kill you.*

He clambered carefully over, eyeing the wire as he swung first one leg over, then the other.

The climb was steeper here and once he had reached the ridgeline, the hillside fell away from the path—now unmistakable, if still unmarked—in a grand sweep. Moments later he came upon the fort foundation on the top of the hill, a wide, roughly circular embankment like a great bowl with the path running around its lip where a stockade had once been. But there was no sign of the horse.

He walked farther along the ridge, the wind even sharper now so that he felt he could lean into it, out over the edge, and be held up. Down below in the steep-sided valley the barman had called "the manger," he could see a narrow black road. And beyond it was a curious little disk-shaped hillock, flat-topped like a green baize table.

"Dragon Hill," the barman had said, because some local story said that this was where Saint George had done his one famous deed. Thomas remembered the way some version of that story had found its way into Spenser's *Faerie Queene*, though whether Spenser knew this place, he had no idea.

A few more steps and he found it. He was gazing off into the distance, searching for it, when he realized that the ground beneath him had changed. He glanced down and found the bright white of the chalk. Up close, it was hard to make out the overall shape of the broken, serpentine lines, but the figure boasted only one dot and it was at Thomas's feet right now. He hadn't seen it coming, but he had wandered right onto the great horse's head and stood now on its eye.

CHAPTER 86

Thomas found a phone box in the nearby village of Wool-stone. He hadn't been sure what he was looking for at the horse, but—as at Hamstead Marshall Park—there was no sign of disturbed earth, and the more he thought about it, the less likely it seemed that anyone could bury anything up there. The horse was, after all, the exposed chalk beneath the grass. How did a couple of bereaved women bury something in solid stone?

"English Heritage," said a woman's voice.

Thomas introduced himself quickly, politely, and got to his question.

"I'm researching the Uffington white horse, but my laptop has died and I don't have a U.K. cell phone," he said. "I wondered if I could ask you a few questions about the scouring and the physical structure of the horse itself."

"I can't tell you much without the files in front of me, but if you call back in about an hour, Grace will be in. She's doing some evening research and will be able to tell you all you need to know."

And more, suggested the slight smile in her voice.

"Grace . . . ?"

"Anson. Grace Anson. Let me give you the number so you don't get trapped at the remote switchboard."

He thanked her, hung up, and checked his watch. There was a pub across the road. He could stop there for dinner. The walk on the hills had tired him more than he realized; a seat and a sandwich sounded perfect. First, one more call. He checked the number, dialed, and went through the usual process of request and patient waiting as the verger was located.

"This is Ron Hazlehurst," said the voice.

"Yes, my ecclesiastical friend," said Thomas. "This is Thomas Knight, your transatlantic nuisance."

Hazlehurst was delighted to hear from him. He asked about his "jaunt" to "the Continent" and the development of his mystery. Thomas gave him the short version and got right to his question.

"Your contact at the Sorbonne who looked into Saint Evremond's papers for you?"

"François, yes," he said.

"Have you spoken to him since?"

"No, why?"

"I'm just curious to see if he mentioned our little quest to anyone else. I got the impression that other people knew I was in the Champagne region and what I was looking for. The timing seemed coincidental at best."

"I can call and ask him," said the verger. "It may take a little time because we're about to start evening prayer. Is there a number I can reach you at?"

Thomas looked around.

"I'm in a village called Woolstone. There's a pub."

"What's its name?"

Thomas peered at the now-familiar image on the sign outside the timber-framed and thatched building.

"The White Horse," he said.

Naturally.

CHAPTER 87

Thomas took his pint of Arkell's best bitter out of the timbered bar to a picnic table outside. He ordered a ploughman's lunch (despite it being dinnertime), sipped his beer, and looked at the garden, which was classically English, complete with vast, fragrant roses and a fish pond where dragonflies maneuvered like helicopters. Down here there was almost no breeze, and the day had stayed comparatively warm. It would be light for another couple of hours, but it was a soft light that was turning slowly to dusk as he sat, and he had the garden to himself.

The ploughman's was a plate of bread and salad that hinged on an excellent dry white cheddar and a brown pickle relish that was sweet and tangy. He was halfway through his second beer when he was summoned to the bar to take a phone call.

The verger sounded sheepish.

"I suppose it's my fault," he said. "I didn't insist upon secrecy."

"Who did he tell?"

"He's not sure, I'm afraid. An American."

"Male or female?"

"Female. Young for a professor, but not inexperienced."

Julia McBride, Thomas thought.

"The thing is," said the verger, "he got the impression that she already knew."

"That I was going to Epernay?"

"No, that the Missing Play might have been sent to France by Saint Evremond and returned to the Champagne region after the revolution. He only told her because he was convinced she'd just made the same discovery."

"She was already there?"

"The papers were checked out to her when he arrived. That's how they got talking. He doesn't remember everything he told her, and even less of what she told him. She was, he suggested, quite charming."

"Yes," said Thomas, "she would be."

As soon as he had finished with the verger, he asked if he could make a call of his own. They could add the cost to his bill.

The barmaid, a pretty girl who he thought might be Russian or maybe Polish, seemed uncertain, but the landlady waved the question away and checked the clock on the wall.

"Hello, Miss Anson?" he said.

"Mrs.," said an efficient voice. "You must be the gentleman inquiring about the white horse. What can I tell you?"

"The scouring," said Thomas. "What is it exactly, and how long does it take?"

"Well, it has varied over the centuries," she said. "Sometimes it was no more than a trimming of the turf and a lot of drinking and revelry, though it probably involved ritual activities and worship in ancient times . . ."

"What about recently?"

"Well, the horse was almost completely overgrown by the end of the First World War and was deliberately covered during the Second, but since English Heritage took over, things are both more regular and more scientific."

"Can you tell me about the scouring in 1982?"

"That's before our time, I'm afraid. English Heritage was established the following year by act of Parliament."

"So who owned it before then?"

"The land around the white horse was donated to the National Trust by the Right Honourable David Astor in 1979, so they actually owned it in '82."

"And the scouring?"

"Since the horse itself was put into guardianship in 1936," said Mrs. Anson, "the duty of maintenance and repair fell on the state. In 1982 this duty would have fallen to the Department of the Environment."

"And local people might have helped?"

"I don't have those records, I'm afraid, but yes, I believe so, if they were supervised."

"Okay," said Thomas. "Thanks."

"Any other questions I can answer for you?"

"No, I don't think so . . ." said Thomas. "Well, perhaps one. If someone was to . . . Let me put it another way. It's not possible, is it, that anything could be buried on White Horse Hill? I mean, it's solid rock, right? Chalk, yes, but still rock."

"You aren't planning to try digging up the ground, I hope," said Anson, her voice stern. "That would be defacing a national monument . . ."

"No, of course not," Thomas insisted. "I'm just wondering if there could be hollows in the rock. Tunnels, perhaps. Places where things could have been interred . . ."

"I doubt it, but you'd have to talk to an archaeologist about that," said Mrs. Anson.

"Of course," said Thomas. "Thank you. You've been very helpful."

He hung up and immediately began to dial Deborah on her cell. It rang for a long time and when she answered she sounded harried. Thomas spoke quickly: Was there any archaeological record of hollows, passages, graves, or vaults under the Uffington white horse?

"Not really a good time, Thomas. Something has happened . . ."

"It's urgent, Deborah. I wouldn't call you, but . . ."

"Thomas, I'm standing on a wooden platform several hundred feet above the Mexican jungle. My site is in a state of chaos . . ."

"I could call back."

She sighed.

"Okay, okay. I'll do my best. What was it called again?"

"The Uffington white horse. Oxfordshire. It's the exposed chalk of a hill shaped like a . . ."

"Horse," she said. "Yes. If I can't find anything online, I

may have to make a call or two. I don't think I have any current books on that area . . ."

"Okay," said Thomas. "Just . . . quick as you can, okay?"

"I'll do what I can."

He gave her the number and hung up.

He spent the next twenty minutes staring at the phone, so that the pretty Polish girl sidled off looking uneasy and whispered to the landlady, who gave him a long, cautious look.

"I'm waiting for a call," he said. "It won't take long. I'll pay . . ."

The phone rang.

He snatched it up.

"Deborah?"

"I can spare you one minute, so you need to pay attention."

"Okay," he said.

"This white horse of yours," she said. "I skimmed some recent archaeological journals online, and I can't find anything about any kind of space under it, but the white part isn't the exposed chalk hill itself."

"It's not?"

"Well, think about it," said Deborah. "Grass can't grow right out of the chalk, can it? I checked. There's dirt below the grass that goes several feet down before you hit the chalk bedrock."

"So the white horse isn't bedrock?"

"Absolutely not," she said, insistent. "There were excavations in the mid-nineties that were trying to figure out how much the horse shape has changed over the centuries— hardly at all, incidentally—and they found that the outline is actually a series of interconnected trenches. Each trench is several feet deep. They were dug into the earth and then backfilled with chalk blocks from a neighboring site. Underneath is a little more earth, *then* the bedrock. The trenches were recently reinforced to prevent deterioration."

Thomas stared at the bar.

"Okay," she concluded. "I really have to go. We've found something here, Thomas. Something big. But it's weird. I'll tell you all about it later. I don't know, but . . . Thomas?" said Deborah. "You still there?"

He said he was, but his mind was already up on the hills where, a quarter of a century ago, two grieving women had found what archaeologists would take another decade to discover.

The chalk horse was not solid. It was packed into the earth by hand. Which meant, of course, that it could be unpacked: dug out and then replaced, piled back in on top of what had been buried.

Thomas thought of the horse's eye where he had stood only a couple of hours before, and he wondered if the book was still there.

CHAPTER 88

In the car Thomas replayed XTC's languid and evocative "Chalkhills and Children," Andy Partridge crooning about being anchored by family and the pale stone of the downs. But for Thomas the chalk was also the Dover cliffs and the fertile underpinnings of the Champagne region. Listening to the song was like soaring over the green fields, eagle-like, looking down on the white horse and what might lie beneath it.

It was nine o'clock by the time he had parked his rental car in the Ridgeway lot. His was not the only one. There was a green Toyota Corolla that was clean enough to be a rental, though he couldn't see a company logo. It might just be some courting couple out for a night on the downs, looking to rediscover the horse's legendary links to fertility. But there was also a familiar bicycle.

Thomas calculated the distance back to Elsbeth Church's house. It was about sixteen miles. It had never occurred to him that she might be here, but it now seemed natural, even inevitable. She had probably been coming here for years, more than ever now that she knew people were searching for what she had hidden so long ago. And if he was right about what was buried under the horse, the women must have had to move it at least temporarily when those excavations were going on. Perhaps that was when it all started, Daniella seeing the little play once more and wondering if instead of reburying it they might not make some money out of it. Elsbeth would have been insistent, of course, but maybe that's when things started to unravel for the two writers.

Thomas left the parking lot at a run. It was getting dark in earnest now and the ground was uneven, but he pounded up the hill as best he could, retracing his steps from the afternoon with a nagging sense that he might already be too late.

He had almost reached the ridgeline when he saw headlights on the road far below him, inching their way through the vale of the white horse toward the parking lot.

Another of the hunters, he thought.

What had looked to be a triumphant conclusion was starting to look like something entirely different, something hurried and dangerous. In desperation, he fished out his U.S. cell phone and powered it on, but there was no signal, and he turned it off again. If he got through the night, he thought, he'd buy a U.K. phone.

He remembered the electric fence just before he walked into it, and he had to force himself to slow down and climb over. He probably should have stuck to the path, but at least this way he knew he'd get there. He was hot and breathless by the time he reached the top, and the light was too low to see if anyone else was up there at the ancient fort. He ran heavily along the close-cropped turf of the ridge and down toward the horse.

A pale moon had risen and the lines of the great chalk figure were uncannily bright, clearer indeed than they had been in daylight. They fluoresced like something unearthly. He turned back, but the parking lot was lost in trees now, and though he strained to hear, there was no sound of an engine running. Perhaps whoever it was had gone somewhere else.

And perhaps they're coming.

He hurried over to the horse's sweeping head and squatted down. If he'd never been there before, he wouldn't have known any difference, but he had, and he was sure. The chalk circle of the great eye was a little more powdery than it had been, a little more mounded. One good rain and it would go back to what it had been, but right now it was just different enough.

Someone had beaten him to it.

Thomas stared at the pale, bluish moon glare on the chalk, and he forced himself to think.

The car and the bike were still in the lot, and he had met no one on his way up. Even though he had missed a small part of the path by cutting across the field, he could be fairly sure they hadn't returned that way.

So where had they gone?

The hill sloped steeply down: open, grassy country with nowhere to go. There was only one path from the top that went anywhere other than the parking lot, and that was the old Ridgeway that slanted west toward Wayland's Smithy. Thomas hesitated, feeling blind and desperate, and then began to run.

CHAPTER 89

The Ridgeway path was broad and straight, a hard compacted earth surface impregnated with stone that had enough chalk in it to glow a little under the moon. To the sides the great irregular hedgerows rose up, shielding the path from dark fields and patches of pine forest. Beyond the sound of his thudding feet and increasingly labored breathing, the night was utterly silent.

He ran on, sweating, wheezing, but maintaining pace, until he figured he had covered about a mile. And then, quite suddenly, off in the open fields to his right was another path and a sign labeled WAYLAND'S SMITHY.

He paused, doubled up, sucking in the night air, and then set off at a jog down the path. A couple of hundred yards farther on was a stand of heavy trees, beeches, he thought, and among them were standing stones. They were not as large as he imagined those at Stonehenge and were less regular, but some were as big as a man, and they stuck upward like jagged teeth tracing what looked to be a long, uneven loop under the trees.

Thomas approached slowly, his eyes flashing around the ancient stone circle, trying to make sense of its shadows. As he got closer he could see that the circle was in fact an elongated oval, and at the near end the ground in the center rose up in a long mound with a stone mouth. Beside it, sitting on the ground, were two people.

One of them was Elsbeth Church, and the other was Randall Dagenhart.

They watched him approach in silence.

"When shall we three meet again?" said Dagenhart.

His voice seemed to unwind out of the darkness, drifting

like smoke, and though he was being arch, Thomas found the quotation unsettling.

"What is this place?" he said.

"A barrow," said Dagenhart. "A Neolithic burial mound."

He spoke as if this were all quite normal, as if they had arranged to gather in this unearthly place at this ungodly hour. It was the first time since they had first met at the Drake that Dagenhart didn't seem angry and dismissive of him. He seemed, in fact, quite calm.

"And what are you doing here?" Thomas said, taking a step toward them.

"Oh, I think you know that, Mr. Knight," said the professor. "I'd introduce you to my friend, but I believe you have already met."

Thomas said nothing. He considered Elsbeth, who was not looking at him, but was clutching something in her hands. It was a plastic bag, stained with dirt and the pale streakings of the chalk, wrapped tight upon itself. It was about the size of a slim paperback. By her side was a pickax or a mattock, one end of the head sharply pointed, the other flat, chisel-like, and bright from use.

"So you found it," said Dagenhart to him. "I had a feeling it would be you. You always were too clever for your own good, even if it wasn't the kind of intelligence that made a scholar. And you were determined. The moment you showed up I knew that while the academics were mulling the clues and turning them over and over for nuance, you'd get in there and start tearing at the earth with your teeth till you found it."

"So what do you plan to do now?" Thomas said.

Church stirred and her gaze flashed past where Dagenhart sat, and Thomas saw for the first time a rusted metal can labeled PETROL. He stared.

"You're going to burn it?!" he said. "That's . . . that's crazy!"

"Perhaps," said Dagenhart. "I used to think so. A long time ago."

He shot Elsbeth a look, but she remained blank.

"But this is Shakespeare!" said Thomas, aghast. "Isn't it?"
Dagenhart just nodded.

"And you've built your life around Shakespeare!"

"Parts of it," Dagenhart corrected. "But the key is in the other parts."

"What are you talking about?" said Thomas, suddenly angry. "People died over this!"

"Exactly," said Dagenhart, and his look at Church was longer this time.

Thomas continued to stare at him, fumbling for words he couldn't find, and then he saw that Dagenhart was crying, silently, his body quite still, but the tears on his cheek undeniable. Thomas, who had been motionless since entering the barrow, felt suddenly exhausted, and he sat on the edge of a long narrow stone. His eyes never left Dagenhart, and once he was sitting he said, quietly,

"You set the school fire in '82. You didn't mean to kill anyone. You just wanted to scare them away and leave their copies of the play behind. You had been having an affair with Daniella Blackstone and she had mentioned what the kids were doing. She probably hadn't thought much of it, may not even have known what Alice had found among her great-grandfather's things, but as soon as you saw it you knew right away, didn't you? Maybe she showed you a bit of it and . . ."

"Alice showed me," he said, and his voice was empty like a barrel rolling through a cellar. "I asked her for it and she gave me one of the copies. And then I thought that if I could hide that away, say I lost it, and get rid of the other copies, I might make something of it. Of myself. They had written them out by hand, you know? These sixteen-year-old girls had transcribed every word, each word enough to generate an article, each sentence a book, each page a career . . ."

He spoke with awe in his voice as he remembered, and there was something almost like pleasure in the memory. It didn't last.

"They were rehearsing in the school hall," he said. "They left all their things—including the scripts—in a cupboard there every evening. I thought they were gone. Normally they would have been, but they decided to stay late and they were in the back room . . . I just thought that if I could destroy the others and keep the original, then that would be it . . . I could see the cupboard from the window. There was no one there, so I threw in a bottle of gas and a burning rag, but . . ."

He broke off, but not because he was overwhelmed. Despite the tears, there was a deadness in his face that corresponded with Church's.

"When did they find out it was you?" Thomas asked. "The mothers, I mean."

"Almost immediately," he said. "I told them, actually."

"And they didn't take you to the police?"

"They did not," said Dagenhart, and he sounded utterly miserable, as if he wished for nothing more than to have been brought to justice. "They could see what it had done to me, and a part of Daniella still felt something for me. We came to an agreement. They buried the play, and I went away, back to my hateful job and my hateful wife with her hateful cancer."

"Cancer?" said Thomas, brought up short by the word, stung by it.

Dagenhart blinked and looked at him, as if confused.

"So?" he said.

"I knew she was sick for a long time, but . . ."

"She's dead now," he said, flat. "At last. The final act, at last."

For a second Thomas was confused and silent and the three of them sat there, still as the stones, till he pressed the point again.

"But why do you have to destroy the play?"

"Because," croaked Elsbeth Church, speaking for the first time in a level voice that sounded like it had said these words a thousand times before, "if it survives, people will profit from it: profit from my Pippa's death. My child was thrown into the fire. That will not make a penny for anyone."

"But your daughter loved the play!" said Thomas. "She wanted to bring it out into the world."

"She was sixteen," said Dagenhart. "She wasn't old enough to see it for what it was."

"And what was it?"

"A lie," said Dagenhart.

Thomas looked at him.

"A lie?" he said.

Here it comes, he thought. *The secret they want buried.*

He waited for what seemed like a minute and then prompted again: "What lie?"

"Happiness. Comedy. Love, the greatest lie of them all," said Dagenhart. "*Love's Labour's Lost* is life. Death, misery, work, disappointment, fruitlessness, emptiness. The tale told by an idiot, full of sound and fury, signifying nothing." He paused, and looked at the little book. "But when love triumphs, when its labors are won, when the couples ride off in wedded bliss, healthy and full of joy, then, Mr. Knight, we are in a fiction, a fiction that can build only disappointment. The world has too much Shakespeare as it is. It needs no more lies about the power of love."

Thomas couldn't believe what he was hearing.

"That's it?" he exclaimed. "That's what this has all been about? That's the big secret you want to keep buried because you don't agree with it? That *Love's Labour's Won* has a happy ending?"

"Not that the *play* ends happily," said Dagenhart. "That *life* ends happily. That love fixes everything."

"This is nuts," Thomas said. He was shouting now, suddenly angrier than he could have imagined. "It's a love story with a happy ending, and you want to destroy it because yours didn't? Literature isn't there merely to confirm what you already believe. It's there to challenge, open up new possibilities . . ."

"Don't lecture me, Thomas," said Dagenhart. "And don't suggest mine is just one jaundiced view. Love cools, friendship falls off. Everyone knows that. We just pretend not to because the writers and the moviemakers and the goddamned greeting card manufacturers have told us that there's something better out there: Mr. or Mrs. Right, the soul mate who will take your shitty little life and make it all better. Except that they won't. You'll get bored of each other, irritated.

Maybe you'll slap each other around or—more likely—you'll just stop talking: two people merely coexisting, blots on each other's consciousness. Maybe she loses her job, or you can't sell your house, or one of you is struck down by some hellish, ravaging disease. Either way, life intervenes, and love can do nothing about it except make it all worse.

"You ever noticed, Thomas, how Shakespeare is only interested in love till the couple get married?" he continued. "That's where the comedy ends and the tragedy begins. Romeo and Juliet are fine till they get together. Think of the comedies. *Much Ado About Nothing, As You Like It, Twelfth Night*. Once they get to the altar, the story has to stop, because Shakespeare—with his second-best bed in Stratford and his London exile—knew what his comedies pretend not to: that love is unsustainable, that it is all wild hope and impossible expectation, and that it drags misery and despair and futility after it like a great chain, each link a poem, a film, a play . . ."

"And you think that destroying this text will change that?" said Thomas.

"No," said Dagenhart. "But I refuse to add to the chain."

He reached behind him and picked up the corroded gasoline can. As he fumbled in his pocket for a lighter, Elsbeth Church unwrapped the play.

She laid it on one of the fallen stones like some Druid priest preparing a sacrifice, backing away from it, eyes down.

Thomas got to his feet. The book was small and brown and nondescript.

"Let me read it!" he said on impulse.

Dagenhart looked at him, then took a step toward the stone where the play rested.

"You're an addict, Knight, you know that?" he said. "Cut it out of your life and see the world as it is."

He unscrewed the cap off the can and, like a priest sprinkling holy water, he splashed the book with gasoline. The scent of it filled the air.

"Now, Mr. Knight," said Dagenhart. "Step back."

Thomas thought for a second and was beginning to move forward when something heavy and pointed tapped the back of his head. He clutched the back of his skull and turned to see Elsbeth Church leaning into him, her eyes wide, the mattock grasped tightly in both hands.

But as he stared at her he caught movement between the standing stones. Someone was there. Someone whose head was strangely distorted and oversized in the darkness.

CHAPTER 90

There was space between the trees, and the moonlit field showed his silhouette as he crossed between the sarsen stones, else Thomas would never have seen him. He moved easily and silently, and Thomas knew him at once as the man who had shot him through the shoulder back in Chicago, but now he also knew whose face was under the night vision goggles. For a split second, before the adrenaline kicked in, before the dread of how it would all end got a foothold in his mind, before all the panic and the terror, he felt a momentary pang of sadness and wondered if Dagenhart was right after all.

And of the four of us here now in the dark, how many will see the dawn? Half? Less, probably.

Church and Dagenhart didn't know the masked man was there, and Thomas said nothing. It was like he was waiting for something decisive to happen before taking action, something that would justify whatever brutal force he might have to use.

But then there was a snap and the stone circle suddenly flickered with the candleglow of Dagenhart's cigarette lighter, and by the time Thomas had started to move and shout, it was too late. There was another light—this time momentary and brilliant. It came from the edge of the circle and was followed by an explosive crack like a tree riven by lightning. It was loud and flat and short, so that it was gone before he had a chance to respond to it, and Thomas was still wincing away from the sound of the gunshot when he realized that Dagenhart was crumpling to the earth.

The lighter flame died before he hit the ground. As Elsbeth Church spun toward the stones where the shot had been fired, Thomas turned and stooped to Dagenhart. It was dark now, too dark to see much of anything with the trees shading out the moon and none of that urban glow in the sky that he was used to on the darkest nights in Evanston. So it was with his hands and his ears that Thomas discovered that Dagenhart had been shot through the chest and was quite dead.

CHAPTER 91

"The next person to make so much as a movement toward that play will go the same way as Dagenhart," said the man with the gun in his hands. "And Miss Church, put the pickax down."

Thomas heard her do so.

The gunman's voice was even and just unfamiliar enough in its composure that Thomas wondered if he had been wrong after all, but he knew he only thought that because he wanted it to be true.

"Put the gun down, Taylor," said Thomas. There was a momentary silence.

"You expected me?" said Taylor Bradley.

"Yes."

"Why's that?"

"Because of David Escolme," said Thomas. He was stalling. "He said he gave some names to Daniella Blackstone. People who could help her authenticate the play quietly. I was one of them because I had been his high school teacher. Dagenhart was another, but he was the last person Daniella wanted to involve in her plans for the play. I couldn't think who else David would have known, but then I remembered that David would have been in Dagenhart's lecture class, a class that always had graduate student teaching assistants . . ."

"Okay," said Taylor. "Yes, very clever. I was Escolme's TA and he came to me because Daniella had told him not to go to Dagenhart."

"Come on, Taylor," said Thomas. "Put the gun down. More killings will only make it worse."

"Really?" said Taylor Bradley. "What's that Macbeth

line? 'I am in blood stepped in so far, that should I wade no more, returning were as tedious as go o'er.' I've racked up quite the tally, Thomas, and without being caught. I spared you in Evanston for old times' sake. But you've made things difficult. I have nothing to gain by sparing you this time, and a good deal to lose."

"You know how else I knew it was you?" said Thomas. "You never asked why I was here. I told you about Kumi, remember? We were in the Dirty Duck and I told you about . . . all of it, and you *knew* her. You knew us as a couple. But you never said, 'Hey, Tom, why don't you go be with her?' It struck me as weird even then. 'Maybe he doesn't want to pry,' I thought, 'But still . . . Why doesn't he tell me to go to Japan or have me take her back to the States?' But you wanted me here. Back in Chicago, you were prepared to kill me because you thought I already had the play, but once you realized it was still hidden you wanted me pottering around, seeing if I could turn it up. *Then* you would kill me, but not before. So you never suggested I should go be with my wife while they cut her open to take out her cancer."

He had started speaking just to keep him talking, a conventional ruse borrowed from just about every murder mystery he had ever read, but as he framed the words something had happened. The realization he had carried in his head had settled in his bones and made him angry.

Bradley didn't seem to hear it. He moved to the center of the barrow and stooped to the play, shaking off drops of gasoline as he picked it up.

"Why do you want it so badly?" said Thomas.

"Oh come on now, Thomas," said Bradley. "We're not going to play that Agatha Christie crap. You know why I want it. I'm a badly paid assistant professor at a tiny school with barely literate students, with a four-four teaching load, and a third-year review that says that if I don't generate a 'significant scholarly achievement' in the next two years, I won't get tenure. Can you believe that? *A significant scholarly achievement!* They mean, of course, a book. There's no one on the staff who could understand the damned book if I did write it,

and my students are too busy texting each other and plagiarizing their papers from the Internet to know we even have a
library, let alone consult its books. But a book is what they
want, and my theater work is not considered 'reviewable academic product.' "

"Discovering a lost play saves you from having to write a
book?" said Thomas. "That's why all those people died?"

"It will keep me in the classroom and in the theater, which
is where the real work of Shakespearean academia is done.
They want treatises on obscure Renaissance fishing manuals
and deconstructive essays that we only read so we can foot-
note them in our own pointless essays. It's insane. They call it
research, like it's going to save lives or build fuel-efficient
cars, or something, but it's really just the profession's secret
handshake. It has no connection to real education, and it has
nothing to do with what these plays originally were. Yes, I'll
publish the play, which will get me tenure, and probably
move me to a better school where the kids give a rat's ass, but
I'll also get to stage it, show it to the world as it was meant to
be seen, as a piece of performed art, not the raw material
used by scholars to further their own careers by parading
their cleverness."

"You are going to stage it?"

It was Elsbeth Church's voice, and underneath the blankness was something else, something dark and wrathful.

"Of course, I'm going to stage it," said Bradley. "It's a
play. It's supposed to be seen in the theater, not read in some
study armchair . . ."

Church flew at him, fingers splayed. The speed and wildness of the attack caught him off guard, and she was almost
upon him when the first shot rang out.

CHAPTER 92

Thomas ducked as he heard the bullet careen off the standing stone to his right, dropping almost to the ground. His knuckles brushed the haft of the mattock Church and Dagenhart had used to unearth the lost play, and he grabbed it as another shot tore the night apart.

It was followed by a keening wail.

Elsbeth Church had been hit. There was a silence, and then Thomas could hear her fighting for breath where she lay.

Taylor Bradley had been knocked onto his back, the night vision goggles wrenched from his face by Elsbeth's ravenous nails, but he still had the gun, and he was already scrambling to his feet.

Instinctively, Thomas rolled right, moving fast and low past one stone, then another.

Bradley, sensing the movement, fired twice, behind him.

Thomas, now at the mouth of the barrow's burial chamber itself, threw himself to the ground and lay quite still. For a moment there was nothing, and then he heard Bradley's voice.

"Come out, Thomas," he said. "Let's not make this any more difficult than it has to be. We were friends, once."

The strangeness of the remark struck Thomas. There had, after all, been no falling out between them. They had been friends until the moment Bradley tried to kill him.

But there was something else in the voice. Something deliberately casual that sounded fake.

Thomas focused his thoughts, and they came to rest on the night vision goggles. Even if they had survived the fall, Bradley wouldn't dare try to put them on now. It would take too much attention, and with Thomas only a few feet away, he wouldn't dare let down his guard.

And if he had been wearing them for several minutes at the very least, his eyes would have grown accustomed to them. Now he was in a very different kind of darkness, and his eyes were still getting used to it.

Thomas inched around the cave mouth, scuttling as quietly as he could across the gap to the next stone. He could hear Church's ragged breathing in the center of the clearing. He moved again, and this time he thought he heard Bradley react, turning for signs of movement.

But there was no shot. Bradley didn't know where he was.

Instead, he spoke softly.

"You of all people should know why this play has to be brought out where people can see it," said Bradley. "You can't let people like Dagenhart dictate the nature of art. Come out, and we'll introduce *Love's Labour's Won* to the world. Together. A celebration of love and life. It would be tribute to everything you value, Thomas. Think of it as a memorial to Kumi."

The last words pinned Thomas against the rock, rooted his feet to the earth. His mouth fell open and locked in a silent cry, eyes clenched. But only for a moment. Then a terrible anger welled up in him.

Thoughtlessly he sprang from his hiding place and burst into the circle.

Bradley wheeled and fired at him, but Thomas kept going, not knowing—not caring—if he had been hit. Four more yards, and then he swung the mattock in a broad, lethal arc, its bit catching a sliver of moonlight so that it flashed like a spark as it hit Bradley's outstretched hand.

Bradley gave a shout of rage and pain and the gun clattered away into the darkness and was lost.

The two men fell on top of each other, rolling and scrambling, the mattock gripped by its handle between them as they each tried to press it against the other's windpipe. Thomas used the breadth of his shoulders, but his right side was still weak, and he could not push the wooden haft down. Taylor

Bradley's eyes—only inches from Thomas's—flashed with triumph, and he grinned as he pressed back, twisting the mattock till Thomas was rolling back and under him, his shoulder burning.

He brought his knee up hard, and Bradley's grip faltered. Thomas released the mattock handle and punched with his left. Once. Twice. Then they were up, the mattock abandoned, the two men gripping each other like exhausted prizefighters, flailing and butting desperately.

Bradley kicked, a neat, hooking stab with his foot, that whipped Thomas's right leg out from under him, and then they were down again, scrambling, and Thomas knew he was going to lose. He took a blow beneath his left eye, and the sky went white for a moment. Then another. And another, and he could feel himself sliding toward unconsciousness.

He reached for a weapon but could find nothing. His strength, already taxed to the limit, was failing. The blows kept coming, and Bradley's face—merciless now—swam in Thomas's vision.

Then there was something else. A sudden moist coldness and an acrid stench so sharp it acted on his senses like smelling salts. He flinched away from it, and he saw Bradley hesitate, his face moving from confusion to terror in a heartbeat.

Gasoline!

Then the mattock head swung into view above them. It was a weak blow, carried more by the weight of the weapon itself than any great force from the wielder, but it caught Bradley behind his left ear and he rolled sideways, half stunned, half furious.

Thomas squirmed out from under him, and there was light, first a speck, yellow and uncertain, then sudden blossoming above them. As Thomas fought to make sense of what was happening, he saw by the light in her hand, Elsbeth Church, wild as Margaret of Anjou or the weird sisters of Macbeth, blood streaked, her face crusted with dirt, her hair blown into a tangled fury, holding the burning play aloft.

"No!" screamed Bradley, staring at her.

"Yes," she muttered.

Then she threw it to him, its flaming pages still just held together, and as he snatched it, the gasoline with which she had doused him exploded into flame.

CHAPTER 93

Thomas stumbled out of the stone circle and onto the path back to the Ridgeway with Elsbeth Church slung over his left shoulder. She had not spoken since collapsing back to the ground as Bradley became a screaming, flaming torch, and he was not absolutely sure she was still alive. The bullet had hit her low in the belly, and she had lost a lot of blood. He had no idea what kind of damage had been done inside, or how much his lugging her back to the car might yet do, but he knew she would die if he left her there, and no one else was around. He had taken off his shirt, torn it, and bound the wounds as tightly as he could. He doubted it would be enough.

Bradley had not survived the fire. The burning was bad—so bad that Thomas was glad of the night so he wouldn't have to see it all—but he suspected his old friend had died of shock or heart failure.

The play, of course, had been incinerated utterly.

Dagenhart was dead too, though Thomas suspected that his last thoughts—if he had had time to realize he was dying—were probably of relief.

He reached the Ridgeway but knew with certainty that if Church was still alive, he could not get her the mile or so back to the car by himself without taking more time than she had. He couldn't see more than a few yards ahead of him and wished he had brought Taylor's night vision goggles. Still, he blundered on, sightless and determined, though he walked as if wrapped in failure. He trailed a chain of corpses, and the one thing he had sought to save had been lost to the fire. He had achieved nothing.

He pressed on between the hedgerows to a place where fields stretched out on his left-hand side and dense young pines rose up on his right. And then, as his legs began to wobble under the weight of his burden, as he weaved from one side of the path to the other, he saw two men approaching at a run. They were big men. Out here in the moonlight he could see them quite clearly as they got close. One was bald and wore an earring.

Thomas slowed to a halt and gradually lowered Elsbeth Church to the grass under the hedgerow. He thought her eyelids fluttered as he set her down, but he could not hear her breathing.

The two men had spread out a little as they approached. They still crammed their square bulk into coats and suits as they had when they had chased him through the ruins of Kenilworth Castle, and they had that watchful caution, as if they were penning a wild animal.

But Thomas felt anything but wild. He was exhausted. His legs trembled and he doubted he could have carried Elsbeth any farther even without their appearance. He had no energy to fight or fly, and he felt only desolation and despair. He bent down and found himself laughing, at the futility of his predicament, at his failed mission, at himself.

CHAPTER 94

"What's so funny?" said the bald man.

The other nodded, his eyes still on Thomas. He had a tiny goatee.

"Yeah," he said. "Forgive me for saying so, Mister Knight, but you don't seem to be in what you might call a comic situation."

Thomas laughed all the more at that.

"Neither, for that matter, is the lady," he added. "Take a look at her, will you, Mr. Wattling?"

Thomas stopped laughing at that. He hoped the name was an alias. If they were calling each other by their real names, they didn't expect him to be able to pass the information along.

"I don't have it," he said. "The play. I don't have it."

"Didn't think you would have," said the man with the goatee. "No offense."

"None taken," said Thomas, feeling the urge to laugh again. "It got burned. In Wayland's Smithy. Doused with gasoline and burned to nothing."

"Well, that is a shame," said the big man, his eyes still on Thomas. "Gasoline. That's petrol, right? Funny, isn't it, how we come up with different names for the same stuff."

Thomas considered him. The whole encounter was feeling increasingly surreal.

"How is she, Mr. Wattling?"

"Not good," said the bald man, straightening up. "Alive, but only just. Gunshot wound to her stomach."

"Where were you going to take her?" said the man with the goatee.

"To my car," said Thomas, bewildered.

"That won't do at all," said Mr. Wattling. "She needs to get to a hospital."

"I don't have a cell phone," said Thomas.

"You hear that, Mr. Barnabus?" said Mr. Wattling. "He don't have a mobile."

"Mr. Barnabus" pulled one from his pocket.

"Oh dear, oh dear," he said, dialing. "Living in the twenty-first century with no mobile? And you an American! Got to live in the present, Mr. Knight. Time marches on, isn't that right, Mr. Wattling?"

"Right and correct, Mr. Barnabus," said Mr. Wattling. "Time's wingèd chariot . . ."

"Waits for no man," concluded Mr. Barnabus.

He turned sharply and spoke into the phone.

"Yes, we need an ambulance, please," he said. "We're on the Ridgeway between White Horse Hill and Wayland's Smithy."

As he gave what details he could and promised to try to move Church to the nearest road, Thomas stared from one to the other. The bald one with the earring—Mr. Wattling—gave him a nod.

"Apologies about last time, Mr. Knight," he said. "We rather got off on the wrong foot."

"You tried to kill me."

"Not at all," he said, waving the remark away as if nothing could be further from the truth. "You're a big man. I had to take the initiative, as it were. Just wanted to scare you a little into telling us what you knew. Or, failing that, just scare you. Our employer thought that would put you off the scent a bit."

"It didn't," said Thomas.

"Evidently," said Mr. Wattling, with a rueful look down the Ridgeway.

"Who is your employer?"

"Now that would be telling, wouldn't it?" said the bald man with a boyish smile.

"I think you owe me that much," said Thomas.

"It's not like we were really trying to kill you," said Mr. Wattling.

"Felt real enough to me."

"Well now, that was the idea, wasn't it? But you know we weren't actually trying to kill you because, well—you know—if we had, you'd be dead, like, wouldn't ya?"

He grinned, ear to ear.

"Ambulance is on its way," said the other. For a long moment, they all just stood there in silence, looking at each other. "So," he added, looking back in the direction of Wayland's Smithy. "How many bodies are back there?"

"Not including any that were buried there—like—a million years ago," Mr. Wattling inserted, helpfully.

"Two," said Thomas.

"Villains?"

Thomas didn't know how to answer that. He guessed the word was commonly used in England to mean little more than *criminal*, but it was hard not to hear overtones of Iago, Iachimo from *Cymbeline*, or Edmund from *King Lear*. Neither Dagenhart nor Taylor Bradley seemed to fit the role. In answer, he simply said their names.

"Bradley?" said Mr. Wattling, his eyebrows raised. "Didn't see that coming."

"Still," said Mr. Barnabus, "the thing has a certain—whatsitsname?—closure. Justice served, dead villains, and Mr. Knight here will live to fight another day. Very neat. Very—dare I say it?—Shakespearean."

Thomas laughed again at that, laughed hard, till he started to cough. There was another long silence, and Thomas stopped wondering if they were still going to attack him.

"Gresham," said Mr. Wattling, suddenly.

"The film guy?" said Thomas. "He hired you?"

"That's right," said Mr. Wattling.

Thomas looked at Mr. Barnabus, who was watching his colleague thoughtfully.

"Why are you telling me now?" asked Thomas.

"Like you said," said Mr. Wattling, "owe you that much. But I wouldn't share that information with anyone else."

"Yeah?" said Thomas. "Why's that?"

"Mr. Gresham . . . Miles, his first name was—didn't know

that, did you?—was ambitious, sometimes a little shady, but no more than most successful people. He was also married with two kids: eight-year-old girl and a twelve-year-old boy. The boy plays football for his school."

"Soccer," Mr. Barnabus clarified.

"Right," said Mr. Wattling. "Thank you, Mr. Barnabus. I didn't know they played soccer in school over there much, but there you go."

"Why are you telling me this?" Thomas asked again, heavier this time.

"Just thought you should know," shrugged Wattling. "Wouldn't want you thinking of him as another villain, or just another victim. Faceless, you know? I know quite a lot about Mr. Miles Gresham. Like to hear some of it?"

Thomas shook his head.

"I think I get it."

"That's all right then," said Wattling.

Two silent minutes later Thomas caught the sound of the hospital's recovery helicopter thrumming its way over White Horse Hill toward them.

"See?" said Mr. Barnabus, gazing off to where the helicopter's lights were stooping over the trees. "All's well that ends well."

"Wrong play," said Thomas.

The helicopter came roaring overhead, then—once its floodlights had found them—veered off into an adjoining field and set down there. Thomas was watching the stretcher bearers hunkering down beneath the rotors when he realized that apart from the huddled form of Elsbeth Church, he was alone.

He spun around, but the two men who had been with him had melted into the pine forest at his back and completely disappeared.

As a pair of the paramedics—or whatever the Brits called them—were ministering to Elsbeth, and others were walking down the Ridgeway toward Wayland's Smithy, Thomas stopped the policeman who was escorting them.

"One of the men killed back there was Professor Randall

Dagenhart," he said. "He has a laptop computer. It may be in his car, or back at the Shakespeare Institute in Stratford. It's important that you get hold of it before anyone hears he's dead. In the interest of closure. When you have it, I'd like to talk you through what it contains, and make you a proposition."

The policeman fumbled for his notebook.

"And you'll want to talk to Daniella Blackstone's steward," said Thomas. "I think you'll find he's been blackmailing Dagenhart, trying to get him to reveal the whereabouts of a certain play."

"A play?"

"Yes," said Thomas. "It doesn't matter now. It's gone."

"And he was blackmailing Dagenhart about Daniella Blackstone's death?"

"No," said Thomas. "About something that happened before that. A long time ago."

He began walking along the dark path toward White Horse Hill, and he thought of the way all those lives had tied together, the academics and the students, the living and the dead, all somehow melded by contact, by shared history, and the words of that Paul Simon song floated back up into his mind. Something about taking two bodies and twirling them into one . . .

Very true, he thought. *Very Shakespearean.*

PART V

Let me not to the marriage of true minds
Admit impediments. Love is not love
Which alters when it alteration finds,
Or bends with the remover to remove:
O no! it is an ever-fixed mark
That looks on tempests and is never shaken;
It is the star to every wandering bark,
Whose worth's unknown, although his height be taken.
Love's not Time's fool, though rosy lips and cheeks
Within his bending sickle's compass come:
Love alters not with his brief hours and weeks,
But bears it out even to the edge of doom.
  If this be error and upon me proved,
  I never writ, nor no man ever loved.

—Shakespeare, "Sonnet 116"

EPILOGUE

1. One week later

It was hot in Chicago. Even down here by the lake it felt muggy and oppressive. The traffic was backed up all along Lakeshore Drive, and with the Cubs making a bona fide bid for the NL Central Division title, it would get worse as game time approached.

Thomas wasn't sure why Polinski had suggested they meet here, where they had last seen each other. There would, perhaps, have been neater closure—what Mr. Barnabus would have called *Shakespearean* closure—in ending it where it had begun, at his own house, but Thomas had his doubts about how much real closure Shakespeare's plays ever truly had, so he preferred it this way. Over the last few days he had thought a good deal about what had happened, how he had gotten pulled into it all, and what—if anything—he had achieved, and he found that much of it came back to Escolme.

The play, which had been lost, was still lost, and the one copy that they knew had existed was gone. Blackstone was dead, as were Escolme, Gresham, Dagenhart, and Taylor Bradley.

A body count worthy of Hamlet.

Were any of those his fault? None directly, he thought, except Bradley, and who knew, maybe it would have been worse if he hadn't gotten involved. And he had uncovered things—truths of a sort—that were valuable, even if they couldn't resurrect the dead or restore a lost play by Shakespeare, and wasn't that the core of his job as a teacher: finding truth, passing it on, or encouraging others to seek it out for themselves?

It was easy to forget that, probably worse in academia, he thought, with all the fuss about publication and tenure, and

Thomas found himself reluctantly sympathizing with Taylor Bradley's skepticism about what he had to do to maintain his position. Taylor had been passionate and excited about Shakespeare, but it hadn't been enough, hadn't even been right. Perhaps if he had taught high school or worked at a theater, and his place had been filled by someone writing about the gender and class dynamics of the Renaissance as happened to be manifested by a few plays by someone called Shakespeare, maybe no one would have died.

Thomas also sympathized with Taylor's outrage at the burning of the play, an act of cultural vandalism that no amount of personal hardship on Dagenhart's part could justify. In the last few days Thomas had been playing XTC obsessively, buying up all their albums and downloading video clips from the Internet. There he had stumbled on their song "Burning Books," which deftly slid between the torching of text to the torching of the people who wrote or read them. Though Dagenhart had never meant to kill the girls or even Taylor, his fanaticism had burned as hotly and as dangerously as any religious or political ideologue's.

Words, words, words. Mightier indeed than the sword and at least as lethal, though Thomas thought that Andy Partridge's assessment of the printed word as more than sacred was the only useful way to think of them. Burning books—whatever the motive—could only ever be the act of a barbarian or a dictator.

That morning he had called Deborah Miller in Atlanta to thank her for her help and to play her the song, but she was still in Mexico and Tonya had no idea when she would return. He thought he heard some concern in her voice under the playful remarks about Deborah sunning herself on some Cancún beach while Tonya kept the museum on its feet.

"Running up and down some Mayan pyramid, more like," he muttered aloud, watching the soft lapping of the water on the lakeshore.

"Talking to yourself now, Knight?"

He hadn't seen Polinski approach.

"Hey," he said.

"Rehearsing your next interview?" she said, her wide mouth buckled into a smirk. "I can't turn on the TV without seeing you these days."

"Awful, isn't it?" he said, meaning it.

She was wearing a pantsuit with a light gray jacket that bulged where her gun was, and she looked hot and flustered. "But you helped clear Escolme's name, showed he was telling the truth. All that crazy stuff about the Shakespeare play. No wonder you're famous."

"I guess so." Thomas nodded.

"And from what I've heard, the search isn't over, right?"

"It is for me," said Thomas, "but the news that one copy of the play survived has spawned a lot of searches for others. People are badgering Elsbeth Church for what she remembers of it, but I doubt she'll tell them anything. It's going to be quite the cottage industry on the fringes of academia for a while."

"And you think they'll find it?"

"Who knows. There may be one out there somewhere, in some uncataloged archive or forgotten loft storage . . . Who knows?"

He and Polinski had talked several times daily since that night on the Ridgeway, often in conference with representatives of the English and French police, as coordinated by Interpol. Together they had helped put all the pieces together. Bradley's face had been identified on CCTV at the Demier cellars, and his booking confirmed at the Drake during the National Shakespeare Conference. Most of the evidence was circumstantial, but it was enough to build the case against him, and forensics would fill in some holes. Elsbeth Church—who would make a full recovery—had told the Newbury police that she had invited Thomas into her house, and though they knew this was a lie, they had been content to drop the charges against him. The case was effectively closed. Thomas didn't know what they still had to talk about, but Polinski had been insistent that they meet face to face on his return to the States.

"It mattered to Escolme that he was proved right," said Polinski.

"You know that for sure?"

"I do, actually," she said, taking an envelope out of her breast pocket. "Escolme didn't have much, but he suspected he was in danger and made provisions. The day he wrote to you, he also wrote to a lawyer with what amounts to his last will and testament."

Thomas stared at her, wondering where this was going.

"In the grand scheme of things," she said, "it doesn't amount to much—a few thousand dollars' worth of assets— and there was a condition attached. He had no family and no close friends. His estate, such as it was, was to go to you, if you were able to prove that his story about the play was true and that he had not killed Daniella Blackstone. You did, so it's yours."

Thomas stared at her. They were standing only yards from where Escolme's body had been found.

"There's another catch," she said, and she was frowning now as she checked the wording of the letter. "The money should be used by Mr. Thomas Knight to fund his exploration of future cases, which he should pursue in the manner of a consulting detective."

She gave him an ironic look.

"You've got to be kidding me," he said.

"I kind of wish I were," said Polinski, "because I know you are the kind of guy who will take this request-from-the-grave stuff seriously."

In his mind Thomas heard Escolme's bad British accent over the phone: "*You see but you do not observe*! Great stuff."

He supposed it was.

"A consulting detective?" he said.

"Forget it," said Polinski. "The last thing I need on my beat is some clown who thinks he's Sherlock Holmes."

"You think I'm a clown?"

"I think you're a high school teacher," she said, smiling.

"I am," he said, returning her smile. "And proud to be one. But," he added with an uncharacteristic wink, "I get the summers off."

2. A month later

Thomas turned the campus map around till he had himself oriented and made a beeline for a string of three-story brownstones shaded by maples. It was dry and the trees were starting to droop and yellow before their time. The English department had seen better days, and its once luxuriant marble floors were cracked and stained. The stairs to the third floor were tight and rickety, and the tiled hallway at the top rose and fell in great, sagging waves.

Julia McBride was sitting at her desk, pen in hand, leafing through a stack of brownish books each tagged with a library call number. She didn't look up at his knock, but told him to come in before she realized who he was.

The play of emotions on her face was quick and complicated. Thomas thought he saw surprise, even concern, then restraint, and finally a familiar flirtatious attention.

"Tom Knight," she said, beaming. "Well, I'll be damned! But then you knew that already. To what do I owe this visitation? I rarely have celebrities dropping by, except academics, and we all know *they* don't count."

"I just wanted to tie up a few loose ends," said Thomas, smiling and watchful.

"For whom?"

"Mainly for myself."

"Indeed?" she said, shifting and settling in her chair as if still unsure of what tone to strike. "Aren't you the bloodhound? I was sorry to hear about old Randy Dagenhart. Very sad. And that young man, *Bradley*, yes?"

She said it as if she had to reach for the name and Thomas felt his knuckles tighten on the chair arm.

"Taylor Bradley," said Thomas. "Come now, Julia. You knew him as well as everyone else did."

She swallowed and adjusted.

"You're right, of course," she said. "Funny, isn't it? Some people want to suggest they knew him better than they did, and some—like me—want to get away from him."

"That is funny," said Thomas.

"Human nature, I guess," she said.

"Yes?"

"What?"

"I didn't think you believed in human nature," said Thomas. "I thought everything was temporally and culturally specific. I thought that 'human nature' was just one of those catchalls that white men used to claim that their values were universal."

She considered him shrewdly.

"Is there something you're getting at?" she said.

"Not at all," said Thomas, smiling. "What would make you think that, dearest chuck?"

She stared at him.

"What?"

"*Dearest chuck*, I said," Thomas repeated, his smile smaller now, more careful. "That was what Bradley called you back in Stratford. It struck me at the time because it seemed friendlier—more intimate—than your relationship deserved, considering he was the lowly assistant professor at the no-name school and you were the big-name scholar. But then there was the fact that he knew what that obscure cocktail of yours was, though I'm pretty sure the recipe came from the Drake. So you'd spent a little more time together than you suggested. Still . . . *dearest chuck*?"

"He was joking," she said. "And drunk. Trying out his Britishisms."

"Yes, I thought that too," said Thomas. "But it turns out that *chuck* isn't a common Britishism in the South at all. More a northern thing, apparently. Liverpool and places like that. Taylor Bradley hadn't been anywhere north of Stratford."

"Maybe he got it off the TV," she said. She shifted in her chair. "Are you going somewhere with this?"

"The thing is," said Thomas, ignoring her impatience, "it wasn't so much the phrase as your response to it that stuck in my mind. You looked—I don't know—irritated, but more than that. Alarmed."

"Why on earth would I be alarmed?" she said. Her face was white.

"That's what I kept wondering," said Thomas. "And then I

remembered where I knew the phrase from. 'Be innocent of the knowledge, dearest chuck, till thou applaud the deed.'"

There was a long silence. Thomas counted the seconds. Three. Four. Five.

"So?"

"So, that was what Macbeth says to Lady Macbeth after he has sent killers after Banquo and his son."

She stared at him. Another three seconds passed and then, her voice level and clear, she said, "I think it's time you left, don't you?"

"Could be," said Thomas. "I just wanted to say hi."

"You've already told this harebrained rubbish to the police, no doubt?"

"No doubt," said Thomas.

"And they thought it worthless, so you came here by yourself."

"Actually they found it quite interesting, but probably unprovable. So, barring new forensic evidence, holes in your alibis, or telling phone or bank records—none of which I expect them to find—you're probably in the clear."

"Naturally," she said, smiling like a snake.

"Naturally," Thomas said. "But I'm curious. How would you have shared the play? Only one career would have been made by its discovery, and I doubt it would have been Taylor's. He wasn't an idiot, and though I'm sure you charmed him, he must have known that."

She smirked.

"Taylor was never what you might call a leading man," she said. "I was pretty sure that if he ever came by the play, I could talk him into—er—sharing it with me. He was one of those needy, malleable young men. He was—at the risk of sounding like Eliot—not so much a Hamlet as an attendant lord."

"How convenient."

"I didn't kill anyone, Mr. Knight," she said. "I may have shared some professional fantasies with a man who turned out to be unstable to the point of being a sociopath, I may have bent a few rules in following you to France, and I may have committed the occasional sin of omission by not confiding all I feared to the police, but that's all. Such deeds I did, they are not near my conscience. And no, I don't sleepwalk."

"Of course not," said Thomas.

"So," she said, "let be."

"I may have to," said Thomas. "But I keep coming back to the first murder. I can believe that Bradley hunted Gresham down in the cellars, and I'm sure it was he who killed David Escolme and tried to kill me in my house, but the first killing—Daniella Blackstone—that seems different to me. The others were methodical, ruthless, but Blackstone was killed on impulse, hit over the head with a half brick. Now Daniella talked movie deals to Gresham and publishing rights to Escolme, but I don't see why in her quest to get a Shakespearean on board she would have gone to—as you put it—an attendant lord. Escolme might have thought Taylor was a real Shakespearean because he looked up to him as only an undergraduate can, but Daniella would have taken one look at his résumé and known he couldn't help."

"She must have talked to Dagenhart."

"Dagenhart had known about the play for twenty-five years, and he would have seen it destroyed before Daniella—or anyone else—made it public. He had made a vow."

"He would," she said, her lip curling. "Dagenhart always was a sentimental old fool who could find ways to dignify his basest urges."

"I think he read through the prism of his own experience," said Thomas, "like we all do."

"Then he really was a fool," she said. "In the end, it was just a book. For him to withhold it, to *destroy* it, because of what it meant to him was absurd and typically self-involved."

"You would have shared it with the world, no doubt?" said Thomas.

"I would have done with it what people do with Shakespeare these days: they use it to talk about things that interest them. Welcome to academia."

"I think Taylor sent her to you," said Thomas. "Someone with a reputation she would respect."

She laughed then, a high musical laugh, part delight, part derision.

"I already told you I didn't kill anyone, so if you are looking to worm a confession out of me, you can forget it."

"Sorry," he said. "Congrats on your new article, by the way."

"Article?"

"On servant clothing."

"Oh, the Cambridge book," she said, pleased. "How on earth did you know about that? I don't even have a contract yet."

"Word gets around," said Thomas. "That was what Chad was working on, right? Servant clothing. Livery."

Her eyes narrowed.

"He was my research assistant for some of it. Why? What did he tell you?"

"He told me it was all your work and it was right that you made him take stuff out of his Chicago paper."

"Well, it wasn't really his, was it?" she said. Her eyes held his, but it seemed to take an effort, like they were in some children's staring contest.

"No doubt," he said. "But then . . ."

"What?"

Thomas reached into his inside pocket and drew out a pair of letters on heavy paper.

"I got a couple of rejections today," he said. "One from *Shakespeare Survey*, the other from *Quarterly*."

She seemed caught off guard by the admission.

"You are still writing articles for journals?"

"Well, that seems to be the question," he said.

"I don't follow."

"I couldn't understand why Chad was buying you a jump drive," said Thomas, putting the letters in his lap for a moment.

"I'm sorry," she said, her confusion seeming genuine enough. "What are you talking about?"

"Back in Stratford you sent him out to buy you a jump drive, right after you blocked him from answering questions on servants' clothing. He, loyal lackey that he is, did as he was told, but I saw it, and I couldn't help wondering why. The only computer I saw the whole time I was there was Randall Dagenhart's."

"So?"

"He used to leave it out, Mrs. Covington said. She couldn't decide if he was admirably trusting or out of touch with the twenty-first century."

"And?"

"Probably a bit of both, I think," said Thomas. "Anyway, after he died I had the police impound the computer. I was kind of hoping that there'd be information there that would help them complete the picture of what had happened—connect the dots, as it were, but there wasn't really. What there was, of course, was his most recent work."

"And?"

She had become quite still now and her voice was low.

"I got them to agree to my performing a little test. I found an article he was writing on *Love's Labour's Lost*. I took his name off it and put mine in its place. Then I sent it to every major journal in Renaissance literary study. This morning I got the aforementioned rejections."

"I'm sorry to hear they didn't like it," she said, eyes and voice quite blank.

"It wasn't that they didn't like it," he said. "It was that they had recently received the same submission from someone else."

She breathed then, as if she had been holding it for a long time, and then she sat back in her chair and all the tension left her body. She looked away, and when her eyes came back to him, she was smiling.

"I knew you were going to be a problem," she said. "And it only got worse when you started feeling guilty about being attracted to me."

He smiled at that.

"The police won't prosecute you for plagiarism, Julia," said Thomas, getting to his feet, "and they almost certainly won't prosecute you for conspiracy or murder, but I'm afraid your career as an academic is over."

"We'll see," said Julia. The words could have been defiant, but sounded merely uncertain.

Thomas took a step to the door, then stopped and turned back to her.

"I have to ask," he said. "Why did you do it? You are a well-respected critic, and I know you haven't spent your professional life plagiarizing other people's stuff. Why now?"

For a moment she just looked at him, as if deciding whether to throw more defiance at him. Then she shrugged.

"Academia isn't interested in what you published five years ago, Thomas. At the top, it's about what you are working on right now, and scoff all you like, but women don't get to sit on their laurels like men do. A year or two of professional silence, and they'll knock you right off the heap. It used to be easy for me. I'd wake up with a paper half written in my head, or the germ of a book. But the ideas and methods I was trained in are already old hat, and keeping up with what's new, what's hot in Shakespeare studies seems to get harder each year. Chad is only moderately intelligent, but he is already doing work I should be doing. Angela outstripped me before she had finished her prospectus. I know more, and I have more . . . more *poise*, more professionalism, but as a mind . . . I may not look it, but I'm getting old."

"Aren't we all," said Thomas. "Cormorant devouring time."

"A true humanistic sentiment," she said, smiling. "Now, if you don't mind, I have a resignation letter to write."

3. Two months later

Westminster Abbey was darker than he had remembered it, cooler, but the fall was well under way in London and the sun set earlier. The green-blazered marshals were warning the tourists that the church would shortly be closed to all not attending evening prayer.

Kumi drifted by Thomas's side, her hand clasped in his, pausing to remark on the occasional monument or tomb, but generally silent, absorbing the place. They lingered over the great poppy wreath on the tomb of the unknown soldier, and Thomas thought of Ben Williams.

> *The evil that men do lives after them;*
> *The good is oft interred with their bones.*

They moved through the Lady Chapel, where Elizabeth, Mary, and James lay, past the throne of Edward I, the tombs of Henry V and Richard II, and into Poets' Corner. Ron Hazlehurst was waiting for them under the inscription to Charles de Saint Denis, Lord of Saint Evremond.

He smiled at them and shook their hands. For a few moments they talked about their immediate plans, how long they had in London, and Thomas's intent to walk Kumi up White Horse Hill.

"It's a ridiculous amount to do in four days," said Kumi, "but he's insistent. Has to show me everything."

Thomas said nothing, just smiled and shrugged, but he knew in his heart that he had to share it all with her, or it would somehow be less real.

"And how *are* you?" the verger asked Kumi without preamble. He was serious, even grave. "If that's too personal a question, don't answer, but I feel I have known you for some time now and it matters to me."

Kumi looked taken aback, but unoffended. Thomas looked quickly away.

"The surgery went well," she said. "And I've just completed a course of radiation. Hopefully we'll get by without chemo. Then . . . we wait. Lots more tests to come, but—for now—we're good. Tired, but good."

The verger nodded.

"That *is* good," he said. "Very good. I don't understand these things. I don't mean scientifically, though that is also true. I mean, cosmically. Theologically. But I will thank God for your recovery and pray that you have heard the end of it."

Kumi nodded, smiling, though her eyes had suddenly filled with tears and she could not speak.

"Well," said the verger. "Perhaps you'd like to go through.

I doubt we'll be short of chairs, but you never know. Once in a while a school group shows up for evening prayer because they don't want to pay general admission, and suddenly it's standing room only."

He motioned them into the center of the nave—the choir on one hand, the sanctuary, with its shrine to Edward the Confessor, on the other—the massive vaulted ceiling soaring above them as it had for a thousand years.

As the organ began to play, Thomas thought of the odd hit men or whatever they were—the police had found no trace of them—who had called themselves Mr. Barnabus and Mr. Wattling and the jumbled quotation that had been one of the last things they had said to him:

Time's wingèd chariot . . . Waits for no man.

True enough.

Almost immediately the minister, reader, and choir processed in and the service began. There were six men in the choir, and they were accompanied by the great pipe organ. The music was exquisite, a lilting, heartbreakingly beautiful sound, and Thomas was alarmed to find himself close to tears.

Why? He wondered. It's only music. And, as seemed to happen all the time now, he heard Shakespeare again, this time Orsino opening *Twelfth Night* . . .

> *If music be the food of love, play on;*
> *Give me excess of it, that, surfeiting,*
> *The appetite may sicken, and so die.*
> *That strain again! it had a dying fall:*
> *O, it came o'er my ear like the sweet sound,*
> *That breathes upon a bank of violets,*
> *Stealing and giving odour!*

He thought back to the production he had watched with Taylor Bradley in Stratford, how it had moved them both, how they had talked of melancholy and loss, and he knew why it was so painful to hear the music.

Because it won't last. Because it will fade and die, devoured by time, by mortality. Because everything ends. Because no matter how long you have, it will always be too short to make a world-without-end bargain in.

He took his wife's hand and gripped it in his so hard that she turned to look at him.

"Okay?" she whispered.

He nodded furiously, so that he would not have to say the word. And when the service ended and they stepped blinking out into the late-afternoon sun, she put her arms around his neck, and he could think only of one more line from Shakespeare, a line said by a flawed and faithless husband at the moment he got back the wife he did not deserve:

"Hang there like fruit, my soul," he whispered, "till the tree die."

She looked at him, and smiled that distant and knowing smile of hers.

"If you don't start using your own words instead of someone else's," she said, "I'm going to ask for a divorce. And, while you're finding some thoughts of your own, you can wipe that dopey, tragic look off your face."

"I just keep wondering how much time we have," he said, "I mean, even if everything is okay—with you, I mean. Your health. It just makes me think that time is short and . . ."

"Yes," she said. "It is. No matter what happens. And you could get hit by a bus tomorrow. So let's not waste time waiting for things to get worse. Okay?"

He looked into her eyes, her face framed by the vast and storied shell of the abbey, its stones rooted in times and lives past, and he nodded.

"Okay," he said.

"Good," she said. "Now, where can we get a glass of champagne?"

ACKNOWLEDGMENTS AND
BACKGROUND INFORMATION

This is, of course, a work of fiction, and all the characters in it are imaginary. Much of the story is inspired by fact, however, so let me clarify what is and isn't real. Shakespeare was a man from Stratford who wrote poems and plays (like Thomas, I have little patience with conspiracy theories challenging his authorship). One of those plays was *Love's Labour's Lost*. The evidence for the existence of *Love's Labour's Won* is as represented in the novel. I believe the play existed and that it was not an alternative title for another play (say, *Twelfth Night* or *The Taming of the/a Shrew*). We don't have it, but it may still exist. Somewhere.

The movements of the surviving copy in the novel are fictitious, though Charles de Saint Denis of Saint Evremond was real enough, and except for his dealings with *Love's Labour's Won*, everything I say about him is true. There really is a Saint Evremond champagne sold under the Taittinger label, and though the Demier company is my invention, the cellars are modeled on those belonging to various houses in Epernay. Taittinger is, of course, a respected maker of fine champagne and would not indulge in any of the activities I have attributed to Demier.

The Shakespeare Institute in Stratford is real, but I have manipulated it a little for my purposes, and there is—alas— no Mrs. Covington. All the scholars with whom I populate the novel are wholly fictitious. Honest.

XTC are one of the great British pop bands, and I strongly advise all readers to seek them out if they don't already know them. If I had pursued a life as a musician, this is the kind of stuff I'd aspire to write. I'd like to thank Andy Partridge and Colin Moulding (and the band's erstwhile members Terry

Chambers, Barry Andrews, and Dave Gregory) for the enjoyment and stimulation their evolving music has given me over the years.

I will post links on my website to XTC song lyrics and to images of the various locations, particularly the Uffington white horse, Westminster Abbey, and some of the sites in Epernay and Reims: www.ajhartley.net. Readers with comments and questions can reach me there.

As ever I would like to thank all who helped me in the research and execution of the book, including the marshals and vergers of Westminster Abbey, and Christine Reynolds, assistant keeper of muniments there. I am grateful also to Chris Welch of English Heritage, the Ancient Monument Inspector responsible for Oxfordshire who helped me fill in some details of the white horse's recent history; to Sarah Werner at the Folger, who clarified the tortured history of the Shakespeare folio once thought to have been in the library of Louis XIV; and to Anthony Hartley and Retired Detective Inspector Jim Oldcorn (Lancashire Constabulary), who ensured that I got current British arrest procedures right.

It is daunting to write a novel (a mystery/thriller, no less) involving material that I write more soberly about in my Shakespearean hat, and I am especially grateful to my academic colleagues who read the manuscript and gave me feedback, notably William Carroll, Ruth Morse, Tiffany Stern, Lois Potter, and Skip Shand. I would also like to thank my style gurus Edward Hurst, Bob Croghan, and Phaenarete Osako.

There is nothing remotely fictional about the seeming randomness of breast cancer, though—as everyone surely knows by now—the key to survival is early detection and treatment. I am only a novelist, but I would ask those who read this to support cancer research and ensure that they get regular examinations.

Thanks for reading.

A. J. Hartley
July 2008

A boisterous fantasy adventure from
New York Times bestselling thriller writer

A. J. HARTLEY

Act of Will

IN HARDCOVER MARCH 2009

Will Hawthorne, a medieval actor and playwright on
the run from the law for sedition (or playwriting),
finds himself inextricably bound to a group of high-minded
adventurers on a deadly mission. In the course of Will's
uneasy alliance with his new protectors, he must decide
where his loyalties really lie, and how much he is prepared
to do—and believe—to stand up for them.

"I was amazed by these vividly knowledgeable
adventures of a youth living by his wits in a world
much like Elizabethan England."

—David Drake, bestselling author
of *The Gods Return*

"A. J. Hartley is a rare discovery: a writer capable of
challenging a reader as much as he thrills."

—James Rollins, *New York Times* bestselling
author of *Black Order*

978-0-7653-2124-4 • 0-7653-2124-6
tor-forge.com • penguin.com

M339JV0908

BEHIND EACH SECRET IS A TRUTH.
BEHIND EACH TRUTH IS A SACRIFICE . . .

ON THE FIFTH DAY
A. J. Hartley

The mysterious death of a Catholic priest has been met with suspicion by his brother, Thomas Knight—and the grave silence of church authorities. All Thomas knows is that his brother died in the Philippines, the last stop of an international trek researching the history of Christian symbols. But Thomas and curator Deborah Miller aren't alone in retracing the priest's perilous and labyrinthine path. Their every move is being shadowed by a fanatical cabal of agents who are desperate to hide the astonishing secret Thomas's brother stumbled upon—and willing to kill to keep it buried in the shadows of history forever.

"Terrific plotting, first-rate suspense.
On the Fifth Day is a ripping good read."
—Kathy Reichs

penguin.com

A RIVETING THRILLER FROM
A. J. HARTLEY

THE MASK OF ATREUS

"An exhilarating thriller
rooted in the dark side of history."
—Jeff Long, bestselling author of *The Wall*

"Move over Michael Crichton—
A. J. Hartley is right at your heels."
—J. A. Konrath, author of *Whiskey Sour*

penguin.com

Penguin Group (USA) Inc.
is proud to present

GREAT READS—GUARANTEED

We are so confident you will love
this book that we are offering a
100% money-back guarantee!

If you are not 100% satisfied with
this publication, Penguin Group (USA) Inc.
will refund your money!
Simply return the book before
March 6, 2009 for a full refund.

M193G0508